Praise for the novels of

"*Sisters of the Great War* offers a meticulously researched portrait of the first World War, while providing marvelous insight to the lives of female nurses and ambulance drivers who served at the front. You'll root for Ruth's dream of becoming a doctor, Elise's right to be herself, and for both sisters to find love! Perfect for fans of *Lilac Girls*, *The Alice Network*, and *Girls on the Line*."
—Suzanne Rindell, author of *The Two Mrs. Carlyles*

"*Sisters of the Great War* is a war novel like no other. As with Feldman's previous novel, *Absalom's Daughters*, a harrowing time in history is perfectly rendered and fearlessly explored through the lives of two sisters, in this case the horrors and challenges of the Great War. Ruth volunteers as a nurse, Elise as an ambulance driver. Their lives are utterly transformed in a riveting narrative that redefines who the true heroes of war are. *Sisters of the Great War* is an experience I shall never forget."
—Dennis Danvers, author of *The Perfect Stranger*

"More than a century since the guns of the Western Front went silent, World War I continues to horrify and illuminate. *Sisters of the Great War* shows us why, through the rich, gripping stories of heroes and siblings Ruth and Elise Duncan. Humanity as a whole may've reached its nadir during these dark years of industrial slaughter. But brave, committed people still found purpose and resolve amidst all that ruin. What a striking novel about war, love and hope."
—Matt Gallagher, author of *Youngblood* and *Empire City*

"*Sisters of the Great War* is a deeply life-affirming book, the kind that will sustain you through the darkest of times. This novel is grounded in history yet boldly contemporary in its depiction of the two female protagonists. It shines the spotlight on women in active roles at the front as a nurse who is also doctor-in-training, and an ambulance driver. These women are real and vulnerable, yet they never lose sight of their priorities and of the people they love. I couldn't help falling in love with them, both for their vulnerabilities and their strengths. This book is immersive, profoundly affecting, and transformative in appreciating and understanding women of the past."
—Olga Zilberbourg, author of *Like Water and Other Stories*

Also by Suzanne Feldman

Absalom's Daughters

Look for Suzanne Feldman's next novel
available soon from MIRA.

SISTERS
of the
GREAT WAR

SUZANNE FELDMAN

mira

mira™

Recycling programs
for this product may
not exist in your area.

ISBN-13: 978-0-7783-1122-5

Sisters of the Great War

Copyright © 2021 by Suzanne Feldman

This edition published by arrangement with Harlequin Books S.A.

For questions and comments about the quality of this book, please contact us at
CustomerService@Harlequin.com.

Mira
22 Adelaide St. West, 40th Floor
Toronto, Ontario M5H 4E3, Canada
BookClubbish.com

Printed in U.S.A.

For Vicki, Forever and Always.

SISTERS

of the

GREAT WAR

AUGUST, 1914

God said, "Men have forgotten Me:
The souls that sleep shall wake again,
    And blinded eyes must learn to see."

So since redemption comes through pain
He smote the earth with chastening rod,
    And brought destruction's lurid reign;

But where His desolation trod
The people in their agony
    Despairing cried, "There is no God."

VERA MARY BRITTAIN

IN FLANDERS FIELDS

In Flanders fields the poppies blow
Between the crosses, row on row,
   That mark our place; and in the sky
   The larks, still bravely singing, fly
Scarce heard amid the guns below.

We are the Dead. Short days ago
We lived, felt dawn, saw sunset glow,
   Loved and were loved, and now we lie,
   In Flanders fields.

Take up our quarrel with the foe:
To you from failing hands we throw
   The torch; be yours to hold it high.
   If ye break faith with us who die
We shall not sleep, though poppies grow
   In Flanders fields.

JOHN McCRAE

Part One

CHAPTER ONE

Baltimore, Maryland
August 1914

Ruth Duncan fanned herself with the newspaper in the summer heat as Grandpa Gerald put up a British flag outside the house. If he'd had a uniform—of any kind—he would have worn it. People on the sidewalk paused and pointed, but Grandpa, still a proper English gent even after almost twenty years in the US, smoothed his white beard and straightened his waistcoat, ignoring the onlookers.

"That's done," he said.

Ruth's own interest in the war was limited to what she read in the paper from across the dining table. Grandpa would snap the paper open before he ate breakfast. She could see the headlines and the back side of the last page, but not much more. Grandpa would grunt his appreciation of whatever was inside, snort at what displeased him, and sometimes laugh. On August 12, the headline in the *Baltimore Sun* read, France And Great Britain Declare War On Austria-Hungary, and Grandpa wasn't laughing.

Cook brought in the morning mail and put it on the table next to Grandpa. She was a round, gray-haired woman who left a puff of flour behind her wherever she went.

"Letter from England, sir," Cook said, leaving the envelope and a dusting of flour on the dark mahogany. She smiled at Ruth and left for the kitchen.

Grandpa tore open the letter.

Ruth waited while he read. It was from Richard and Diane Doweling, his friends in London who still wrote to him after all these years. They'd sent their son, John, to Harvard in Massachusetts for his medical degree. Ruth had never met John Doweling, but she was jealous of him, his opportunities, his apparent successes. The Dowelings sent letters whenever John won some award or other. No doubt this was more of the same. Ruth drummed her fingers on the table and eyed the dining room clock. In ten minutes, she would need to catch the trolley that would take her up to the Loyola College of Nursing, where she would be taught more of the things she had already learned from her father. The nuns at Loyola were dedicated nurses, and they knew what they were doing. Some were outstanding teachers, but others were simply mired in the medicine of the last century. Ruth was frustrated and bored, but Father paid her tuition, and what Father wanted, Father got.

Ruth tugged at her school uniform—a white apron over a long white dress, which would never see a spot of blood. "What do they say, Grandpa?"

He was frowning. "John is enlisting. They've rushed his graduation at Harvard so he can go home and join the Royal Army Medical Corps."

"How can they rush graduation?" Ruth asked. "That seems silly. What if he misses a class in, say, diseases of the liver?"

Grandpa folded the letter and looked up. "I don't think he'll be treating diseases of the liver on the battlefield. Anyway, he's coming to Baltimore before he ships out."

"Here?" said Ruth in surprise. "But why?"

"For one thing," said Grandpa, "I haven't seen him since he was three years old. For another, you two have a common interest."

"You mean medicine?" Ruth asked. "Oh, Grandpa. What could I possibly talk about with him? I'm not even a nurse yet, and he's—he's a doctor." She spread her hands. "Should we discuss how to wrap a bandage?"

"As long as you discuss something." He pushed the letter across the table to her and got up. "You'll be showing him around town."

"Me?" said Ruth. "Why me?"

"Because your sister—" Grandpa nodded at Elise, just clumping down the stairs in her nightgown and bathrobe "—has dirty fingernails." He started up the stairs. "Good morning, my dear," he said. "Do you know what time it is?"

"Uh-huh," Elise mumbled as she slumped into her seat at the table.

As Grandpa continued up the stairs, Ruth called after him. "But when is he coming?"

"His train arrives Saturday at noon," Grandpa shouted back. "Find something nice to wear. You too, Elise."

Elise rubbed her eyes. "What's going on?"

Ruth pushed the letter at her and got up to go. "Read it," she said. "You'll see."

Ruth made her way down Thirty-Third Street with her heavy book bag slung over one shoulder, heading for the trolley stop, four blocks away, on Charles. Summer classes were almost over, and as usual, the August air in Baltimore was impenetrably hot and almost unbreathable. It irritated Ruth to think that she would arrive at Loyola sweaty under her arms, her hair frizzed around her nurse's cap from the humidity. The nuns liked neatness, modest decorum. Not perspiring young women who wished they were somewhere else.

Elise, Ruth thought, as she waited for a break in the noisy traffic on Charles Street, could've driven her in the motorcar, but no, she'd slept late. Her younger sister could do pretty much anything, it seemed, except behave like a girl. Elise, who had been able to take apart Grandpa's pocket watch and put it back together when she was six years old, was a useful mystery to both Father and Grandpa. She could fix the car—cheaper than the expensive mechanics. For some reason, Elise wasn't obliged to submit to the same expectations as Ruth—she could keep her nails short and dirty. Ruth wondered, as she had since she was a girl, if it was her younger sister's looks. She was a mirror image of their mother, who had died in childbirth with Elise. Did that make her special in Father's eyes?

An iceman drove a sweating horse past her. The horse raised its tail, grunted and dropped a pile of manure, rank in the heat, right in front of her, as though to augur the rest of her day. The iceman twisted in the cart to tip his hat. "Sorry, Sister!"

Ruth let her breath out through her teeth. Maybe the truth of the matter was that she *was* the "sorry sister." It was at this exact corner that her dreams of becoming a doctor, to follow in her father's footsteps, had been shot down. When she was ten, and the governess said she'd done well on her writing and math, she was allowed to start going along on Father's house calls and help in his office downstairs. Father had let her do simple things at first—mix plaster while he positioned a broken ankle, give medicine to children with the grippe—but she watched everything he did and listened carefully. By the time she was twelve, she could give him a diagnosis, and she remembered her first one vividly, identifying a man's abdominal pain as appendicitis.

"You did a good job," Father had said to her, as he'd reined old Bess around this very corner. "You'll make an excellent nurse one day."

Ruth remembered laughing because she'd thought he was joking. Her father's praise was like gold. "A nurse?" she'd said. "One day I'll be a doctor, just like you!"

"Yes, a nurse," he'd said firmly, without a hint of a smile. It was the tone he used for patients who wouldn't take their medicine.

"But I want to be a doctor."

"I'm sorry," he said. He hadn't sounded sorry at all. "Girls don't become doctors. They become nurses and wives. Tomorrow, if there's time, we'll visit a nursing college. When you're eighteen, that's where you'll go."

"But—"

He'd shaken his head sharply, cutting her off. "It isn't done, and I don't want to hear another word about it."

A decade later, Ruth could still feel the shock in her heart. It had never occurred to her that she couldn't be a doctor because she was a girl. And now, John Doweling was coming to town to cement her future as a doctor's wife. That was what everyone had in mind. She knew it. Maybe John didn't know yet, but he was the only one.

Ruth frowned and lifted her skirts with one hand, balancing the book bag with the other, and stepped around the manure as the trolley came clanging up Charles.

CHAPTER TWO

———————————————————

That evening, Elise was hunched over the motorcar on Charles Street where the engine had conked out. Father had come home irritated and sent her out after supper to fix it, or retrieve it, or *something*. Just have it ready for calls the next day.

With her stained blue mechanic's apron covering her long dress, Elise peered around, expecting the stares of passersby— a *woman* working on a *car*? She was used to the scorn. Once, while she was driving, someone's snotty brat had thrown a rock at her, missing her, but leaving a little dent in the shining black body of the car. Here, so close to the university, the least she expected was mocking comments from passing fraternity boys. That'd happened more than once. In her experience, though, the women were the worst, with their silent, judgmental eyes. Elise could almost read their thoughts—almost. When they stared at her, she felt accused of something—taking a man's job? She wasn't sure. The women put their noses in the air and hustled their children along, as though just the sight of her working on a car would somehow scar them for life.

At this point, it was so late, hardly anyone was on the street. There were no hecklers, so she focused on the engine again. Smelling of gasoline, black with oil, it was barely visible in this dark space between streetlamps.

She found the fuel line by touch—where the problems with the motorcar usually began—and was just detaching it, when a shadow fell over the already shadowy engine. She looked up and found herself staring into the amused eyes of a man in a pin-striped suit.

"Do you need help, miss?"

This happened all the time, too. Men who knew nothing about engines were always ready to dive right in, assuming she was a damsel in distress.

"No, thanks," said Elise briskly. "I know what's wrong with it."

"It was an empty offer, actually," said the man. "I don't know a thing about motors." He smiled at her. His lips were full and his face round. He had beautiful eyelashes. "You must be quite an expert," he said.

Elise made herself look away, back at the grimy innards, the invisible fuel line. "I've been working on this one ever since my father bought it."

"Your father's a mechanic?"

"He's a doctor," said Elise.

"A doctor? Then who taught you what to do?"

Elise spared him a glance. Was he flirting with her? *That* would be a first. "I just watched what the mechanics did." Should she tell him the details? The men laughing as she unscrewed the spark plugs when she was ten, and the subsequent streaks of grease on her sundress? The way Father had sold off old Bess and the buggy to the milkman as soon as he was convinced his daughter could fix the car? How the small stable behind the house smelled of gasoline now instead of hay and leather?

"Really," she said down into the engine, "I just like to fix things." She wished he would go away.

"How extraordinary," said the man in an entirely different tone—sweeter, higher, utterly fetching. "Maybe you could come and fix my motorcar sometime."

Elise looked up. At first she wasn't sure. Then her mouth opened as she saw through the *him*, into the *her*.

His—her—smile widened, and the man—the *woman* dressed in a pin-striped suit—grinned. "The thing breaks down all the time. Maybe," she said, "it just needs a loving touch."

Elise straightened, wrench in her hand. The back of her neck prickled. The prickle shivered down her spine, lower and lower, until it ended up all funny and tingly. Elise could feel herself blushing deeply in the dark.

"Do your friends fix cars, too?" the woman asked.

"I don't…have many friends," Elise replied.

"And the ones you do have, don't understand you," the woman said. She raised an unmistakably suggestive eyebrow. "They think you're peculiar. What about your family?"

"My—my father sent me out to fix—you know." She gestured at the car, its open hood. "This."

"So he at least understands."

"Understands?" Elise asked.

"You don't have to hide it from him."

"Hide?" Elise repeated. "Hide what?"

The woman let out an easy laugh. "Come with me," she said. "I'll show you." She turned and started walking away.

"Hey!" Elise shouted. "Wait! I can't just leave the car."

The woman beckoned, her smile wide and languid, as though every question could be answered just by following.

Elise, speechless, looked at the car, and then at the pin-stripes disappearing into the night. With the wrench still in her hand, she followed.

Elise trailed the woman at a distance, across Charles Street, through Wyman Park, and down Howard Street, through thin crowds into a sketchier neighborhood, where she had driven but never walked. Houses around her became store-fronts, then drinking establishments. Elise wanted to pause and get her bearings, but couldn't lose sight of the pin-striped suit. Streetlamps cast hard shadows, and she hurried though them, bumping into people—women in low-cut blouses who might have been prostitutes and men who might have been their customers. Ahead of her was the woman dressed as a man, making her way down the street, strutting as though she owned it.

Elise followed until the woman stopped in front of a bar marked with a single purple musical note painted on the door. She waited until Elise was close enough to see her open the door and go in.

Elise stopped in the middle of the sidewalk, aware, finally, of her racing heart, the wrench in her hand, and her surroundings. Between her and the door were four or five couples, women in nice dresses, men in smart suits all out of place in this run-down part of the city. It took her a moment to ask herself the blindingly obvious question, and in that moment, their eyes turned to examine her. Heat rushed into her face. What did they see? An eighteen-year-old girl dressed in a mechanic's filthy apron, her long brown hair tied back. And what did she see? For the first time in her life, Elise saw through their disguises. These people could be anywhere. Walking down the street. Driving in cars. Shopping at the market. She realized she was holding her breath—perhaps everyone was— and then one of the "men" bent to kiss one of the women on her full, painted lips. Elise let her breath out in a gasp. The woman giggled. The two of them separated long enough to stare at Elise.

"Girl," said the one dressed as a man, in a low but distinctly female voice. "You simply *must* make up your mind."

Elise stifled the blurt of words brimming in her mouth, turned and ran. She ran, not knowing if she would have spoken or screamed. *Make up my mind about what?* She bolted up the length of Howard Street until, panting, she had to stop and walk. She walked in the dark until she found her father's car and hunched over the engine, breathing in its fumes.

In her heart, she knew the answer to the question, and had known for quite some time.

CHAPTER THREE

September 1914

Dr. John Doweling, Ruth noted, was tall, sandy-haired, with large, practical hands and a shy smile. She, Elise, Father and Grandpa met him as he got off the train. John hadn't eaten since breakfast, so they took him out for a late lunch at Sunny's, a not-too-fancy restaurant within walking distance of Penn Station.

Over sandwiches, they quizzed him about the war.

"Will they send you directly to the front?" Grandpa asked. "Or will there be some training first?"

"I suppose they'll have to teach me how to march," John said, over coffee. Ruth had expected him to order tea, but he'd been in the States for years now, and said he'd developed a taste for it. He took a sip. "I'll miss coffee when I get back home, but it's not a proper meal without a cup of tea."

"It's hard to get a good cup of tea in America," said Grandpa. "No one knows how to make it. Too strong, too weak, the water's the wrong temperature. You'll appreciate it when you get back to London."

"I imagine I will," said John. "And I imagine it'll be near impossible to get a cup of coffee at the front. It'll be tea and Bovril."

"What's that?" Elise asked around her sandwich.

"It's a sort of instant broth," said John. "Easy to send in packages. I hear it's a staple for the soldiers."

Ruth hadn't spoken yet. She was evaluating him. So far, John seemed nice, not stuck-up or snooty. In fact, if anything, he seemed quietly worried. "What else do you hear?" she asked.

"Well," said John, "I hear that the war is a glorious endeavor. Everyone in my parents' neighborhood is signing up to go. But I also hear the Germans have machine guns that can cut down a hundred men in minutes."

"*Machine* guns?" said Grandpa. "That sounds dreadfully unsporting."

"I'm not sure this is a sporting war." John put his sandwich down. "Some say the casualties will rival those of your Civil War."

Father looked up in surprise. "But that was tens of thousands of men."

"A machine gun is a bad bit of business, Dr. Duncan," said John. "And if you believe what you hear, entire villages of civilians have been shot by the Germans simply because one person is suspected of spying."

"I've heard that," said Grandpa. He seemed to have finished eating even though half a sandwich still lay on his plate. "People are fleeing their homes. I've seen the photos in the newspaper."

Ruth had, too, across the dining room table. Awful pictures of refugees—orphans with bundles, entire families with their belongings loaded into a donkey cart, people on foot who'd escaped with nothing but their lives, all searching for safety between the German advance and the barrier of the English Channel. All they'd found was a little town called Ypres, in Belgium, where the British and French had dug in to hold off the Bosch.

Ruth cleared her throat. "I'd like to talk to you about medical school."

John seemed to brighten, and he looked straight at her for the first time. "Yes, of course," he said. "You're the nurse, is that right?"

"For now," Ruth started, "but I really want to be a—"

"That's enough," said Father sharply. "I'm sure Dr. Doweling is quite tired from his journey." He got to his feet. "It's time to go."

The next day, Sunday, Father told Ruth to show John the sights, but because Father took the motorcar—and Elise, in case it broke down—they could only walk. Grandpa was assigned as chaperone.

John and Ruth were free to amble along the leafy streets while Grandpa strolled behind, well out of earshot, as though they were courting.

Maybe they were, Ruth thought. John was handsome enough, but she wanted to talk about medicine, not romance.

"What would you say if I told you I wanted to be a doctor?" she asked as they were walking down the tree-lined boulevard that was Thirty-Third Street.

Traffic was light. A few drivers were out in their cars, but mostly it was carriages pulled by horses, and a few other people out on foot. It wasn't noisy, but still, John said, "What?"

Ruth repeated herself, making it sound like a joke this time. She was afraid he would laugh at her.

"I would say you'd better start soon," he answered seriously. "It takes years to earn a medical degree."

She was taken aback. "But there aren't any medical schools for women."

"There are," he said. "In London there's a women's medical college, and I know they train women as doctors in France. There are some here in the States, too."

Ruth stopped in her tracks. "Father told me there were none."

John stopped, too. "That just isn't true." He waited for Grandpa to catch up and said, "Do you know that your granddaughter wants to be a doctor?"

"She's been through this with her father," said Grandpa. "Why do you ask?"

"Why didn't you tell her about the schools here in the States?" asked John. "And what about the one in London? Why've you let her spend all this time becoming a nurse instead of what she really wants to be?"

"What school in London?" Grandpa said blankly. He listened as John told him. "Well, I had no idea about anything like that," said Grandpa, somewhat in a huff. "But I suppose these are different times."

John turned back to Ruth. "With your training, the women's college would certainly consider you. You could come to London and stay with my family. What would your father say to that?"

Ruth swallowed hard and told him the truth. "He would say *no*."

That evening, Ruth sat with John and her father in the parlor. It was just the three of them, but Father was talking as though she wasn't even in the room.

"This is all very well and good," he said, when John told him about the medical colleges for women, "but what will she do for a husband? She's not likely to meet a man in a school for women, is she?"

"Father," Ruth started, but he motioned at her to be quiet.

"And even if she was accepted," said Father, "I've heard about those places. Their focus is on female patients. She wouldn't even learn how to treat men. That's not real medicine. Besides, nursing school is expensive enough."

"There are always scholarships," John persisted. "My family couldn't afford Harvard without them."

"You were a gifted student," said Father. "Ruth is good at the basics—it's all she needs. She makes good grades and she does well, but darling," he said, finally, to Ruth, "I don't know if you would stand out in a crowd."

"But," said Ruth, "I'm at the top of my class!"

"You're in a small school," said Father. "And though I'll admit you have some talent, we've talked about this before. You are a nurse, and a nurse you shall be. You might as well get used to that idea, because I will not be sending you to England to fulfill some girlish fantasy."

Ruth sat up very straight in her plush Victorian chair, trying to keep the tears out of her eyes.

The rest of the week passed slowly. Ruth showed John monuments, museums and churches. Grandpa was always there to take them out to lunch. Ruth pretended to enjoy herself, but inside she wanted to go to her room and curl up under the covers until John was gone. He had held something out to her, all in innocence. She found herself sitting in silence at lunch while John and Grandpa talked. John had worked with an X-ray machine, been trained in new surgical techniques, saved limbs, hands, even eyes. She had no doubt he would be a good doctor on the battlefield, though he seemed sad when he talked about it. *There will be so many*, he said. *It'll be like the medicine of the Napoleonic Wars where you would just cut off the wounded limb. Everything I've learned will be for nothing.* Those words went to her soul, and she stared at her uneaten sandwich. His training, like hers, might turn out to be useless.

The next Saturday, they were waving their goodbyes from the dock as his ship sailed out of the harbor. No one seemed happy, even though people threw confetti and streamers from the ship to the crowd gathered below. The departure was muted and sad, and when the ship was out of sight, the crowd dispersed into an early autumn rain. Elise drove them home in silence.

Ruth stared out the car window feeling like something had been pulled from her, like a feather plucked out of a wing. She had found, as John's boat sailed away, that she was more than sorry to see him go. He had shaken Grandpa's hand, then Father's, then Elise's, smiling and saying his thank-you's, his goodbyes. Ruth had reached out, expecting his firm, friendly grip. Instead he held her hand for a long moment, his gray eyes meeting hers. With his other hand, he had smoothed a lock of loose hair behind her ear. The touch was like a bolt of lightning. She couldn't say anything. She could hardly take a breath.

She would write to him, she decided. She would see if he wrote back, and if this incomplete feeling was mutual.

Ruth spent a week composing her first letter. It was harder than she'd thought, skirting the issue of feelings in favor of friendly information. In the midst of her indecision and different versions of the same *how are you*, a letter arrived from John.

Dear Ruth,

I have enlisted as an officer and been sent to camp to train. I hope never to have to shoot this gun they have saddled me with. Your grandfather was right—I did miss good old English tea and particularly teatime, which we have daily no matter what drills we are performing. We march, we crawl through mud, and though I have an orderly who washes my clothes, I must admit I never feel fully clean. I imagine this is only a taste of what awaits me at the front in Ypres in Belgium where I am to be stationed. I pretend that I will be able to maintain sterile conditions there, but I don't have much hope. My orderly has been to the front and returned with a wound in his leg that makes it impossible for him to do much but totter about. He doesn't speak of the war very often, but when he does, he makes it sound most awful. I don't know if he is trying to frighten me with his expertise, or just with honesty.

On the home front, my parents are well, but sad to see me leave. I know they will write to me, but I hope you will, too. I would be very glad to hear from you. Tell me about your studies. Tell me about your plans to become a doctor, for I have confidence in you, and would like to know more.

Yours most sincerely,
John

At supper that evening, there was nothing but talk of the war until Grandpa pointed to Ruth and said, "You could go over. You could serve in the hospitals. Represent the family."

"Good heavens," said Father, his fork halfway to his mouth. "Don't put crazy ideas in her head! She hasn't even finished nursing school."

"She's studied with you since she was a child," said Grandpa. "How much more ready can she be?"

"Absolutely not," said Father, looking right at Ruth. "Absolutely *not*," he said again as she began to think about what Grandpa was suggesting.

★ ★ ★

Ruth and Elise sat together in the parlor that night. Father had gone to his study. Grandpa was in the kitchen, having another piece of Cook's irresistible peach pie, Ruth suspected. She was leafing through her anatomy book. Elise had her bare feet up on the sofa, which Father hated, and was flipping through a magazine. It was after dark and the gas lamps were lit, giving the room, lined with bookshelves, a warm glow.

Ruth closed the anatomy book, marking her place with her thumb. "What would you say if I told you I was going to volunteer for the war?"

Elise turned the page. "I'd say, why would you volunteer for anything after all the money Father's spent on your school?"

"I think I want to go to Belgium," said Ruth, and hearing the words come out of her mouth made her heart flutter. "I want to help the wounded, with John."

"I'll tell you what I think," said Elise, and she turned another page. "You're sweet on him. I saw how he looked at you when he left. But have you really thought about it? I doubt it would be anything like nursing school—do you even study bullet wounds or sword wounds, or what're those things called? Bayonets?"

"That's for the doctors," said Ruth. "All I know how to do is stand by and hand them instruments. How am I going to learn to do anything more except by getting my hands dirty? I could get medical experience in Belgium I wouldn't get anywhere else."

"Why would they let you do anything over there?" Elise asked. She cocked her head. "Let's say I went, too. What would I do except watch some man work on an engine while I handed him tools? It wouldn't take long before he decided he could pick his own tools out and I'd be peeling potatoes and doing his wash."

The parlor door opened and Grandpa came in, wiping his whiskers with a napkin.

Elise swung her feet onto the floor and sat up straight. He settled next to her and eyed Ruth. "What did John have to say?"

"He says they're teaching him how to shoot a rifle and crawl in the mud," said Ruth. She looked down at the anatomy book again. "He asked me to tell him my plans."

"Plans?" said Grandpa. "What kind of plans does he think you have?"

"I think I want to represent the family," said Ruth. "In the war. Like John." She took a breath. "I'll graduate in the spring. I'm old enough to make decisions about my own life."

"You heard Father," said Elise. "He'll never let you go."

Grandpa leaned forward on the sofa, elbows on his knees. For a while, he didn't say anything. Then he looked up at the two of them. "Sometimes it's better not to listen to your father."

Ruth's mouth dropped open. "What?"

"You must be patient with him," said Grandpa, "because he lost his wife. My Marie."

Ruth and Elise glanced at each other in amazement. *Marie.* Even eighteen years after her death, Father refused to speak her name, and because of that, no one else dared. The only trace of her was an old photo on Father's nightstand. When they were little, and Father was away on house calls, the governess would sometimes tiptoe Ruth and Elise into his room to see the picture of the soft-eyed young woman with long, trailing hair.

There's your mother, she would say in a whisper, *watching you from heaven.*

Grandpa clasped his hands together. "I won't undermine

him. He is your father. However, sometimes you must have the courage to question him. Because he does make mistakes."

"What kind of mistakes?" Ruth asked, hardly believing her ears.

Grandpa looked over at Elise, on the sofa beside him. "Your mother asked for a midwife when she was in labor with you. Your father refused to call one." He turned to Ruth. "Even though she nearly died when you were born."

No one had ever told her *that*. Ruth eyed her sister. She knew Elise felt guilty about their mother's death, as though she, in taking her first breath, had been responsible. Father had never reassured Elise that this was not true. Now Ruth didn't know what to think.

"Marie wrote me a letter after you were born, Ruth," said Grandpa. "She told me she was afraid to have another child, but that your father wanted a son. And she would try."

"I killed her," said Elise miserably. "And I'm not even a boy."

"You did no such thing." Grandpa put his arm around Elise's shoulders. "She asked for help. If he had listened to her, you might still have a mother, and I might still have my only child."

"But how do you know this?" said Ruth. "She couldn't tell you… Did *Father* say something?"

"He wrote to me just after her funeral, telling me what had happened," said Grandpa in a soft voice. "Of course I was shocked. He was a doctor, after all. But then I thought, *now he's a widower, like me.* Your grandmother died of consumption, and no doctor could cure her. Perhaps having a midwife wouldn't have made any difference. Maybe no one could have saved her." He shook his head slowly. "Your father begged me to come from London and help him. *Live with us,* he said. *Leave your sorrow behind. Watch your granddaughters grow.*" Grandpa let go of Elise and balled his hands in his lap. "He met me at the dock. I'll never forget his face. He was weeping like a child, and I forgave him." He took a deep breath and looked up at Ruth. "I'm telling you this because I know your father loves you. Marie's death nearly destroyed him. If you pursue medicine, I believe he's afraid the same thing could happen to you." He leaned forward on the sofa and said, more urgently, "What if you were to become a doctor, Ruth? What would you do if someone you loved died? Because of something you did—or didn't do?"

Ruth hesitated. The nuns at Loyola often talked about death, but in hushed tones. Not in terms of the body—more the transformation of the soul. The truth was, Ruth had never seen anyone die. Father kept her away from his terminal cases, and at school—well, the doctors oversaw the transformation of souls. Not student nurses.

"What do you think it'll be like in a hospital full of wounded and dying men, Ruth?" said Grandpa. "Think about that long and hard before you make a decision."

CHAPTER FOUR

November 1914

After that conversation with Grandpa, Ruth couldn't concentrate at school. Her normal focus blurred. Her grades plummeted, and the nuns eyed her with either concern or pity. Ruth felt herself moving mechanically through her classes, day by day, asking herself the same question. *What if someone you loved died under your care?*

Advanced nursing students like her were allowed to assist the college's surgeons, but all she did was hand instruments to men in white masks. The surgeons didn't look at her twice, and weren't interested in teaching. Certainly, their thoughts about life and death were hidden from her. Ruth watched as they cut into living flesh, and asked herself if she had the courage to do the same.

The most the surgeons let the nurses do was stitch up incisions, as though sewing was beneath the men. Ruth, grounded in girlhood embroidery lessons, learned from the nuns to put a needle through skin, to make her knots tight and neat. The sisters would nod at her delicacy and skill, but if they knew more about repairing the rest of the human body, they weren't saying.

Ruth did her best to get her hands on the worst cases with Father's patients, but when they needed surgery, he would send them to another doctor at the hospital. One night, after she thought everyone had gone to bed, she noticed that the lights were still on in the office downstairs. When she went down to turn them off, she found her father in the examination room, sitting in the white wooden chair with a roll of gauze bandage in his lap.

"Ruth," he said as she stood, surprised, in the doorway. "Come in here and help me."

"What's the matter, Father?" she said when she saw his bloody wrist. It was the right wrist, and he was pressing the gauze against a wound. "What happened?"

"The MacQuistons' dog," he said. "It took me by surprise."

Ed and Marjory MacQuiston had twin girls, barely three years old and sickly. The dog, small, high-strung and protective, lunged at anyone who came to the house. Father went there often, sometimes twice a week, and always complained about the dog.

"It wasn't locked up?" said Ruth, bending to examine his wrist.

"Obviously not," said Father. "I'll need stitches."

For a small dog, it had left a ragged tear almost four inches long, lengthwise up his arm.

"It missed the artery," said Ruth, gently probing.

"I *know*," said Father, and he pulled away. "That's why I waited so long to do anything about it. Now get the suture kit. You'll be sewing me up."

Ruth blinked, but kept her eyes on the bloodied gauze. Father had never asked her to do anything like this. Despite

her schooling, he was still only letting her mix plaster and
give spoonfuls of medicine. He hadn't asked her for a diagnosis in years, though she would silently offer them. In his
mind, she knew she was supposed to calm the children, the
parents. The dog.

"Yes, Father," she said, and went to get the kit, the alcohol and cotton.

She wanted him to sit on the padded exam table so she could
have the chair and a better angle, but he showed no sign of
moving, so she knelt on the floor at his feet, and gently dabbed
at his wound with alcohol-soaked cotton.

"I know it burns," she said as he winced.

"Never mind that," he said through clenched teeth.

Up close and clean, the cut didn't seem bad. Not only had
the dog missed the artery, but its teeth had just scraped the
tendons. There had been a certain amount of bleeding, but
most of that had stopped.

"You may not need stitches," said Ruth. "A pressure dressing would be fine."

"Are you giving me a diagnosis?" said Father.

Ruth flushed and looked up. "No, Father, I'm just trying
to save you some pain."

"Stitches," he said. "Unless you don't think you can do
them."

Maybe he felt stupid for not seeing the dog coming. Or
maybe he was angry at the MacQuistons. Whoever. Whatever. Now he was angry at her.

"I would do it myself," said Father, "but I would prefer not
to sew with my left hand."

She realized then, with absolute clarity, that he had no faith
in her at all.

But she would do this. Because he had finally asked her to
do something. Still on the floor, she took the curved needle

out of the leather suture kit, wiped it down with alcohol and threaded it with catgut. His gaze was on her like a weight. Ruth took his hand, braced it against his knee, and pressed the point of the needle into his skin. A drop of blood sprang out. She heard him take a breath, and it occurred to her that he had never been hurt like this before—had never had stitches, or had a bone set—that his most serious and lingering injury had been her mother's death.

Just as quickly, she pierced the other side of the wound, and tied the ends of the catgut neatly, precisely, as the nuns had taught her.

They had praised her. He said, "This is not *embroidery*."

Somehow, by doing this the right way, she was making him angrier. Ruth positioned the needle for the next stitch.

"Too far from the first," he said. "Make it closer, or I'll have a scar."

He was going to have a scar no matter what. The thin skin of the wrist was prone to it. Ruth moved the needle. Her palms were sweating. "Yes, Father."

"Get on with it!"

She slid the needle in and out. She tied the stitch, but now her fingers were clumsy and the knot was off.

His irritation was a heat. "Haven't you learned *anything* in that school?"

She couldn't think of an answer. It was as if she'd forgotten everything. She angled the needle, touching skin for the next stitch, but she hesitated. Too close? Too far? And then he moved his hand.

The needle drove into the vein of his wrist. Blood dripped out, and he yanked away from her with a yelp, dragging the needle and catgut out of her fingers.

"Good God!" he shouted at her, on his feet now, blood

running down his arm. "How many hundreds have I spent on you! And this is the best you can do?"

Ruth scrambled up from the floor, her shoes catching in the hem of her long skirt, which made her feel clumsier and even more incompetent. "I'm so sorry—"

"Sorry is not *enough.*" He pointed at the door, the stairs. "Get out. Get *out!*"

Terrified of what he might say next, Ruth fled.

Father saw Ruth's grades at the end of the fall semester and refused even to look at her. The cut on his wrist had become a messy scar, which he showed her on the evening he deigned to notice her again.

"Your grades are abysmal," he said, as they sat alone by the fire in the overheated parlor. "I've paid your tuition through next semester, and you may finish school, but I'll tell you now, your future is clearly not in medicine." He leaned back in his chair, staring into the flames. "I wanted a good, decent life for you, Ruth. I've tried to keep you from being unrealistic, but you've wasted my money and your own time."

Ruth, on the sofa with her elbows on her knees, looked down at the floor. There were so many things in her mind that she didn't have the courage to say—*I never wanted to be a nurse. I wanted to follow in your footsteps, to be a doctor.*

She squeezed her eyes shut, refusing to let herself cry. In the heat of the room, she understood that whether she became a doctor or a nurse, or someone's wife, he would never have a word of praise for her. Grandpa had forgiven him for the unforgivable, widower to widower, but instead of love or compassion, Ruth could see the anger and guilt her mother's death had left in her father. Anger at his wife for having the nerve to die. Guilt for his own responsibility in her death.

CHAPTER FIVE

January 1915

It took Elise a long time to find the door with the purple music note again.

For weeks that winter, she drove slowly down Howard Street whenever she had a chance, but nothing looked familiar except the prostitutes huddled in their tight dresses and fake furs. She was afraid to ask them anything. Elise began to wonder if she had imagined the door, somehow, and the woman dressed as a man—or had been so lost in this bad part of the city that she would never find either of them.

She discovered that she didn't especially want to find the woman dressed as a man. She seemed too bold, too knowledgeable. She had already worked her way into Elise's dreams. The long eyelashes held her like a net. And the lips. There was always a kiss, which left Elise wide-awake and sweating every time. She had to throw off her covers and fling her limbs out like a starfish to let the heat rise from her body, gulping back the words, *Make up my mind…?*

One cold afternoon in January, after she'd dropped Father off at the hospital to check on a patient with some awful disease, Elise made her way up Howard Street, thinking that daylight and a different angle might make the door easier to see.

She cruised past hole-in-the-wall churches and bars, past a music hall she couldn't remember ever seeing before, and finally turned to bump over the trolley tracks into an alley. The alley was strewn with trash and broken liquor bottles, and she was afraid for the tires. She drove carefully, slowly, certain this was *not* the right place, because she didn't remember such a lot of broken glass. But sure enough, at the end of the alley was the door, fastened to a nondescript building, with the purple note, faded in the daylight.

Elise came to a dead stop at the end of the alley by the door, trying to get her bearings. Then the door opened. Her heart gave an enormous *thud*. Instead of the woman dressed as a man, she saw two police officers.

"Lock it up," said one. He was holding a padlock. If he'd looked over his shoulder, he would've seen Elise, staring in shock and surprise.

"But what about the fags?" said the other.

"They're gone. Flew the coop."

"We could wait for them inside, tonight."

"Not worth it," said the first one. "They've seen us. They've gone somewhere else." He handed the padlock to the other officer, who slammed the door.

"Gone where?" said the man, ratcheting the lock into place.

"The usual spots," said the first one. "You know. Don't worry, we'll track 'em down."

"Goddamn fags," said the other, and they both turned down the street, walking away from the alley, swinging their billy clubs.

Elise, frozen in her seat, didn't make a move, or a sound,

until they were well out of sight. Then she let her breath out between her teeth, put the car in gear, and drove, trembling, in the other direction.

Half an hour later, Elise found Ruth standing alone in the blowing cold at the intersection of North Charles and Cold-spring Avenue. Her heavy coat flapped around her as she waited for a trolley home from class. Elise pulled up to the curb.

"Get in!" she shouted over the noise of the engine. "How long've you been standing there?"

"Twenty minutes." Ruth shoved her book bag in the back and practically fell into the passenger seat. "The trolley's always late." She blew on her hands and rubbed them together. She eyed Elise. "What's the matter with you?"

"What?" said Elise. "Nothing."

"You're pale," said Ruth. Her breath came out as steam. "It's freezing and you're sweating. Are you sick?"

Elise shook her head, not trusting her voice. *Goddamn fags.*

"Well, you *look* sick," said Ruth, and she took an envelope out of her pocket. "Here. See if this'll snap you out of it."

"What's this?"

"A letter from John," said Ruth. "It's not long. I don't think he ever has time to write anything long. Read it. It's interesting."

Elise frowned. Ruth was trying to tell her something, but she was so distracted. Elise fumbled the letter open and skimmed two short paragraphs.

"Ambulance drivers...are women?" she said in amazement. "All the men are fighting, so the women are driving?"

Ruth raised an eyebrow. "Maybe you wouldn't have to peel potatoes and do laundry. Maybe you could fix ambulances. Who knows? Maybe there're dozens of girls like you over there."

"What do you mean by that?" Elise said nervously.

Ruth frowned at her. "Mechanics, Elise. What did you think I meant?"

Elise put the letter down. "You're seriously thinking about going?"

Ruth let her breath out in the cold air and nodded, as if reassuring herself. "I'll graduate in June, and then...well, then I'll just *go*."

Elise blinked at the letter. "What if the war's over by June?"

"They thought it'd be over by Christmas," said Ruth. "Christmas has come and gone."

"Father would never allow it. He'd—" Elise heard how her own words sounded and stopped.

Ruth was wiping one eye with the heel of her hand. "I didn't tell you this." She put both hands over her face. "He said medicine wasn't in my future."

"When was this? Why on earth would he say such a thing?"

"He got bitten by the MacQuistons' dog." Ruth dropped her hands into her lap. "He wanted me to stitch him up. I did a terrible job. He wouldn't even let me finish. Then he saw my grades. He thinks he's wasted his money on nursing school." She took a shaky breath. "He's so angry. I just don't think I can stay."

Elise looked down at John's letter. It was like a beckoning finger. "You don't have to go to *war*," said Elise. "We could get a place together." She touched her sister's shoulder lightly, knowing that more would make Ruth break down. "We'll move out. I can find us an apartment."

"Neither of us have jobs," said Ruth. "How would we pay for that?"

"I'll be a—a nanny," said Elise. "You'll be a nurse. We can do it."

Ruth let out a breathless laugh. "A *nanny*?"

"A teacher?" said Elise. "A chauffeur?"

"Oh, Elise," said Ruth. She sniffed hard. Tears were rolling down her cheeks. "You're not that kind of a girl—and you don't need a job. You're going to be the one who stays with Father through sickness and health until the day he dies. You'll get the house. You'll get the car. You'll have an inheritance to get you through your old age. You're special to him…and I'm…not."

"Don't say that," whispered Elise. "It isn't true. Don't even *think* that. Anyway, you're the one who's going to be a doctor."

"Just like him?" Ruth said bitterly.

Someone honked behind them. Elise pushed the letter at her sister and put the car in gear.

Ruth wiped her eyes. "I don't want to go home."

"We won't," said Elise, and she spun the steering wheel to the left. "I know a coffee shop on Calvert. We can go there and talk."

As they got closer to Calvert, the traffic backed up. Carriage horses stood steaming in the cold as their drivers craned their necks to see what was holding things up. Motorcars honked, and even through the closed windows, Elise could hear men yelling. People were walking in the street in their muffs and coats. And hats. There was something about the hats. Women in heavy coats and festive summer hats were blocking traffic, walking in the street with signs that said Votes For Women.

"What's going on?" Elise asked, mystified.

"Don't you ever read the paper?" said Ruth in a tone that indicated that she knew Elise never touched the newspaper. "The purple, green and white? They're marching for women's suffrage. There must be a rally somewhere down the street."

"Suffrage?" echoed Elise.

"The right to *vote*, Elise." Ruth made an impatient gesture at the impatient people all around them. "Surely you've heard about *that*."

Elise didn't say anything. Ruth rolled her eyes at her.

"Where's the coffee shop?" Ruth asked.

Traffic was piling up behind them. There was no way to back out or go forward. Elise pointed in the direction the women with the signs were marching. "Four or five blocks away."

"I guess we can't just leave the car and walk there," said Ruth.

"We're *not* leaving the car," said Elise.

Ruth huddled into her coat. "Then I guess we're stuck."

They watched as a dozen broad-chested policemen shouldered their way between cars and carriages, following the women in the summer hats. Elise shivered. In a minute, there were even more police. Now they were running. Women were running, too. Signs fell to the street, and the winter wind blew them around like trash.

A police officer grabbed a woman on the sidewalk and shoved her against a wall. As though in an awful sort of dance, the woman spun away and fled. The police officer turned, wielding his billy club, searching for his next target. She came almost immediately, hobbled by her long skirt and heavy coat, holding on to her white summer hat with both hands. Elise noticed she had gray hair as the police officer brought the billy club down.

The woman crumpled, out of sight, onto the sidewalk. Elise heard Ruth gasp. The police officer raised the billy club and brought it down again, hard.

"My God," said Ruth, as she opened the car door, letting in a blast of cold air and the sound of muffled shrieks.

"Wait!" Elise yelled as Ruth scrambled out in her school uniform and heavy coat. "No, wait, you can't leave." Elise grabbed for the handle on her side, but Ruth turned once, gave her a paralyzing look, and shut the door.

CHAPTER SIX

———————————

"Stay where you are," said the policeman as Ruth ran over to help the woman he'd beaten to the ground. He brandished his club at her. Ruth glanced over her shoulder and saw Elise, thankfully still inside the car, watching with her hand over her mouth.

"You've hurt her." Ruth tried to make her voice authoritative. "I'm a nurse. I'm here to help."

The woman moaned. There was blood on her chin, and she struggled to sit up. She was not a young woman. Ruth crouched next to her. The policeman took a step back, as though to give her room.

"Where did he hit you?" whispered Ruth.

"Here," gasped the woman, touching her ribs.

"You've *hurt* her," Ruth said, peering up at the policeman. "You must call an ambulance."

"This way!" shouted the policeman. He waved at a horse-drawn van rumbling up the street. It was coming against the stalled traffic, and the driver was making the horses go onto the sidewalk.

An ambulance, Ruth thought, and bent over the woman again. "You'll be all right," she said, trying to keep her tone calm. "But we'll get you to the hospital."

The woman dabbed at the blood, staining her white cuff. "I'm bleeding."

"It's just a scratch," said Ruth, then gasped as the policeman pulled her roughly to her feet. "What are you *doing*?" she demanded, and then she saw that the van was not an ambulance, but a paddy wagon with Police written on the side in white letters. The last thing Ruth saw as she was shoved inside was Elise, openmouthed, still inside the car.

Ruth and the woman who had been beaten sat handcuffed in the paddy wagon with five other women, crammed together in the dim box that smelled of sweat and urine. A dark-haired matron sitting opposite Ruth, so close that their knees touched, looked like she should have been home with half a dozen children.

"Listen," the matron said grimly, "I've told the others, but you two need to know as well—when we're processed at the police station, remember to tell them that you will not be eating the filth they serve in the prison cells. We will not give up our right to protest, and we will be hunger-striking as soon as they lock us up."

Ruth felt her eyes go wide, but she didn't say anything. Prison? Hunger-striking? The handcuffs were so tight. She could only hope that Elise would get home quickly and tell Father what was going on. She held her breath against the stink in the wagon and tried not to think about how angry Father would be.

* * *

The police station was a brick building with heavy wooden doors and barred windows, built like a fort. Inside, dozens of women were sitting on benches, and standing where there was no more room to sit. Some were chained to a metal bar that ran the length of one wall. The room, small with a high ceiling, was noisy and hot and stank of cigar smoke. The police were blots of blue in the crowd of white hats and dark coats. There were other men, too, husbands, Ruth thought, of the women who had been arrested, crowding around the high-set sergeant's desk, trying to get their wives out before they were put into cramped, dirty cells for the night.

Ruth kept her eyes on the station's front door, but the men coming in and out were strangers. Hours passed. The lights came on in the police station as it got dark outside. The woman who had been beaten turned to Ruth at one point and thanked her for coming to help. She seemed calm now. She scrubbed at the blood on her sleeve with spit and her fingers, and said, mostly to herself, "This will never come out."

By the time it was Ruth's turn to be processed, most of the other women had been taken away. Only Ruth and the women from the paddy wagon were left.

Then the heavy wooden door opened, and to Ruth's relief, Father and Elise came in. Grandpa was right behind them. Instead of letting the big wooden door slam shut, he held it so that it closed slowly, without a sound. Then he followed Elise and Father over to where Ruth was standing, cuffed. Ruth was unspeakably glad to see them all, but it was easy to see the dark anger in her father's face.

"Next!" said the sergeant, and Ruth stumbled toward him with the rest of her fellows.

Father went right up to the sergeant's desk. "What's the

meaning of this?" he demanded, before the sergeant could even ask for Ruth's name. "Why has my daughter been arrested?"

The sergeant consulted a paper on the desk and turned to Ruth. "Name?" he barked.

"Ruth Duncan," said Ruth, with all the quiet dignity she could muster.

The sergeant wrote this down. "Sir, she was arrested for disturbing the peace."

"She wasn't disturbing anything!" said Elise. "She's a nurse! She was trying to help a woman who was being *beaten*!"

The sergeant ignored her. "We picked her up at a suffrage demonstration, sir," he said, and leaned forward a bit. "You might want to keep the girls in your family under control. Avoid this sort of thing in the future."

"There will be nothing of the sort in the future," said Father tightly. "What will it cost to keep her out of jail?"

"Bail is ten dollars," said the sergeant.

Father reached for his wallet and took out two fives. He handed them to the sergeant, who wrote a receipt. It seemed to take a long time. Father didn't even glance in Ruth's direction. Grandpa shook his head sadly. Elise crossed and uncrossed her arms. When the transaction for her freedom was finally complete, another officer removed the handcuffs.

Ruth rubbed her chafed wrists. "Thank you, Father," she said. "I didn't mean to—"

"Don't *ever* let me find you in circumstances like this again," said Father in the harshest tone she had ever heard from him.

Without hesitation, he slapped her, once—hard—across the face.

Cook held a supper plate for Ruth, but Ruth couldn't eat and crawled into bed, leaving the ham slice and mashed potatoes untouched. She had homework due the next day, but was too teary to do it. She'd never been hit before. Had never expected to be hit. The fury in her father's eyes, as he'd raised his hand to strike, had terrified her. She cried silently into her pillow and was awake long after she heard the rest of her family come upstairs to sleep. No one came to comfort her.

By the time she fell asleep, it was almost time to get up. Ruth went downstairs hesitantly, dressed in fresh clothes, her face washed, her long dark hair combed out and braided. Her wrists were still red, and she had chosen a blue dress with long sleeves to hide them. She worried about running into Father, but Cook said he was already out on a house call. Neither Elise nor Grandpa was out of bed yet—at least that was normal. Cook smiled at her as though nothing was wrong and gave her a couple of soft-boiled eggs, a biscuit and a mug of coffee.

At school, one of the nuns was waiting for her at the class-room door with a note. Instead of going to class, Ruth was to report to the director of the school of nursing immediately.

Ruth sat in a wooden chair in front of the director's desk, waiting for her. The office hadn't been redecorated since Victorian times, with its walnut walls and gas lamp sconces. The windows were leaded glass, sparkling clean, and on the walls were photos of graduating classes from the late 1800s all dressed in the same white frocks and caps, all arranged with the tallest graduates standing in the back. Ruth had time to take this in before the director came through the door, eased her way behind her desk and sat.

She was an old woman with a ruddy Irish complexion, and Ruth could see the heat of her temper rising around her neck and into her cheeks.

"It's come to our attention that you were in trouble with

the police last night," said the director. She might as well have been talking about a murder, considering her tone. "You were attending a suffrage demonstration. I'd hoped I was mistaken about this, but I don't believe I am."

"Ma'am," said Ruth. "I wasn't attending anything. The police were beating a woman—she fell to the ground! I went to see if I could help."

"What were you doing at a violent demonstration?" demanded the director. "Don't you know those suffragettes are radicals? First, it's the vote. Then women will start doing men's jobs. The next thing you know, we'll have women doctors, and then where will the nurses be?"

Ruth looked down at her hands. "I—I just wanted to help. Surely there's no harm in that."

The director leaned over the edge of her desk. "Ruth Duncan, your tenure as a student here is over. You will pack up your things and leave this campus immediately."

Ruth looked up, not sure she had heard correctly. "My tenure? What do you mean? You *can't* just—"

"I assure you that I *can*," said the director, "and I can assure that you *will* leave immediately and go back to your father. Maybe he can teach you a thing or two that we missed here, but I doubt it." She stood. "I wish you luck in whatever you endeavor to do, but you will not do it *here*."

Ruth waited for the trolley in the cold, feeling devastated and ashamed. What now? Hopeless scenarios went through her mind, but worst of all, what would Father do when he found out? She was tempted to blame the suffragettes for everything, but, the only one she could honestly blame was herself.

She got home, sat down in the parlor and wrote the letter she'd been composing in her head.

Dear John,

I hope you are well, and your family is the same. I have some difficult news for you.

I have been compelled to leave nursing school under some unfortunate circumstances which I will not go into until we see each other again. It's enough to say it was a result of my own foolishness, and not a question of skill. I am still as determined to be a doctor as ever. I am writing to tell you that I have decided to volunteer for service in the war, as a nurse or an aide, or whatever medical position I can get. I need your help for this. I'm afraid I will not be able to depend upon a letter of recommendation from my school, or my father, so I am asking you to speak for me.

Please let me know what, if anything, you can do.
Yours most sincerely,
Ruth Duncan

If Father had been angry about Ruth's arrest, he would be furious about her expulsion. Ruth, afraid of another slap, waited to tell him at supper, across the table and well out of reach. Grandpa and Elise—even Cook—just stared at her, but Father smoldered at the head of the table.

"Go to your room," he snapped, as though she were a child.

She left her dinner on her plate and went upstairs, lay down on her bed and waited for tears to come, but there was nothing in her heart but fear.

Half an hour later, there was a knock on Ruth's door. She sat up and tried to compose herself, but she was completely uncomposed. "Yes?" she said, and felt her heart thud in her chest as her father came in.

He sat beside her on the bed, fists on his knees.

"I've just had a long talk with your grandfather," he said.

"He told me about the conversation you had regarding your mother. About going against my wishes. About going to war."

"Yes, Father," whispered Ruth.

"I loved your mother," he said, without looking at her. "I never laid a hand on Marie, and I'm sorry that I struck you." He took a breath. "But you've left me without a lot of choices." He turned to her on the bed. "Why do you provoke me, Ruth? Tell me, so that I'll understand."

"I'm not trying to provoke you," said Ruth. "I never have."

"But you are," he said. "I see in you this desire to become a doctor—this pointless dream. Women don't have the skills. Women don't have the talent. I've told you over and over. Why don't you listen to me? Why can't you want normal things—a husband and children—like a proper young woman?"

She couldn't help it. "You mean like Elise?"

She could see him bristle. "I've never said this to anyone but your grandfather," he said in a low voice, "but your sister is lacking something." He took a deep breath. "There is a problem in her emotional development. I don't see it often in my patients, but I recognize it when I do."

"What kind of problem?" The nuns had never talked about anything like this.

"A retardation," said her father, almost in a whisper. "She'll never be socially adept, especially with men. She doesn't know how, and she can't learn." He tapped his fist three times on his knee. "I will not have two daughters with the same affliction."

"Neither one of us is *afflicted*, Father."

He narrowed his eyes at her. "You see? There you are, diagnosing again."

"But she isn't *retarded*, Father. She just likes fixing cars."

"You know so little, you don't even recognize your own ignorance." He got to his feet. "I didn't come up here to argue with you. I've apologized. That's enough."

Ruth didn't say anything. She sat on the edge of the bed, rubbing her knees, thinking about ignorance. His. Hers.

He went over to the door and stopped. "You will do one thing for me."

"Yes, Father."

"There are other nursing schools. You will finish your studies. You'll graduate. I'm willing to pay for that, but no more." He opened the door, and in a moment, she could hear him going back downstairs.

"Yes, Father," she whispered, but in her soul, she knew she was lying.

For two weeks, Ruth waited for John's reply, and during that time, she was as docile and quiet as she knew how to be. Whatever her father said, she agreed with. Whatever he told her to do, she did. She looked for other nursing schools and even lined up admissions interviews, but her heart wasn't in it, and none of them accepted her.

Ypres, Belgium.

Finding it on a map was easy. Now the American papers were putting the war news on the front page, with maps showing the movement of troops, and photos of men in trenches, filthy from head to foot. When Grandpa was done with the paper, Ruth read everything she could about the war, but found nothing about the wounded men; just how many had been killed on each side, as though it was a counting game.

Another counting game was how much money she had, and how she would afford a ticket for a ship bound for Europe. She had all of fifty dollars, saved up from the allowance her father gave her and from birthday and Christmas presents. A ticket to England, where she hoped to start her journey as a volunteer, cost sixty. Reluctantly, she called Elise into her bedroom and asked if she had the difference.

"Ten dollars?" said Elise. "That's a lot. What do you need it for?"

Ruth told her.

Elise sat down on the bed beside Ruth. "You're running away from home."

"I don't think I can run away as an adult. I think we call it 'pursuing a calling.'"

"Just a minute," said Elise, and she left. Ruth could hear her rummaging around in her own bedroom. When she came back, she was holding a coffee can. "All right," said Elise. She gave Ruth a fistful of bills. "That's ten for you and sixty for me."

"What're you going to do with sixty dollars?" said Ruth. "And how did you get that much?"

"I get an allowance, just like you," said Elise. "I've been saving."

"But what're you going to do with it?"

"Obviously," said Elise, as though it really was obvious, "I'm coming with you."

John's letter arrived the next day.

Dear Ruth,

How mysterious your circumstances sound—but the point is that you can come and that's what counts. Contact the British Embassy in Washington, DC. Let them know your plans and tell them of your skills. Be sure to tell them that you want to volunteer in Ypres, or who knows where they'll send you.

The work here is hard, but not without reward.

The letter from the embassy came early in March.

Father intercepted it, examined the envelope at the dinner

table and gave Ruth a suspicious look. "Why would the British Embassy be sending you a letter?"

"Perhaps you should open it," she said, her spoon hovering above her soup.

He did, while she sipped. Elise played with her napkin. Grandpa set his spoon down on the table. Cook waited in the doorway to the kitchen while Father took the letter out of its envelope.

"'Dear Miss Duncan,'" he read. "'Thank you for your interest in volunteering as a nurse for the war effort.'" He frowned and read on. "'Thank you as well for the information about your sister, who wishes to volunteer for the Ambulance Corps.'" He stopped. "Elise? What's this?"

"Well," blurted Elise, "she can't very well go over there by herself, can she?"

"Over there?" said Father. "Neither one of you is going 'over there.'"

"What does the letter say, Father?" said Ruth with more courage than she actually felt.

Father scowled at the page. "It *says* there are positions for both of you in Ypres." He folded the letter and held it out to Cook. "Throw this in the fire. Neither one of these girls is going anywhere."

"Yes, Doctor," said Cook and made a move to take it, but Grandpa reached out and took the letter before she could.

Ruth heard Elise gasp and swallowed hard herself. "What does the rest of it say, Grandpa?"

Grandpa stroked his beard. "It tells you where to report," he said. "It tells you who your matrons-in-command will be. It says, 'We appreciate your willingness and your sacrifice.'"

Father's face grew darker, and he glared at his father-in-law. "You've encouraged them. What could you possibly be thinking? Neither one of them is fit for a war! They're just girls!"

"Girls they may be," said Grandpa, "but these are different times, a different war. The Dowelings tell me that their street is emptied out of youngsters. Everyone has gone away to volunteer in one capacity or another."

"This is not *London*," said Father. "They are not *British*."

Grandpa gave the letter to Ruth, whose hand trembled as she took it.

"I will not underwrite this," Father said to her. "You'll not get a cent from me. How'll you get to Belgium without a ship?" he said mockingly.

"I have the money for passage, Father," said Ruth. Something hot was in her throat. It felt like rage. She tried to choke it back.

"But *why*?" demanded Father. "Why are you so eager to get into what's obviously a dangerous situation?"

"I want to be a doctor," said Ruth breathlessly. "You won't hear of it—you don't think I can do *anything*—so I might as well leave."

"You'll *never* be a doctor," Father snapped at her. "I don't care where you go. That's just a *fantasy*."

Ruth shot to her feet so fast that her chair fell over. "All I've ever done is try to please you, Father, to help you, but you *dismiss* me. And now you want me to *stay*? For what?"

He was red in the face with fury. He didn't answer.

He turned to Elise. "What about you?" he demanded. "Driving an *ambulance*?"

"I have to go with her," said Elise in a small voice, like she was admitting to a crime. "I have to. Who'll keep her out of trouble if I don't?"

"We'll take care of each other," said Ruth. "We won't be separated. You'll see."

Father shoved his chair back, threw his napkin to the floor

and stormed out of the dining room. Cook, wide-eyed, watched him go, then disappeared into the kitchen.

The room was quiet for a while, and then Grandpa said, "When will you girls be leaving?"

Ruth, still standing by her overturned chair, breathing hard, looked at the letter in her hands. At the bottom was a short imperative. "Report by April 9." She counted days in her head, something she'd done over and over in bed on sleepless nights. Seven days on a ship. Two weeks in London to get their paperwork in order.

"We'll leave at the end of the week," she said.

Three days later, Father drove the car down to the same dock John had left from. Grandpa sat beside him in the passenger seat, with Ruth and Elise in the back, hugging the luggage that wouldn't fit in the trunk. It was a silent drive, and it had been a tense, silent week. Everyone was biting their tongues, especially now, as they approached the dock. Ruth took a deep breath to brace herself for one last confrontation at the bottom of the gangplank. She knew it was coming. She was pretty sure she knew what her father would say. She just didn't know what she would say back. She would stay calm, she told herself. She would stay civilized. If worst came to worst, she and Elise would just leave without another word. Ruth glanced at her sister as Father parked and turned off the engine. Elise, wrapped up in a coat and scarf, with a suitcase in her lap, was wide-eyed as though she had suddenly realized that she was leaving home and going to some unknown, foreign place. Father and Grandpa got out of the car and opened the trunk. Elise made a move for the door, but Ruth touched her arm.

"Are you all right?" said Ruth softly.

Elise just nodded.

"You don't have to go."

"I want to," whispered Elise.

Porters took their trunks, and Grandpa carried their suitcases while Father lagged behind, rehearsing his objections once again, Ruth thought. Her chest tightened as they pushed through the crowd. Confetti flew in the cold March morning, and colorful streamers were being thrown from high on the stern of the ship by laughing passengers already aboard. Ruth peered to see them, tried to picture herself up there smiling her goodbyes, throwing handfuls of colored paper, and couldn't quite do it. The gangplank loomed ahead, and Grandpa put the suitcases down. As he straightened, Ruth saw the tiredness around his eyes and how his shoulders slumped. He opened his arms, and Elise practically fell into his embrace.

"Oh, Grandpa," she sobbed.

"You'll be all right, my dearest." He reached for Ruth and hugged them both. "You'll be all right." He said it like a prayer. Ruth felt him take her hand, and opened her eyes long enough to see the folded money he pressed into her palm. "Take it," he whispered. "You'll need it in London." He held on to them for another long moment and released them with a gust of a sigh.

Ruth pushed the money into her pocket and turned to Father, to meet his steely eyes.

He took a breath. "You won't change your mind," he said flatly.

"No, Father," said Ruth.

"Elise?"

Elise shook her head, wiping her eyes with the end of her scarf.

"You will write," said Father, in the exact same tone.

"Yes, of course."

Ruth watched, blinking back tears as he swallowed hard. Then he held out his hand, perfunctorily, professionally.

"Good luck," he said. "I do wish you luck."

She took his hand and shook it, unable to say anything. He let go and turned. "Elise?"

"Goodbye, Father." Elise sniffed and awkwardly shook his hand as well.

"Good luck," he said again, and turned to Grandpa. "I believe we should go now." Without waiting, he spun on his heel and began walking toward the car, straight-backed.

Grandpa watched him go and let out his breath in a cloud of steam. "You know he loves you both."

"We know," whispered Elise.

"We know," echoed Ruth.

The ship's horn sounded.

"Best get on board, then," said Grandpa. "Be safe. Be well. Write." He turned and hurried off after Father.

Ruth and Elise hoisted their suitcases and made their way slowly up the gangplank until they reached the deck.

Elise stopped abruptly. "Look," she said, and opened her right hand. In it was a crumpled envelope.

"What is it?" said Ruth. She was expecting a letter—an angry one—filled with the words Father hadn't said on the dock.

Elise opened the envelope. Inside was a stack of twenty-dollar bills. "There must be two hundred dollars in here," whispered Elise.

Ruth looked down at the dock. Far below, she could still see Father and Grandpa, standing by the car.

As the streamers and confetti fell, she watched Father wiping his eyes as Grandpa gripped his shoulder, both of them weeping like children.

CHAPTER SEVEN

April 1915
Ypres, Belgium

Finally, Ruth thought, peering out the window of the train, after the voyage from America, and the red tape of British bureaucracy, here they were in the thick of it.

The sun was up by now, and she elbowed Elise, who'd been sleeping since they'd boarded the train in Calais.

"I'm awake," muttered Elise. "Are we there?"

"Almost." Ruth pointed at the town in the near distance. "I think that's Ypres."

Elise rubbed her eyes. "Look at all the soldiers." She sounded amazed. Even though this train was full of soldiers, as was the ship from Dover, Ruth was just as impressed by how many there were between them and the town. Soldiers in dirty uniforms were marching, riding horses, sitting on the ground and smoking cigarettes, or just standing, watching the train go by. There were more than she could hope to count, driving teams of horses pulling great guns behind them. Ruth twisted in her seat to get a better look at the guns. They were enormous—

like cannons—but so large it was hard to see how even a six-horse team could move them. And there was mud. A lot of mud. The train passed another crew of men with horses and a cannon, struggling to free the wheels of an overloaded cart. Everyone was spattered with mud.

The train slowed and pulled into a station with a bullet-pocked sign that said Ypres.

"Is this where we get off?" asked Elise.

"No," said Ruth, as everyone else in the car grabbed their duffels and backpacks and rifles. "We're supposed to be south of here, where the hospitals are."

"Why isn't the hospital in town?" asked Elise.

"I guess it's nearer the front lines," Ruth said, sounding to herself far more informed than she truly felt.

"Oh," said Elise, leaning back in her seat. "I guess that's where the ambulances are, too."

"That would make sense," said Ruth.

Elise nodded, but she looked jumpy.

Ruth smoothed her hair and tried to fight down her own nerves. She hadn't expected to feel this way. Back in England, everything had been calm, seemingly normal. She and Elise had stayed for two weeks with the Dowelings and even gone sightseeing while their papers were put in order, but underneath the normalcy was an anxiousness that everyone seemed to feel.

"It's the war," Mr. Doweling had told them, while they were sipping tea late one afternoon in the parlor. He had explained to them, grimly, that as Britons, everyone had a duty to King and country. He'd pointed to a photo of King George on the wall and explained that the war was based on honor. The Germans had none. The British had a monopoly on it. The French were certainly doing their bit.

He had shaken Ruth's hand and Elise's. "It was good of you

to come," he'd said as he left them at the train, which had taken them to Dover, where they had watched the white cliffs recede into the distance at dusk, as their ship headed through U-boat-infested waters for the French port of Calais.

Now, hours later, with a mostly sleepless night behind them, it was dawn in Belgium.

Elise leaned across Ruth to get a better look out the dirty window. "Is it my imagination, or does Ypres look a lot like Baltimore?"

The cobbled streets, the brick houses built in rows, even the stone church across from the station seemed like a photo of some part of Baltimore that they hadn't seen before. Maybe Ypres and its countryside would be familiar, Ruth thought, but in her heart, she knew it wouldn't.

All of the soldiers had left the train now. The conductor, also a soldier, came through with his helmet in his hand. "Ladies?" he said, with a British accent. "This is the last stop before the end of the line."

"Is that where the hospitals are?" asked Ruth.

"Aye," said the conductor. He studied them for a moment. "Nurses?"

Ruth nodded, her mouth suddenly dry.

The conductor looked at them kindly. "Keep your heads down," he said. "Good luck, then."

"Thanks," murmured Elise as he made his way briskly to the end of the car.

The afternoon was quiet at Hospital Number Four—about ten miles to the south of Ypres. Ruth stepped out for a much-needed breath of air and found Elise waiting for her, in uniform— a knee-length skirt and a neatly ironed jacket—smart and well turned out, her long dark hair braided and tucked up in a bun.

"Where are you staying?" said Ruth, because the first thing that had happened was that they had been separated.

"I'm about a mile away, by the motor pool in a shack full of bunks," said Elise. "The girls—and they're all girls—are eaten up by lice, and most of them don't look like they sleep much anyway. Half of them smoke." She produced a cigarette from her pocket. "Do you want it?"

"No," said Ruth. "*No*. Are you joking?"

Elise put the cigarette back in her pocket. "Where are you staying? In some posh little room?"

"I share my posh little room with three other nurses. One looks like a snorer."

Elise smiled. It was good to see that, and Ruth hoped she would still be smiling after the next few weeks.

"Have you seen John yet?" said Elise.

"No. He's in Hospital Number Three, up the road." Ruth pointed in the direction of the booming guns, too distant to provide much more than a vibration in the ground. It was unnerving, though, to be this close to them, only a few miles from the front. "That's where they do most of the amputations."

Elise wrinkled her nose. "What about you?"

"This is an abdominal station. We do belly wounds. Chest wounds." She didn't want to describe what was going on in the hospital behind her.

Elise didn't seem to be listening. "Did they tell you about the train for the wounded?"

"No—what train?"

"It goes down to the front lines at night. They load it up with the wounded and bring them in for the ambulances. The ambulances bring them to the hospitals. Everything's supposed to run like clockwork."

"Clockwork?" echoed Ruth. She had seen a man without a face today, still alive somehow.

Elise checked the watch that Mr. Doweling had given her. "I have to go. They're taking me on the grand tour, Hospitals One through Fourteen. I have to memorize the routes. They don't use headlights at night."

"Oh," said Ruth. "Try to be safe."

"I will," said Elise and kissed her on the cheek.

Ruth watched her go down the muddy road until she disappeared behind a group of marching men.

Only a few hours ago, at the train station, an ambulance had picked them up. Since there wasn't room in the cab for three, Ruth and Elise had chosen to ride together in the back, where the wounded would travel from the front lines to the Casualty Clearing Stations, otherwise known as Hospitals One through Fourteen.

The driver, who'd introduced herself as Tippy, was a stout little English woman who looked to be about thirty. She'd dropped Ruth off at Hospital Number Four, as per her orders, and taken Elise on to the ambulance barracks where Elise was going to get a uniform and an ambulance. Elise was part of the Volunteer Aid Detachment now, and committed to at least six months of duty as a VAD. From the sound of Tippy's vehicle, it seemed as though Elise's mechanical skills would come in handy. Even as they had driven off together, Elise in the passenger seat, Ruth could hear them talking about fuel lines and cold starts.

She was afraid for Elise. Her sister had avoided Father's practice diligently her whole life and now, well, now Ruth had the panicky feeling that she should tell Elise that this was all a mistake, that they should pack up and go home before it was too late.

But it was already too late.

Behind her in the hospital, men groaned in agony, desperate for a sip of water. Water wasn't allowed with abdominal wounds. It was the first thing the nurses had told her.

Ruth adjusted her short white nurse's veil, part of her new uniform. She had lied about having a nursing certification from Loyola, and they were so desperate for help here, no one asked any questions. Ruth was now a full-fledged Royal Army Medical Corps nurse, in the blue dress with the white apron. Men already called her Sister. The doctors—Emmanuel, whom they called The Mouse, and MacPherson—had called her Sister.

"Duncan?" said a woman behind her, and she turned to see the head nurse, Mary Gardener, beckoning. Gardener seemed to have a calm and gentle soul, at least at first glance. Ruth didn't know how she managed to stay calm after what Ruth had seen in those hospital beds.

"Teatime's over," said Gardener. "Back to work for you."

"Yes, Sister," said Ruth. "Thank you, Sister."

CHAPTER EIGHT

Elise's ambulance was really just a truck—what Matron called a lorry—with six racks in the back for stretchers, and a big red cross painted on either side of a canvas cover, flapping in a light wind.

Elise, in her new uniform, had been marched out of the barracks with three other women who had just joined the Ambulance Corps. Now they stood in a huddle while their matron, a heavyset woman with a cigarette hanging out of the corner of her mouth, read off the rules and regulations from a clipboard.

"No men in the barracks," she said. "No smoking in the barracks." She took a drag on the cigarette and eyed them, one at a time. "And no quitting. You're signed up for six months. Six months you shall stay."

"Yes, Matron," chorused two of the women, sounding enthusiastic.

Matron scowled at Elise and the willow-thin girl next to

her. There had been no introductions. "Yes, Matron," Elise and the other girl mumbled.

The wind shifted, bringing with it the smell of something burning. Elise glanced down the line of twenty ambulances, thinking that maybe one of them had caught fire. The trucks—lorries—were a haphazard collection of old and new, tires taped against old blowouts, fenders dented. There was no fire that she could see, but what she did see surprised her. Even though they were rim-deep in mud, the ambulances were all spotlessly clean.

Matron continued to read off the rules. The girl beside Elise nudged her with an elbow.

"What do you think happened to the drivers we're replacing?" she whispered.

"Um," said Elise, "maybe their six months were up?"

"No talking!" snapped Matron.

The girl ducked her head. Elise tried to smile. She wanted to be as enthusiastic as the other two women, but something *was* on fire. Smoke was now rising in thick black puffs from behind a grove of mangled trees, and there was a constant low booming that she could feel through her feet. Wasn't anyone paying attention?

"Excuse me," she said, when Matron lowered the clipboard.

"Excuse me, *Matron*."

"Excuse me, Matron," said Elise. "There's a fire—" She pointed to the rising smoke. "Shouldn't we call someone?"

Everyone looked toward where she was pointing. As if to emphasize the danger, something exploded in the distance, throwing flames into the air along with the smoke.

Elise glanced at Matron, who plucked the cigarette from her mouth and flicked off the ash.

"Darling girl," she said, "that's only the war."

★ ★ ★

When Elise got into her ambulance for the requisite hospital tour, she realized that the steering wheel and the gearshift were on the wrong side. Tippy, in the passenger seat, shook her head as Elise ground the gears, trying to find Reverse.

"You know," said Tippy in a snotty-sounding accent, "you *are* supposed to be able to drive."

"I *can* drive," snapped Elise. She shoved the clutch all the way to the floorboard and yanked the gearshift into place, and the grinding stopped. The ambulance coughed. Elise looked over her shoulder to find not a window to see through, but a sheet of metal between her and the back.

"That's to keep them from grabbing you," Tippy informed her.

"Who?"

"The soldiers, of course," said Tippy. "Most of them are hysterical by the time we get them. Some have lost their minds from the shelling. All in all, it's quite horrible, but you must keep your chin up."

Elise swallowed, not sure how much of this was meant to scare her.

Tippy waved a hand. "Let's carry on, shall we?"

"Sure," said Elise. She backed the ambulance up and joined the line of lorries heading for the main road.

Elise had seen a map in the barracks of how the fourteen hospitals were arranged in a kind of long oval, almost like a racetrack, with the ambulance barracks and motor pool in the center. One thin line of road trailed off toward the front, but stopped where hatched lines, indicating the railroad tracks, came in. When Elise had seen that, she'd been relieved. Ambulances met the train and that was that. No driving to the front.

"Remember," said Tippy, "we almost always drive at night, so you must memorize the landmarks for each hospital."

They turned out onto the main road, and Tippy was silent for a while. The road was a mess, full of potholes and mostly mud. Rain, which had started as a drizzle, came down harder, turning the mud into slime. They passed four-horse teams pulling artillery, men making their way on foot to the front in wet uniforms, and twice as many men, bandaged but still walking toward the hospitals, as though this was something they did every single day. One of the horse-drawn wagons was stopped in the middle of the road as the horses struggled in the fresh mud. Tippy leaned over and honked long and loud to clear the road, but the sound of the horn hardly registered under the noise of the engine that was coming from overhead. The horses didn't even flinch at the sound, but Elise stuck her head out the window into the rain in time to see an aeroplane fly past. She watched it with her mouth wide-open until it disappeared into the gray distance.

"Did you see that?" she said to Tippy, who was watching her with undisguised disdain. "Did you *see*?"

"You're lucky that was one of ours," said Tippy blandly. "Otherwise, by now you'd be blown to bits."

"What?" said Elise, wiping the water out of her eyes. "But this is an ambulance."

"The Bosch want to kill us all," said Tippy. Her mouth tightened into a knowing line. "Now. Drive on."

The first few hospitals were visible from the road. One and Two were large wooden sheds with patched tin roofs. Elise stared as they drove by. These dumps were *hospitals*? She had expected something more permanent—built with bricks at least, like the ones back in Baltimore.

"You'll be able to see these in the dark," said Tippy, "most of the time. Unless the aeroplanes are around, and then all the lights are off. But the next ones are set back a bit. You just have to know where to turn." As Elise drove, Tippy pointed to three burnt tree stumps in a row. "That's the turn for Hospital Three," she said. "The one for amputations. Most of the time you'll be going there."

"My sister works at Number Four," said Elise. "She's a nurse."

"Abdominal wounds," said Tippy. "Another popular destination."

Elise couldn't decide if Tippy was being helpful or, for some reason, vengeful. Elise kept quiet for the next two hours as they made the circuit, noting the blown-apart tree that now looked like a witch's hand as the marker for Hospital Ten, where they were supposed to bring men without faces. *Wouldn't they be dead?* Elise wanted to ask, but she didn't think she'd get a straight answer.

At one point, when they were almost back at the barracks, Tippy made her stop by at the biggest intersection Elise had seen so far. There was room for at least four lanes of traffic. A long line of supply lorries drove past groups of wounded men who straggled along the sides of the road.

"Shouldn't we help them?" said Elise.

Tippy shook her head. "They've been through triage at the front, and if the doctors at the front say they can walk to a hospital, then they can walk."

"But we *could* help them," said Elise, and she put the ambulance in gear to do just that.

Tippy put a hand on hers. "No," she said. "I just wanted to show you this. The train—and the front—is that way. You'll become very familiar with this road, and men like those." She nodded at the wounded soldiers plodding toward them. "You must learn one thing above all else."

"What's that?" Elise asked.

"Harden your heart," said Tippy softly. "You can't save everyone."

CHAPTER NINE

Ruth followed the head nurse, Gardener, back into the hospital.

For the second time that day, the smells hit her as she walked through the wide swinging doors and into the main ward. Ruth recognized the faint taint of carbolic acid and lye soap, but over that lay the stink of blood, urine and feces. There was another smell she couldn't quite identify, a kind of fleshy rot. She swallowed hard and wondered if she would ever get used to this.

"The bedpans need to be emptied," said Gardener, seeing the expression on Ruth's face. "You can help the orderlies."

Ruth glanced around the ward. Rows and rows and rows of men wrapped in stained white bandages lay silently in their cots. There were two orderlies that she could see, and two other nurses. The orderlies were emptying bedpans. The other two nurses were not.

Ruth took as much of a breath as she could manage. "I'm

a trained nurse, Sister. Are you sure you don't need me to do something else?"

"Well," said Gardener. "There's certainly a lot to do. I'm about to start administering afternoon medications. Would you prefer to help me?"

"Yes, Sister."

"Good," said Gardener mildly. "This way, then."

Ruth followed her across the ward, between cots. Some of the men were asleep, but most were not, and Ruth saw them follow her with their eyes, some pleading, some glazed over with pain, and some just staring at the hospital's metal roof. There was low conversation, off in a corner. As they passed the cots, to Ruth's uneasy surprise, no matter how awful the wound seemed to be, no one was weeping or screaming.

Ruth licked her lips nervously. "They're so quiet," she said to Gardener's broad white back.

"There's no honor in disturbing an entire ward with your own distress," said Gardener. She stopped and felt one man's forehead. The man blinked up at her, bandaged around his belly and chest. A rubber drain ran out from under his sheet and into a tall flask. The fluid was green, tinged with red, to Ruth's eyes, a sure sign of infection.

"Me temp's down," said the man hoarsely to Gardener. "Feelin' better, I am."

"Very good," said Gardener. "I'll be back soon with morphine." She gestured at Ruth. "This is Sister Duncan. She's just come in from America. Sister, this is Sergeant Hadley."

Hadley touched his temple, either a weak salute, or a tip of an imaginary hat. His face was bloodless. A shadow of stubble made his skin almost blue. "Pleased to meet you, Sister."

"Pleased to meet you," echoed Ruth. She rested her fingers against his forehead as well. He was burning up with fever.

Ruth glanced at Gardener, wide-eyed. Surely she must know, this man was…dying.

"Come along, Sister," Gardener said to her, and turned away.

At the far end of this row of cots were the medical supply cabinets. When the two of them were out of earshot of the men, Ruth whispered, "Hadley—he's in terrible shape. He needs a *doctor*."

"My dear," said Gardener in a normal tone, "he's seen a doctor. The Mouse put him back together yesterday."

"But something's wrong. You felt how hot he is—and that drain…"

"It should be running clear," said Gardener, "but it isn't."

"What are you going to do?" whispered Ruth.

Gardener opened one of the supply cabinets, a white wooden unit with a red cross on it. Inside, neatly arranged, were stacks of bandages, clear bottles of alcohol, white cotton in rolls and a collection of glass syringes in a metal tray. Filling the shelf at eye level were brown vials of morphine.

"Can you give an intravenous injection?" Gardener asked.

Ruth had done this twice in school, on fellow students, with a saline solution. Both had started crying when the needle went in, and the nun had made Ruth stop.

"Yes," said Ruth.

Gardener handed her a vial and a syringe. "Fill it to here." She indicated a tiny number on the glass. "No more. And give it to Hadley."

"That's not going to help him," said Ruth. "He needs…"

Gardener turned to face her. "Surgery?" she said in a low voice. "Any more and he'll die on the table. I'm surprised he survived the night. The Mouse took nine bullets out of him and two pieces of shrapnel."

Ruth wasn't sure what shrapnel was. "But he has an *infection*," she said. "Morphine won't do anything for that."

"Very true," said Gardener. "Nothing in this cabinet will help an infection. In fact, as you're about to find out, we have very few tools for treating these men." She nodded at the syringe Ruth was holding. "Sometimes the best we can do is make them comfortable."

Ruth looked up at her, speechless.

"Until they die," said Gardener softly. "That's right." She put a hand on Ruth's shoulder. "Give Hadley his shot before his last dose wears off. Do a good job, won't you? Don't make a mess of his arm."

Ruth nodded, dry in her mouth. "Yes, Sister."

"Carry on," said Gardener as she turned back to the cabinet.

Ruth stumbled through the ward, trying *not* to stumble, trying hard to walk in a manner that didn't betray that she now knew Hadley was a dead man. And how many of these others were, too? She dared to glance down at their faces. Blank, pained, asleep, but none of them seemed surprised. Because, she realized, they had already faced death at the front, faced death in surgery, and now they were here in the ward, facing death again. The vastness of this understanding made her breathless, like she had run a long way. Breathing hard, she found Hadley's cot. She stood next to him, dizzy.

"Hello again," she said in a small voice. His eyes were closed.

She sat on the edge of the cot, letting the dizziness pass. Hadley didn't budge. Ruth put the morphine bottle in her lap and held the syringe in her left hand. With her right, she touched his forehead again. He was cooler. Which made her afraid. She pressed her fingers to the artery in his neck. She felt stubble, cool skin. There was no pulse. Ruth snatched her hand away.

"Hadley?" she whispered. "Hadley?"

As if by magic, Gardener was standing beside her.

"Is he gone, then?" she said.

Ruth could only nod.

Gardener bent to pull the sheet over his face. She straightened and beckoned to one of the orderlies. "Come along," she said to Ruth. "And bring the morphine."

By the time they broke for supper, Ruth had injected at least twenty men. None of them cried, or even flinched. Every last one of them thanked her before they drifted off to sleep. After her first fumbling attempts, Gardener had showed her how to slip the needle into the vein, gently but firmly. Ruth watched her change the dressings on nightmare wounds—chest and belly, arms, legs—and helped as well as she could, but between the smells and the sights, she thought she might pass out.

At one point, Gardener raised a sheet to show her an unconscious man's side. Ruth had to take a step back. His leg had been removed at the hip, and the wound, like a rip in a piece of cloth, had been sewn shut over a drainage tube. The flask on the floor, where the tube emptied, was almost filled with bloody green fluid.

"Well," said Gardener. "You'll get to know this smell."

Ruth, who had been breathing through her mouth, took a small sniff. Fleshy rot. It was so strong, it nearly brought her to her knees.

"Gangrene," said Gardener. "Here now. Take his pulse."

Holding her breath, Ruth bent to the man's wrist. At first she thought he, too, had died, but then she found it, thready, irregular and weak.

"Remember how it feels," said Gardener quietly. "When the ambulances bring the wounded in tomorrow morning, we will not be operating on men without the strength to stay alive."

"Yes, Sister," whispered Ruth.

"There's one more thing I need to show you," said Gardener. "Follow me, please."

Ruth hurried after her, away from the smell and the imminent death, past the door to the operating theater, past the brick ovens where the other two nurses were busy sterilizing syringes.

Gardener led her to a door in the back, put her hand on the knob and hesitated.

"You've done a good job today," she said. "I'll admit, you surprised me. But you must always remember that this is war. Every day you'll face something you've never imagined." She turned the knob and pulled the door open. "Let's go outside," said Gardener, not unkindly.

Ruth stepped into the fresh air. The back of the hospital opened onto a stretch of churned mud and a grove of trees, just beginning to turn spring green. Beyond the trees was a low hill, and behind the hill the sun was setting in familiar shades of red and orange and violet.

Ruth let her breath out and felt her shoulders slump. At least there was a place to go to get away from the death and silent suffering. To her relief, even in this foreign land, the sun still looked the same. She inhaled deeply—smelled gangrene—and gagged. *You're imagining it*, she told herself. Ruth wanted to thank Gardener for showing her this exit, brief as it was, and turned. Then she saw what she was meant to see.

Next to the door where Gardener was standing was a blue wheelbarrow. The smell—the fleshy rot—was coming from there. Ruth stared at the pile in the wheelbarrow, the heap of bodiless arms and legs. She could see the bloody joints and cut bone, like pieces of meat in a butcher shop. She could see hands. Ruth took a breath to scream. The stink of rot

rushed into her, caught in her throat. Ruth fell to her hands
and knees in the mud and vomited until she thought her
heart would break.

CHAPTER TEN

The sound of Matron's whistle went through Elise's sleeping body like a knife. Elise jerked upright, wide-awake in the sudden brightness of the barracks bunkroom, as all around her, women shot out of their beds, fully dressed, and bolted for the door. Elise, also fully dressed—no one wore pajamas here—shoved her feet into her muddy shoes. The whistle sounded again, for anyone who could've slept through it the first time. Elise got to her feet and ran outside.

She had no idea what time it was—just night—as she clambered into her ambulance, the third one from the front of the line. She yanked the starter and pumped the gas, and the engine roared to life. The lorry in front of her jerked forward. No headlights, no taillights. Elise raced not to lose sight of it.

Out on the main road, it was a quick right turn, a mile or so to the big intersection, and then down the shallow hill, another two miles, to where the train tracks ended and the wounded began. Elise's heart pounded as she drove, practically nose to tail with the ambulance in front of her. Her mouth was absolutely dry. She tried to tell herself, *all you have to do is get them to the hospitals*, but in her gut, she knew there was going to be more to it than that. Something that Tippy knew, but hadn't mentioned. Elise thought about the soldiers they'd seen straggling along the road, and then her right front wheel hit a hole so big, she thought she'd driven into a ditch. Gritty black water splashed in through the window that wouldn't close, wetting her jacket and skirt. Elise hit the brakes and looked out into the dark. Was she off the road? A soldier with a bandaged face stared back. Elise yelped in surprise.

"Take me to the hospital," mumbled the soldier. Caked blood showed like black tar on the bandage.

"I can't!" Elise shrieked. "I'm on my way to the train!" The ambulance behind her honked. There was a huge sudden booming and she had to scream to hear herself. "I've got to go!" The soldier seemed to evaporate into the night, and Elise slammed the accelerator to the floor.

The ambulance lurched forward. A blaze of light exploded overhead like fireworks, and in that moment, she realized the soldier wasn't alone. Dozens of them—maybe a hundred—were stumbling up the hill, some by themselves, some being carried by two others. All were bandaged. Some were just lying on the side of the road, as though too exhausted to take another step. *Those are the dead ones*, said a knowledgeable voice in her head. The blaze in the sky dimmed to nothing, and Elise crept on, desperate to find the ambulance in front of her, terrified of driving over a corpse.

The two miles to the train seemed to take hours. Every time a shell burst in the sky, Elise saw more and more men she wasn't allowed to help. She finally crept up to the tail end of the next lorry and stayed there until she saw a soldier in a white helmet directing traffic to the left. The ambulance in front of her turned, and Elise, close behind, followed. Another shell exploded, and she saw the train.

In the first flash of garish light, Elise counted at least nine cars. In the second, she could see that the train was actually much longer, extending far into the darkness that ended at the front. Along the side of the train, men on stretchers were being unloaded and placed on the ground in neat rows. That was where the ambulances were headed.

It seemed logical enough in the beginning. The first two ambulances stopped in front of the first train car, and another soldier in a white helmet waved Elise toward the second. With no one ahead of her, she could see more clearly. The rows of men on stretchers went on and on. They seemed so carefully arranged. Perfectly placed. Waiting for her. But the men on the stretchers weren't lying still—they were writhing in the flashes from the shells, their mouths open in awful screams, and that was when Elise realized how loud it was. She couldn't even hear them.

An orderly with a tattered coat and a gray beard came running up to her on the driver's side.

"Over there!" he shouted in her ear and pointed in the opposite direction she thought she was supposed to go.

"But what about these men?" she shouted back.

"They're dead." He pointed again, stabbing his finger into the dark. "Now go!"

She twisted to watch him running for the ambulance behind her, then looked forward again, at the men on the stretchers. Flares shot up into the sky, illuminating everything in shades of red. The men she'd thought were writhing were still now, as if they'd died suddenly, just because the orderly had said that they were no longer alive. She hadn't been wrong about their mouths, though. They were wide-open. Their eyes were open. Their limbs were splayed like their bodies had fallen from a great height. Elise felt a panicked cry rising in her chest and gunned the ambulance, bumping between bodies and holes until she saw another orderly—another graybeard—waving her in with wide sweeps of his arms. She stopped next to him.

"Get out," he shouted. "Lend a hand."

Elise shoved the door open and stepped into ankle-deep mud. The men on stretchers were lying in that same mud. There were three orderlies. Two of them grabbed a stretcher at either end and began running toward the ambulance. Elise had the presence of mind to open the back gate. The men shoved the stretcher in, and ran to fetch another.

"Come with me," said the first orderly. He grabbed her arm, and the two of them ran for the neat rows. Mud filled Elise's shoes immediately. She bent to help lift a man from the mud. The man, even missing a leg, was incredibly heavy, too heavy for her. Elise tried hard to lift him, and couldn't. Tears started streaming down her face. Someone shoved her to one side. Another aging man took the end of the stretcher away from her and helped the first orderly angle the soldier into the ambulance. To Elise's surprise, three of the six racks were already full. Another stretcher came past her, and this time she could hear the soldier. "My leg, my leg—please don't take my leg!"

Two more stretchers and her ambulance was full, sagging over its tires. Two soldiers hobbled over and sat on the back gate. One had his arm in a sling. One had no hands. Elise looked into his face. Or the dark that had been his face.

"Go!" shouted the first orderly. "Hospital Three!"

Elise fled through the slop to the cab. The engine was still running, but when she put the lorry into gear, it didn't move. She downshifted and tried again. Her tires spun uselessly, spewing mud. Behind her, she heard the orderlies yelling as they heaved the ambulance forward. The tires got a grip on something dry, and Elise shot away, winding through the slime, up the hill, and away from the shells and flares.

In the cab, there was no escaping the smell of vomit and gasoline, no way to shut out the hammering of the bombardment around the battlefield. Worst of all was the sound of men dying in the back of the ambulance as she drove with nothing but the thin metal partition between her and the noises she couldn't do anything about. She drove faster over the uneven, muddy road, but that seemed to hurt them even more. What was she supposed to do? Slow down and let them die? Or get them to the hospital as soon as she could, and do more damage to damaged men? These two impossible things were expected of her. This was what Tippy had neglected to tell her. Elise wiped her eyes with muddy hands and made the turn at the three burned tree stumps, just as the hot edge of the sun appeared over the horizon.

CHAPTER ELEVEN

The next morning—and it was finally, mercifully, morning—
Ruth hovered over the brick ovens that stood in the middle
of the hospital. Orderlies stoked the ovens day and night to
keep the place warm, but also to keep water boiling for the
sterilization of instruments. Ruth had been up all night. Now
she was resting while waiting for a dozen water-filled trays of
glass-and-steel syringes to come to a boil. *A watched pot*, she
thought, and glanced around the ward.

The orderlies were emptying the bedpans again, moving
like clerks through a department store of horizontal man-
nequins. The next wave of wounded soldiers would be here
within the hour, but Ruth couldn't imagine where they were
going to put them. The hospital was absolutely full. There
wasn't a spare bed. Were they going to place the casualties
on the floor? Ruth eyed the rough wooden planks. As far as
she could tell, the floorboards were lying on top of dirt, and
every time it rained, the dirt turned into mud. The building

seemed to have been put together for some altogether different climate. Over the course of the night, Ruth had seen the tin roof shuddering and literally lifting off the rafters in a strong wind. She had seen rain falling on her patients. When she'd pointed this out to Mary Gardener, Gardener had given her a towel to dry the men off. That was all.

Ruth rubbed her eyes. The water in the instrument trays was boiling now, and she checked her watch. It was five thirty in the morning. She wondered where Elise was. She wondered what John was doing. She thought of the arms and legs and hands in the wheelbarrow and tried not to think anymore.

When the water had boiled for an eternal five minutes, she used sterile tongs to place the instruments on clean towels. There were bottles of saline, morphine and carbolic acid, and she filled each syringe according to its label, separating them out on the towels so no one would get confused in the chaos she could only imagine would occur when the wounded arrived. Gardener came by and surveyed her work.

"Well done," she said. "You have about fifteen minutes." She tilted her head toward the far end of the hospital. "Check on the boy."

"Yes, Sister."

The boy was a civilian, about eight years old with tousled blond hair, and blue eyes that had dulled over the hours. His father had brought him in sometime around midnight, then disappeared. As far as anyone could tell, the boy had been caught outside during one of the bombardments. He was Belgian and spoke French. The only word Ruth understood was *mama!* The rest was a garble. He had been hit by shrapnel—and now Ruth knew what *that* was. Mary Gardener herself had washed his wounds with carbolic acid, and bandaged him, but the boy was pale, less and less responsive.

One of the other nurses came over when she saw Ruth with

the boy. She touched his hand and smiled at Ruth. Her name was Helen Thompson, and she was Ruth's bunk mate in the nurses' quarters—a place Ruth hadn't seen yet. Like Gardener, Helen seemed unfazed by the horrible things all around her. Like Gardener, she didn't seem to need sleep.

"It's a blessing he doesn't understand English," said Helen quietly. "Gardener sent an ambulance to town for his mother last night, and she refused to come. She and her husband run a bar about a mile from here, and they have five other children. I guess losing one isn't so noticeable." Helen was a tall, broad-shouldered Englishwoman. She looked as strong as any man. Ruth thought that if Helen had gone with the ambulance to get the mother, the mother would have come, five children or not.

"I can't believe she wouldn't come for her own little boy," said Ruth.

"I can't believe a lot of things," said Helen, "but I do know, mothers should be with their children at times like this."

Ruth glanced around at the ward. So many boys without their mothers.

"Ah," said Helen. "There's The Mouse. That means the ambulances should be here any minute."

Ruth saw Dr. Emmanuel, coming in from the officers' mess, wiping his mouth with the back of his hand. When she'd met him yesterday he'd been wearing a white operating gown with a surgical mask down around his neck, his fluffy gray hair sticking up at odd angles. He'd shaken Ruth's hand and welcomed her. He had tired brown eyes and delicate hands, but the nurses affectionately called him The Mouse because of his outsized ears. He wasn't a big man—no taller than Ruth, no heavier than Elise—but Gardener had told Ruth that she'd seen him subdue Viking-sized soldiers with a few words and a wad of gauze soaked with chloroform.

Now The Mouse looked up from checking on a soldier and saw them watching him. He came across the ward and bent over the bed between Ruth and Helen. He pressed lightly on the boy's bandages. The boy didn't move.

"Not good," said The Mouse. He raised the boy's eyelid. Even from where she was standing by the foot of the bed, Ruth could see that his pupil wasn't changing with the light.

"What shall we do, Doctor?" Helen asked.

"Morphine," said The Mouse. "It won't be long. He should have no pain."

"Yes, Doctor," Helen said, and she left to get a syringe.

Ruth sank down on the edge of the boy's bed and held his limp hand until the ambulances arrived.

The ambulances came in a wave of exhaust fumes. Instead of sirens, Ruth heard the cries of wounded men, and the shouts of orderlies. Ruth followed Gardener as she hurried toward the open doors, morning sunlight and the endless thunder of heavy artillery.

"Now," Gardener said over her shoulder to Ruth as they went outside. "They have triage doctors at the front, and supposedly they've separated out the abdominal wounds for us, but things are a bit chaotic when the ambulances pick them up, so we can get pretty much anything. Here, for example." She pointed to a man whose face was swathed in bloody bandages. The orderlies had put him on the ground, in a neat row with at least a dozen other men. "He should've gone to Number Ten, but we'll help him as best we can. And here," she said as they hurried along, indicating a man whose skin was horribly blackened and blistered. "That's from a flamethrower."

"A *flamethrower*?" Ruth exclaimed.

"The Germans use anything they can think of," said Gardener. "Of course, now we have flamethrowers, too. Here."

She stopped abruptly and knelt by a soldier bandaged over

his belly. He was barely conscious, covered with mud and missing a boot. He rolled his eyes at them like a frightened horse.

"Take his pulse," commanded Gardener. "And remember the man from yesterday."

The one who hadn't had the strength to stay alive. Ruth swallowed and crouched down. Was *she* going to be the one who decided if this man lived or died? Is *that* what they did here? She found his pulse. Rapid and strong. Gardener was watching her, her face inches away.

"Yes," whispered Ruth.

Gardener took his pulse on the other side. She nodded at Ruth. "You'll be all right," she said to the soldier. "We'll take good care of you." In the chaos of the triage tent, she gave the soldier a warm smile.

More and more wounded men arrived, dozens, then a hundred, then too many to count. Inside, they were lined up on the floor in rows, head to foot, with only enough space between them for the nurses to step, to take pulses, to stop the bleeding, to decide who was going into surgery first and who was going to die. More were outside, on the bare earth in the overflow areas, which were covered by nothing but a canvas tent.

"Ah," said Gardener, and she knelt next to a muddy soldier with a bandaged head. "Here's one you need to see."

Ruth reached breathlessly for his wrist, but Gardener caught her hand. "This is a head wound," she said, and lightly touched the bandage, blood-soaked all the way around. "Tell me what you see," said Gardener in a perfectly calm voice.

"He's *dying*," said Ruth. "We have to *help* him."

"Tell me what you see," said Gardener.

Ruth gulped. "He—he seems fine except for his head."

"What else?"

"Blood," said Ruth. "He's bleeding from his ears."

"It's likely this bandage is all that's holding his skull together," said Gardener in a low voice. "I don't know why he's here. The triage doctors could have let him have a decent, quiet death without the trauma of being in an ambulance." She got to her feet, brushing off her long blue skirt. Her white apron was dotted with red.

"But," said Ruth, still on the floor, "surely there's something we can *do*."

"Check his pupils," said Gardener, already moving on.

Ruth pushed the soldier's eyelid up. The pupil was wide and slack. She felt for his pulse, *willing* him to be responsive. But there was no pulse.

"He's dead," she whispered, but Gardener was already gone.

Ruth stumbled to her feet and almost knocked over one of the ambulance drivers. This one was maybe eighteen, willowy and blonde, sobbing.

"You have to help *him*," the driver wept and pointed to the head wound. "They wanted to leave him to die, but I *insisted*."

"I'm sorry to tell you," said Ruth, "but he's...he's passed on."

"You would have done him a favor by leaving him behind," said Gardener over her shoulder. "You don't belong in here, young lady. Go back to your ambulance."

"But I *know* him," said the driver. "We had dinner together. We—"

"Don't get involved with them," said Gardener. "Hasn't anyone told you that yet?" She beckoned impatiently to Ruth.

Ruth gritted her teeth against her sympathy and pushed past the girl to kneel beside the next man; a belly wound had bled through the bandage. She fumbled for his pulse while Gardener eyed the retreating, weeping driver.

"No doubt one of those privileged daughters." She sighed. "From some country manor or other. Half of them don't last, you know. They haven't the stomach for it." She turned to Ruth and lowered her voice. "The other half are daredevils and ne'er-do-wells—worse than men."

"My sister is a driver," said Ruth.

"Is she?" said Gardener, almost conversationally. "Then I wish her the best." She nodded at the wounded soldier Ruth was hovering over. "And this man?"

"Yes," said Ruth.

"Good," said Gardener. "Come now. You'll need to see the operating theater."

The operating theater was in the back of the hospital, behind a double door. Inside were three steel tables and two doctors—The Mouse and MacPherson—already gloved, gowned and masked in white. Behind Ruth and Gardener, the orderlies were bringing in the first patient—walking him in—a huge man with red hair. The man was bent double with pain, leaving a trail of dark mud behind him, but he straightened when he saw the doctors.

"Rosa!" he shouted, and yanked against the orderlies in a panic. *"Rosa!"*

His wounds weren't bandaged—he must've just been thrown into an ambulance to get him out of the way. The orderlies held on to him like he was a wild animal. *"Rosa!"* His body heaved, and blood rushed from under his muddy coat. As she backed away, Ruth could see a deep wound in his chest, full of grime and bits of his own uniform.

"Get him to the X-ray," shouted MacPherson.

"Let me sedate him first," said The Mouse.

"'E won't fit on a stretcher," grunted one of the orderlies. "We just got to git 'im on the table—"

"No!" shouted the man, and he threw off the two orderlies like they were rag dolls.

The Mouse came forward and stood right in front of the terrified soldier. He pulled his mask down. "Soldier," he said calmly. "Do you want to see your Rosa again?"

The red-haired man nodded once, breathing hard. Ruth could see that he was having trouble staying on his feet. If he fell, it would take four or five men to pick him up. That would take time. Other men would die.

It took all her courage to step up beside him. She took his sweaty, bloody hand in hers and looked into his face. He was like a giant.

"I'll help you," she said, her voice shaking. "I'll help you get onto the table. You don't need to be afraid."

His hand tightened. He peered down with bloodshot blue eyes. His grip was crushing.

"You'll see her again," whispered Ruth. "I promise."

She felt the strength go out of him. She took a step into the operating theater, and he followed, swaying like a tree about to come down. She led him to the closest steel table, and he toppled onto it. The Mouse appeared at Ruth's shoulder with a wad of gauze. He pressed it against the soldier's nose and mouth, and after a moment, the man went limp.

"Gardener," said The Mouse. "Put on a gown and mask. I'll need you to assist today."

"Yes, Doctor," said Gardener, and she turned to Ruth. "Tell Helen she's in charge, won't you?" And she shut the double doors of the operating theater in Ruth's face.

CHAPTER TWELVE

In daylight now, Elise climbed into the ambulance cab and started the engine. In the back, a burned man screamed that he couldn't see, and someone else told him to *shut the 'ell up*. But he didn't. He couldn't. Elise stepped on the gas, behind the next ambulance in line, heading up the dirt road toward the hospitals. All around her, bands of soldiers were heading away from the battleground, like shift workers going home. They were filthy, caked with mud, marked from their labors with the machine that was the war. In the meantime, the next batch of soldiers marched in to replace the ones who were leaving. They were clean. They were the ones she would be picking up tonight, Elise thought, exhausted, horrified and sad.

The lorry in front of her honked at the new recruits, and they spilled to either side of the muddy track. The first ambulance surged forward, and Elise gunned her engine to follow. Tires and horses and men had churned the road into a deep muck. There was barely any purchase for her wheels as she slithered up the hill, her windshield sprayed with mud from the ambulance in front of her, the men in the back crying out as she hit whatever bumps were left. Elise urged the ambulance forward, rushing as well as she could to the top of the hill and off to the right.

Twenty minutes later, she found Hospital Four, where Ruth was stationed—a conjoined collection of sheds with a wide front door. Another ambulance was already there, with an anthill of activity around it. Elise pulled up just behind. Orderlies, all old men, descended on her ambulance to pull out the wounded and get them inside. Elise jumped out of the cab and ran to see what she could do to help.

The hospital doors were propped wide-open, and inside she could see a carpet of wounded men arranged on the floor, the nurses moving among them like quick birds, bending here, running there.

She spotted Ruth crouched on the floor in the midst of the stretchers. Ruth glanced up, and their eyes locked across the open, chaotic space. Elise blinked. She had seen her sister angry, happy, focused, but never so utterly intent as she was right now. There was something different about her face. It was as though Elise had never really seen her sister before.

"Ruth," said Elise, but nowhere near loud enough.

Ruth looked away, raised a man's arm and took his pulse.

One of the orderlies stopped next to Elise, breathing hard. "Where's the other driver?" he demanded.

She tore her eyes away from Ruth and glanced at the ambulance in front of hers. It was blocking her in. "How should I know?"

"*There* she is," said the orderly, answering his own question.

The driver, the blonde, impractical-looking girl who had spoken to Elise yesterday, ran out of the hospital in tears. She climbed into the driver's seat and shot off down the road, steering wildly between the ruts and bumps.

Elise got back into her own lorry and headed down the dirt road toward the train. She stopped her lorry in the loading area and got out to find the girl sobbing against the side of her ambulance even as the orderlies loaded it up.

"What's the matter?" Elise shouted over the bedlam around them. It sounded like a stupid question the second it was out of her mouth. What *wasn't* the matter?

"They wouldn't help him," the girl said, weeping. "They were going to let him die out here, but I got him to the hospital, and they still wouldn't help him."

Elise glanced back at her own ambulance. Stretchers were being loaded with mechanical speed. "What's your name?" shouted Elise.

"Hera Montraine," said the girl, and she sobbed into her dirty hands.

"You have to pull yourself together!" said Elise. "There's no stopping now—your ambulance is full!"

A sergeant came running over. His arm was in a sling, but he was still carrying a rifle over his shoulder. "Driver!" he bellowed at Hera. "Hospital Five. You!" He pointed to Elise. "Number Eight!"

"You'll be all right," said Elise. "Just get going!"

Hera wiped her face with her sleeve, got into her cab, started the engine and drove off in a cloud of exhaust.

When the horrors of the day were over, Elise figured she'd made at least ten trips to Hospitals Four, Six and Eight. She'd lost track after that. It was almost evening now, and she'd missed both breakfast and lunch. There was no way she was going to miss supper, or be the last to show up. The cook, as Elise had already discovered, tended to underfeed the hungry women who descended on the mess hall after their runs were over. Besides, to call this woman a cook was to overstate her capabilities.

Elise parked in the line of ambulances that would have to be washed out and inspected by the matron before any of them could go to bed. It was either a mercy to get to eat first, or a punishment, as cleaning out the ambulances was a gruesome task better done on an empty stomach. But there was no time for thinking like that. Elise switched off the ignition and went to the mess hall.

Inside it was subdued and smoky as women ate and puffed on cigarettes. Dinner was stew of some kind, with rock-hard bread. Elise found Hera at the end of a table with the drivers from her bunking unit, Tippy, Victoria and Edna. All of them were smoking. Elise brought her plate over. Without a word, they made a place for her, and she sat.

"The bread is a week old if it's a day," said Victoria. She was the daughter of a duke and spoke with a high-society accent. This much Elise had learned already—who had what kind of accent. "My advice is to let it soak in the stew until it falls apart."

Hera, who was sitting next to Tippy, hadn't touched her food. Her bread had sunk to the bottom of her stew bowl and lay there like a lonely crustacean.

"We keep telling her she has to eat," Tippy said to Elise. "Maybe you can convince her."

"The food makes me sick," said Hera in a small voice. "I don't think I can take much more. It…it runs right through, if you know what I mean."

"That just means you need to harden your very bowels," said Edna. "Think of the rest of us. You don't imagine we didn't go through the same thing? Eat it. You'll toughen up from the inside out."

"You can't *not* eat," said Tippy. "You'll be ill and end up in hospital. All you'll do is take up a bed someone else needs more. Just because of an upset stomach."

Hera reddened at this, as though she would never take up an unnecessary bed on purpose, and dipped her spoon into the stew. She tasted it, and her mouth tightened. She swallowed and said, "I guess it's not so bad tonight."

"Not so bad," said Edna. "Now have a bit of potato. There's no way to ruin a potato."

Hera obeyed, and little by little she ate the stew until everything but the meat was gone.

"I'm afraid it's horse meat," she said.

"No doubt it is," said Victoria. She took Hera's bowl, and high-class English daughter that she was, ate every bite.

Elise had finished hers by then, including the bread and the questionable meat. There was a time limit on meals. Soon the matron would blow her whistle, and it would be time to wash the ambulances out, getting them ready for inspection.

Victoria decided there was time to light another cigarette. She and Tippy handed it back and forth, eyeing the matron and the cigarette to see which would be finished first.

"Here now," said Tippy to Elise and offered her the cigarette. "It's a filthy habit, but think how sophisticated you'll be when you get home. Think how you'll impress the boys. Smoking makes one seem worldly, don't you know."

"I'm worldly enough, thanks," said Elise. "And if I ever get home, it'll be a miracle. As for the boys, my mechanical skills *always* impress them."

The other women laughed, but Victoria said, "Come check my lorry tonight. It's been running rough. There was a time or two today I didn't think I'd make it up the hill."

"I'll look at it," said Elise. "Maybe it's your fuel line."

"I'd be utterly grateful," said Victoria, and at that, Tippy stubbed out the cigarette.

"Here we go," she said, and the matron's whistle screeched through the mess hall.

"Ready, girls?" said Tippy. "Time to drag your sorry carcasses out there and do the dirty business."

The dirty business was all that and more and involved buckets of soap and disinfectant, and scrub brushes. The inside and the outside of the ambulances had to be cleaned, and it took the last reserves of energy Elise had. She could hear Hera retching as she worked in the next lorry over, and that didn't help her insides settle around the so-called stew and lump of bread. Poor girl, she thought, and wondered how long Hera would stay. People had their reasons for being here. The men couldn't help it—but the women seemed to be here for the grim glory the war afforded them, or else, as Elise suspected in Hera's case, to find a husband.

Elise scrubbed at the mud, and whatever else was caked onto the ambulance's tires. This was no place to find a husband.

One could end up a bride and then a widow in an instant.

CHAPTER THIRTEEN

Two long days later, Ruth was standing by a tree stump just outside the hospital's front door. She was sipping a hot cup of tea, wrapped in a greatcoat against Belgium's April chill, when an ambulance pulled up and John stepped out.

"Here you are," he said. "Safe and sound."

She swallowed her mouthful of tea. She had written him a rushed note as soon as she could. *We are here.* Now she was surprised at how much thinner he was, how deeply shadowed under his eyes. They hadn't seen each other since he'd left Baltimore for Belgium last fall. His letters had been full of praise for his colleagues in the hospital, but he'd never mentioned how much death there was every day. Today, Ruth could see the things he hadn't written about etched into his face.

He took her cold hand in his warm glove. "But why're you drinking tea outside in the cold?"

She didn't want to tell him it was because the smells in the hospital made her sick to her stomach. "Do you want some?" she said, instead of explaining. "Let's go in."

The two of them walked through the abdominal ward and into the duty mess between the operating theater and the officers' quarters. She let his hand slip out of hers just before they entered. Even after just a couple of days, Ruth understood that there was no privacy here, only gossip. John seemed to understand this, too, and sat across from her at the long table. Orderlies served hot tea and cold scones, and Ruth introduced John to the two surgeons.

"Dr. Emmanuel," said John, "Dr. MacPherson. I hear nothing but good things about your work."

"You're one of the arm-and-leg men, aren't you?" MacPherson said, dismissively.

"I am," said John.

"A good clean cut is a blessing to all," said Emmanuel, and raised his teacup in a kind of salute.

John smiled at him, and then Ruth. She relaxed a bit. His hands were still practical and calm, and his sandy hair still fell over his frank gray eyes. He was the same man. She wondered about herself, if the awful things she'd seen had already changed her.

"Have you heard from your parents?" Ruth asked as she broke apart one of the scones.

"I have two letters from home that I haven't had a chance to open," said John. "How were they when you were there?"

"They were so proud of you," said Ruth. "They couldn't stop talking about you."

John gave her a wry smile, and Ruth thought of the wheelbarrow full of arms and legs.

"How's Elise coping with all this?" John asked.

"I've barely seen her," said Ruth. "I'm so worried about

her. She didn't have any idea of what she was getting into. She really just wants to work on cars."

"Why on earth did she come?" John frowned as he sipped his tea. "She could work on cars in Baltimore."

"She could work on *Father's* car," said Ruth. "I'm convinced that's what he would've had her doing for the rest of her life."

"What about marriage?" John asked. "Didn't she have a beau?"

"Not that I ever knew about," said Ruth. "But then, Elise can be very secretive."

John looked puzzled. "About what?"

"If I knew that," said Ruth, "she wouldn't have any secrets."

Mary Gardener pushed open the thin door in a rush. "Doctors," she said abruptly to Emmanuel and MacPherson. "You're needed. Right now."

Ruth got to her feet, but The Mouse waved her back into her seat. "Take your time, my dear," he said, and hurried out the door, leaving John and Ruth alone.

The floor of the mess vibrated dully from distant explosions, but other than that, it was quiet. Ruth looked up at John, and then down at her half-eaten scone. "I have to tell you something."

John sipped his tea. "You have a beau."

"What?" She blinked in surprise. "No!"

"Then it can't be bad news," said John.

"It is, though," said Ruth. "I—I lied to you in my letters. The ones I sent from home."

John cocked his head and sipped.

Ruth hesitated, wondering which lie she was going to be honest about. She lowered her voice. "I was kicked out of nursing school. Before I finished. I don't have my degree. You're having tea with a fraud."

He raised his eyebrows like he'd misheard. "But why?"

Ruth swallowed. "I was arrested. For being at a suffrage rally."

John seemed to consider this. Ruth held her breath.

"Your father must've been displeased," he said after a moment.

"He was *very* displeased," she said in a rush. "He came to get me at the police station. And not right away, either. I thought I was going to spend the night in a cell. He paid my bail and then he came over to me, and then he..." Ruth stopped and swallowed. She didn't want to make her father into a villain, but here it was, months later, and she could still feel the burning sting of the blow.

"Then he what?" said John.

Ruth couldn't say anything, just frowned at her own lap.

"He hit you," said John.

"Yes." She couldn't tell how he felt about it—a perfectly acceptable punishment, or a mean trick delivered by a man who wanted to control his daughter.

John didn't say anything for a while, but she could see that his mouth was a tight, straight line. "That's inexcusable," he said finally.

"Yes," said Ruth, as lightly as she could. "I thought so as well."

"And that's why you left home," said John.

"I left home for a lot of reasons," said Ruth.

John got up and came around to her side of the table and sat, close, but not touching.

"Ruth," he said in a low voice, "show me where he hit you."

"Here," she whispered, and touched her left cheek.

He kissed her there, warm and soft. She shut her eyes, turned her head and kissed him, tenderly, on his mouth. It felt so brave to do so. She'd never kissed a man before. John touched her shoulders, then pulled her close, his mouth at her ear.

"I will never hurt you," he whispered.

CHAPTER FOURTEEN

On Sunday, at the end of her first week in the barracks, Elise was instructed to bathe.

She had no idea what to expect. At home, when they were little, Grandpa would wash her and Ruth in the tub. She remembered the floating fairy islands of bubbles and the lush warmth of the towel afterward. This wasn't going to be anything like that.

When bath time came, she stood by her bunk with her uniform balled up against her body, covering her nakedness as the rest of the women briskly stripped down to nothing and sloshed water into metal bathing pans—*pans*—no wider than the bottom of a barrel, no taller than the length of her hand.

Hera, bare and pink, her hair gathered up on the top of her head, grabbed Elise's arm. "Don't just stand there! Let's get some hot water before it's all gone." She threw Elise's clothes onto the nearest bunk, exposing her pale lankiness to everyone.

Elise followed her over to the stove, where four teakettles were on the boil. Hera grabbed a kettle with one hand and gave Elise a push with the other. "Go on—get a pan. I'll scrub your back."

Elise got a pan from a stack of perhaps a dozen, and the two of them pushed through the crowd of naked women to a corner of the barracks.

"You can go first," said Hera, pouring the steaming water.

"But it's too hot," said Elise.

"Not for long." Hera handed her a rag that had probably been torn from a towel, and a bar of sweet-smelling soap. "My mother sent that," she said. "She has no idea what we're washing off out here. Of course, I never tell her the truth in my letters. She'd be mortified."

Elise put a toe into the water. It was hot but not scalding. She put her other foot in and crouched in the shin-deep water, somehow chilled to her nipples. She sopped the rag and scrubbed it with scented soap, trying not to look at the nudity around her. She had seen her sister—curvy and well-built—without clothes on, but that was it. She'd never seen a man naked, and certainly not so many women. She couldn't help but stare. Tippy was edging toward fat, even on barracks rations. Edna was thin as a whip with knobby knees and visible ribs. Victoria had slender hips and remarkably large breasts. Even Matron was naked, cigarette in her mouth, a towel just barely around her ample waist. There were tummies and buttocks, pubic hair, nipples with tender dark areolas. And then there was Hera, her blond hair curling. Elise pressed the soapy rag against her face and rubbed hard, eyes shut. Her heart, she realized, was pounding.

"Do you want to do your hair?" Hera asked, behind her now.

All Elise knew was that she needed to get her clothes on as

quickly as possible. She shook her head into the rag, sloshed the already gray water over her face and began washing the rest of her body as fast as she could while Hera scrubbed her back.

"Get that engine oil out from under your fingernails," Hera advised. "You might as well have a couple of hours with clean hands."

Afraid her voice would tremble, Elise obeyed wordlessly. Hera rinsed Elise's back and stepped away for a moment to get a towel, leaving Elise to stand in what was now cold, brackish water.

Hera offered her a towel. Elise quickly wrapped herself in its thin scratchiness. "Now," said Hera, "let's dump this out, and then it's my turn."

The two of them dragged the pan to the back door of the barracks, which opened onto the latrines. Hera peeked out. "I don't see any boys," she said, and opened the door wide. Together they hurled the water into a soapy pool that was forming outside. Hera slammed the door shut. "The boys just *know* when it's bath day. Last week, Matron opened the door, stark naked, and there was a whole platoon! You should have seen her face." She giggled but stopped abruptly. "You don't think it's funny?" she said. "I didn't know you were a prude."

"I'm not a prude," said Elise. "I'm just—I'm not."

"Well, good," said Hera. "Let's get some more hot water."

Elise helped Hera wash her hair, scooping up water from the least soapy side of the pan with a ladle, which, she thought, could easily have come from the barracks kitchen. The idea of soap mixed with soup made her want to gag. She grimly soaped Hera's back while the water was still warm, and Hera sighed with pleasure, which made Elise's heart pound, as though in fright.

But it wasn't fright. She knew what *that* was. Her heart was in her throat most of the time between the front and the various hospitals. This wasn't the same. This was like the time back home, in Baltimore, the night she'd followed the woman dressed as a man.

Elise shut her eyes and squeezed them tight, smelling the combination of aromatic soap and sweaty bodies. The images of that night were burned into her mind. Knowing about the disguises had made her see the world in a completely different way. Now, as she opened her eyes again, and let the gray water sluice down Hera's alabaster back, she wondered if half the women in the barracks weren't hiding something.

CHAPTER FIFTEEN

May 1915

Ruth woke up at some wee, dark hour of the morning. Helen was snoring away in the bunk above her. The vibration of the big guns seemed closer, and shook dust out of the thin bedding overhead. She pushed away the pillow she had brought from the Dowelings' house—it was full of lice—and covered her head with her thin sleeping bag. She tried to ignore the hammering of the artillery, but couldn't. Ruth wondered how Helen could sleep. She had four weeks in Belgium to Helen's six, and the nights were still loud and frightening. The thought of the war grinding up soldiers like a machine made Ruth sick to her stomach. Was John sleeping, or in the midst of cutting off an arm or leg? There was a talent wasted, she thought, and huddled deeper into the sleeping bag. All that medical education, and the best the Royal Army Medical Corps could do was make him an amputator?

Helen let out a choking snore in the bunk above her, and Ruth pushed herself up to sit on the edge of the bed. She felt around for the stump of candle on the floor by her bunk and the box of matches beside it. She struck one and lit the wick. The flame stretched up, long and smoky, casting leaping shadows around the small room. Helen grunted in her sleep, but didn't budge. Ruth took the candle over to the table, where unanswered letters were piled up, and picked out the one that Grandpa had sent at least a week ago with a box of Cook's homemade goodies. It was his third letter since she and Elise had left Baltimore, and she hadn't had time to answer any of them. He—and Father—probably thought she was dead by now. She wondered if Elise had found time to write and doubted it.

She found a clean sheet of paper, a pen and ink in a stoppered bottle and began.

Dear Grandpa, dear Father;

Thank you so much for the cookies and sweets. We have shared them around, and everyone agrees that Cook's baking skills are unparalleled. Even the women here who are Ladies at home in England agreed that they have never tasted better.

    As you can imagine, we're terribly busy and don't get many chances to sit down and write a letter, so this one will have to be short. I am well, and so is Elise. Her duties keep her far away from the Front, as do mine, and we are out of harm's way. Please don't worry about us. We see each other often, and Elise is thriving as a driver and mechanic for her ambulance squad. She has made a number of friends, as have I.

Ruth paused. Helen had stopped snoring. Was it worth trying to get back to sleep? It must've been three in the morning. She looked down at the letter, which was almost a complete lie, and decided she had to end with something honest.

We send all our love and will write whenever we can.

Your faithful daughter,

Ruth

Ruth sighed and folded the letter in thirds, pressed it into an envelope and addressed it.

"You're awake?" mumbled Helen from her bunk.

"Sorry," said Ruth. "I thought I was being quiet."

"It's not you. It's the guns. They sound closer." Helen sat up and cocked her head. In the candlelight, her eyes looked sunken, like an old woman's. Ruth was pretty sure she looked the same way herself. The war would age them all.

Helen rubbed at her hair. "God," she said. "These lice."

"I know," said Ruth. "My pillow's infested."

"My hair's infested." Helen clambered down from the upper bunk in her long nightgown and came over to the table. She pushed aside the papers and teacups until she found a pair of shears.

"What're you doing?" Ruth asked.

"I'm going to cut the lice out," said Helen, her voice still gravelly from sleep. "Would you like to join me?"

Helen had beautiful long blond hair. It fell almost to her waist, but most of the time she kept it tied up in a tight, impervious bun. Ruth could hardly believe her ears. "You're dreaming," said Ruth.

"I'm having a nightmare," said Helen. "And you're as full of the vile little beasts as I am." She scruffed at her head. "God. Can't you feel them crawling?"

Ruth touched her own hair. She'd done her best to ignore the crawling, but every time she combed her hair, the lice… well… She was infested, just like Helen said. She thought of John, on the docks in Baltimore, smoothing back her hair. Then she wondered if he had lice, too.

"Yes," she said.

Helen got the empty washbasin from the table, put it on the floor and knelt next to it, like a penitent. "We'll need paper."

Ruth shuffled through the letters on the table until she found a copy of the *Herald*, two days old, which had come with the post from London. She knelt across from Helen on the rough wooden boards.

Helen took three sheets and crumpled them into the basin. Headlines about attacks, trenches and the number of Germans killed showed in the flickering candlelight. She handed the shears to Ruth. "Here," she said. "You do mine. Then I'll do yours."

"You're sure?" said Ruth.

"Absolutely sure." Helen bent her head. "I do hereby give myself to the war, body and soul," she intoned. "I sacrifice my hair for victory. And if I have to, I'll do what the ancient Amazons did before they went into battle."

"What's that?" Ruth asked.

"Cut off a breast," muttered Helen. "The better to draw a bowstring."

"Good God," said Ruth. "Nobody's going to do *that*."

"Just cut," said Helen.

Ruth took a handful of thick blond hair and sank the shears into it. Hair fell in clumps onto the sheets of newspaper. She cut again, and again, while Helen breathed heavily into her hands. She cut until all that was left was a choppy blond brush.

Helen sat up and ran her fingers through it. "Good," she said. She looked different now—harder. Less likely to dispense mercy. "Now you."

Outside, through the single window, the night sky went bright with the bombardment, and a deafening crash shook their little shed to the splintery wooden floor. Light shot over the bunk beds, the tiny gas stove in the corner, the table with its unanswered correspondence. The flash outshone the candle's warm glow, and for a moment it looked like broad daylight.

The light faded, and Ruth pushed her hair forward until it was a thick, mahogany veil across her face. She bent down hesitantly. This was not what she'd gotten up in the middle of the night to do.

"Are you afraid?" Helen asked.

"Of course," said Ruth, "I've had long hair my whole—"

"I don't mean your hair," said Helen. "I mean, are you *afraid*?"

"Well, of course," said Ruth, staring at her own knees. "I'm scared to death of the bombs, and the poor men. All that blood…"

"Do you know what I'm afraid of?" said Helen, cutting.

"What?"

"Losing this war," said Helen. She dropped a hank of dark hair into the basin. "If we lose, the world will change. And I don't just mean that we'll all be speaking German. I mean you won't be able to call yourself an American anymore, and I won't be able to say that I'm British. We'll be subject to the Bosch, and everything they stand for. Every evil thing. What they've done to the Belgians—raping and looting and burning—shooting entire villages to kill one spy—that'll be the world, my dear. And that is what we have to defeat." She cut deeply, ferociously, and the last of Ruth's hair fell away. "We must burn them to the ground," said Helen grimly, and she took the candle off the floor, touched the flame to the edge of the paper. "Like the vermin that they are."

Ruth sat back on her heels as the fire shot up from the enamel basin, smoking and stinking of burnt hair.

"It's not just a war," she said.

"Oh, no," said Helen darkly, watching the flames. "It's all of civilization."

The two of them watched as the fire shrank and smoked out, leaving an ash-black stain in the washbasin.

"Let's go," said Ruth. "I don't think I can get back to sleep." She touched her hair, or what was left of it.

"You look absolutely topping, darling," said Helen, and she got up to get dressed.

Ruth cracked open the door of the nurses' quarters a sliver and stepped outside. In the predawn dark, another distant *boom* sounded, farther from the hospital this time, away from their shack, one of a dozen shacks along the sloppy mud of the main road.

"The calm before the storm," said Helen, adjusting her nurse's veil over her short hair.

"What do you mean?" said Ruth.

"The ambulances won't be here for another three hours," said Helen. "It's quiet in the hospital. The night nurses have the easy work."

Ruth doubted that. Nothing here was easy.

"Let's go," said Helen. She hitched her skirt high above her ankles and waded into the mud.

Ruth followed. "What were you doing before the war?" she asked, stepping carefully, trying not to slip. "Why did you come to Belgium?"

"I was a nurse," said Helen. "I worked with pregnant women, and I was on my way to becoming a midwife. When the war started, I worked in a munitions factory with my sister, but she convinced me I could do more good out here." She stopped in the dark, in the middle of the road. "What about you? America's not even in the fight. Why would you want to be in a place like this?"

"Oh," said Ruth, "I came out here for love."

Helen laughed. It was the first time in weeks that Ruth had heard anyone laugh. "The fellow from Hospital Three?" Helen asked, still standing in the middle of the road. "The amputator?"

"He's a good surgeon," said Ruth, defensive. "Besides, he—"

"He what?" Even in the blackout dark, Helen was grinning, Ruth could tell.

"I—" said Ruth. She was afraid Helen would laugh even harder. "Well. I want to be a doctor one day. He said I could."

"What kind of doctor?" Helen asked, not laughing.

"A surgeon, I think," said Ruth breathlessly, as though she was admitting to something indecent.

"You'd better tell The Mouse," said Helen. "MacPherson would never let you do more than hand him a scalpel, but Emmanuel was a professor at one of the medical colleges. He's got Gardener in the operating theater, and I know she's doing more than just holding his instruments."

It sounded almost dirty the way she said it. "What do you mean?"

"I *mean*," said Helen, "she wants to be a surgeon, and he's teaching her."

Ruth blinked in the dark. "What should I say to him?"

"Exactly what you said to me," said Helen. "Come along, now. There are bedpans to empty." She sloshed toward the hospital, and Ruth hurried after.

The Mouse came in from the officers' mess just as the first wave of ambulances arrived, so Ruth didn't get a chance to talk to him. There was no break for lunch, or even tea. It wasn't until the end of the day that there was a slowdown.

Helen, bandaging wounds a few beds away, pointed at the

operating theater door and mouthed *now*. Ruth swallowed, straightened up from the man she had just injected with morphine and made her way to the far end of the hospital.

The door to the operating theater was wide-open, and Ruth's heart pounded. This was not her father's neat little office. The floor inside was slick with blood. The three steel tables were splashed with it. She could smell the chloroform and the now-familiar stink of gangrene. Gardener, in a smeared white smock, was wiping down one of the tables with a rag, while The Mouse and MacPherson bent over the last patient— an unconscious soldier no older than Ruth. He had curly brown hair, and a bloody, hand-shaped print on the side of his face, as though he'd touched his wounded abdomen and then his face in disbelief.

Gardener saw Ruth and beckoned. Ruth stepped inside, and Gardener handed her the rag. "Start cleaning up in here," she said—although this was a job the orderlies did. "They're almost done." She took off her bloody smock and left the room.

"I'll take care of this one," said The Mouse, and for a moment, Ruth thought he was talking about her. She turned to see him and MacPherson staring at her.

"Yes?" said MacPherson.

"I—I had a question for the—for Dr. Emmanuel," said Ruth.

"Go on," said The Mouse to MacPherson. "You look like you could use a drink."

"I'll see you at the club," said MacPherson, and he pushed past Ruth, leaving her alone with The Mouse and the unconscious soldier.

The Mouse's surgical mask was down around his neck. "Yes?" he said.

Ruth was suddenly aware of her rumpled uniform dress,

her stained apron—her hair. She licked her lips. The soldier on the table would die if he wasn't helped, and soon.

"Dr. Emmanuel," she said, as quickly and as firmly as she could, "I want to be a doctor." She swallowed. "I've spent all this time being a nurse, but—"

"A doctor?" said The Mouse. He put his mask back on and turned to his patient. Ruth's pounding heart sank.

"This man has a piece of shrapnel in his belly," said The Mouse. "I'll show you the X-ray. You can help me open and close."

Ruth's eyes went wide. "What?"

"Put on a gown and mask," said The Mouse. "They're by the door. And gloves. Don't forget to put on gloves."

Ruth turned to the pile of sterile gowns and pulled one on, then a mask. The gloves were rubber, thick, too big for her hands. Already The Mouse was holding up the glass plate of the X-ray for her to see. The shrapnel showed as a sharp white blot on a black background.

"Stand next to me," instructed The Mouse. Ruth obeyed and watched, holding her breath as he removed the bandages from the soldier's belly, and cleaned it with cotton and alcohol. The wound was a long, jagged tear, like someone had taken a piece of broken glass and tried to gut this man like a fish.

"I'm going to put my hand inside his wound," said The Mouse. "The X-ray makes the shrapnel easier to find—it's just under the skin—but I still have to put my hand on it. Understand?"

"Yes, Doctor."

He slid his gloved hand into the wound, and Ruth remembered to breathe as she watched him grope inside. Her father would've been shocked at the ham-handedness of his technique, but then, her father was shocked that she was even here.

"Now," said The Mouse in an absolutely even tone, "I'm

going to take my hand out, and he's going to start bleeding. You're going to clamp the artery so we don't lose him. Very fast."

"Yes, Doctor." Ruth reached for a clamp on the spattered metal tray next to the table.

"Put your hand in here," said The Mouse. "You'll feel my fingers and the shrapnel. Quickly now. Let's see what you're made of."

Ruth swallowed and slid her fingers into the man's belly—something she'd never been allowed to do in nursing school—but here she was, up to her wrists in the warmth of a human body. Blood flowed into the ends of her sleeves, high above the cuffs of the gloves. Already the hem of her skirt was wet with blood from the floor. She found The Mouse's fingers and then the knife-edge of the shrapnel. Even through the thickness of the glove, she could feel the artery next to the shard, leaking and about to give way. With the clamp in her other hand, she squeezed gently down on the artery. It slipped away.

"Be assertive!" snapped The Mouse. "This is no time for silly games."

She found the artery again, and clamped it. She found gauze on the small stand beside the operating table and soaked up the blood so The Mouse could see what he was doing.

"Good," said The Mouse. He pulled his hand out of the boy's innards and showed her the shrapnel. It was about an inch square, burned black, sharp as a knife all the way around. "He was lucky," said The Mouse, "this is all he had in him. Some come in with five, six pieces. We can still save them, but it takes longer. Sometimes too long. Now. You can suture, I assume?"

"Only flesh wounds—I've never—"

"Today you'll learn internal sutures," said The Mouse, "and

if that doesn't make you faint, I'll have you in here tomorrow, yes?"

"Yes, Doctor."

"This is your chance, then. Gardener's good, but her hands
are too big. She gets in the way. You're smaller. Small hands.
You could do very well. Now watch."

She watched as he made the tiny stitches needed to sew up
the artery. He gave her the needle and let her do one, then another. Her hands shook, and her stitch was nowhere as neat as
his, but she didn't faint, and he didn't yell at her, even though
all she could hear inside her head was her father's fury.

"Good," he said. "Very good. You'll be in here tomorrow.
What's your name?"

In a wavering voice, she told him.

"Duncan," he said. "Good. Get Gardener to help you clean
up this mess." And with that he shed his bloody smock, turned
on his heel and left.

The orderlies helped Ruth clean up the operating theater,
and Gardener was there, too, but she mopped and wiped with
a forced sort of energy and didn't say much. She certainly
didn't congratulate Ruth on her first surgery. Initially, Ruth
put her attitude off to just being tired. Ruth herself was exhausted. But the thrill of clamping an artery—doing internal
sutures!—had left her light on her feet. It wasn't until the un-
pleasant business of cleaning the operating theater was over
that it occurred to Ruth that she'd taken Gardener's place at
The Mouse's side. Had Gardener been told that her hands were
too big? Had she been told she was in the way? Ruth scrubbed
in the washbasin in the nurses' washroom, making sure to get
the blood out from under her fingernails. Gardener scrubbed
right alongside her, saying nothing.

"Sister," Ruth started, meaning to say *I'm sorry*, but she wasn't, and she wasn't sure what to say.

"Don't 'Sister' me." Gardener shook water from her hands and turned to Ruth. "Do you know what I was before the war? I was a private nurse to a baron, a very sick man. I cared for him until the day he died, six months ago, and then I came here. Do you know, I'd never wanted to be in the operating room? It sickened me. But Emmanuel took me on. He taught me how to see past the blood and the suffering, and showed me that I was doing some good. Now you're here. You're obviously more qualified than I am—and you're younger and prettier."

"I don't think that has anything to do with—"

"Oh, but it does," said Gardener, and she toweled her hands angrily. "Men are men. I don't care how old, or where they are—operating theater or front lines. Just you wait—if this war goes on long enough, it'll happen to you, too."

Gardener left the washroom and slammed the thin door behind her.

Ruth straightened and looked at herself in the smudged mirror. Her veil was askew, revealing her cropped hair. She took the veil off. It was spotted with blood anyway. The thrill was waning, but there was something she needed to do before she collapsed for the evening, and that was to go see John.

It was almost dusk, and outside, the June air was soft and smoky. Uniformed men meandered past Hospital Four, heading for their barracks and supper. Number Three was a mile away. Ruth wondered about walking a mile in her bloody shoes, with her hair cut down to a man's bristle. Surely she would attract stares. She also wondered, in a rush of anxiety, how John would react to her haircut, and wished she'd kept her veil on.

Ruth started walking, following the soldiers to the main road and turning right at a wooden building marked Headquarters. Here, sitting outside on mismatched chairs, the officers smoked. One was missing a leg. Two had their arms in dirty white slings. She expected their gazes to follow her, but they didn't. Perhaps they'd seen stranger things today.

Hospital Number Three came into view, just past a ruined farmhouse. John had described it, so even though there were no signs marking it as a hospital, Ruth knew he would be somewhere in the big, low-slung barn. There was a concrete apron to one side, where once cattle had entered and exited. Now a weather-worn dining table and chairs occupied the space. A couple of ambulances were parked in front of the barn, empty of both drivers and patients. Two men leaned against one of the ambulances, one smoking, one looking at his own feet. At first Ruth thought they were orderlies, but as she got closer, she saw their doctor's coats. Closer still, she saw that the man looking at his feet was John.

She called his name, and he straightened, smiled, then frowned.

"Ruth?" he said. "Your hair!"

"The lice finally got to me," she said, coming up to them, suddenly unsure of herself. She happened to glance at John's army-issue boots. They were stained with dried blood. The cuffs of his trousers were caked with it.

"I think it's very becoming," said the doctor next to him, an older fellow with a moustache. He took another drag on his cigarette. "I hear short hair is all the rage in London these days."

"It'll grow out again," Ruth said to John. "It's just so hard to stay clean."

"Believe me, I know." He smiled again, which made her

heart rise up, as though her choppy haircut was more than forgiven. "Allow me to introduce you to our head surgeon, Dr. Nelson Talley."

Talley gave a slight bow. "Head of the knives and saws, if you please," he said. "We really don't do surgery here unless the boys at the front get confused and send us a lorry full of abdominal wounds. But that doesn't happen too often, does it, Doctor?"

"No," said John. "That's Ruth's job. She's at Number Four."

Ruth was aching to tell John about the surgery she'd helped with, but she hesitated to say anything in front of this other doctor.

"Number Four," said Talley. "You see, young fellow, that's where you should be. Obviously the most attractive nurses are down there." He stubbed out his cigarette with his heel. "Well, I'll leave you two alone. Unless, Doctor, you need a chaperone?"

"Not at all," said John, and smiled again, but this time his fatigue showed.

The two of them waited until Talley went through the door and into the barn. Then John took her hand. It was hard for her to imagine so gentle a touch sawing off anonymous limbs. Tentatively, she squeezed his warm fingers, while men, mule-drawn carts and belching lorries rushed by.

"Do you want to go for a walk?" said John. "I really need to get away from this place for a while."

"Of course," said Ruth. "Which way?"

"I'll escort you back to Number Four, if that's all right," said John. "It's growing dark. I wouldn't want you to get run over."

The two of them turned down the main road, the way Ruth had come, still holding hands. Troops whistled at them from a passing lorry.

"It's so good to see you," said John as they stepped around

puddles. "I've had the most discouraging day, and here you are, to brighten things up."

She blushed, glad she made him feel that way. "I just wanted to tell you about—about something Dr. Emmanuel let me do."

"For heaven's sake, spit it out," said John. "I'm quite sure you're shaking."

She told him about the surgery, how The Mouse had told her she'd done a good job and asked her to come back into the operating theater the next day.

"Good for Emmanuel," said John, serious now. "You know, he was a professor of surgery. There's a lot he could teach you."

"Do you—do you think I could learn to be a surgeon before the end of the war?"

John let out a short laugh. "How long have you been here?"

She looked down at the mud, at her feet, the puddles she was avoiding. "Four weeks or so."

"And do you ever have a chance to speak with your patients?"

"Not usually," said Ruth. "They're always so—so wounded. They don't say much. And so many of them die…"

"Amputees are far more talkative," said John. "We hear a lot of chatter from the officers, and do you know what they say?"

"What?" Ruth asked, mystified.

"That this war is at a stalemate. The front lines don't move. The men don't move. It's just the generals on both sides throwing troops at each other, fodder for the cannons." John squeezed her hand. "The generals won't give up until they literally run out of men, and that means this war could go on and on. If Emmanuel chooses to teach you, you may well have time to learn everything he knows about abdominal surgery. But Ruth…"

"Yes?"

John stopped her. She turned toward him and found herself

looking into his eyes. "Don't let your ambitions crowd out your humanity. I cut and saw all day, like a machine, but I try to remember that every fellow I work on is someone's son or husband or brother. You need to do that, too."

Ruth swallowed. "Of course."

"I don't mean to lecture you. I'm sure you've thought about this yourself."

"I have," she said. "At first I was so afraid to touch them. I was afraid I'd hurt them even more."

"Now you hardly see their faces."

Ruth nodded slowly. "The same with you?"

"The same with me."

They walked along in silence for a while, past the officers smoking their cigars in front of the headquarters building, until the shed that was Hospital Four came into view.

John stopped. "I don't think I've congratulated you on your first surgery. Congratulations to you, the future Dr. Duncan."

Ruth smiled. He put his arms around her, and she nuzzled into his coat. She shut her eyes and held him as tightly as he was holding her.

For a moment, there was no war. Only peace in her heart.

CHAPTER SIXTEEN

June 1915

Elise was in her bunk trying to catch up on a tremendous amount of missed sleep when Matron's heavy footsteps approached the side of her bunk.

"Duncan," said Matron.

Elise rolled over in her thin sleeping bag. There was no mattress between the bag and the boards of the bed, and her elbows and knees ached constantly. She had brought a pillow from the Dowelings' house in London, on Mrs. Doweling's advice. Now it was infested with lice, or bedbugs, or both. She was filthy and tired all the time. "Yes?" said Elise.

Matron, as always, was fully dressed and smoking a cigarette. "That idiot, Montraine, is stuck out between Hospitals Ten and Twelve. I need you to go out and fix her damn ambulance. I want her back before roll call."

"What time is it?" asked Elise.

"Six in the morning," said Matron. "You've got two hours. Get a move on."

Elise struggled out of her sleeping bag wearing her shirt, underwear and a pair of dirty socks, and reached for her uniform skirt and jacket. Elise wondered how long she could possibly last in these conditions. She had promised herself that she would stick it out here as long as Ruth could, but Ruth was made of pretty stern stuff.

Elise buttoned her jacket and pulled on her shoes. She smoothed her long, uncombed hair, and tied it in a knot. Matron tapped the watch on her wrist.

"We don't have time for vanity, Duncan."

"Yes ma'am," said Elise as she hurried past the less mechanically inclined sleepers.

Outside it was just dawn and it looked like rain, but then, it almost always looked like rain. The Belgian summer was not sunny and steamy, like Baltimore. To Elise, it seemed nasty and wet, rarely clearing into blue sky. And when there was blue sky, it was almost always stained by smoke coming from the battlefield. At night the stars were hidden by flares and explosions and fire in the distance, and there was always the noise of the artillery, hammering away, day and night. It was enough to drive a person out of their mind.

The ambulances were parked in a neat line in front of the barracks, nineteen of them instead of twenty, all spotlessly clean. Elise picked the one she had cleaned last night, got in and started it up.

Sometime during the planning of the war, someone had had the foresight to arrange the hospitals in a sort of ring around the ambulance barracks, and so the distance to Number Six, for example, was about the same as the distance to Number Twelve. Without traffic, Elise thought, she would be able to get to Hera in half an hour. Then maybe an hour to fix the engine, then another half hour to get back before roll call. She shifted gears and gunned the ambulance down the muddy road.

She resented Matron calling Hera an idiot. Hera seemed to be a lot of things—young and silly, for one. There were even nasty rumors that she was a "loose woman." But she wasn't like that. The two of them had bonded, as well as anyone could bond in a place like this. They sat next to each other at meals, pocketed stale scones for each other when one missed teatime, helped each other with the miserable business of cleaning the ambulances after supper. Elise wanted to introduce Hera to Ruth, but there was never any time. She rarely saw her sister except at a distance, during ambulance drop-offs. They had taken to sending each other notes via the hospital courier, but those notes were few and far between. Elise knew that Ruth was helping in surgery now—her gruesome dream come true at last—but Elise hadn't told Ruth about Hera. She wasn't sure why.

Elise made the turn toward Hospital Twelve. The ambulance's bald tires skidded in a slick of mud, and Elise slowed to steer through it. On either side of her, wooden crosses stretched as far as the eye could see, bright red poppies waving over their grisly fertilizer.

The wooden crosses fell behind her, giving way to bivouacked troops on either side of the road. Their tents were dirty, torn-up little things, and every once in a while, there would be a group of wooden boxes in a field, each the size of a large crate. Each had a man sitting on it with his pants down around his ankles, usually smoking a cigarette, staring off into the morning. Toilets. Out in the open. Elise averted her eyes, though in her heart she knew no one cared. She could stare all she wanted. Privacy was nonexistent here. She was lucky to have a latrine with doors. She was also lucky not to be sleeping on the ground, like these men obviously were.

After another bumpy half mile, she saw Hera's ambulance, off to the side of the road, its right-side wheels sunk in mud. Hera was slumped in the front seat, sleeping, or sobbing. It would be one or the other.

Elise honked, and Hera straightened, wiped her eyes and waved energetically. She slid out of the cab and pushed her blond hair back as Elise drove up and stopped.

"I'm so glad it's you," said Hera, sounding genuinely relieved. "Anyone else would've shouted at me for breaking down. It wasn't my fault," she added. "The stupid thing just died."

Elise took the tool kit out from under the passenger seat and climbed out of the cab. Hera looked dirty and exhausted. "What're you doing out here?" she asked.

"Some major wanted a ride to see his brother in Hospital Twelve. He couldn't walk there on his own two feet. I'm the most useless," Hera said forlornly, "so Matron sent me."

"You're not useless." Elise went to the front of the ambulance and opened the bonnet. Underneath, the engine was cold, blackened with oil, and smelled flooded. "How long have you been sitting here?"

"At least a couple of hours. Some fellows on horses came by just before dawn and told me they'd ride down to the barracks."

"Have you tried to start it since then?" said Elise.

Hera shook her head, came over to stand beside Elise and peered at the engine. "Can you fix it? You're such a magician with these cranky old things."

Elise had to laugh. "Try it now. Let's see what happens."

Hera got back into the cab. Elise heard her yank on the choke and press the starter. The engine churned half-heartedly, then stopped.

"I've broken it," said Hera. "Matron will kill me."

"I think the spark plugs are fouled." Elise groped in the tool kit for the right wrench and started unscrewing the first one.

"Is that bad?" said Hera.

"No," said Elise. "It's easy."

Hera got out of the cab and stood next to her. "How do you know what to do?" she asked. "At home the chauffeur took care of the car. I never even knew what was under a bonnet until I got here."

"Well," said Elise, "when I was little, I took things apart and put them back together again. And they worked. I thought it was the most fun thing in the world." She eased the spark plug out. It was covered with oil and the gap was, indeed, fouled. She wiped it off with a rag and examined the hole it had come out of. "You may have an oil leak, too."

Hera didn't seem to be listening. "When I was little, I played hospital with my dolls. I gave them the most grievous diseases."

Elise smiled and started on the next spark plug. "You wanted to be a nurse?"

"No," said Hera, "I wanted to be a committee lady, like my mother. She serves on three hospital boards. When I was small, she was so busy, Nanny and I hardly ever saw her. Probably like your father—always out on some emergency or other."

"Father always took me to the garage when the car broke down," said Elise. "The mechanics would let me shift gears and do things like this." She wiped down the next plug. "I would get grease all over my dress—I guess they thought it was cute."

"But you learned how to fix cars," said Hera.

"I did," said Elise. "And Father stopped having to go to the mechanics."

"And he was so proud of you," said Hera, propping an elbow on the fender. "You were like a son to him."

Elise eyed her. "What a strange thing to say."

"Well?" said Hera. "Don't you think he was proud? And every man wants a son. Even if it has to be a daughter."

"I guess he was proud," Elise said slowly. "I mean, he never said anything like that. It was expensive to get the car fixed. I think he was glad to save the money." Elise screwed the spark plug back in and took out the last two. Both were a mess. "What about you? Were you the son or the daughter?"

"The daughter," said Hera, without hesitation. "My father adores me. He's mortified that I'm here in the bloody old war, but I couldn't just sit it out at home. Everyone has a duty, even him, and he's a lord. He watches for zeppelins at night from our highest tower."

Elise suppressed a grin. Whenever Hera talked about home, it sounded like a castle. Maybe it was. Elise preferred her fantasy and had never asked.

"Don't laugh at me," said Hera. "At least I *know* why I'm here."

"You think I don't?" said Elise in surprise.

"You're certainly not here to improve your mechanical skills," said Hera. "Anyone can see that driving an ambulance scares you to death. America's not even *in* the war. So why *are* you here?"

"Because Ruth's here," said Elise. She wiped down the spark plugs and screwed them in hurriedly. "I couldn't let her go to Belgium by herself."

"Oh, please," said Hera. "I really want to know. Aren't you here for a husband?"

"No," said Elise, "and you can start this thing now. It's fixed." She pushed the bonnet down and bolted it shut.

Hera got behind the wheel, pulled out the choke and pushed the starter. The engine sputtered and turned over. It wasn't exactly purring, but it would run. "I really want to *know!*"

Hera shouted over the noise. "If you're not here for a husband, are you here for..." She gunned the engine and the rest of her words were lost.

"I can't hear you!" Elise shouted. She grabbed the tool kit, ran back to her own ambulance, slid into the cab and started it up. She had to turn around to get to the barracks, but Hera roared past before she could even put the lorry into gear. She looked up just in time to see Hera blow her an exaggerated kiss, and it occurred to her that what Hera had said was, *Are you here for...a wife?*

But that was ridiculous. Wasn't it?

CHAPTER SEVENTEEN

Elise was sound asleep, dreamless, for a change, or more accurately, free of nightmares. Something heavy moved on her sleeping bag, and thinking it was a rat, she opened her eyes and her mouth to scream. A cool hand closed over her mouth, and Hera's voice hissed, *"Don't yell, for heaven's sake."*

Elise shoved herself up straight in the hard bunk. It was the absolute middle of the night. Somewhere in the distance, a bomb exploded, shaking the rafters. Hera, nearly invisible, climbed into the bunk with her and pushed a cool metal shape into her hand. Elise recognized it by touch. A hip flask. The top was open. She smelled it. Some kind of liquor.

"What the hell?" she whispered. "What're you doing out of bed?"

"I can't sleep," said Hera softly, and in fact she sounded wide-awake.

"And you're *drinking*?"

"Only a bit."

"Matron would *murder* you if she finds out," Elise whispered. "My God, what if she blew the whistle right now?"

Hera sighed and moved closer to Elise. Elise pushed the flask back at her. Hera took it. Elise heard her take a gulp and hiccup.

Elise gauged the snores around them, the sounds of women turning sleepily in their hard bunks. "Give me the flask," she whispered. "You've had enough."

Hera handed it over, and Elise tucked it into a corner of the bunk where no one would see it if the lights suddenly came on.

"I hate driving the ambulance," Hera hissed, close to Elise's ear and scented with booze. "I hate it so much. And all these girls are so short with me. Except for you. You're my only friend here." In the dark, she put her arms around Elise's shoulders. She pressed her face against Elise's neck, and Elise felt hot tears rolling down to her collarbone, soaking into her shirt.

"Don't cry," Elise whispered, "for God's sake. You'll wake everyone up." But her arms went around Hera's waist, awkwardly, seemingly on their own. The contact, warm skin to warm skin, was electric for Elise, but seemed to make Hera weep even harder. She buried her face in Elise's neck and snuffled there, her body shuddering with suppressed sobs.

"I want to go home," Hera wept into Elise's ear, "but Mother would never have it. Father would disapprove. I'd be an embarrassment to my family."

Elise wanted to tell her that she wasn't an embarrassment—could never be. Who could blame her for being young and scared in a place like this? Elise wanted to tell her that she felt the same way, but none of those words made it out of her mouth. Hera's heart pounded against her own chest, and the warm, soft swell of Hera's bosom pressed against hers. Elise held Hera as tightly as she dared, not saying anything, her heart thundering in her ears, her mind racing, back and forth between the beckoning glances of the woman in the pin-striped suit, and the women all around her in the shoddy barracks bunks. She ran one hand hesitantly up and down Hera's back, and Hera seemed to calm down. Her body relaxed against Elise's, hot and damp. Hera pushed away long enough to wipe her face.

"You're a good friend," she sniffed. "We should make a pact."

"A pact?" echoed Elise. "What do you mean?"

"Like the soldiers do," said Hera. "Two of them pledge to protect each other in battle, to fight back-to-back. Nothing comes between them. And if one of them is killed, the other writes to his family and tells them how brave he was. We could do that." She collapsed back onto Elise's shoulder.

"We could," said Elise, softly, into Hera's hair, "but I don't intend to be fighting."

"Silly," whispered Hera, "it's just a figure of speech. It just means we'll be watching out for each other." She let out a teary little snort. "No one else is going to do it."

"Don't start crying again."

"I won't." Hera sniffed hard. She was quiet for a while. "Can I stay here until the whistle blows?"

Elise gulped dryly. "What would Matron say if she found us together like this?"

"She would call me a coward," said Hera bitterly. "She's already said as much. But it's true. I am a coward. I know I'll never sleep if I go back to my own bed. And then what good will I be when we're out doing our runs?"

Elise let out all her breath, wanting to tell her no, but she couldn't. Maybe she was a coward as well. "All right," she whispered.

"Oh, good," Hera whispered back and planted a damp, jolting kiss on Elise's cheek. "I knew you were a friend." She slid down in the bunk and blundered into Elise's sleeping bag, which wasn't even close to being big enough for two. Elise slid down as well, and the two of them struggled for a moment, thigh against thigh, arm under back, until Hera was comfortable, and Elise was contorted. In no time, Hera was breathing quietly, sound asleep against Elise's neck. Elise tried hard to relax, but it was absolutely impossible. She tried to imagine that Hera was a man, and that she was in the same exact position. That didn't help either, and just made her more tense.

Above, in the upper bunk, Tippy snored hard, oblivious of everything. Elise lay where she was, eyes open in the dark, listening to the sounds of breathing, in her ear, all around her, until much later, when the whistle blew, just before dawn.

In the chaos of dressing and fleeing to the ambulances, no one seemed to notice the two women jumping out of one bed.

CHAPTER EIGHTEEN

Ruth sat at the table in the nurses' quarters, staring alternately at the short, sputtering candle and the blank sheet of paper in front of her. The candle quivered every time a bomb exploded, outside, not so far away, in the middle of the night.

Helen was snoring in the upper bunk, just a shadow in the shadows. Ruth had been afraid of waking her up with the sound of a striking match, but their shift at the hospital had been more brutal than usual. Helen was down for the count.

Dear Father and Grandpa, Ruth wrote. She wasn't sure if it was the noise or the guilt that had woken her. There were three unanswered letters from home on the table, one for each of the last three weeks. She shut her eyes for a moment to see if she could sleep sitting up, but both the noise and the guilt made her open them again.

I hope you both are well.

That was a good start. She made herself write some more, trying to stick with pleasantries.

> *Elise received the package you sent with the chocolate and cookies, and we were glad to see it. The food at the hospital is bearable, but Elise and the ambulance drivers are a step "below" us, and she never stops complaining about what they're given to eat.*

So much for the pleasantries. Was it time to be honest for a change?

> *I have time to write to you now because though the wounds we're seeing are very bad, our caseload is light at the moment. The Germans used gas on our lines for the first time last week and most of our boys— the Tommies, the French, even the Armenians—ended up dead in their own trenches. Not just a few, but hundreds, perhaps a thousand men must have died along five miles of the front here. I can hardly bring myself to describe what we've seen. Men with their faces swollen, blinded from mere contact with the stuff, coughing their lungs out, but the worst thing is we don't have a treatment for them. We wash them down with fresh water and try to make them comfortable with morphine, but in most cases, it is just an act of futility. If they're wounded in addition to the gas, the gas seeps into the wound and makes it gangrenous. Whole areas of tissue have to be cut away just to clear the wound, and then the man dies anyway. It's horrible.*

Were those tears dripping on the letter? She wiped her tired eyes.

> *We have all been issued gas masks, but these are just a pair of goggles with burlap cloth hanging down to cover the nose and mouth. The soldiers say that one must urinate on the cloth to neutralize the effects of the gas, and when I told Elise, she gave me a look I can't describe. She, of course,*

is closer to the front lines than we are at the hospital and more likely to come in contact with gas—even loading patients into the ambulance is dangerous because the gas hangs around the men, even as they are evacuated.

Of course, she could easily describe the look on Elise's face if she wanted to. Awful disbelief.

One would think that by now we would be overrun with Germans with so many casualties, but from what I hear, the Germans were unprepared for the success of their own weapon and didn't drive into the holes in our lines. For this we are intensely grateful, but it does make one wonder what will happen next time. Now there is a gong that they ring down at the front to warn of incoming gas. The sound of it makes the men hysterical, as there is no way to shoot back against gas. No amount of "over the top" will stop it, and hiding in the trenches only makes it worse. There are so many dead men, I can hardly convey it to you.

So many dead men.

It is at times like this I don't feel as though I'm practicing medicine—just helping men along into death. I think that we will never win this war unless we are prepared to fight gas with gas, which seems so dishonorable to me.

Honor, on the other hand, seems to have been left behind. I have seen too many deaths by machine gun and flamethrower and strafing by aeroplanes to believe that there is any honor left on either side. Last week, I had a cavalry officer here who was telling me about the old days when he and his chaps could actually ride into battle with flags waving and trumpets calling. He was so sad about the way war is now that he broke down and wept in my arms. What was worse was that this man, who had fought so valiantly under other circumstances, struck me as naïve under those given here. To think that his horse, which was shot out from under him, could carry him past the muck of no man's land and over the German trenches like it was a magical thing. The old wars seem like fairy tales to me, hardly worth reminiscing about since they have so little bearing on reality these days, and the gas just tops it all off. One can only wonder what the Germans will come up with next.

I wish I could end this letter on a lighter note, but I don't feel light. I'm heavy with the pain and suffering I see in the hospital and about which I can do so little.

And now, Ruth thought bitterly, more pleasantries.

At any rate, I hope you both are well. Despite the bad food, Elise and I are keeping our spirits up.

We miss you very much.
Love,
Ruth

Ruth read over what she had written. Too honest, she thought. Too honest by a long shot.

She took the letter by its corners, tore it to shreds, and burned it, bit by bit, with the shuddering candle.

CHAPTER NINETEEN

July 1915

Elise lined up with the rest of the Ambulance Corps volunteers at the eight o'clock roll call. It was a hot July morning, and Elise was almost used to the routine by now. The matron, on the other hand, normally brusque and opaque, looked nervous as she let her cigarette burn to ash without taking more than two puffs.

"You'll all be down at the front lines today, tomorrow and for the foreseeable future," she said, and there was an audible gasp from the line of women. "The bloody Germans managed to blow up the train tracks last night." She took a drag from the flagging cigarette. "I won't try to tell you it won't be dangerous. I encourage you to write to your families. You have about half an hour. They're trying to clear the road for us as we speak." She took another puff and threw the cigarette on the ground, crushing it with her heel. "Dismissed."

Back in the barracks, no one was talking, just scribbling down their last words to friends and family. The matron's nervousness had rubbed off on everyone. The woman with such steely resolve was scared, and she had scared everyone else.

Elise sat next to Hera on Hera's bunk. "We'll be all right," she said in a low voice.

"What if we're not?" whispered Hera. She had a blank piece of paper in her hand and a pencil in the other. She took a breath and pushed the paper at Elise. "You write mine. I'll write yours. Like we said. In our pact."

"But we aren't dead," said Elise.

"Yet," replied Hera. "Please. Do it for me."

Elise took the paper. "I'll watch out for you today," she whispered. "You don't have to be afraid."

Hera just swallowed and nodded and took another sheet of paper out from under her bunk. Elise watched her write, *Dear Messrs. Duncan…*

Elise frowned at her own paper and wrote, unsteadily, over her own knees,

Dear Lord and Lady Montraine,
My name is Elise Duncan, and I am Hera's friend from the
Ambulance Corps. I am writing to tell you that Hera was…

What should she say? Elise swallowed and made herself put down *killed today while rescuing wounded soldiers from the front.*

Elise wiped tears from her right eye, which was stinging for some reason. She wanted to see what Hera was writing, but she didn't dare look over.

She was heroic. She was always incredibly brave, even when she
was scared to death.

Elise erased *to death.*

She was a very dear friend to me. I have never known anyone like her. She didn't have many friends here because she was so new, but we bonded very quickly.

Bonded wasn't really the right word. Elise chewed on the end of her own pencil, trying to come up with something more accurate. She erased *bonded*, and wrote *we became like sisters*. But that wasn't right either. There was something more that she didn't have the words for. Elise finally wrote,

I am so sorry for your loss, and mine.
Sincerely yours,
Elise Duncan.

She straightened and saw Hera folding her own letter in half. "Aren't you going to let me see?" whispered Elise.

Hera gave her an unhappy look and handed her the letter. Elise opened it to find it spotted with tears.

Dear Messrs. Duncan,
I am so very sorry to let you know that your daughter, Elise, was killed today while evacuating wounded soldiers from the front lines near Ypres. She was the bravest, strongest person I've ever met. I came to the Ambulance Corps alone and frightened, and she immediately took me under her wing, even though she was brand-new as well. She was terribly talented with her mechanical skills, and it is due to her efforts that our ambulances ran at all.

I did not know her as long as I would have liked, but I want you to know that she was more than just appreciated. Your daughter was dearly loved.

Yours in sorrow

Elise blinked away her own tears. Hera, silently weeping, put an arm around her shoulders. Elise took her sweaty hands.

"Please be careful today," Hera whispered. "I can't lose you."

Elise squeezed Hera's hands wordlessly.

"Will you write to your sister?" said Hera. "Or do you want me to?"

"I can do it," said Elise. She let go of Hera and took another sheet of paper, and found that she had no idea what to write. *I love you* seemed too simple, and too obvious. If these would be her last words, what did she really want to say to Ruth? Elise held the pencil over the paper on her knees and scribbled, *You are so much better at this than I am.*

She folded the paper in half as Hera watched.

"That's all?" said Hera.

Elise nodded, unable to say anything.

Around the room, others were laying their letters on the table, putting on their hats and uniform jackets, ready to drive into the throat of the war. Elise shrugged into her jacket, put her hat on and went outside without waiting for the whistle. Hera trailed her, wiping her eyes.

The first three miles were the same three miles they always drove, and aside from a few fresh craters, nothing was different. Everyone kept nose to tail as the bombs whistled overhead. The ground shook under Elise's ambulance, but at least it was dry today. Mud would've made everything even worse. There was probably plenty of mud along the track to the front, though. It was just a matter of time.

Up ahead there was some kind of congestion, and Elise craned her neck to see the new troops coming in, from off to the right. There were so many of them. Hundreds of them, so many that perhaps there were a thousand, jamming the road.

Elise had never seen so many people in one spot, not even on a busy Baltimore afternoon, and her stomach sank. Some men were in new uniforms, fresh recruits. Some were muddy veterans. Some were singing as they marched toward the front, and their voices sounded high and frightened over the shelling and the engines. An almost visible shudder went through their lines as they saw the number of ambulances headed in the same direction they were, and the singing seemed to stop. Still, Elise could hear echoes farther back, where perhaps reality hadn't sunk in yet, and all was camaraderie and brave souls.

Someone blew a whistle, loud and piercing, and the ambulance line began to move forward with a little more speed. The troops split around them, still marching in formation, often with officers on horseback leading them. From what she had heard about the trenches, Elise couldn't imagine what use the horses could possibly be—just a hindrance—and another casualty. She passed an officer on an especially beautiful white horse, already dirty to its knees, on a tight rein as bombs continued to whistle overhead and break into pieces in the near distance, shattering the air, shattering the ground. Elise's heart pounded in a new and dreadful way. She tried to look into the eyes of the soldiers she passed, hoping to see some courage she could borrow. What she saw was the same feeling as in her chest—tightly controlled fear—and determination to get the job done.

The next turn in the road brought the ambulances into new territory, past where they usually went down the hill to the trains. She could see the railroad tracks now, a twisted mess of rails and boards, the whole area pocked with craters. Train cars were smashed and on their sides. Everywhere, the trees, which had been leafed out and shady, were now stripped, like the masts of ships and burned until only the charred trunks remained. And then there were the dead men, still lying on the ground while the repair crews rushed around, clearing this tangle of metal, piling that mass of wooden ties. The burned tree trunks came between Elise and her view of the tracks, and someone honked. She focused her attention on the road again and caught up to the ambulance in front of her, edging up behind it, keeping her distance at just a few feet so that the marching men wouldn't get between her and the next vehicle. They would only slow her down.

Then suddenly, there was the front, burning and smoking like a vision of hell. Elise took a quick breath and found herself choking on the stink in the air—gunpowder mixed with fear and rot. She'd had dreams about the front, but none of them matched what she was looking at right now.

Trees had been blasted away to blackened stumps, giving a long view onto the trenches below and the hordes of men filling them. Everywhere there was movement and smoke and the racket of falling shells. The morning sun laid long, reddish shadows over the tangle of barbed wire. Beyond the wire was the churned muck of no man's land and beyond that, more wire and surprisingly, at least to Elise, a faint view of the German front lines. She could just see the Germans, tiny figures wreathed in smoke from the British bombs and missiles. Their trenches, like the wire, stretched as far as the eye could see in a landscape stripped of anything green or living. It was high summer, and there was not a single blade of grass or a flower to be seen. Just heaped brown sandbags here on the British side, and sticks woven together like a basket to keep the earth in the trenches from caving in.

From her vantage point, up on this hill, Elise could see the wounded and the dead lying in the craters and ditches of no man's land. Some were still crawling. Some lay still in pools of water. Here and there were groups of soldiers who had died together. The sun gave one last bloody glare and rose into a black haze of smoke. Half the sky went dark, and the shells arced overhead, leaving trails of light like fireworks. They exploded so close by, Elise swore she felt pellets of dirt patter against her face. The noise was deafening, and she could hardly hear the whistle blowing from the lead ambulance. She didn't know she was supposed to move until the ambulance ahead of her gave a jolt and pitched forward toward the low ground of the front. Elise saw the soldiers erupting from their trenches, over the top, running toward the German lines. She saw them mowed down by what she could only guess was machine gun fire, and then there was too much smoke to see. Smoke enveloped everything, and she followed the ambulance in front of her, down the hill, into the muck, to retrieve the wounded.

For the first time, Elise saw what triage was like. From the train, when it had been running, it was a mad rush to get everyone on the ambulances, hopefully in the correct order, to go to the right hospital. Here it was just madness.

Corpses lay among the living, and the living were moaning, sobbing or, worst of all, silently grinning. Elise couldn't even see any orderlies. What she could see, in the thick haze, was a sort of slow-motion dance that the doctors at the front did around the bodies lying on the ground, tagging them with paper slips—who would stay and die and who would get a chance to be saved. Who would walk to the nearest hospital and who would be driven. Wounded men helped other wounded men to their feet, two together, sometimes two supporting a third between them, all walking away from the front, partly bandaged, partly bleeding, all staggering under the weight of the fighting and the smoke.

Orderlies suddenly appeared and began to load her ambulance. The noise was overwhelming, and what she thought was a whistling shell was actually a blast on the whistle from the matron, standing right next to her.

"Duncan!" shouted the matron. "Hospital Ten, double-time!"

The gate of Elise's ambulance slammed shut—a jolt to the frame of her lorry rather than a noise she could hear—and a ghost-faced sergeant waved her on with a white stick, which looked like he was waving a human bone. Elise shot up the hill, her tires spinning in the mud and debris, and managed to get to the top without hitting any of the wounded soldiers making their way on foot ahead of her. She honked uselessly for them to get out of the way. No one could hear anything over the raging of the guns.

On the way back, a corporal with white gloves, standing on an empty cart, seemed to be directing traffic, surreal in the murky air, like a pair of hands and a white, terrified face floating above everything else. A riderless horse came galloping through the lines, heading away from the battle. It got caught up in the mass of men headed toward the front, and someone tried to grab its reins, but the horse reared and kicked and ran off the road, away from everything. Elise gunned her engine and drove as fast as she could. The smoke made her eyes feel like they were made of gritty glass. There was no ambulance in front of her that she could see, no one to follow, but she could sense that there was a line behind her and she had to move faster. She pressed her foot down on the accelerator and hit bumps on the road. She heard the men in the rear cry out. Even though she had been aware of them before, it was the first time she could actually hear them.

"Mercy!" they screamed at her. Elise drove even faster, tasting blood in her mouth from having bitten into her own cheeks.

Hospital Ten was the farthest from the front, and it took almost forty-five minutes to make it those six miles. At last she saw the open doors and an ambulance ahead of her, unloading.

Victoria was the driver, and she was standing outside the cab with a cigarette, shaking visibly. Elise climbed out and ran over.

"Are you all right?" said Elise.

"I'm all right," said Victoria. "But they're bombing hospitals. I was supposed to go to Number Four. They'd been shelled. They told me to go somewhere else, so I came here." She dragged deep on the cigarette and got back into the cab.

"Number Four?" Elise shouted. "But that's where Ruth is."

"Your sister? I know," said Victoria. "I didn't see her, but I saw that doctor they call The Mouse. He was evacuating the place. He was bloody all over, but it could have been someone else's blood. I don't know. Oh, my dear," she said, "I hope she's all right." She started the engine and took off into the smoky daylight. Behind Elise, the orderlies were shouting that she was clear and had to go, too.

"I'm going!" she cried. "I'm going!" She followed Victoria away from the hospital, and at the turnoff, she headed left, for Hospital Number Four.

CHAPTER TWENTY

Ruth heard the shell hit before she saw it, and when she did see it, she couldn't believe her eyes, because it just sat there, unexploded, half buried in the splintered wooden floor.

It was a huge thing, half the size of a hospital bed, and it landed in the middle of the main ward, tearing through the tin roof like it was made of paper.

The patients saw the shell hit the floor. There was a moment of complete silence, and then pandemonium. Men with abdominal wounds threw off their drainage tubes, got up and ran, as best they could, out the doors. The blinded ones groped their way out of their beds, and since they were grouped together, found each other by touch. Crying out, they stumbled around, knowing there was a bomb but not knowing where it was or how to get out. All of this happened in the moments that Ruth and Helen and Mary Gardener stood frozen, holding each other, waiting for the thing to go off.

When it didn't, Ruth let go of Mary. "We have to get everyone out of here," she whispered. "Where's The Mouse?"

"I'll find him," said Mary, and she ran to the operating theater.

Ruth and Helen turned to the chaos around them and looked for the orderlies. The four old men were standing in stunned silence, and one by one they looked at the women as though they would know what to do. The only saving grace, Ruth realized, was that the walking wounded had been cleared out of the hospital in the days before this attack, and instead of having a hundred beds to clear, there were only about thirty. If they crept around the bomb very quietly, maybe it would stay exactly as it was, and not explode in their faces. She went over to the orderlies and put her hands on their shoulders.

"Get the stretchers," she said over the shouting of the soldiers. "Take the worst ones outside. I'll take care of the blinded ones."

They turned to obey just as Mary, The Mouse and MacPherson came running in from the direction of the operating theater. The doctors both stopped short when they saw the bomb, sitting there like an unwelcome guest, at an angle to the ground.

"Where are the orderlies?" demanded MacPherson. "We've got to clear this place."

"They're coming with stretchers," said Ruth, and she turned to Helen. "Help me with the blind ones. At least we can get them outside."

"What about the patient in surgery?" said Helen.

"We lost him," said The Mouse. "Don't worry about him."

The orderlies appeared with armloads of folded stretchers. Each of the doctors grabbed the end of one and hurried over to where the legless cases were.

Ruth and Helen ran over to the blinded men, and Ruth

took the closest by the hand. They had stopped shouting now and stood together in a group—there were twelve of them—breathing like runners.

"Come with us," said Ruth in her kindest yet most commanding voice. "There's an unexploded bomb in the hospital, and we need to get you to a safe place."

The blinded men followed wordlessly as Ruth led them through the door and across the road to where the nurses' quarters were. Helen followed at the rear of the line, holding the last man's hand as he and the others stumbled over the caked ruts in the road.

"Careful," said Ruth, her heart pounding. "The road's very rough. Lift your feet!"

She opened the door to the nurses' quarters, and together she and Helen got the men situated on the lower bunks, where they sat quietly with a mumbled, "Thank you, Sister."

As Ruth and Helen ran out, an ambulance was just pulling away, revealing The Mouse standing in the road, still wearing his bloody smock. It took Ruth a moment to realize that he had just turned away a full ambulance, not an empty one. There were no empty ambulances coming.

Already a dozen men were lying on the other side of the road from the hospital, on stretchers. None of them were far enough from the building to be safe if the bomb exploded, and any of them who were conscious knew it. The ones who had gotten out by themselves, earlier in the immediate chaos after the bomb had fallen, hadn't gotten much farther, and under the racket of shelling, Ruth could hear them groaning with pain. She heard a man vomiting. She heard a man sobbing for his mother. Two of the orderlies burst out of the hospital with another man on a stretcher and raced across the road to lay him in a row with the rest.

Shells burst overhead, and Ruth wondered how long until the next one fell on them.

She ran over to The Mouse. "How many are left inside?"

"Just three," said The Mouse. "We have to get the rest of them farther away. If that thing goes off, we'll all be flattened."

MacPherson came out of the hospital as the orderlies raced back in. "We have to get them out into the field," said MacPherson, meaning the area where the dead were buried. "We can stage them from here and get them out of harm's way."

Unless the cemetery was shelled, thought Ruth, but she followed Mary in, and the two of them grabbed a stretcher.

Ruth eyed the bomb as they tiptoed past it and prepared herself to die. Surely it was just a matter of time until the bomb went off. Even if it didn't, there were so many other bombs falling around them, one of them would get her. It wasn't beyond the Germans to send a shell into a cemetery. She'd heard plenty of stories about soldiers hiding in grave-yards during shell attacks, only to find themselves in craters with a coffin for company, sometimes already emptied of its contents, sometimes not. For all she knew, they would just be taking the men to their graves a little early. The man on the stretcher, an abdominal wound from Suffolk, looked at her with pleading eyes, and Ruth did the only thing she could think of. She smiled at him.

"Don't worry," she said, "we'll have you out of here and over in the field in no time." He was heavy and made her slow as she stumbled under his weight, frightfully slow, slow enough to invite death, but she kept smiling, radiating as much calm as she could, and finally he smiled, too. It was a pained smile, but he let himself lie back on the stretcher and be car-ried out the front doors of the hospital and deposited on the other side of the road where his mates were.

The Mouse came over and lowered his voice so only Ruth and Mary could hear. "If we could just get them into another hospital, we might be able to save most of them. The fact is, out in the field, they're just going to die. And slowly, too."

Helen hurried over. "The nearest phone's at Hospital Three." She looked like she was ready to run for it, her hair bristling out from under her nurse's veil, her clothes all awry. Ruth could only imagine that she looked the same.

"Listen," said MacPherson, "even if we had a phone, all the ambulances are out on runs. There's no way to contact them and tell them to come here. We have to wait for one to show up and tell them to send an empty one."

"We need at least two," said The Mouse. A shell whistled overhead, flying in the general direction of the cemetery. It hit the ground with a flash and blew up with such force that it pushed them all to their knees.

Ruth stood unsteadily against the ringing in her ears. So much for the idea of putting the wounded into the cemetery. She and The Mouse, MacPherson, Helen and Mary looked at each other. Ruth glanced around at the men lying on the ground, lined up along the side of the road. The orderlies brought the last two cases out, put the stretchers down and came over to the group of doctors and nurses.

Another bomb shrieked overhead and landed square in the field where the bodies were buried.

"They're aiming at us," shouted The Mouse over the noise. "It's just a matter of time until we're hit again." He glanced over his shoulder, where there was fire now in the field. "It's been a pleasure working with you all," he said in a perfectly calm voice.

Ruth felt like she was in a dream. She reached out and took Mary Gardener's hand, which was cold and sweaty. The nurses, doctors and orderlies stood there together in the noise, and the stink of burning dirt, and waited. Behind them, lying on the side of the road, the wounded were quiet, as though they'd reached the same conclusion as The Mouse and were just waiting for the end.

More bombs were screaming overhead. "Perhaps we should pray," MacPherson said. Ruth felt her knees go weak, and she fell onto them. MacPherson clasped his hands and began to say the Lord's Prayer when suddenly there was a different noise and a different smell. It was the chug of an engine and the whiff of exhaust. An ambulance veered into view and came to a skidding stop. To Ruth's amazement, it was Elise who jumped out.

"What the hell are you doing?" Elise shouted over the shelling.

"We can't take your men," The Mouse shouted back. "We've got an unexploded bomb inside."

"I'm empty!" Elise shouted. "I can take a dozen!"

Ruth scrambled to her feet. The orderlies and doctors did the same. There was a flurry of action as stretchers were picked up off the ground and loaded into Elise's ambulance. In moments it was so full, the lorry sagged over its tires.

"I've got room for one more in the cab," said Elise, "two if they're skinny."

"The blinded ones!" said Ruth. "They're still in the nurses' quarters."

"How many?" Elise asked.

"Twelve!" said Ruth, and hurried to get them.

Inside, the nurses' quarters smelled of cigarettes. The blinded men, smoking, their eyes covered with bandages, were absolutely silent.

"Listen," said Ruth. "There's an ambulance here. She can take two of you, but the rest are going to have to walk with me to the nearest hospital. It's a mile away. We're being shelled, as you've no doubt noticed. It won't be an easy walk, but we don't have any other choice."

The men shuffled to their feet. "We're ready, Sister," said one with a distinct Cockney accent and sergeant's stripes on his uniform. "You pick who goes in the ambulance. The rest of us'll walk with you. We've been shelled before, 'aven't we, boys?"

The rest muttered in agreement. Ruth picked the two thinnest and led them outside.

She squeezed the two blind men into the passenger seat in the cab. The space was so tight, they practically had to sit in each other's lap. Elise got in and started the engine.

"What're you going to do?" she said to Ruth. "Where're you going to go?"

"We'll take the blind up to Hospital Three," said Ruth, sounding calmer to herself than she actually felt. "They can walk the mile. When we get there, we'll get a bomb squad to disarm the damn thing."

"Be careful," said Elise, and she shoved the ambulance into gear.

"You too," said Ruth as Elise roared off.

CHAPTER TWENTY-ONE

They formed a line—MacPherson and The Mouse in front, the ten blinded men in the middle, and Ruth and Helen and Mary with the orderlies behind. Overhead, the rockets and shells were like pinwheels against the clouds, which would've been beautiful at any other time, Ruth thought as she tightened her grip on the man's shoulder in front of her. Now the streaks in the sky were like the hands on a clock, ticking toward the second when one would come down right behind them and blow them all to hell.

It occurred to her then that the Germans might be winning, and this made her feel so low that she struggled to keep the tears from her eyes. All this work, all this blood—just to be defeated? Ruth stumbled on the uneven dirt road and felt Gardener grab her arm to steady her. It was then that she noticed they weren't alone. The wounded from the front were walking with them—two men supporting a third, individuals hobbling along with a stick of wood for a crutch.

There were bodies along the road as well, and Ruth recognized some as patients from Hospital Four, amputees who had tried to escape and had died by the roadside, their wounds betraying them. Some, she thought, had simply bled out. Some had been hit by shrapnel. A few still had their drainage tubes attached. Tears ran down her face as she walked, slowly, as though in a funeral procession. Mary was still holding on to her, and her fingers dug in painfully, but Ruth didn't care about that. She clenched the man's shoulder in front of her and hung on to him as though he was a lifeline in a very dark and watery place. In turn, his free hand came up and covered hers. All of his humanity and concern flowed through that touch. All his fears and experiences on the battlefield came to her. He was blind now, but still walking, and Ruth found some strength in that. She squeezed Mary's hand, and Mary squeezed back. Ruth sniffed hard and kept going. If they got to the next hospital—and it was a big *if*—they would need her in one piece, not sniveling like a little girl.

A bomb whistled overhead, very close, and the soldier in front of her stopped suddenly. "You'd better get down, Sister." He turned and yelled, *"Down, boys!"* and the blind men dropped to the ground as the bomb hit, just up the road. The force of it knocked Ruth off her feet, into a heap with Gardener underneath her, Helen and the orderlies behind. A wave of dirt rushed over them, and the noise left her deafened. The force left her with spots on her eyes, and her head felt like the inside of a metal bell.

"Helen!" she shouted. "Mary!"

Mary pulled herself out from the tangle of limbs. The now familiar smell of incinerated soil came over them, but there was more than that—the smell of blood and the echoing sound of shrieking men. Ahead there was fire and thick smoke—trees were burning. One fell and crashed onto the road. The fire showed four men lying sprawled under a cover of dirt, as though they'd died and been instantly buried. None of them were moving. Ruth knew that two of them were MacPherson and The Mouse.

She and Mary and Helen struggled over to them. Mary was bleeding down the side of her face. Ruth tasted blood inside her mouth and felt something warm running along her left arm, but there wasn't time to see what it was—she knew anyway. She knelt near MacPherson and dug at the dirt across his face. His eyes were still open. His mouth was open, but he wasn't breathing. She crawled over to where Mary was with The Mouse. She still couldn't hear anything, just high-pitched ringing in her ears while Mary screamed over the noise, mouthing the words, *He's still alive!* And he was, clawing at the dirt that buried him, his face covered, his mouse ears filled with it. Ruth crawled over to the other two men who had been leading the blinded column. There was no hope for them.

The burning tree blazed ahead of them. Beyond that was an enormous crater. Around it, dead men lay in heaps.

They were down to eight blind men, four orderlies, a wounded doctor and the three nurses. Hospital Three seemed like it could be a hundred miles away, and there was no guarantee that it hadn't been hit either. Behind her, the blind sergeant was back on his feet, arms out, feeling the air for his companions. Ruth left Mary on her knees beside The Mouse, and rushed over to him. Other blind men were on their feet now, too, and so were the orderlies.

"Sister!" shouted the blind sergeant, "Sister, is that you?"

Her hearing was coming back. "Yes," she shouted. "We've been shelled. Two of your men are dead."

"Are you quite all right, Sister?" shouted the sergeant, as though they were in Piccadilly Circus and she had tripped on the sidewalk. She almost laughed, but it came out as a hysterical cry.

"Listen to me, Sister," shouted the sergeant over the ringing in her ears. "Are there any wounded to carry?"

"No—everyone's dead or able to walk."

"There's no walking in shelling like this," said the sergeant. "We need to find a hole and get into it. Is it evening yet?"

"Not yet—not for hours, I think."

"Then let's find a ditch," said the sergeant. "In the evening, the shelling may stop for a while, and we can get to where we're going. In the meantime, it's better to stay put."

The closest ditch was the shell hole just beyond the burning tree. Ruth turned for the orderlies and saw that they were gone, run off into the fields on either side of the road. Only Ruth, Mary, Helen, The Mouse and the blind men were left.

They formed a line again, this time with Ruth and The Mouse, who seemed too stunned to do anything but follow, in front. Mary and Helen were behind with the blind men. They all made their way around the tree and into the crater, where the dirt was still warm from the impact, still smoking around the edges. In the middle was a pool of water. Ruth, Mary and Helen helped The Mouse and the blinded men into the hole, then slid in themselves, up to their shins in water, covered with dirt and ash. Overhead, shells continued to arc and fall.

Ruth wondered where Elise was.

The blind sergeant groped for her shoulder. "Hunker down, miss. Don't think about anything. The chances they'll hit this hole again are one in a million." He squeezed hard and let go, pressing himself down into the dirt, and Ruth did the same. She spared a look around for Helen, who was so covered in mud that she was almost invisible, and for the other blinded men who had curled into the sides of the crater like it was their mother. Another shell whistled down and hit not far away.

The earth shuddered and sparks rained over them, but the hole in the ground protected them from the force of the blow.

All day long, the shelling went on, and Ruth no longer had to imagine what it was like at the front. The front was all around them. Trees burned, ash drifted over them and dirt spattered on them. When evening finally came, it came with a thunderstorm, like heaven competing with the heavy artillery. Lightning flashed against the slashes of fire in the sky, and thunder rolled with the steady *boom* of the guns. The storm gained strength and poured rain into the muddy crater. Ruth's ears rang, and her body was bruised from the pummeling the earth had taken. She had wept for MacPherson when she was sure that no one could hear her, and now her body was empty. The storm rolled over them and into the dusk, where it became a line of retreating clouds against the steady light of sunset. The blind sergeant had been right; the shelling seemed to stop, or at least the noise seemed more distant. Ruth really couldn't tell. She dragged herself out of the mud and over to Mary, who was covered from head to foot in muck. The only part of her white uniform that was still relatively clean was the part that had been rained on.

"Mary?" She touched her shoulder, and Mary looked up from the muddy side of the crater.

"You're alive," wept Mary. "I thought we'd all been killed."

Ruth could hardly hear her. "Get Helen. Get The Mouse. We have to walk. We have to get to Hospital Three."

Mary nodded and struggled to stand. Her face was streaked with tears, and Ruth could see how hard she was working to keep herself under control. The three of them got the remaining blind soldiers and The Mouse on their feet, and together they crawled out of the muddy hole and formed a line.

Now that she had a chance to get her bearings, Ruth could

see how far they'd come, which wasn't far at all. In fact, Hospital Four was still in one piece, less than five hundred feet behind them. The hole in the roof was clear, and through the wide-open doors, she could still catch a glimpse of the unexploded bomb. Between them and the hospital, all over the road, were bodies. The side of the road had been blown into a huge hole. Based on the size, the shell must have killed everyone nearby. That was what was behind them. Ahead, there were more shell holes, more bodies and the remains of burned trees, some of which were still standing, smoking. There was movement ahead as others crawled out of shell holes and began their march to the hospital. There was no sign of ambulances, no sound of engines. As the ringing in Ruth's ears began to wane, she turned to the muddy blind sergeant and put her hand on his arm.

"You saved our lives," she said. "If we hadn't been in that hole, we all would have died."

"I've been in a lot of holes, Sister," he said. "We woz lucky, that's all."

"But you said the chances of being hit again were one in a million," said Ruth.

"I lied," said the sergeant. "There's no safe place in hell."

Miraculously, a mile away, Hospital Number Three was unscathed. Even the trees were fine. Ambulances pulled in and away like delivery wagons. The casualties were so high that the staff was lining the wounded up outside the barn that was the hospital. Tents had already been hoisted over the overflow areas. Hospital Three was taking up the slack of Hospital Four.

Ruth tried to see if any of the ambulance drivers was Elise, but she didn't recognize any of them. It was as though after a mile of walking and a nightmare of shelling, she and her filthy clothes had passed into a different country where she knew no one and no one even saw her. In her exhausted mind, she wondered if she had somehow turned invisible to the rushing orderlies and nurses. She and Mary, Helen, The Mouse and the blind men came to a halt in front of the hospital and stood there until finally an orderly noticed them.

"Hey, Sister," he said in an American accent, "these three are women!"

"We're nurses from Hospital Four," said Mary, with more presence of mind than Ruth possessed.

"We're here," said Helen and her voice quivered. "We're here to help." And with that she burst into tears.

CHAPTER TWENTY-TWO

Elise gunned the ambulance up the hill toward Hospital Number Three. Shells were falling all around her, close enough to shake the lorry to its very bolts and rattle the teeth inside her head. Beside her, the two blinded men huddled together in the passenger seat, trying to take up as little room as possible in the cramped cab. Behind her, in the back of the ambulance, the men were silent, and she could almost smell their fear. Smoke blew everywhere, and Elise coughed over the steering wheel, her palms slippery with sweat. Trees burned on either side of the road. Wounded men trudged toward the relative safety of the next hospital, holding each other up.

"Get in!" she had shouted at Ruth as the last blind man was loaded. Ruth had run off like she hadn't heard, and it occurred to Elise that she should have simply shoved Ruth into the ambulance and taken her along. In her gut, Elise knew Ruth would never have come. Sisterly devotion or not. Bombs or not. Raging fires or not.

Finally, finally, there was Hospital Number Three, doors open, lights shining as though nothing was wrong. Already, though, they had lofted the tents atop the overflow areas, and other ambulances were stacked up, waiting to unload. Elise pulled up as close as she could, jumped out of the cab, and ran up to an orderly who was already at one end of a stretcher.

"Hospital Four's been bombed," she said, her voice shaking more than she'd expected. "The bomb hasn't gone off yet, or at least I think it hasn't gone off. Someone's got to get down there and disarm it!"

"You'll have to speak with someone in charge, miss," said the orderly, a man with a gray mustache. "Find the head nurse. She'll help you."

Elise hurried back to her ambulance instead. It would be too easy for her load to be overlooked, especially in this over-crowded chaos. She glanced around for someone she knew, and spotted Hera. Elise shouted at her until Hera turned around, bewildered and terrified. She ran over when she saw Elise.

"They're bombing us!" she cried. "They're *bombing* us!"

"I know," said Elise. "It's bad. Have they unloaded your lorry yet?"

"Yes, but—"

"Go find the head nurse," said Elise. "Tell her there's an unexploded bomb sitting in Hospital Number Four. She needs to get on the phone and tell someone to go disarm it."

Hera, already pale, blanched even more and ran back to the hospital.

The two blind men had climbed out of the cab and were standing, holding on to the edge of the door, their eyes covered with bandages. Orderlies were already running toward them with stretchers. As Elise stood by, they emptied her lorry, man by man, until all that was left was the smell of blood and chlorine gas. Even though it would've taken half an hour of time she didn't have, Elise wanted desperately to clean out the inside of the lorry before the next batch of wounded had to travel in it. She wanted even more desperately to see if Ruth was all right. But there were no choices anymore. She got into the driver's seat, started the engine and began driving, toward the fire and the deafening sounds of the war.

CHAPTER TWENTY-THREE

Ruth never saw the blinded men again. The Mouse was taken away on a stretcher. She and Mary and Helen were bundled away by the orderly and taken to the nurses' quarters, where kind but rushed hands stripped them of their dirty clothes and washed their bodies until the stink of burned earth was gone. Another nurse found them fresh clothes, and a third found beds where they lay down and slept like the dead.

When Ruth woke up, she thought it was only a few hours later, but a nurse told her that it was in fact the next day, and would she be able to give a hand with the wounded after she ate something? Ruth went into the nurses' washroom and fixed herself up as best she could with a basin of water while the nurse made her a cheese sandwich and a cup of tea. Ruth didn't see Mary or Helen anywhere and asked where they were.

"They're already out on the floor," said the nurse who introduced herself as Rose. She was a young thing, aged around her eyes. Ruth sat down at the table and ate the sandwich and drank the tea while Rose watched. She hurried knowing Rose would only be waiting because there was so much to be done and no time for dawdling over food.

"What about The Mouse—I mean Dr. Emmanuel?" Ruth asked.

"The doctor you came in with?" said Rose. "He's already been evacuated."

"He was all right?"

Rose shrugged. "He was walking last I saw."

"My sister, Elise Duncan, was driving an ambulance here during the shelling," said Ruth. "Have you seen her? Do you know if—if she made it?"

"I don't know," said Rose. "I don't know any of the drivers."

Ruth washed down the last of the sandwich and got up to follow Rose into the wards.

The wards were overflowing with men. They lay on the floor on stretchers and even on the bare boards. The beds were filled. The overflow areas were filled. Ruth couldn't imagine why they'd let her sleep so long with all this work to do. The smell of carbolic acid, bowel and blood was familiar and overwhelming.

"Where do you want me to start?" she said.

"You're Ruth Duncan, aren't you?" said Rose.

"Yes."

"Dr. Doweling would like you in the operating theater. They say you're very good and assisted down at Number Four."

John. John had requested that she be able to rest so that she could help him. She was unspeakably glad to know that he was all right.

"Where is he?" said Ruth.

"Follow me," said Rose.

The operating theater was a disaster. Orderlies mopped the floor as fast as they could, working around three doctors. John was just finishing the amputation of an arm, and the smell of cauterized flesh filled the air.

"Remind him," he said to the orderlies who took the man out, "that he may not be so lucky about the arm, but he's lucky to be alive." John saw Ruth. Over his surgical mask, his eyes narrowed with relief. "You're all right," he said. "We weren't sure yesterday."

"I'm fine," said Ruth, though truthfully, she felt like she was jumping headfirst into a pot of boiling water. "I'm ready to start."

"Get a gown and a mask on," said John. "We'll begin with this poor bastard."

She obeyed while the orderlies put the next man on the table—an abdominal wound. John put the man under with chloroform, then began to examine the man's torso with his hands. It was then Ruth realized that they didn't have an X-ray machine here. No quick way to check for shrapnel or bullets. Just manual exploration. It took time the man on the table didn't have. He began to shudder despite the chloroform. Blood ran more freely from his wounds. John picked up a scalpel and stood over the man's trembling body, still caked with mud from the trenches.

John hesitated and looked at Ruth. "I could cut him, you know," he said in a quiet voice, "but he would just bleed out more quickly. Tell me. What would you do?"

Ruth swallowed hard. It wasn't her place to make these decisions, but she knew what to say. "First, do no harm," she said.

"Exactly," said John. He put the scalpel down. "Orderlies!"

he shouted, and two men appeared in the doorway. "Take this soldier out. Make him comfortable. If he comes to, give him morphine."

The two orderlies obeyed and in moments were back with the next one, this time a man still conscious, both legs broken below the knee, hanging at odd angles to his body.

"Don't take my legs!" the man cried. "Don't take my legs!"

Ruth soaked a gauze pad with chloroform and pressed it over his nose and mouth. Her feet were slipping in the blood on the floor. The man went limp under her hands. "Will we have to take off his legs?" she asked.

"No," said John. "They're not shattered. We'll set them both and have the nurses put them in casts."

Afterward, she could remember the first dozen cases but not the next forty, or fifty, or however many they'd had. Her hands were busy, handing instruments to John, but also pulling bullets and shrapnel out of bodies. Once he saw how she could work, John told her where to cut and where to sew, and the two of them went twice as fast, working as a team. Behind her, the two other surgeons worked nonstop, each with the help of a nurse who rotated out after a certain number of hours, but Ruth stayed until she realized it was dark outside. She stayed until it was light again. She remembered someone coming in with cups of tea and hunks of bread. She remembered Rose coming in regularly to help everyone change into fresh surgical gowns. She remembered seeing the hem of her skirt crusted in blood and thinking how pointless it was to try to remain sterile in an environment such as this. And when it was finally over, she lay down on the floor next to a bed already occupied, tears leaking out of her eyes for Dr. Emmanuel and Dr. MacPherson. And Elise. What had happened to her? She hadn't heard a thing about the ambulances. Was that good? She closed her eyes over hot tears and wept for all the ones who'd had to die today.

CHAPTER TWENTY-FOUR

Two days later, the bomb at Hospital Four had been disarmed and removed. The roof had been fixed as well as it would ever be. The entire ward was empty and clean. The orderlies had been found, and now the only people missing were the doctors. That was why, Ruth realized, there weren't any patients yet. The Mouse was gone, and MacPherson was dead, and no one knew who was going to replace them.

She wrote to Elise, if only to prove to her sister that she was still alive. *I'm hoping they send John down from Hospital Three, but it isn't likely. The army, in its wisdom, wouldn't do something so sensible. This means I'll have two new doctors to break in, to prove myself to in the operating theater. It'll be like starting all over again.*

Elise's answer was short and to the point. *Just be glad you're in one piece.*

In fact, the army, in its wisdom, sent only one replacement for MacPherson and The Mouse. The new doctor was tall, middle-aged, with a drinker's nose, who smelled of whiskey when he passed. His name was William Fellowes.

Ruth introduced herself as he sat in the hospital mess, eating a sandwich and drinking tea. He did not invite her to join him.

"I used to help the last team of doctors with the surgeries," she said. "I'd like to do the same for you, if I might."

"You mean assist?" said Fellowes. "I can always use a good nurse."

Ruth took a breath. "I know how to open and close a patient. I know how to remove shrapnel and bullets with the least possible harm—and I know how to do internal sutures. I would be a valuable asset to you in the operating theater."

Dr. Fellowes gulped his tea. "Where I come from," he said, "doctors are doctors and nurses are nurses." He looked at her with hard blue eyes. "That's not going to change while I'm here."

Ruth bristled. "You think because I'm a woman, I can't handle it."

"I never said that." Fellowes drained his teacup. "I've seen your kind before. You can't keep up. You break down and start to panic. The wounded pile up, and cases that could be saved tend to die. I've seen plenty of doctors, men through and through, who have the same problem. They don't belong in this kind of hospital."

"I see," said Ruth tightly.

"Do you? I'll tell you what. There's a big push coming in the next few days. The generals always think throwing in a few more divisions will win this war." He snorted like this was a joke to him. "I'll let you assist. We'll see how you respond to pressure." He stood and gave her a sloppy salute. "You're dismissed, Sister."

The next morning when her shift started, Ruth felt a bone-deep fatigue that she was starting to think of as a bottomless sort of hopelessness. She had sent three notes to Elise, but gotten no response. Her sister was probably cleaning her ambulance under Matron's watchful eye. The Drinker, as she had started to think of Dr. Fellowes, hadn't emerged from the officers' quarters yet, and she wondered if he was getting quietly drunk before starting rounds.

She did the best she could, overseeing two new nurses: Danforth, a dour, middle-aged woman with short brown hair, and Benson, a glamorous-looking redhead, who froze like a surprised rabbit every time a new load of wounded men came in.

Ruth wiped her forehead against the heat of the Belgian summer. Nothing had been the same since the dud bomb. Mary Gardener and Helen had been transferred to different hospitals. Even if they were still here, even if MacPherson had survived, even with The Mouse, things would still be different. There was something about the tone of the war that had changed. It had crawled into bed with Ruth like an unwelcome insect. She hadn't really believed in valor and honor before she got here, or so she had told herself, but she had held fast to her faith in a decisive, glowing victory. Now that faith was ebbing, replaced with a sense of cynicism that none of this—the caring for the wounded, the heroic actions in the operating theater that pulled men from the brink of death—would really amount to anything in the end. If there was to be an end.

That afternoon, stretchers of groaning, weeping men covered the floor. In the distance, the artillery roared. The wind shifted to carry smoke and the smell of gunpowder into the hospital.

Ruth pulled on her gown and mask. Benson, the redhead, stood at her elbow, shaking.

"Just be calm," Ruth said to her, hardly calm herself. "You'll be all right."

Benson, her pretty green eyes huge in her small, pale face, just nodded.

Ruth stepped into the operating theater as the orderlies brought in the first man. His right arm hung at a broken angle.

Fellowes was already standing by the operating table, his surgeon's kit open beside him, saws and scalpels gleaming. The man saw them and let out a terrible cry.

"Don't take my arm!" he shrieked. "I'm a miner. How'll I take care of my family? Don't take my arm!"

"Nurse!" Fellowes snapped at Ruth. "Put this patient under."

Ruth soaked a wad of gauze in chloroform and pressed it gently over the soldier's face. His eyes were wild, then glazed as he panted in the fumes. Then his eyes closed. His face relaxed. His body went limp on the table.

Fellowes picked up his tissue knife, preparing to take off the arm.

"Wait," said Ruth. "Aren't you going to examine him?"

"I don't need to," said Fellowes, muffled behind his mask. "The arm is coming off. Speed is the key. You know how many men are out there."

Not knowing what else to do, Ruth cut through the muddy fabric of the man's uniform until the broken arm was free. Without the sleeve, she could see the break was a straightforward one, in his upper arm—easy to set and bind up in a cast, but Fellowes was already pushing her out of the way, ready to slice into the man's flesh.

"No!" said Ruth, trying to stand between him and the arm. "Look—the nurses can set this break! You don't have to touch him!"

The orderlies were already bringing in the next man, an abdominal wound, still conscious and moaning.

Fellowes narrowed his eyes at Ruth, blade at the ready. He glanced at the broken arm.

"There isn't even a bullet wound," said Ruth. "He must've fallen—or something. Put him in a cast, and in six weeks he can be back on the line."

Fellowes frowned and spoke to the orderlies. "Get this man out of here. Tell the nurses to set his arm." He turned to the abdominal wound on the next table as the orderlies took the man with the broken arm away. "I'll give you that one," he said to Ruth, "but the next one is mine."

"Yes, Doctor." Ruth shut her eyes briefly in relief. Maybe she'd done the miner a favor. Maybe not.

She put the next man under, and helped pull away the fabric of his uniform to expose the mess of his belly. "I'll get the X-ray ready," she said to Fellowes.

"Don't bother," he said. "I don't need a damned X-ray to know where to put my hands."

Ruth swallowed her reply as Fellowes bent over the man, groping for shrapnel. He brought out two pieces, then three, skillfully, neatly, and she had a glimmer of hope. Maybe he really did know what he was doing. She had seen The Mouse work like this. Maybe Fellowes just had a terrible bedside manner. She was ready to admit that she'd misjudged him, when the man on the table began bleeding profusely from just underneath his diaphragm, right where Fellowes had his hands.

Fellowes pulled out a fourth black metal shard and eyed the pulse of bright red blood. "Bad luck," he said. "That last one must've nicked the artery."

"I have sponges," said Ruth quickly. "I have sutures ready."

Fellowes ignored her. "Bring in the next one," he shouted over his shoulder to the orderlies, who hurried to obey.

"But what about this man?" said Ruth.

"He's done for," said Fellowes, stripping off his gloves. "Obviously he's bleeding from a greater wound than was immediately obvious. There's no hope for him. Now get me a clean pair of gloves." He threw the bloody ones on the floor.

"But, Doctor," Ruth said in amazement. "*You* nicked the artery. You *have* to sew it up!"

He turned to her. "Nurse," he said, coolly. "I don't *have* to do anything. This man is as good as dead."

Ruth opened her mouth. "But he *isn't* dead! You can't just abandon him!"

Fellowes reddened behind his surgical mask. "You think I should spend an hour sewing up a patient who's beyond help, while a dozen more die out there?" he shouted at her. "This is *war*, woman! If you can't face that, go out there and find me a nurse who *can*."

Ruth swallowed, though she thought she might vomit. He was right. But he was also wrong, in so many ways.

The orderlies hurried in with the next man. Both his legs hung at awkward angles. Fellowes picked up the tissue knife. "You'll assist," he said sharply, "without a *word*, or you'll leave."

"Yes, Doctor," said Ruth breathlessly.

And then, as if to push her as far as he could, Fellowes reached under his surgical gown, and pulled out a metal flask. He unscrewed the top, lifted his mask and took a long swallow of what Ruth could only imagine was whiskey.

"Doctor," whispered Ruth.

"Nurse," he snapped back. "I warned you. Now you will leave this operating theater, and you will send the other nurse. Benson, I believe is her name."

Benson. She would never talk back. Younger, prettier. Mary Gardener's words burned in Ruth's ears. She turned and stumbled out of the operating theater.

★ ★ ★

When the endless day was over, she went to find John.

It wasn't difficult. He was doing his own rounds in Hospital Three. She came up behind him and touched his arm. He turned and for a moment didn't seem to recognize her. Then he leaned over to envelop her in his arms. She embraced him, holding him with all her remaining strength. They stood together for a long while.

"What brings you to our corner of no man's land?" he said in her ear.

"Let me help you with rounds," she murmured, "and then I'll tell you over a cup of tea."

CHAPTER TWENTY-FIVE

She told him about Dr. Fellowes. She didn't bother to hide her feelings.

"He's very quick to cut," she said as an orderly poured her a steaming cup of tea. "Very quick to criticize a—a point of view."

John handed her a scone. "You mean he won't let you in the operating theater."

"I'm just another nurse now that he's in charge."

"You want me to come down there," said John. "You think it would be better that way."

"I *know* it would."

John studied his scone. "The army moves exceedingly slow when it comes to relocating personnel. It could take months for them to move me a mile down the road."

"You've done enough abdominal wounds for them to at least consider you," said Ruth. "Will you apply for the transfer?"

John nodded and bit into the scone.

★ ★ ★

Now it was all about the waiting. The next morning, Ruth was helping Danforth change dressings when the sound of heavy guns rattled the windows and shook the floor. They both paused. Ruth straightened. Every head that could be lifted from a pillow was up and alert.

"Our boys are going over the top," said Danforth. "In an hour we'll have a hundred men in here."

Ruth ran to the officers' quarters. She knocked on the wooden door, which provided about as much privacy as a stretched sheet.

"Dr. Fellowes?" she called through the door. "We're expecting wounded—" She wasn't sure what to say next. *Are you ready? Are you drunk?* "Dr. Fellowes?"

The door swung open, and he stood there. He looked sober enough, which gave her hope, until he opened his mouth, and the smell of whiskey took all the optimism out of her.

"Get th' operating theater ready," he roared. "We'll show the Bosch who's in charge around here!"

Ruth turned to Danforth. "Make sure the operating theater is ready. I have to make a telephone call."

The telephone, which had been installed after the dud bomb was removed, was wired into the wall near where the instruments were put to boil for sterilization. The phone had been put in a public spot to keep people from making private calls, and that had worked well until now. Ruth clicked the receiver handle until she got a cheerful "Hello?" from one of the operators.

"Connect me with Medical Headquarters," said Ruth. There was a long silence, then a click, then a male voice with a heavy Irish accent said, "Medical Headquarters."

Ruth told him who she was and which hospital she was

in. "We're expecting a flood of wounded, and we only have one doctor here."

"I'm sorry, Sister," said the voice on the other end. "We don't have spare doctors to send around."

Ruth held the receiver closer to her mouth. "But our doctor is drunk," she said. "I don't think he's fit to operate."

There was a brief silence on the other end as if papers were being consulted. "This is Fellowes we're talking about, at Number Four?"

"Yes."

"Fellowes has a reputation," said the man on the other end of the line, "but he's not too bad, even if he is loaded."

Ruth felt her mouth drop open. "You can't let a *drunk* perform surgery!"

"I assure you, Sister," said the man, "it's far more common than you might imagine. Everything will be fine. Just try to calm down."

The line went dead. Ruth hung up the phone and looked around the ward. An ambulance had arrived, and orderlies were unloading the men into rows on the floor. The sound of groans and cries began to fill the air, but Ruth hardly heard it. She could do one of two things: sort casualties with Danforth and Benson, and hand them over to Dr. Fellowes, or put on a gown and a mask and face him down in the operating theater.

Her feet seemed to make the decision for her, carrying her to where the surgical gowns were stacked in their sterile pile. She put one on, numbly, and tied on a mask. She stepped into the operating theater, and Dr. Fellowes turned to her.

"You're here to assist?" he said in a loud voice. "I don't need a damned assistant."

"I'm not here to assist." Her heart was pounding. "I'm here to do surgery."

"But you're just a nurse," said Dr. Fellowes. He started laughing. "Get out of here and bring me a patient."

"Sir," said Ruth. "Sir, you are drunk."

"I am not *drunk!*" he bellowed. "Now get *out*, bring me a patient, and stop wasting time!"

Two orderlies stood in the doorway with a soldier on a stretcher. The bandaging around his belly spelled an abdominal wound.

"Take him to the X-ray," said Ruth breathlessly.

"Bring him *here*," ordered Dr. Fellowes.

The orderlies stood where they were, frozen.

"Take him to the X-ray," said Ruth again. "This man is drunk on duty."

Because they knew her and could tell something was wrong and because they trusted her, the orderlies took the soldier to the next room. Ruth hurried after them, out of Fellowes's line of sight for the moment. There was another patient right behind this one, though. They would put him on the Drinker's table, where who knew what would happen, but this was the best she could do for now, Ruth told herself.

In the room with the X-ray machine, she cleared the soldier's chest and belly of his tattered clothes and exposed the X-ray plate. It took moments to see the bullets and shrapnel in his body. There was so much of it—some dangerously near his spine, some right next to his heart. She glanced back at her unconscious patient. All she really had to do was kneel down, reach in and pull the pieces out. And then he would die. She already knew he was going to die. Even a doctor like The Mouse wouldn't have been able to save him, not with all the time in the world.

The orderlies were waiting impatiently, ready to bring in the next case.

"Take this man out," said Ruth. "Tell the nurses to give him morphine. Make him as comfortable as possible."

One of the orderlies knelt on the floor and took the soldier's pulse at his throat.

"There's no heartbeat, Sister."

Ruth knelt beside him to be certain. He was right. The man was dead. Nothing she—or Dr. Fellowes—could have done would have saved him.

"Shall we bring in the next man, Sister?"

"Yes," she said. "Yes."

Back in the operating theater, Dr. Fellowes was cauterizing the stump of a leg. The air stank of scorched flesh, but Ruth didn't have time to think about it. The next case was already on her table, a big man with blond hair, writhing in pain. His right arm was bound up in bloody rags, and Ruth could see the bone sticking out above the elbow. Blood was streaming down his arm, dripping off his fingertips. He'd been shot through the hand as well. The whole arm would have to come off.

She didn't want to do it, but there was no choice. Ruth opened the surgeon's kit and took out a long, sharp tissue knife. When the man on the table saw it, he screamed.

"Hold him," said Ruth to the orderlies. "I'll put him under." The orderlies gripped the man by his shoulders and held him still as Ruth administered the anesthesia. He struggled and made muffled noises through the cloth until the chloroform took hold and his body slumped on the table.

"Wait a minute," said Dr. Fellowes, wiping off his knives with alcohol-soaked rags. "I'll be right there."

"No," said Ruth. "You take the next one—" The next one was already in the doorway. "I'll take this arm."

"Now *listen*, girl," shouted the Drinker. "You're no *doctor*.

I *order* you to get out of this room *at once* and tend to your duties as a *nurse!*" He held up his knives, almost as a threat.

Ruth's stomach went tight. "You, sir, cannot *possibly* see to all the men who're about to come through here. I know enough to take off arms and legs. You may see to the more severely wounded ones."

"Oh, I *may*, may I?"

Ruth turned away, pulled the tourniquet out of the surgeon's kit and wrapped it around her patient's upper arm. The bleeding slowed. The tissue knife was close at hand. She took it and made the cuts, fast, around the part of the bone where she would have to saw. Blood covered her gloves. She knew that The Mouse could've done a procedure like this in ten minutes or less. She needed to be that quick. The knife handle slipped in her hands, but the cuts were done. She took the saw and began to slice, hard against the living bone. The man lay limp, unfeeling, unknowing.

She held on to the arm until bone and sinew gave way and the arm came off in her hands. She let it slide to the floor and grabbed the tray with the sutures.

Ruth picked one of the needles and surgical thread and began sewing the arteries closed, fast but neat. How long was this taking? She knew the Drinker's eyes were on her as she worked, judging her on time, technique, everything. She finished the sutures and felt the heat of the cauterizing iron at her side. She pressed its flat, scorched surface against the sawed end of the arm. The smell was overpowering, but when she took the iron away and inspected her work, it looked good. No bleeding, only burned flesh.

"Take him out," she said to the orderlies. "Have his wound bound." She eyed Fellowes, who was standing by his own patient with his arms crossed. "Bring me the next amputation case," she said.

"Very well," said Fellowes. He made his way to the third table, where a soldier lay, muddy in his tattered uniform, pale, watching everything, too frightened or too deeply in shock even to react. "I'll take the bellies. You take the limbs. Nurse!" he shouted to Benson, who had come in and was standing right beside him. "Put this man under."

"Yes, Doctor," replied Benson, and went to get the chloroform. She had to press past Ruth to do this, and as she went by, she gave Ruth the subtlest nod.

By the next morning, Medical Headquarters must have figured out they'd done something wrong, because John Dowling showed up at the door of the hospital with his surgeon's kit and his captain's uniform. He tipped his cap to Ruth.

"Looks like someone cut through the red tape. I'm here now."

"Thank God," she said. "Go to the officers' quarters and see if Fellowes is drinking."

"You look like you could do with a drink yourself."

"Don't even joke about it," she said. "Please. Just check on him."

"Will do," he said and saluted smartly, then headed for the thin wooden door.

Fellowes didn't come out of the officers' quarters that day.

"Couldn't get him out of bed," John told Ruth later that morning, over an unconscious patient. "He smelled like a distillery."

Ruth eyed the orderlies as they brought in the next man. "Lucky it's slow," she said.

"Quite lucky," John agreed.

By afternoon, all the critical cases had been dealt with, and the minor ones had been cleared out. The nurses and orderlies cleaned the beds and floors. Ruth washed down the operating theater herself, while John sterilized every blade. By three o'clock, there was actually time to have a cup of tea. John followed Ruth into the mess and sat down across from her. Benson and Danforth sat nearby, at the other end of the table.

"We're not supposed to fraternize," Ruth admonished him, glad to the soles of her shoes that he was there.

"But we haven't had time to talk shop," said John. "For example, the X-ray machine. We don't have one at Hospital Three. We find the shrapnel and the bullets with this." He held up his forefinger. "And let me tell you, our infection rate is skyrocketing, because this—" he nodded at his finger "—is never completely sterilized before it goes from one patient to the next. They just come in too fast."

"I'll show you how to use the X-ray," said Ruth.

Benson and Danforth smiled at her, a little too knowingly, and Ruth felt herself flush. She finished her tea and a piece of toast. "Come on," she said to John.

He drained his teacup and followed her out.

In the X-ray room, Ruth showed him the controls, the light-sensitive plates and how the patient would be positioned. "A nurse will do this for you," she said, "but it's a good idea to know what to do in case you end up having to do it yourself."

"Won't you be there?" said John. "I'd assumed you'd be assisting me."

She hadn't, she realized, told him about taking charge in the operating theater yesterday, with Dr. Fellowes drunk. She explained what had happened and watched the expression on his face change from bright interest in the X-ray to a dull worry.

"How well did your patients do afterward?" he asked.

"They were fine," she said. "Most of them were evacuated this morning."

"Show me the ones who're left."

They went out to the ward and examined her amputee cases. By the time they were done, they had seen seven men, all in good shape, though not happy at losing an arm or a leg.

They went back to the operating theater, where they could be alone, and John took her by the hands. "Listen to me," he said. "It's a miracle you didn't kill anyone yesterday. It's also possible that a limb might have been saved."

"The real miracle," she said coldly, "is that Dr. Fellowes didn't manage to murder more of his patients. I had to do the amputations *and* keep an eye on him."

He put his hands firmly on her shoulders. "That's over for now," he said. "I know you want to be a doctor, but you can't be. Not yet. What you did yesterday could very well be considered heroic. No—it *was* heroic. But I'm here now, and you can't operate on your own anymore."

She looked at the freshly scrubbed floor. It occurred to her that if she hadn't pursued John, if she had left the Drinker doing operations…

"You'll still let me help," she whispered. "You'll teach me."

"I will do that," he said. "Rest assured, I will do that."

When her duties were done for the day and it was getting dark, she went to see Elise.

Ruth found her alone, sitting in one of a dozen muddy-footed chairs in front of the ambulance barracks. Light from the barracks' windows shone on the side of her face, deepening the shadows under her eyes, making her almost unrecognizably thin and tired.

"Elise?" said Ruth. "Are you all right?"

Her sister blinked, as if coming out of a daze. "What're you doing here?"

Ruth sat in the chair next to her. "To tell you the truth, I came to complain. But you look terrible."

"Thanks," said Elise. "You look just topping."

Ruth smoothed her dress, as if that might make a difference, and found there were spots of blood all over it. "I've had a strange couple of days." Ruth told her about the conversation she'd just had with John and found herself wiping away tears.

Elise crossed her arms, unsympathetic. "Why're you crying? Finally you have John in the same hospital as you. He's willing to teach you, and here you are sobbing your eyes out."

"I'm not sobbing my eyes out."

"You are. Not only that, you're crying about the wrong thing."

"I am *not*." Ruth scrubbed her eyes with the heels of her hands and took a couple of deep breaths. "Why? What do *you* think I should be crying about?"

"You're tired," said Elise, and she reached out to ruffle Ruth's short hair. "God knows, we're all bone-tired. This'll probably look better in the morning, but let me just say this."

"What?"

Elise eyed her. "You have to make up your mind. Do you want to be a doctor, or do you want to be a doctor's wife?"

Ruth eyed her right back. "There's no reason I can't be both."

Elise laughed.

"I know this'll sound stupid to you," said Ruth, "but I'm in love with him. I want to stay with him."

Elise didn't say anything, just studied her hands in her lap.

Ruth stared at her for a long moment. "Oh my God. What about you? Have you found someone? Please—not a Tommy."

"Not a Tommy," said Elise. "It's nothing, really. Not like you and John."

"But someone you met driving the ambulance?"

"Sort of," said Elise. "Like I said, it's nothing."

"An orderly?" Ruth asked. "Did you at least find a young

one? All of ours are old men. If it's not a Tommy, then there's not a lot to pick from. Unless you landed a doctor." She reached over and took Elise's hands out of her lap. "Come on—I've just told you everything. Anyway, you know you can't keep secrets from me."

Elise pulled away. "It's not a doctor. It's more like wishful thinking than anything else. I mean, my God, who'd be stupid enough to fall in love in a place like this?"

"I would," said Ruth blandly, "and I'm a lot smarter than you."

Elise snorted. "Well then. You should tell John about your plans. See if he approves of that wife-doctor idea."

"He would never stand in the way of me going to medical school."

"Even if you had a baby?" said Elise. "What would he say then?"

Ruth hesitated. "There are ways to…to avoid having a baby."

Elise shrugged. "Better ask him about that, too."

"I don't have to depend on his permission," Ruth said hotly. "These are modern times."

A shell exploded in the sky, cracking like a thunderbolt, littering the night with fire. Inside the barracks, someone pulled the blackout curtains closed, leaving the two of them in utter darkness. The barracks door opened. A triangle of light spilled out and disappeared just as quickly as someone came outside and shut it.

"Elise?" a woman called, and she came over to where they were sitting in the dark. "Elise," she said, sounding worried. "You'd better come in." Ruth almost recognized her voice. "Who's this?" said the woman.

"My sister, Ruth," said Elise. "Ruth, this is Hera Montraine."

Ruth stuck her hand out into the night, and a shadow shook it—light and ladylike. From the handshake, Ruth wondered how this girl had the fortitude to drive an ambulance. Another shell lit the night, revealing blond curls, a slender figure.

Hera reached for Elise. "You should come in, darling. It's bloody dangerous."

"I will," said Elise. "I'll be there in a minute."

Hera stood where she was, arms at her sides. "Hurry, won't you?"

"Sure," said Elise. "Of course."

Hera headed for the door, showed briefly as a silhouette, and vanished.

Ruth turned to her sister. "'Darling?'"

"You've been here long enough. You know how they talk," said Elise, in darkness. "Darling this and darling that. Bloody this and bloody that." She was talking so fast, she was practically babbling. "The English. You know—they just blurt things out."

Ruth frowned. *That* had certainly not been her experience.

"Anyway, she's new. Newish. We started at about the same time. I guess we kind of—got to be friends. I fix her lorry. I fix everyone's lorry."

Ruth tried to see her sister's face. Impossible. "Good lord, Elise, you're allowed to have friends. You've *got* to have friends in a place like this."

A bomb went off in the distance. Artillery answered with hard white flashes.

Ruth heard Elise let out her breath. "You should go," she said tightly. "I'll drive you."

Ruth groped for Elise's hand and held it. "Are you sure you're all right?"

"How I want to get out of here," whispered Elise. "And how I want to stay."

"Me too," Ruth whispered back.

CHAPTER TWENTY-SIX

Someone touched her arm in a dream. John. In the dream, she smiled at him. He held her hand and squeezed just enough to wake her up. Ruth opened her eyes, and he was bending over her, in her bunk, in the nurses' quarters, in the middle of the night, whispering.

"Are you awake?"

He was holding her hand. Ruth pulled her sleeping bag up to cover herself—she was in her underwear. "What're you doing here?" she whispered back.

"Get dressed," he said softly. "Come to the operating theater."

"What? Is there an emergency?"

"Just come," he whispered, urgent now. He let go of her hand. Then he was gone, out the door, into the night.

Ruth pulled on her clothes in the dark, not wanting to wake Danforth in the bunk above. She put on her shoes and quietly went out, across the road to the hospital.

The lights were on in Hospital Four. The lights were always on. Inside, both night shift nurses gave her curious looks, which she returned. She'd only ever seen them sleeping. They'd only ever seen her sleeping. It was like the meeting of two different worlds. Ruth tried to collect her wits. She grabbed a sterile gown, gloves and a surgical mask on her way into the operating theater.

John was there with a dead man.

She could tell he was dead by his wounds. His chest was open. His belly split. There was no hope—had never been any hope—for him.

"What's going on?" said Ruth, almost breathless. This seemed to be verging on a nightmare she couldn't wake up from.

John wasn't wearing a surgical mask. His face was tight and tired.

"I thought about what I said to you today—about it being a miracle that you hadn't killed anyone while you were doing amputations on your own."

Ruth could only nod.

"Dr. Emmanuel was teaching you surgical techniques," said John, as though stating a fact.

"Yes. He was."

John gestured at the dead man. "I need you to show me what you know."

Ruth eyes widened. "On *him*?"

"He's beyond feeling," said John. "You can't hurt him."

Ruth's heart sped up. "But what about Dr. Fellowes?"

"He's asleep," said John. "He's dead drunk, and he's not going to bother us."

"And the other patients?" There was a full ward out there.

John shook his head. "All taken care of. The ambulances will come in the morning, but tonight…" He turned to his surgeon's kit, opened it. The scalpels and retractors gleamed. He'd cleaned and sterilized everything—for her.

Ruth looked at the dead man's ruined body. His face, she saw now, was covered with a white towel, as were his privates. "I..." she said, "I don't know where to start."

Something in John seemed to relax. "Let's start with sutures," he said, not like her father, who would've snapped at her, but in the gentle tone of a teacher.

Ruth took a breath. If this was a nightmare, she would take charge of it. Control it. End it.

"Internal?" she asked. "Or external?"

CHAPTER TWENTY-SEVEN

October 1915

Autumn was the season for war, and both sides sank their teeth into it. It didn't matter that all they gained or lost was a few yards on either side of no man's land. Word was that the fighting wouldn't slow until winter set in. Over those months, John came to the nurses' quarters once or twice a week to wake Ruth and take her to the operating theater. Each time there was a different dead man.

If Fellowes had any inkling about their midnight sessions, he never said anything. He conveyed his feelings with dirty looks and off-color remarks during meals, when they all sat together. The other nurses ignored him. John studiously ignored him. And so Ruth tried to ignore him, too.

There came a point during one of the big pushes when there were so many wounded men that John finally sent Ruth to work on the casualties who were carried in to the third table in the operating theater, the one where they had to wait because there were only two surgeons.

Fellowes glared at Ruth as she bent over her first patient of the day, already limp from chloroform. John had stepped back plenty of times and let her do surgeries herself, but this was different. There would be no other hands to help if she ran into trouble. All she had was Danforth, the dour, doubting nurse who would hand her instruments.

Her patient had already been x-rayed, and Ruth could see the piece of shrapnel, close to his heart, showing as a white stain on the black glass plate. His clothes had already been cut away, like a muddy cocoon. Danforth swabbed his wound with alcohol, and Ruth pulled on a fresh pair of gloves. Danforth handed her a scalpel, and Ruth made an incision below the soldier's breastbone, just wide enough to admit her fingers. She reached inside the man whose face she hadn't even glanced at. Organs gave way at her touch—things she couldn't see but knew by feel. She found the resisting piece of metal, and the pulse of his aorta only an inch or so away. She wrapped her fingers around the shrapnel and carefully guided it out of his body. It was like all the other pieces of metal she and John had pulled out of so many soldiers—black and evil-looking. She gave it to Danforth, who put it in a metal pan with a sharp clink and an inscrutable expression. Ruth cleaned the wound and sewed the soldier up. He would have a fist-sized scar on his chest, and he would spend the next month or so in a convalescent hospital in England, but once he was healed, he would probably go back onto the battlefield. She was sorry for him even as she was elated for herself, having completed this task without asking for help from anyone.

When the day was over, she had worked on ten men. She had been slower than John or Fellowes, but she had done her share by the time they stopped for supper. John had been over to check on her several times. He never got in her way and only gave advice when she asked for it. Fellowes, on the other hand, ignored her completely, both in the operating theater and the mess. It was because of him that she sat with the nurses, at the other end of the table from the doctors. She wasn't intimidated by him. She just didn't like him, and couldn't stand to watch when he took a hip flask out of his pocket and drained it before the meal was over. He obviously didn't care if anyone knew or was taking note.

So it went on, for weeks, until a pair of generals showed up one day to pin medals on soldiers' pillows. The hospital was still a wreck from the push, with soldiers lying on the floor on stretchers, blood not mopped up. Not what the generals were used to seeing. Furthermore, there was no doctor on hand to show them around and comment upon prognoses, so they had to rely on a nurse, which didn't please them at all. When they got to the operating theater to see what the doctors could possibly be doing with their time, they found John and Fellowes performing surgery as usual, and Ruth, up to her wrists in a third soldier's belly.

"What's going on here?" demanded one of the generals, the fatter of the two, with mustache and muttonchops joining together over his ruddy cheeks. "What's this *nurse* doing with this patient?"

"Operating, sir," said Fellowes before John could answer.

"She's just doing some suturing," said John, but Ruth could tell, he knew this was trouble.

The two generals strode over, unmasked and un-gowned, to lean over the limp form of the man Ruth was working on. She couldn't stop or he would bleed to death.

"Good morning, sirs," she said as they breathed their germs on her patient.

"By whose authority are you performing surgery on this man?" demanded the thinner general, the one with the most ribbons on his chest.

"Mine, sir," said John. He came over to Ruth's table with his hands up by his shoulders to keep from contaminating anything, but it looked like he was surrendering. "Sister Duncan has the most experience of any of the nurses here. When we need an extra pair of hands, she steps in."

"Duncan?" said the fat general. "Ruth Duncan?"

"That's right, sir," said Ruth, hands still busy, sewing.

The fat general took a piece of paper out of his pocket and consulted it. "We have a medal for you," he said, "for bravery under fire."

"For what?" she asked, and finally looked up.

"The day Dr. MacPherson was killed," said the thinner general. "You led a group of blinded solders to the next hospital, under heavy shelling."

"But that was in July!" said Ruth.

"Nevertheless," said the fat general, "you are to be decorated for it."

The thinner general opened a black leather folio he was carrying and took out a medal with her name tagged onto it with a bit of string. He pulled off the name tag and pinned it to her spattered surgical gown. "For conspicuous gallantry displayed in the performance of your duties on the occasion of hostile air raids on Casualty Clearing Stations in the Field."

Ruth blinked at the medal. A bronze disk hung from a striped ribbon. There was an embossed portrait of King George on the disk. It glimmered in the light. "Thank you, sir," she said, unsure what to do next. Didn't the soldiers salute?

"Thank you, sir," said John, and he seemed ready to say more, but the thinner general stopped him.

"You, Captain," he said, "are allowing a *nurse* to perform operations? This will stop immediately." He turned to Ruth again. "And I mean immediately."

"Her skill level is very high," said John. "She's qualified—she just doesn't have the degree."

"And she will stop doing these surgeries," said the fat general. "For precisely that reason."

"But we need the extra hands, sir," said John. "If you're going to take her out, at least send us another doctor."

"There are none to spare," said the thinner general. "And you, Captain, are on the verge of insubordination."

John reddened under his mask. He took a breath and said to Ruth, "Step out, please, Sister. I'll see to your patient."

"Yes, Doctor," she said, and wondered how much of a game this was. Would she be back as soon as these two buffoons were gone? She stripped off her gloves, mask and gown and went out into the ward. She let the door to the operating theater swing shut, and breathed deep the smell of disinfectant.

Behind her, she could hear the muffled sounds of an argument.

John was losing. That was all she knew.

Later, when the generals were gone, John came to find her. He'd taken off his surgical smock and gloves, but his mask still hung around his neck.

"I'm so sorry that happened," he said.

"You shouldn't be sorry. I got a medal out of it." She was fully prepared for the worst—that she would never see the inside of an operating theater again.

"I have bad news for you," he said.

"I know," said Ruth. She didn't want to make this any harder on him than it already was. "I'm a nurse, and a nurse I shall be."

His shoulders relaxed visibly. "There's no reason you can't continue to assist," he said. "There's no reason for you to stop learning. And God knows, we need help in there."

She nodded, too upset to say anything more. Of course, they were generals, and of course John would try to make the best of it.

"Come on," he said. "Get gowned up. I finished your fellow, but there's plenty more where he came from."

CHAPTER TWENTY-EIGHT

December 1915

In mid-December, the nurses began decorating the wards for Christmas. Despite being so far from home, Ruth found some joy in the season. She helped string green-and-red paper chains up over the beds along with cut-paper stars and snowflakes. Snow and sleet had made fighting impossible, and the wards were emptied of the cases that could travel. The war seemed to diminish as the holiday took hold.

Someone found an old gramophone, and someone else came up with records with songs popular before the war. None of them were Christmas songs, but the men in the wards sang along with them anyway. The music brought a sense of nostalgia over the whole hospital, which made the decorations, as simple and as thin as they were, seem more poignant than they had any right to be.

"You know what's missing," John said to Ruth on the afternoon of December 23.

Ruth was changing the dressing on a man's foot—he had

frostbite. She hadn't seen a bullet wound in a week, and she was grateful. John had been following her around for the last half hour, chatting about this and that. He seemed fidgety, like he was waiting for her to finish. She had a lot to do. She was almost irritated with him.

"What's missing?" Ruth asked.

The man with frostbite, an officer, looked up at her. "A tree, Sister. It's quite obvious."

"*Quite* obvious," said John. "Hospitals Six and Fourteen have two trees each. We don't even have one. It would do the lads good to have a tree. They could decorate it."

"Where are you going to find a tree?" Ruth asked. "Everything's been burned to the ground."

"I'll make a phone call," said John, as though he'd been waiting for her to say exactly that. "I'll be right back."

Ruth sighed and finished wrapping the officer's foot. If John wanted to go and find a tree, this was the time to do it. Dr. Fellowes would be in charge, but with all the emergency cases shipped off, there wasn't much harm he could do. Maybe there was a single surviving pine tree out there somewhere. How would John cut it down? She wondered if he would use a bone saw.

John returned, light in his step, a glint in his eye. A bone saw, wrapped in clean rags, was in his hand. "Are you ready?" he said, smiling. "Your horse and carriage are waiting."

"My what?" She gestured at the packed ward. "I can't go— look at all these men!"

"Your shift ended an hour ago," said John. "There aren't any emergencies. Come on."

"Go on, now," said the officer. "You don't get a horse and carriage every day."

There was nothing she could say, really. She and John got their coats and went outside.

In front of the hospital, an ambulance driver climbed out of her lorry and stuffed her hands into her pockets.

"You're sure there's a bed I can use?" she said. "Because I'm sick of the fleabag."

"Ask the nurse in charge," said John. "Tell her I said you could sleep as long as you like."

"Thank you, sir," said the driver and disappeared inside.

"You're going to drive?" said Ruth. "We could've called for Elise."

"Let Elise rest," said John. "Let the poor thing stay warm." He held the passenger door open for her. "Are you coming?"

"If you insist," said Ruth.

It was very cold. The snow was three feet deep in places, and the ambulance jounced over ruts in the frozen mud. The sky was flat and gray, and its grayness reflected in the snow, making the whole landscape as dreary as it could possibly be. Burned trees stood like grave markers, and as John drove, Ruth wished she'd stayed in the hospital with its ersatz decorations and sentimental music. She didn't see anything that remotely resembled a Christmas tree, and couldn't imagine how they were going to cut one down anyway. She was about to say something to John when he said, *"Aha!"* and turned off the main road to follow a two-wheeled track. He steered right, and they came upon a widely trampled patch of snow with exactly three pine trees growing in it. Four others had clearly been sawed down.

John gave Ruth a delighted smile. He helped her out and led her over to the trees.

"Which one do you like?" he asked.

One was bigger than the rest but lopsided. She could see why the other tree hunters had left it. The smallest was only shoulder-high but perfect. The other was bigger, but dead on one side.

"Let's take this one," she said, pointing to the smallest.

He went to the ambulance, got the bone saw, knelt in the snow beside the tree and began to cut. Ruth had expected him to go at it with the gusto of a lumberjack, but he was being careful, almost so as not to hurt the tree. She realized he was using an amputation technique, and she had to laugh. In the gray landscape, under the leaden clouds, out in the middle of a snowy nowhere, she couldn't help but laugh.

"What's so funny?" said John, sawing and now breathless. "It's starting to fall. Aren't you going to help?"

She shuffled through the snow and held the tree up so it didn't bind at the base where he was cutting. He looked up to see her smiling.

"It's good to see you happy," he said, from the ground.

"I'm not happy," she said. "I just think it's funny to watch you amputating a tree."

He gave a couple of strong thrusts with the saw. The trunk gave way, and the tree sagged against her. John got to his feet, tucked the saw under one arm and brushed off his knees. He grinned, his cheeks pink. "Come on," he said. "You take that end. We'll get it into the ambulance."

Her end of the tree was heavier than she'd thought. "What're the men going to decorate this with?" she puffed as they dragged it to the lorry. "All we have is paper and rags. The only shiny things are the surgical instruments."

"They'll come up with something," said John. "They're clever fellows." He got the gate of the ambulance open, and they shoved the tree inside. The tree lay on the floor like an unsecured patient. He slammed the gate shut and hurried to open Ruth's door for her.

She got in. "Such a gentleman!"

He tipped an imaginary hat at her, and shut the door. He came around to his own side, got in and started the engine.

Immediately the windscreen fogged. Ruth wiped her side with her sleeve, and he wiped his side with his. Instead of clearing, the fog turned to ice.

"Do these things ever warm up?" said John.

"You'll have to ask Elise," said Ruth, "but I would say the answer is probably no."

He stopped wiping the windscreen and turned to face her. "Can I be very forward, Sister?"

She liked him very much at that moment. The things she remembered from the first time she had ever seen him, his gray eyes, the honest turn of his mouth, were the things she saw now.

"Of course you can," she said.

He put his hand in the pocket of his woolen coat. "I have an early Christmas present for you." He took out a small white box tied up with a crumpled gold ribbon. "I hope you like it," he said, and gave it to her. "I'm sorry it's gotten a bit mashed."

Ruth found she wasn't able to say anything. She pulled at the ribbon and then the lid. Inside was a thin golden chain with a single pearl attached.

"It's a necklace," he said unnecessarily. "I asked my parents to send it."

She took it out of the box. It was the most delicate, exquisite thing she'd seen since she'd come to Europe. "Will you put it on me?" she said with cold lips.

He reached over to push away her short hair, the collar of her coat, the layers between the winter and her neck. He fumbled with the clasp, took off his gloves and fumbled a bit more, then leaned back in his seat. The pearl came down to the space between her collarbones. She could feel its smooth coolness there, and she touched it with cold fingers, but the rest of her body felt suddenly flushed.

"I love it," she whispered. "It's beautiful."

"I think you're beautiful," he said.

No one had ever told her that before—not Father or Grandpa—no one. She touched her hair, self-conscious, but he took her hand and held it against his chest.

"Not just beautiful," he whispered. "You're brave. You're bold. You terrify Dr. Fellowes." He smiled at this, and she let herself laugh.

"Do I terrify you?" she whispered back.

"Only a bit." He raised her hand to kiss her chapped knuckles. "Your poor hands."

"Is that how you're going to kiss me?" she whispered. "Like a queen?"

He shook his head and pulled her close. He pressed his warm lips against hers. Ruth held him, drinking in the heat of his body. Her heart thundered. Or maybe it was his heart, pressed right up against hers. His lips touched her ear and stayed there.

"Ruth Duncan," he murmured, "I'm in love with you."

"Thank God," she said, her face buried against his neck, "because I've been in love with you since I first saw you."

He laughed softly. "Me too. You were so serious in your school uniform. And then you told me you wanted to be a doctor, and I thought, *Now, here's a modern woman.*"

"You want a modern woman?" Ruth said, eyes shut tight, hoping for the right answer.

"More than anything," he said, and kissed her on the lips again.

She kissed him back with all the passion she could muster inside the freezing ambulance.

He pulled away, breath steaming, eyes bright. "Ruth Duncan, I want you to marry me."

She took a breath. "I will." The relief of being able to say it made her dizzy. "I want that so much. I thought you'd never ask."

He hugged her tight, then held her at arm's length. "There's one problem," said John, and he looked into her eyes.

"What's that?" she asked, her head still spinning.

"The Women's Medical College," said John, "won't admit married women."

The cab of the ambulance was all steam and ice now. Ruth took a breath. "What?"

"It's their policy," John said softly. "A woman can't study properly with a family making demands on her time."

"So they only take single women?" said Ruth in disbelief. John nodded.

"But that's ridiculous. You wouldn't be a—a burden. If anything, you could help me."

"That's true," said John. "But to get in, you have to be single."

"I have to make a choice?" said Ruth, appalled. "Be a doctor or be a wife?" The romantic mood inside the cab was rapidly evaporating.

John's arm slipped away. "I wanted to tell you," he said unhappily, "in case you didn't know. I didn't want to…to lead you on with expectations."

"I just can't believe it. It's so old-fashioned." She balled her hands in her lap.

"There may be other options," said John.

"Like what?" Ruth asked, fighting back against the burning in her throat.

"We could wait to get married," said John quietly. "They can't tell you what to do with your life after you graduate."

"But that's years of study," said Ruth. "What do we do in the meantime—live together in secret? In sin? What would my father say? And how long could we keep it quiet?" She covered her face with her hands. "If we got married—here—with just a priest and no one else—and the Women's Medical College somehow found out about it, I'd be kicked out." She started to cry.

His arm came around her shoulders, honest in its weight, but that just made her cry harder.

"Ruth," he said at last, "none of that changes the fact that I love you. I want to marry you. I'm willing to wait for as long as it takes."

"You are?" She leaned against him and sobbed into his chest.

"Oh, my dear." He stroked her short, choppy hair. "I am."

CHAPTER TWENTY-NINE

For Elise, Christmas came without a tree or decorations. For her, Christmas came in a box from home. Inside was a note. *Hope you are doing well—write more often! Share this with your sister. Love, Father and Grandpa*

The box was bigger than any of the other boxes that had come for the Ambulance Corps, and Elise dug in with relish. There were a dozen pairs of woolen socks—enough to share with Ruth—and two scarves. There was a sheepskin hat with fleece on the inside, and she put it on as soon as she got it out of the box. The hat had warm, thick earflaps that made all the other women jealous, which made Elise grin because her choice of clothing had never *ever* made another woman jealous. There were two heavy sweaters, homemade jam and a big tin of cookies. She wished there was a long letter, not just the note, but even when she searched the box thoroughly, she didn't find one.

The other drivers were making delighted noises over their

own boxes. Hera had gotten a new dress, a practical one, with pockets and a high, warm neck. It still had a modern look, and as she modeled the dress, stretching it out across her body without actually disrobing in the chilly barracks, she moved like she was dancing, which made everyone laugh.

Elise stuffed six pairs of socks, one of the scarves, a sweater and half of the goodies into the box and put on her coat. It was a mile to Ruth's hospital, but since driving the ambulances for personal reasons was forbidden, she would walk there. She hitched the box up on her hip and set out.

By now she was used to the snow and the frozen mud of the road and the heaps of ashes the soldiers threw down for traction on the ice. She trudged along under the gray sky, through the dirty snow, trying hard to think of a Christmas song, and finally came up with "God Rest Ye Merry Gentlemen." She got through the chorus, in her mind, not singing aloud, because that just wasn't appropriate for this weather or this place, and discovered that she couldn't remember the words for the entire song. What was stuck in her head was the chorus. "O tidings of comfort and joy, comfort and joy." Elise slogged onward and thought about how uncomfortable and joyless she was and how Christmas here was little more than a mean joke. She shifted the box to her other hip and kept going. She hoped Ruth was in a better mood.

By the time she got to the door of the hospital, her boots were crusted with slush, and it was snowing again. There was an ambulance parked in front of the hospital, driverless, without patients, and she wondered what was going on. Then she heard the singing coming from inside.

Elise opened the door to see every soldier in the ward clustered at the far end, singing "Silent Night" in perfect harmony. She went over as quietly as she could and stood on the edge of the crowd with the nurses. There, at the end of the ward, was a dwarfish tree, glittering in the hard electric lights. It had been decorated with medals. All the soldiers, thought Elise, had hung their medals on the tree, and now they were singing their hearts out. She put the box down and sat on the floor next to it and started to cry. She felt stupid for crying because she couldn't quite put into words why she *was* crying, but the tears rolled down her cold cheeks and into the new scarf Father had sent her.

One of the nurses came over and sat down next to her. It was Ruth. Ruth put an arm around her and held her like she was a little girl, until the urge to cry wasn't quite so strong.

"We got a box from home." Elise sniffled and pushed it at her. The men were still singing. "I brought you half of everything."

"Jam," whispered Ruth, "and cookies and *socks*."

"He must've bought the socks," said Elise, "but Cook made everything else."

"We'll share it with the men," said Ruth. "Except for the socks." She got to her feet and pulled Elise up. "Come over here. I have to show you something."

The two of them went over to the sterilizing stoves, which were burning high to warm the building. It was almost stifling, but, Elise thought, it was good to be hot enough to sweat.

Ruth unbuttoned the top of her dress. A pearl hung from a thin gold chain, just at her throat.

Elise loosened her scarf and pushed her new sheepskin hat away from her forehead. "John gave that to you?"

Ruth nodded and touched the pearl.

"Did he ask you to marry him?" said Elise.

Ruth looked up at her with a serious face. "He did."

"Well," said Elise impatiently. "What did you say?"

"It's complicated. They don't let married women into the Women's Medical College."

"So you said *no*?"

"Not exactly," said Ruth. "We sort of decided to wait."

"For the end of the war?"

"For the end of my medical training," said Ruth.

Elise raised her eyebrows. "Won't that take years?"

"Of course," said Ruth. "But we love each other. We can wait."

"Did you at least decide to get engaged?" said Elise. "I mean, is that what the necklace is for?"

Ruth let her hands drop to her sides. "We didn't actually make it official."

Elise cocked her head at her sister. "So maybe he's not as serious as you think he is."

Ruth opened her mouth to say something, but no words came out.

Elise went on. "Maybe he doesn't really feel the same way about you. I don't know how anyone can feel anything anymore—you've got dying men on your hands every day. I know you don't feel the way you did when you first got here. It's a war. Things change."

"You weren't there when he gave me this," Ruth snapped, loud enough that heads turned in their direction. "You have no idea what you're talking about." She lowered her voice. "Anyway, what about your little friend, Hera?"

Elise caught her breath. How much did her sister know? How much had she guessed?

"Why can't you be honest with me?" Ruth hissed. "You've always had something secret going on. Even back home. But you don't trust me enough to tell me, even here, where one of us could get killed."

"There's nothing to tell," Elise stammered, heat all through her face and neck. The sheepskin hat was making her sweat. "Hera's just a friend. I fix her lorry. I have lots of friends like her."

Ruth arched an eyebrow. "Really? Then you're doing better than I am. All I have is John."

"What do you think I am?" whispered Elise, burning in her cheeks. "What do you think *she* is?"

Ruth took Elise by the shoulders. "I don't know the word for it, but I know *you*. And I'm telling you to be careful. Like you said, we have our hands on dying men every day, and we don't even feel it anymore. Isn't that so?"

"Stop it," whispered Elise. "Let me go."

"You may feel something for her, Elise, but the Ambulance Corps is full of—I don't know—daredevils and ne'er-do-wells—and privileged daughters..." Ruth stopped, breathing hard.

"You don't know what you're talking about," whispered Elise.

Ruth let go of her shoulders, and Elise took a step away from her sister. Her heart was racing. "We shouldn't be fighting on Christmas."

"We're *not* fighting," said Ruth. "You're not *listening* to me."

Elise pushed the box from home across the floor in Ruth's direction with her foot. "Here. Do what you want with it." She turned for the door and practically ran out into the cold, the men still singing behind her.

CHAPTER THIRTY

January 1916

Weeks later, the memory of her Christmas conversation with Ruth still left a bitter taste in Elise's mouth.

Her ambulance full, she pulled out, up the same snowy, slippery hill as she did every night. Elise told herself again *not* to think about Ruth. It was too dangerous to focus on anything but the driving. Soldiers were everywhere in the darkness, rushing to the trenches into the winter push. It was all Elise could do to avoid running into them with the ambulance, and they banged on her fenders with the butts of their rifles, making the men in the rear yelp with terror.

"Get out of my way!" shouted Elise. "It'll be you next time!"

The men parted around her and she struggled on, shifting gears in the frozen mud until her wheels found a dry bit of ground and she surged forward.

There were aeroplanes out tonight. She could hear them roaring overhead but couldn't see them. When they swooped down to strafe, she could see fire spitting out of the guns, which made the planes seem magical and terrifying all at the same time, like dragons in the air. She forced her eyes away from the aeroplanes and back to the road, white with snow, blackened by tire marks. It was too dark for anyone to see the red cross on the side of the ambulance, and no one had had the foresight to put one on the top, where pilots could see it. Not for the first time, Elise found herself scared to death as she drove along the rutted road toward the hospital, but this time it was different. This time she was deeply afraid she and everyone else in the lorry might actually be shot. She gunned the engine, and the ambulance lurched forward into the dark.

She didn't see the aeroplane come in from behind, and the pilot, she thought, probably mistook her for a supply lorry. From so far up, men and machines must seem like ants, easy to crush. Bullets suddenly pocked through the canvas, hitting the men in the back of her ambulance. The aeroplane roared past, turned, and this time came straight at her, guns blazing. Bullets pierced the windscreen on the passenger side. Something hit her thigh so hard, it knocked the breath out of her. She had time to grab the door handle and open it. She fell out of the cab and onto the frozen track. Her ambulance careened to the side of the road and rolled to a stop. Men were climbing out of it, running in all directions.

Elise lay in the cold mud, holding her leg, blood pulsing out of her thigh. She clamped her hands around the top of her leg and started screaming for help. Her screams evaporated into steam in the night air, and she realized the aeroplane was coming back. She crawled to her ambulance until she was underneath it. The aeroplane went by for the third time, swooping low, shooting deafening bullets that rang off the metal parts of the lorry. Elise held her leg and watched as the aeroplane, finally caught in spotlights, rose and flew away into the blackness.

Another ambulance pulled up. Hera jumped out and came running over. Her face was like a pale moon, her eyes wide.

"I'm shot," shrieked Elise, and she crawled, as best she could, out from under the ambulance. "Help me! Get a tourniquet—quick!"

Hera dashed away and returned with a length of rope. She tried to help Elise wrap it around the top of her thigh, but Hera's hands shook, and there was so much blood. Elise pulled the rope as tight as she could and knotted it off. Her leg felt like it was twice its normal size and it *hurt*, just above her knee at first, then everywhere.

"Get me to Hospital Four," Elise gasped. "Get me to my sister."

The next thing she was aware of was being carried by orderlies into the hospital. They were rushing. When they laid her on the floor, they were not careful, and her leg hurt even more. She was surrounded by men, groaning and breathing hard against their pain. The man on her right was bandaged around his belly, but his face was bloody, too. To her left, a man lay with his mouth slack, glazed eyes open, clearly dead. She looked around wildly for Hera. Hera was nowhere in sight.

"Ruth!" she screamed. *"Ruth!"*

One of the nurses started to shush her, then stopped. "You're no soldier," she said. "What're you doing here?"

"My leg," Elise wept. "Get my sister, Ruth Duncan, my sister, *please!*"

The nurse hurried away, and after what seemed like a very long time, Ruth appeared. Her cool hands probed Elise's wound. "For God's sake," she said to the nurse, "get her to the operating theater immediately."

The nurse motioned to the orderlies, and the orderlies wound their way between the live and dead bodies. They picked up her stretcher again, gently this time, and carried her across the ward. Elise's heart pounded. She couldn't see Ruth anymore, and black spots were floating across her field of vision. She gathered her breath for the last thing she had the strength and consciousness to say, the same thing she'd heard a hundred men say as they were loaded into her ambulance.

"Please, don't take my leg!"

CHAPTER THIRTY-ONE

Ruth had the orderlies put Elise on the third table in the operating theater, the one where they put the patients who could wait. But Elise couldn't wait. Bullets had pierced her leg to the bone.

"John!" Ruth called. "Elise is here—she's been shot in the leg!"

John looked up, his concerned eyes showing over his surgical mask. "I can't stop," he said. He was in the middle of a belly wound, blood up to his elbows.

Fellowes came over and took a quick look. He pressed around the wounds, and more blood flowed. "Femoral artery," he said. "Get a tighter tourniquet on her before she bleeds to death. I'd do it myself, but I've got to take this man's arm." Fellowes went back to his own patient and brandished his saw. "We're backed up in here. No one gets special treatment."

Ruth knew that meant he would take Elise's leg off. Which made Ruth furious. Special treatment? She'd show them special treatment. She hadn't been allowed to work on her own since the generals had come. Now she signaled to Benson, the nearest nurse.

"Put on a fresh gown," she said. "You'll be helping with this one."

The bleeding was bad, but Fellowes was wrong—the bullets had missed the femoral artery. Ruth cut away the rope and applied a tighter tourniquet instead—a sterile one—and the bleeding slowed.

"Put her under," Ruth told Benson, "and be careful. This one's an ambulance driver."

The biting smell of chloroform drifted from Elise's face. Ruth probed her leg with gleaming metal tweezers and found bullets, just under the surface of her skin here, much deeper there. Her thigh bone, the femur, was broken, but everything below seemed intact. Elise's leg was salvageable, but it would take time. That was time Ruth didn't have, but time she would make.

She cut into where the bullets were and swabbed out the wounds, careful and neat. Behind her, John was starting on another abdominal case, and Fellowes was taking off yet another limb. She was ten times too slow, but she kept on working, suturing neatly, precisely, so that there would be no mistakes to clean up after, no secret bleeding that would leave her sister a pale corpse.

"Now," she said to Benson, "we'll set the leg."

"You'll do no such thing," said Fellowes, somehow instantly beside her. "This leg is a loss. You should have cut it off twenty minutes ago."

"I'm going to set the leg," said Ruth, and to the nurse she said, "Get the plaster ready."

"There's no time for that," said Fellowes. He pulled off his mask. He was so angry, his drinker's nose had turned even redder.

"Leave her alone," said John from across the small room, bent over his patient. "Let her set her sister's leg."

"Look," said Fellowes to John, "I don't care what you and this—this *floozy* do outside the hospital, but in here, you do what's right, and setting a leg in a surgical situation *isn't right!*"

"Then I'll take her outside," said Ruth. "I'm only a nurse anyway. Setting bones is what I ought to be doing, not surgery."

"That's what I've been *telling* you!" shouted Fellowes. "Get her out of here!" he yelled at Benson, who flinched and nodded. Two orderlies appeared and took Elise out to the ward. Ruth threw off her surgical mask and gown and followed, hands shaking, her whole body shaking.

She and Benson carefully bound Elise's leg, making sure the bones were in their proper places, then added the gauze and plaster to secure them. On the other side of the ward, men groaned in agony and died on the floor. Yet her sister's leg would be repaired. Ruth would never be allowed inside the operating theater again, but her sister's leg would heal correctly. It was Elise that mattered right now. Nothing else. Ruth patted Elise's cheeks until she woke up, groggy from the chloroform.

"Am I all right?" she asked weakly.

"Yes," Ruth said, "you're all right."

Tears ran down Elise's cheeks. "I'm so sorry I said those things to you at Christmas."

Ruth wiped the tears away with the heels of her hands, ready to break down herself. "Don't cry, Elise. Don't worry. Please. I still love you."

"I still love you, too," wept her sister.

★ ★ ★

Elise was evacuated with the rest of the wounded early the next morning, loaded onto a train that would take her to Calais, and then to London via Dover. Ruth wrote a letter to the Dowelings, letting them know she was coming, but not knowing which convalescence hospital Elise would end up in. She hoped the Dowelings would try to find her so Elise would have some familiar company. She started to write a letter to her sister, and found she had no idea what to say. Ruth sat at the table in the nurses' quarters, a blank page in front of her and a candle burning down to nothing. In her mind, she had started the letter half a dozen times. *Dear Elise, I'm so sorry.* But she wasn't quite sure what to be sorry for. She had saved her sister's leg—possibly her life. Probably her life. Ruth frowned at the erasures on the paper that was too rare to waste. *I'm sorry I insinuated those things about Hera.* But she wasn't going to write to Elise about Hera, for heaven's sake. Ruth had only seen the girl twice since Elise's injury, and both times, Hera had just stared in her direction as though she had an important question, but not enough courage to ask it. The minute their eyes met, Hera had fled. How was Ruth supposed to write about that?

In the end, Ruth put her head down on the table and slept, and hoped she would dream the proper thing to say.

Elise's letter arrived at the end of the week.

Dear Ruth,

First of all, I want to apologize for the things I said to you at Christmas. I was wrong to criticize you. You have plans with John. He seems like an honorable man, and I don't want to second-guess you. I'm very sorry, and I hope you will forgive me.

Second, I want to tell you how impressed my nurses are with how you treated my leg. They say it's rare for someone with a wound like mine ever to be able to walk normally again, but they say my prognosis is very good and that I must have had a good doctor. I thought you should know. I'm up and about on crutches. They don't want me to lie around for weeks and weeks. They say that I need to stay strong, and I stay strong by dragging this great old cast around.

Speaking of being impressed, I was awarded a medal for being wounded in the course of duty. A general came by just like they do with the men, and pinned it to my pillow. Now I wear it wherever I go, and next Christmas, I will be pinning this glittery little thing to the tree.

They say I'll only need ten weeks to fully recover, so I won't go home to Baltimore. If all goes well, I'll be able to return to the Ambulance Corps. I don't know if I'll be mentally ready, but because of you, I will be ready in my body.

Your most loving sister,
Elise

CHAPTER THIRTY-TWO

April 1916

Elise, back from London, took the train from Calais to Ypres, with chickens, cavalrymen and their horses. While she was standing at the window of one of the passenger cars, she worked up the nerve to ask one of the cavalrymen why he thought it was a good idea to waste a horse on trench warfare.

He was a lieutenant, a proper, monocled gent with a waxed mustache and riding breeches. "The Germans are on the run," he said. "There aren't any trenches where we're going. It's going to be like the old days where we can simply run down their troops and take their positions."

"What can you do against a machine gun?" Elise asked hopelessly. The horses were corralled in a separate, open car, tied to an improvised fence rail, and beautiful to look at.

"There will be no machine guns," said the lieutenant. "We're cavaliers. They wouldn't send us in if we couldn't be effective."

"I've seen horses sink into the mud of Flanders," said Elise.

"The horses and their wagons, too. Completely. They disappeared without a trace. It was a miracle their drivers got out of the mud alive."

"You've been listening to mad soldiers' tales," said the lieutenant, and he smiled at her in her Ambulance Corps uniform, as though she was just a little girl. "Don't you worry about us, young lady. We and our horses will do just fine." He left her alone at the window of the car, which was passing through the wreckage of the Flanders countryside, where the only color was the bloodred of poppies.

Elise watched the flowers as the train rushed past, along with the ruins of little villages and their churches. Nothing had been spared. The train passed the bullet-pocked sign for Ypres, and Elise felt her heart begin to race. It was fear, for sure. Nowhere she was going would be safe. But then again, there was Hera.

An ambulance was waiting at the train station at Ypres, and Elise went straight to it. To her surprise and delight, Hera was driving. The two of them hugged for a long time.

"It's so good to see you," said Hera, finally letting go. "How's your leg?"

Elise patted it. It was still sore, but she was no longer limping. "Good as new!"

"Everyone will be so glad. We were terrified they'd have to take it off." Hera shaded her eyes to look at the train. "Good heavens, is that the *cavalry*?"

Elise followed her gaze and saw the men unloading the horses. "It certainly is. And what a bunch of snobs they are."

"This is bad news." Hera got into the ambulance.

"Why bad?" said Elise, climbing in next to her.

"Because we'll be moving soon. They say the Germans have been beaten back, and the next place for the hospitals is in an old hotel. We were going to be billeted in the barn, and now the cavalry will want it." She put the ambulance in gear. "We'll have to tell Matron so she can fight them for it."

Elise laughed at the very idea of the matron fighting for anything except a place at the head of a food line.

"Don't laugh," said Hera. "It's very serious. Our only other option is a chicken coop."

"Bad news," said Elise, smiling. "That train is full of chickens."

Ruth was waiting when Hera dropped Elise off. Elise hugged and kissed her sister until Ruth, laughing, pushed her away.

"I'm glad to see you in one piece," she said. "Come inside and get a cup of coffee and a piece of cake before it's all gone."

"There's coffee and cake?"

"One of the nurses got a package in the mail. She's sharing." They hurried inside to the mess. A small chocolate cake sat on one of the tables. A teakettle covered in a towel was beside it, along with a few chipped dessert plates. A hand-lettered sign next to the cake said Share and Share Alike.

"That means we're supposed to have very small pieces," said Ruth, "and very small cups."

"Is there cream?" said Elise, incredulous.

"Don't be ridiculous." Ruth poured out approximately three sips each of coffee from the teapot and cut two thin slices from the already decimated cake. "Savor it," she said, like she was telling a patient to take their medicine, and handed Elise a plate.

Since there were no forks, Elise ate with her fingers. The cake was a little dry from sitting out, but it was good chocolate, and the coffee was delicious. When she had savored the entire piece, she drained the coffee cup and licked the plate.

Ruth smiled faintly at her manners. "How was London?"

"I wasn't out much," said Elise. "People told me that the zeppelin bombings have stopped. They told me you can't get sugar for love or money, and dogs and cats are getting scarce."

"Even you don't believe that last one."

"I don't," admitted Elise, "but I was around a lot of soldiers. I heard a lot of stories."

"I can imagine."

"It was very international, too," said Elise. "There were African soldiers, and Greeks."

"It's like that here now," said Ruth. "They're throwing in all the reserves. Everyone they can get their hands on. We have Australians, and three Americans."

"From where?"

"New Jersey. They're in bad shape and they may not last, but they might like to hear another familiar accent. It could do them some good."

"What about your accent?" said Elise, teasing. "Didn't that do them some good? Or are you getting to be more of a Brit with each passing day?"

"I could ask you the same thing," said Ruth. "John said his parents came to see you when you were in London. They wrote him a letter."

"What did they say?" said Elise, eyeing the cake.

"They said you were up to your waist in a plaster cast, and you ate everything they'd brought with them."

"True," said Elise sheepishly. "They kept handing me scones. I didn't realize I was supposed to save them for later. Did they say I was rude?"

"No," said Ruth. "But they said you must've been hungry."

"Well," said Elise, "the food in the hospital was a damn sight better than the stuff we get in the barracks, but it still didn't compare to Cook's back home."

"Father sent us a box," said Ruth. "There's no chocolate cake, but there are a lot of sweets."

Elise perked up at this. "Enough to share?"

"Plenty. I put half aside for you." She hesitated. "I'm sure Hera would appreciate some. Did she write to you while you were away?"

"She sent me a couple of postcards," said Elise. "You know, 'Having a lovely time, wish you were here' kinds of things." Elise gave her sister a searching look. "What're you trying to say?"

"Nothing," said Ruth. "I was just wondering who was fixing her ambulance while you were gone."

"I don't know," said Elise. "They probably brought in some man who was too wounded or too old to be in the trenches."

"You may have to fight to get your old job back."

"That may be," said Elise. "Speaking of the fighting, Hera said the Germans are being beaten back, and the lines are moving."

"Don't get too optimistic," said Ruth. "It's just a rumor. If we're moving at all, it isn't far. They tell me there's a hotel just on the other side of the German line that we'll be set up in."

"So we'll still be together," said Elise with relief. "We're supposed to be in the barn—or the chicken coop."

"For your sake," said Ruth, "I hope it's the barn."

CHAPTER THIRTY-THREE

May 1915

Rumors of a move proved to be just that.

The new fever that was racing through the soldiers in the trenches, on the other hand, was all too real.

At first, the doctors didn't know what it was. Fellowes took one look at the soldiers suffering horribly from diarrhea, vomiting and rashes, and declared them to be infected with dengue.

"But where would he get dengue?" said John as they examined one of the Tommies, burning with fever.

"From the Africans," said Fellowes, as though it was obvious. "They're here, and they brought their diseases with them."

"But dengue is transmitted by mosquitoes," said John mildly. "Do you think they brought those as well?"

"Don't be pigheaded," said Fellowes. "The symptoms are staring you in the face. The diagnosis is obvious."

"I just don't see it." John turned to Ruth. "Treat this man

for typhoid. Keep him away from the others. Give him aspirin for the fever and keep him hydrated."

"Yes, Doctor." Ruth was confined to the wards now, a
nurse among nurses. John didn't dare work with her in the
operating theater, and the skills that he had taught her over
the months were fading. She gestured at the orderlies, and
they came over to take the sick man to a bed at the far end
of the ward.

When he came to, the man, whose name was Wentworth,
began to cough and retch. He couldn't keep the aspirin down,
and his fever only got worse.

"You don't think it's a new kind of gas?" asked Ruth.

"No," said John, "and I'm not sure it's typhoid either."

Elise was wearing a surgical mask when she dropped off the
next batch of wounded. Except they weren't wounded. They
were sick. Elise waited at the back of the ambulance while the
orderlies unloaded, and Ruth stood by, watching.

"Are any of them still alive?" Elise asked, muffled through
the mask. "They were so quiet on the way up."

Ruth knelt and felt for pulses. There were now dozens upon
dozens of men with the same symptoms, and it was impossible
to keep them isolated from each other. Four out of Elise's six
were dead, their faces still hot from fever.

"Great," said Elise. "Now we're not even ambulances. We're
just hearses." She got back into the cab.

Ruth shaded her eyes at the day. This was the first time
she'd been outside in twenty-four hours. The sky was bright
blue. The crocuses were blooming. The smell of freshly turned
earth was in the air, coming from behind the hospital, where
orderlies were digging graves. Inside, the operating theater
was at a virtual standstill as the doctors tried to decide what
disease they were facing.

Ruth came over to the driver's side of the ambulance and leaned on the door. "What do you hear?" she said. "What do people say it is?"

Elise pulled down her mask. "We thought it was gas at first. But if it is, it's different from anything else. The triage docs are saying cholera, but they're not sure either." She leaned closer to Ruth. "Hera says it's probably spread by contact with blood, so be careful."

Ruth bit her lip against the urge to tell Elise that Hera didn't know what she was talking about.

Elise eyed her and her skepticism. "You wanted to know what I've heard."

Ruth straightened. "Be careful yourself. If it is typhoid—or cholera—boil any water you plan to drink."

"I'll remember to do that," said Elise, "in my copious free time."

Whatever it was, it was soon epidemic in the lines. Now, instead of falling in the trenches due to gas or gunfire, men fell sick. Even the German prisoners were sick. There were so few survivors, the nurses at Number Four knew them all by name. The survivors watched with quiet horror as the soldiers around them coughed and died, no matter what the doctors did.

Elise came by with another load of warm corpses later that day, more upset than Ruth had ever seen her. She pulled off her dirty surgical mask, and wiped her face with her sleeve. "I've never felt more useless," said Elise.

"Are you sick?" Ruth asked and automatically touched her forehead.

Elise brushed her hand away. "If soldiers on both sides are dying like this, how long can the whole mess go on? And that doesn't include the wounded." She lowered her voice. "We should get out of here before we catch it, too."

"If we leave, we'll be on a ship full of sick men," said Ruth. "Is that really where you want to be?"

"Well," said Elise, "no."

"I don't want to be here either," said Ruth. "We're practically a morgue, but I can't think of anywhere safer."

"London would be safer," said Elise. "Have you thought about that? You could be in medical school. I could be driving an ambulance around Piccadilly Circus. I hear there're plenty of women doing that." She took off her hat and smoothed her hair in the fresh May breeze. Her face showed nothing but frustration.

"What about John?" said Ruth. "I can't just leave him."

"Listen," said Elise, "if you could get into medical school, don't you think he'd be happy for you? It's not like you two wouldn't ever see each other again."

"But what happens if he gets sick?" said Ruth.

"Who'll take care of him?" Elise laughed. "Everybody would. Your guy's a favorite. Not like Fellowes. At the barracks, they call him a regular hammer-and-saw man."

"How do they even know that?"

"Amputees can still talk," said Elise. "You should hear them on the way to the evacuation trains."

"Another reason I can't leave," said Ruth.

"As if you're keeping him from sawing off all those arms and legs," said Elise. "You really need to think about what you're going to do next, and when you're going to start doing it. One day soon the fighting will have to stop. Where do you want to be when that happens?"

Ruth let her breath out between her teeth. "I should write to the Women's Medical College."

"Please do," said Elise. "As soon as you hear something, I'll apply for a transfer to London. We can go together."

Later that day, when she was off shift, Ruth sat down at the table in her quarters and composed her letter to the Women's Medical College. She tried to make it short and concise, keeping her experience at the front lines and her time in the operating theater foremost, but it turned into a longer letter. She found herself writing about the wounded and how in the beginning she had felt for each and every one of them, and how now she barely had time to look at their faces. She wrote about the new illness and how it was turning the war into an entirely different kind of killing ground. In the end she reread what she had written and decided it was terrible. It expressed everything in her heart, but it wasn't a proper letter of application. She put the letter aside and started again.

To Whom It May Concern:

I am a nurse in a front line hospital (a Casualty Clearing Station), and am interested in becoming a doctor. I have had extensive operating theater experience, not just assisting, but actually performing surgeries. I was able to do this until I was forbidden to do so by the general in charge of our hospital. Since then I have been restricted to nursing, which I do with pride but also frustration. I wish to apply to your college. If you would be so kind as to send instructions as to how I should proceed, I would be most appreciative.

Sincerely,
Ruth Duncan

She mailed the letter the next afternoon just before tea, and walked back to the hospital from the shabby old postal building. Lorries and ambulances roared by, splashing mud and spewing exhaust, but the truth was, traffic was thin compared to pre-illness days. In the wards, only one man was left alive from the first group, and now that he was healthy, he was due to go back to the line. Ruth took the turn that would lead her back to Hospital Four, and found herself dragging her feet. The whole situation—the grime of spring, the men literally dying as she tried to help them, the futility of the war itself—made her want to scream with despair. She saw John standing by the hospital door with a teacup in his hand. He was staring off into the distance.

Ruth carefully crossed the road and called his name. He seemed to come back into himself.

"Where did you go?" he said.

"I told you. I mailed my letter to the Women's Medical College."

He gave her a long look, and Ruth could see his frustrations and doubts were the same as hers.

"Are we actually helping anyone at this point?" she asked.

John sipped his tea like it was bad-tasting medicine. "We're making them comfortable. Sometimes that's all you can do."

She stood closer to him as a horse-drawn cannon rumbled by, and took his hand. "You could apply for a medical position in London. You've been here for so long, who would say no?"

He took a long swallow of tea. "As tempting as it sounds, I think I'm staying for the duration."

Almost two weeks to the day from when she'd sent her letter, the Women's Medical College replied. The envelope was thin and made of wartime paper. Ruth opened it hesitantly. Inside was a short, handwritten letter.

Dear Miss Duncan,
We are very pleased to hear of your interest in our

institution and impressed at your level of experience.
Though we would be glad to have you as a student, and
we have enclosed an application, we are not currently
training doctors. Our professors are engaged in wartime
activities and, unfortunately, they are unable to perform
both patriotic and academic duties. We are, however, still
training nurses, and if you wish to take a degree with us,
we would be pleased to review your application.

Yours most sincerely,
Cynthia Perkins
Dean of Admissions

Bitterly, she showed the letter to John over tea the next day. He read it and gave it back. "At least they didn't say no."

"They might as well have." She wanted to tear the letter up. She felt absolutely pinned down by the war, like a man in a trench.

John put down his teacup. "Let's go for a walk."

"Where?" she said. "The cemetery? The road? We'll get hit by a lorry or run down by horses. What's the point of going for a walk?"

"The point is, you need to clear your head." John got up and took her hand, pulling her to her feet. Everyone in the mess— the other nurses, Fellowes—watched with gossipy interest. In addition to her irritation with the letter and John's silly suggestion of a walk—her head did *not* need clearing—Ruth began to feel embarrassed. His grip tightened, but kindly.

"Come on," said John, and she let herself be led outside, into the damp-smelling air.

"Where are we going?"

"There's still a bit of woods behind Three," he said. "I thought it might do you good to hear the birds."

Ruth almost laughed. "Are there any birds left?"

John stopped, turned to her and let his hands drop to his sides. Even though the war had added lines to his face, he still looked vital and young. Now, though, he seemed vulnerable and perhaps even close to tears.

"Maybe I'm the one who needs to hear the birds," he said quietly.

She was used to seeing firm efficiency, calm maturity. "Are you sick?" she asked in a whisper.

He shook his head and put his arms around her. She held him tight, her face against his shoulder. Traffic thundered past them. Men whistled from a lorry. She raised her lips to meet his. They were warm and soft, and she allowed herself to imagine the two of them far away, on an island maybe, where it was quiet, where they could be alone. They held on to each other for a long time until a passing driver threw mocking kisses at them, and then she let go. John was smiling, and a warm rush went through Ruth's body. The war seemed to have lifted off his shoulders for the moment.

"Shall we go and listen to the birds?" she said.

In the shred of woods behind Hospital Three, flowers bloomed under the newly leafed trees. Songbirds trilled over the distant sounds of artillery.

"They're nesting," said Ruth wonderingly. "Even in all this."

They found a cool, mossy place and lay down next to each other. John propped himself up on one elbow, his other arm around Ruth's waist. He kissed her again, but differently this time, starting at the line of her jaw, moving to her cheek, then her lips. The tip of his tongue brushed hers.

Ruth squeezed her eyes shut and held her breath. Her pulse beat hard, like the heartbeat of a dying man. But she wasn't dying. Something new was happening inside her body. John's arm slipped under the small of her back, raising her from the bed of moss. Her stomach tightened, her thighs opened, and there was a new kind of heat in the part of herself never discussed in nursing school.

He pulled away and she opened her eyes to see his, deep and gray. She realized she would give anything for the taste of him again. Her hands, at his shoulders, came to his face, both sides of his face. Without a sound, she pressed herself up, opening her mouth against his, tasting, then consuming. His supporting arm crumpled, and all at once she was on top of him, belly to belly, his arms so tight she had to pull away. His grip loosened and she sat up, breathing hard, her knees on either side of his hips in the green moss. His hands were on her thighs, grasping her skirt, and a presence, hard and warm, pressed up against her own heat.

He looked at her with a kind of knowledge, a kind of innocence, and an astonishment he couldn't hide. The presence throbbed under her. She wanted to kiss him again, but as she leaned forward, the presence pushed hard between her thighs, rocking her back with a sensation that made her gasp. John's hands came to her hips, and he pulled her tight, tighter, until she was pinned against the presence, rocking, finding the right place for it, losing it, finding it again, losing it. He sat up, pinned between her thighs, face sweaty against her neck. His teeth slid over her skin, down to her collar. She thought he would bite her, and that thought, the throbbing and the perfect angle of her body all came together at once. She surged against him, struggling in his arms, making sounds she'd never heard before, blinded by what was happening to her, new, all new, happening again, and still new.

Finally, when their strength was gone, the two of them rolled down onto the moss, clinging to each other.

"I love you, Ruth," John whispered.

"I love you, too," she said.

All through the summer, when they could get time, Ruth and John would make their way to the woods behind Hospital Three. The illness, now dubbed "trench fever," waned in late June, and the war picked up where it had left off, with John in the operating theater and Ruth in the wards. Her frustration level depended on the day. Sometimes she was resigned. Other times she would insist on going up to the woods.

"We need a chaperone," John said breathlessly in her ear, one stolen afternoon on the bed of moss.

"We're old enough to know what we're doing." Ruth reluctantly pushed him away and sat up. Her dress was twisted around her waist. She stood and shook it out, brushed off the leaves, and sat down again, her thigh touching his. "We both know I can't afford to get pregnant."

"I know." He leaned over and kissed the pearl at her throat. His shirt was untucked. He'd kicked his shoes somewhere. "I can dream, can't I?"

"Do you dream about me?" she teased.

He smiled and ran his hand through her short hair. Her nurse's veil lay in the moss. "You dream about being a doctor."

"No," she said, abruptly serious. "I dream about the men. There's nothing I can do for them, and they just die."

"Every night?" he asked, and she nodded. "Those are nightmares," said John. "No wonder you look so tired."

She kissed him again. "We should be getting back. Fellowes hates that we do this. I'm sure he's calling the generals right now."

"The generals have better things to do than check on us," said John. "I hear there's a push coming. The Germans are weak, and the lines are about to move."

"Where did you hear this?"

"From the source of all rumors," said John. "Who else, but the Ambulance Corps?"

CHAPTER THIRTY-FOUR

August 1915

Late in the summer, the Germans were beaten back, and the front finally moved east, away from Ypres.

As the lines moved, so did the hospitals, which, for Ruth, meant packing up surgical tools and the operating theater. Orderlies helped pack mattresses and bed frames into the ambulances. When Elise's lorry was full and ready to go, Ruth climbed into the cab with her sister, headed to the main road to follow the caravan of ambulances, supply trucks and horse-drawn carts toward the barbed-wire ruins of no man's land.

Neither of them could remember the big guns being silent for such a long time.

"It's eerie," said Elise, as they drove. "I swear I can hear birds singing." She turned to Ruth. "I didn't think there were any birds left."

Ruth, thinking of the patch of woods, the moss that she might never see again, flushed and didn't say anything.

Engineers had chosen the narrowest part of the marshy,

mile-wide strip that was no man's land and flattened the shell craters into something resembling a dirt road. They'd laid down gravel to keep the heavier lorries from sinking, but every once in a while, there was a supply truck or a horse-drawn cart, off to the side, up to the tops of its wheels in muck, the horses struggling uselessly in sucking mud.

"It's like quicksand," said Ruth. "I feel so sorry for the horses. You know they'll just shoot them."

"I know," said Elise. "Let's not talk about that. I've seen too many dead horses here to ever want to talk about that again."

"Poor Elise," murmured Ruth. "And I thought you only cared about engines."

"So did I," said Elise, "until I got here. Speaking of which…" She revved the engine, which coughed and sputtered.

"Oh, please ,God," said Ruth, "please let us get to the other side before the ambulance breaks down."

"It's been acting up all day," said Elise, shifting up, then down again. The lorry in front of them inched ahead. "I think I can fix it if we pull off someplace."

"Please not here."

"No," said Elise, mostly to the ambulance, "please not here."

The lorry in front moved ahead, and Elise followed, double-clutching to keep the engine running. In a moment they saw the remains of the German barbed wire, then the trenches themselves.

At first glance, the trenches seemed to be the same as on the British side, with parapets to shoot over, and underground bunkers farther back. But there was a sense of vastness to these trenches that was lacking on the British side, Ruth thought, as though a great deal more was hidden under the barren ground than met the eye. One of the things that met her eyes, however, was the bodies, lying as they had fallen while the rest of their forces retreated.

"Damn it," said Elise, "we're going to have to stop." She steered out onto the hard ground of the former German front line, got out of the driver's seat and opened the hood of the ambulance. Ruth heard her swearing and got out, too. Under the hood, it was just a mess of oily innards as far as she could tell, but as always, Elise seemed to know what she was doing.

"How long is this going to take?" Ruth asked.

"Not long. I just have to clean the damn spark plugs. Maybe twenty minutes."

Ruth took a step away, in the direction of the trenches and the unburied bodies.

"Whoa," said Elise, looking up. "Where do you think you're going?"

"To find survivors," said Ruth, and she turned and climbed down into the nearest trench.

To say that the trench smelled of death was an understatement. There were bodies everywhere between the narrow earthen walls. When she dared to look at their faces, she was shocked at how young they were—some looked no more than fourteen years old. She came to an intersection and made a right, away from the British lines and no man's land, toward the bunkers. She stooped to peer into the first sandbagged doorway, and squinted into the dimness. Chairs lay on the floor. A table was tipped over. The corners of maps were all that remained of plans that had been nailed to the wooden walls. Either the Germans had ripped them away before running, or British soldiers had taken them.

There was another opening in the back of the room. Ruth ducked in under the low door and picked her way around the fallen furniture. What she found was yet another bunker, this one with a bare stump of a candle in a saucer, and a box of matches. She lit the candle and looked around. The place was empty except for benches where troops probably sheltered during bombardments—room for thirty men. There was yet another door beyond this one, and she found the same thing—a room dug deep into the hillside, safe from the battering of artillery. The candle was in danger of dying, and she checked behind her to make sure she knew the way out. There was just enough daylight coming in the first door to guide her. She went to the back of the third room and found yet another shelter for the German troops and another door beyond that. The candle flickered and went out, and Ruth turned to go. Anyone who had been safe here, in what was perhaps miles of tunnels, had left long ago. The ones in the trenches had been ordered to stay and hold the line, and they had done that to the best of their young abilities. She wondered if they had done so willingly and had her question answered as she came out of the trench past a machine gun nest with two dead boys in it. They lay on their backs, their eyes still open, gazing at the sky.

Their legs were chained to the heavy tripod of the machine gun.

Part Two

CHAPTER THIRTY-FIVE

August 1918

Once there had been chandeliers.

Ruth could see the shadows of their settings in the high white ceilings of the Hotel St. Jacques, but those were long gone. There probably hadn't been actual guests here, or in the nearby town of Lozer, in the last three years. One of the nurses had told her the hotel had been a popular spa, famous for its mineral waters, and wouldn't that be helpful for the wounded? Ruth wasn't sure what mineral waters would do for gangrene and amputees, but as long as it was boiled and sterile, she was willing to give anything a try.

The makeshift hospital was only a scant two miles behind the new front, and, though stripped by German troops, it still maintained a degree of luxury in its flocked wallpaper and intricate parquet floors. She and John helped set up the operating theater in the kitchen, where there was still, miraculously, running water, presumably from the mineral springs. Twenty operating tables were being crowded together in the hotel's big kitchen. All the surgeons from Ypres were there, except for Fellowes, who had been found drunk on duty by the very generals he had called on Ruth. When he heard the news, John had enthusiastically invited Ruth back into the operating theater.

She was sterilizing instruments on the old-fashioned wood-burning stove when the orderlies were directed to go out and cut down whatever remaining trees they could find. There was a wall of windows at the back side of the room—very grand for a kitchen—and Ruth could see the grounds from where she stood with the other nurses, over the boiling trays. There had once been a garden back there, and pathways and hedges were still visible amid the weeds.

Ruth lifted hot instruments out of the water with tongs and put them on a sterile towel. She made herself promise to get John out of the operating theater, to do some exploring if there was ever a slowdown. Then she heard the sound of an ax from nearby and turned to see a tall, beautiful yew tremble under the orderlies' blows. When they were done, the garden, too, would be stripped. She focused on what she was doing, trying not to think about the woods behind Hospital Three.

By the time the instruments were boiled and the X-ray machine had been made to work properly, the first of the wounded were coming in.

Surgery went on well into the night and didn't finish until two in the morning, when a full moon had risen into the clear night sky. Ruth didn't feel the least bit romantic after more than twelve hours on her feet. What she really wanted was a hot bath and a clean bed, but John took her hand and led her into the ruined garden.

Outside, it was easy to hear the familiar distant booming of the artillery, hammering German positions. It took the ardor out of the air for Ruth, but John put his arms around her and pulled her close. She leaned against his shoulder.

"You did well today," he said quietly. "No one in the operating theater could have done better than the two of us."

"We'll do it all over again tomorrow," she said, muffled against his shirt. "We should get some sleep."

"I could sleep right here in the grass."

"Did you drink the water?" she said. "Maybe it's affected your mind. We're sleeping upstairs on real beds." She pulled away. "Really. I need a bath and some rest."

He leaned down to kiss her. "I'll walk you upstairs."

Inside, they located the servants' stairway, which led up steeply from the empty kitchen to the upper floors of the old hotel. The stairs hadn't been swept in an age, and tracks showed where others had gone before them. At the very top were the servants' quarters, a narrow hallway with doors on either side, all closed. Snores came from behind the doors. It seemed that every room was occupied.

"This is what we get for admiring the moon," whispered Ruth.

"Let's go down a flight and see what we find," John whispered back.

"But those beds are for the patients."

"We'll be patients soon enough if we don't get some sleep."

She had no better suggestions. Ruth followed him down one flight and though a door marked 6th Floor.

Not a soul was there. The entire floor was empty, the beds perfectly made, waiting for patients. Wallpaper sagged, and water stains crept down some of the walls, but carpets had been rolled away, and the floors were swept.

They found a room with a bath attached. There was a tub, and Ruth turned on the water. She put her hand under the stream and waited without much hope. Was it too much to wish for a decent wash? To her amazement, the water turned hot. She plugged the tub and gave John a push. "Go find your own room," she said. "I'm a decent girl. I intend to have a bath and go to bed."

John glanced at her and then the tub, and gave her a mischievous smile.

"No," she said. "No. I'm exhausted."

"Good night, then." He winked, turned and closed the door behind him.

Ruth stripped off her clothes and eased into the bath. There was no soap, but it didn't matter. The hot water lifted the grime and God knew what else from her skin. She combed through her hair with her fingers until it lay flat and wet against her neck. She realized there was no towel anywhere in sight and sat in the tub a while longer, silently cursing but too tired to be really angry. She got out of the tub and pulled up the drain plug. She was sure there would be a ring of filth and felt guilty about dirtying something that someone else would have to clean. She wiped her body as dry as she could with just her hands and then peeked out the bathroom door.

There was John, lying in the bed, still in his clothes, absolutely sound asleep. It was as if he'd sat down for a moment, then collapsed onto the pillows without even knowing it. He was snoring lightly.

Ruth stood behind the bathroom door and wondered what to do next. What they'd done together in the woods was one thing. Being in bed with him—naked—was something else entirely. The inevitable gossip didn't bother her at this point. Everyone knew something was going on between them, and they certainly weren't the only nurse and doctor involved in a romance.

It was the idea of waking up with him that made her heart

quail, and pound at the same time. She touched the pearl at her throat, the only thing she was wearing. How bold could she be? How bold *should* she be? And what about him? Would he be embarrassed to find himself next to her, bare to him, in the morning? Or would he touch her, caress her, like in the woods...

Ruth bit her lip, and turned back to the bathroom. Her underthings and uniform dress were draped over the towel rack. Nothing was clean, but she put everything on anyway and peered out the door again. She was so tired, her mind was going in circles—to get into the bed or to sleep in the tub. She rubbed her eyes and pushed the door all the way open. It creaked loudly, but John didn't budge.

"John?" she whispered.

He snored.

"John?" she said, in an almost normal tone of voice.

He was sleeping so deeply, he looked childlike. Ruth walked over to the bed, barefoot, and realized she'd never seen him asleep before. The way he was now, head to one side, hair awry, he was so young and defenseless. Her heart went out to him, and just standing there in a stupor of exhaustion, she realized how in love she actually was.

To say it in the woods after all...that...was one thing. *I love you.* She'd meant it every time. But to look down at him and *see* him was different. So intimate. She could stand right where she was for the rest of the night, and just study the boyish face he kept so perfectly concealed behind his knowledge, skill and sympathy. *This* face was for her, alone. This was her husband's face, not just her lover's. She would grow old with *this* face.

The understanding was so deep that it made her sink onto the side of the bed. The mattress shifted under her. John

snored. She wanted to shake him awake, to tell him everything on her mind, but she didn't have the heart.

Let him sleep, she thought, and she closed her eyes, just
for a minute.

It was morning all at once, and someone was knocking on
the door.

Ruth opened her eyes and sat up in a rush, in her clothes,
thank God.

"John?" The bed was empty. "Come in?"

A tall girl in a VAD uniform opened the door, balancing
a tray.

"Your suitcase is here," said the girl, "and the gentleman
doctor asked that you have this." She put the tray on the bed.
There were tea, bacon and scrambled eggs.

"Eggs?" said Ruth, dazed. "Where did you get eggs?"

"All I know is that they're serving them in the officers'
mess," said the VAD girl, sounding unmistakably jealous.
"There must be chickens somewhere."

Ruth touched the edge of the tray to make sure it was real.
"What time is it?"

"Just past seven thirty, Sister."

It was like being in a Victorian novel, Ruth thought, as the
VAD girl waited to be dismissed. "Thanks," she said. "Tell
the gentleman doctor I said thanks. No, wait. Tell him I send
him my *compliments*."

"Yes, Sister," said the VAD girl, and she disappeared out
the door.

Had he kissed her goodbye? Ruth touched the pearl at her
throat. Of course he had. He had watched her sleep, the same
way she'd watched him.

The savory smell of the bacon distracted her for a moment,
and she grinned at the thought of him sending the tray up to

her as though she was a fine lady. She ate everything on the plate and then gulped down the tea. She found her suitcase at the foot of the bed, and dug out her comb and a change of clothes. Ruth dressed, and went downstairs to see what would come with the new day.

CHAPTER THIRTY-SIX

The first bomb that fell from the German aeroplane missed the hotel but fell on its circular drive, killing the wounded who were waiting there. The force of the blast knocked down the columns of the hotel's fine portico. When those were gone, the portico itself collapsed, crushing two orderlies and a nurse. The noise from the explosion burst into the crowded kitchen operating theater, and dust drifted in, along with the cries from the men and nurses in the ward.

Ruth and John were hunched over the soldier they were sewing up. The kitchen windows rattled in their frames, and plaster dust shuddered down from the ceiling. The two of them looked at each other over their masks, and Ruth could almost read John's mind: *That's just the first one.*

"Hurry," he said, and the two of them stitched as quickly as they could, so the man could be moved. John glanced around for the orderlies, and that was when the second bomb fell, this time squarely on the roof of the hotel.

Windows shattered. The floor shook, and chunks of plaster fell from the ceiling. Doctors and nurses flung themselves over their patients. One chunk of the plaster ceiling fell onto the stoves where the instruments were boiling, and suddenly there was scalding water and hot metal flying everywhere. The stove, burning high, emptied its flaming innards onto the wooden floor, and in moments the floor was on fire.

Bedlam broke out. There were only two doors to the kitchen. One led to the garden, and one opened into the wards. Doctors and nurses carried the men draped over their shoulders, forming a crush at either door. A pair of orderlies tried to rush in with a stretcher, saw the fire, dropped the stretcher and shoved through the crowd to quench it with buckets of mineral water. As they did, smoke filled the kitchen, and that was when Ruth heard one of the nurses scream. She saw why. The fire was licking up the walls, starting on the wooden cabinets.

"We have to get out," said John. He was carrying their patient in his arms, just a boy, maybe nineteen. "This way." He pushed over to the garden side of the room, weaving through the other operating tables. Instead of going for the doors where the rest of the doctors and nurses and patients were crammed together, he turned to Ruth. "Grab a sheet," he said. "Wrap your arm in it."

Ruth caught up a sheet from the nearest operating table and obeyed, making a muff around her right arm. She already knew what he wanted her to do. She rushed ahead of him to the wall of glass between them and the garden. She thrust at the thin wooden frames and jagged shards of glass with her wrapped arm. The windows gave way easily, and she swung her arm until there was enough room to safely step outside. Others followed suit, and soon the entire wall of windows was just a shattered mass. Ruth turned to take the boy's limp form as John stepped through the broken window, and she heard the sound of the aeroplane's engine overhead.

They both looked up. High above, they could see the damage done to the roof and top floors of the hotel. Bricks had fallen together at crazy angles. One end of a bed hung out of what had been a window. The servants' quarters, just under the roof, were gone. Everywhere people were shouting for help.

John carried the boy to the far end of the garden and put him down in a bed of weeds. Others followed. Soon the garden was covered with groaning men, and men still limp from anesthesia. Surgeons who'd had the presence of mind to hold on to their surgical tools knelt and continued to operate while smoke billowed from the kitchen.

"We have to get everyone out," panted Ruth, shading her eyes at the hotel, where the roof was now burning.

John was on his knees beside the boy, and got to his feet. "Come on," he said. "Let's see who we can save."

Back in the kitchen, orderlies were throwing water on the fire. Ruth and John blundered through the smoke until they found a hysterical nurse and an old man, an orderly, in the lobby. Smoke pressed against the high, ornate ceiling. The blast from the front of the building had left a pile of rubble inside the front door almost too high to climb over.

"Sister!" John said to the sobbing nurse. "Is anyone evacuating the upper floors?"

"Only a few," she wept. "Only a few got out."

John turned to the orderly. "I want you to go to Lozer as fast as you can. Tell the officer in charge we need help. Tell them we have men trapped in here."

"Yes, Doctor," said the old man. "Yes, sir!"

Ruth started for the grand staircase with John right behind her. All she could think about was the dud bomb at Hospital Number Four and the hours it had taken them to travel the single mile to Number Three. How would that old man get to Lozer—which was at least that far away—in any amount of time?

She held up her skirt and ran up the stairs. There was smoke at the first landing, but the second floor seemed untouched by the bombing, and nurses were helping the wounded out of their beds.

"Take these men through the kitchen," said John to the closest nurse. "You won't be able to get out the front door."

"Yes, Doctor," said the nurse, and turned to pass the message along.

Ruth and John headed for the next flight of stairs. To get to the third floor, they had to pass a floor-to-ceiling window that looked out onto the carnage where the bomb had dropped in front of the hotel. There was a muddy crater at the far end of the circular drive, and dead men radiating out from it, their bodies twisted by the force of the blast. From the window, Ruth could see the orderly John had sent to get help in Lozer, hobbling along between the bodies, still on the near side of the crater.

"Come on," said John, and he put a hand on her shoulder.

"Wait," she said. "Do you hear that?"

"Hear what?"

She looked from the orderly to where the sound was coming from, in the sky, a faint buzz, and then she saw the aeroplane, heading purposefully toward the hotel.

"Oh my God," said Ruth. "He's coming back!"

John's grip on her shoulder tightened. "Get down!"

The two of them huddled near the floor, but Ruth could still see what was going on outside. The aeroplane loomed against the clear blue sky, flying closer and closer. It angled downward, and over the engine noise came the sound of shooting. Flashes of fire burst from the plane. Clods of dirt popped up where bullets hit the ground, heading in a straight line, right for the orderly. The orderly threw himself to the ground and covered his head with his arms. Bullets cut right through him. The aeroplane veered away, loud, just in time to avoid hitting the hotel itself. Through the window, Ruth could see the face of the pilot as he swiveled his head around, searching for his next targets. He was so young, and his teeth were set in a grimace of victory.

Suddenly John was no longer at her side. He was running down the stairs against the tide of doctors and nurses racing up to evacuate the rest of the floors.

"What're you doing?" she shouted after him. "Where're you going?"

"He's still moving!" John shouted back, and he was gone.

Through the window, she saw the old man had turned over, arms outstretched in the middle of the road.

"Wait!" she shouted after John. "Wait!" Ruth ran after him, down the stairs, shoving through the crowd. She couldn't get through fast enough, and by the time she got to the ruins of the front door, John was already running across the circular front drive, his surgeon's gown flapping in the mild, smoky summer air. Ruth clambered over the pile of rubble that had been the portico of the hotel, tearing her dress. She scrambled over loose stones and plaster and heard the roar of the aeroplane as it returned yet again.

"John!" she shrieked.

"Stay where you are!" He turned to the bleeding orderly, and the aeroplane swooped in from overhead, following the same path it had before, shooting as it came.

Ruth didn't think. She just ran. She ran straight for the plane and for John, who was leaning down to gently retrieve the old man. Bullets went through John's body as though he was made of fabric, but Ruth still ran. John collapsed on top of the orderly, and Ruth felt a despairing fury. She ran even faster, hands out toward the murderer in the aeroplane.

"Stop!" she screamed at him. *"Stop!"* The plane was almost on her. He could've killed her, but for whatever trace of gallantry was left in him, he didn't. He stopped shooting. The aeroplane swept upward, pushing her to her knees in the dirt with its noise and wind and gasoline stink. Ruth crawled for John, no more than ten feet away, crawled in her torn dress and knelt beside him.

His right arm was soaked in blood. He was lying over the orderly on his belly. Blood bubbled from a wound in his back, just to the left of his spine. With all her strength, Ruth turned him over to see if he was still alive.

He was. He looked stunned.

"I'm shot?" He stared up at her in surprise. "What about the orderly?"

The orderly lay with his mouth and eyes open, clearly dead.

"He's gone," said Ruth, louder than she meant to, her voice shaking. The front of John's surgical smock was smeared with the orderly's blood, but the bullet that had gone in through his back had come out the front, and there was more blood—John's blood—oozing from his belly. She tore his smock and shirt away to see how bad the wound was. The bullet had gone through his gut. A single bullet wound with no shrapnel could be repaired, but—she looked over her shoulder at the burning hospital. Two doctors were running toward her. One was carrying a medical bag. A nurse was close behind. Ruth turned back to John, his right arm flung over his head.

The arm was terribly broken. He was staring up at her, dazed.

"I love you," he said. "I wish I'd married you."

"You're not going to die!" She practically screamed it.

Footsteps pounded up behind her, and one of the doctors

shoved her out of the way. He dropped to his knees in the dirt while the other hovered with the medical bag. The nurse caught Ruth by the arms and pulled her to her feet, but Ruth was too unsteady to stand. She fell to the ground by the doctor who was tearing away the rest of John's shirt and probing the wound with his fingers. Dirty fingers, Ruth thought, fingers that had recently been in the bowels of some other patient.

"Doweling, old man," said the doctor who was still standing, "you've been shot through the gut. And through the arm." He knelt beside John. "We're going to sew you up out here, but I'm sorry to say, old boy, we have no chloroform. You'll have to keep a stiff upper lip and all that." He reached into the medical bag and handed Ruth a piece of wood, no longer than her hand and no thicker than a broom handle. It had strange marks in it.

"Nurse," he said to her. "Put that between his teeth until he passes out. The sooner the better."

She took it and swallowed hard.

"Nurse," said the doctor to the other nurse. "Stop that confounded bleeding in his arm."

"Have you a tourniquet?" she said.

"No," said the doctor with the medical bag. "You must improvise."

The nurse frowned, but Ruth began tearing at her skirt, ripping out strips of blue fabric. "Here," she said, "and here, and here. Just save his arm."

The nurse gave her a frankly doubtful look, but took the pieces of Ruth's dress and began tying them above John's elbow.

"Put the bit in his mouth," said the doctor with the dirty hands to Ruth. "Wilson, hand me a scalpel. We'll do this as fast as we can."

Ruth pressed the wooden bit between John's teeth as the

scalpel slid through the flesh of his belly. He stared up at her, eyes wide, as though he couldn't believe what was happening. Blood spilled out, staining the dirt and the doctor's knees. There was no gauze to sop it up.

Ruth tore off another piece of her dress. "Use this."

Wilson, the doctor with the medical bag, had pulled out retractors and clamps. He gently soaked up the blood so the other could see what he was doing. The retractors and clamps went in as Wilson threaded a needle for internal sutures.

"What do you think?" said Wilson, handing over the needle.

"Is he still conscious?" said the doctor with the dirty hands.

Ruth looked down at John, panting, eyes squeezed shut, straining at the wooden bit. "Yes," she said.

"Keep fighting, old boy," said the doctor. "But save your strength. You'll need it."

Ruth knew what he meant, but wouldn't say in front of a conscious patient. Nothing here was sterile. John's wounds would become infected. His drains would run green instead of clear. He would develop a high fever and die. Just like a thousand other men. These two doctors were John's friends and countrymen, and they wouldn't just let him bleed out, but no one could deny that they might very well be working on a corpse. John must have known it, too. He let out his breath in a rush and went limp against Ruth's leg. The bit fell out of his mouth.

"He's unconscious," said Ruth. She'd expected to be in tears by now, but she'd seen this procedure so often, she was hardened. Dry-eyed, she knew that the doctor sewing up John's intestine was rushing. She swallowed and made herself say the things her father had said to her, so long ago.

"Your stitches are too big," she said harshly to the doctor

with dirty hands. "They're uneven. You're making a mess of his gut. He'll have peritonitis. You're killing him."

The doctor stopped sewing. "And who the bloody hell are you to be telling me how to stitch up my patient?"

Ruth straightened. "I'm Ruth Duncan. I'm his fiancée. I've been working in this madhouse for a year, and I've been working in medicine since I was a child."

The nurse stared at her. "Sister!" she said. "You're *never* to speak to a doctor in that way."

"He's not a doctor, he's a butcher," snapped Ruth.

"Butcher or not," said the doctor blandly, "I'm the best hope you have for saving this man's life. Whatever life he'll have, of course, since we'll be taking off his arm as soon as we get him to a place where Wilson can start sawing."

Ruth looked up. "Dr. Wilson," she pleaded. "Surely you can see what he's doing wrong."

Wilson shook his head, unable or unwilling to go against his colleague. "I'm just a bone-saw man. I'm not qualified to say."

"Wait just a minute," said the doctor with his hands inside of John's belly. "You're Duncan? The nurse who Doweling's been handing off his patients to?"

The way he said it could not have made Ruth angrier. "He's been *training* me. And you're wasting *time*."

"Well," said the doctor, "if he's been *training* you, and you think you can do a better job…"

"Get out of my way," said Ruth, clenching her teeth, "and I will."

The doctor took his filthy hands out of John's abdomen and handed her the needle.

The stitches were worse than she'd thought—widely spaced and uneven. A recipe for an intestinal tear. "Nurse," she said, trying to stay calm. "Please come over here and assist me."

The nurse looked at the doctors for permission. Ruth eyed Wilson long enough to see him shrug and move out of the way. The nurse knelt opposite Ruth.

"What do you want me to do?" she said, almost sulkily.

"What you would do for a doctor, of course," snapped Ruth. "Find something to clear out this blood, so I can see what I'm doing."

The nurse hesitated, then tore away the hem of her dress. "Will this do?"

"That'll be fine," said Ruth. "Now let's get to work."

She sewed while the two doctors watched, waiting for her to fail. They were waiting for her hands to shake, for her to miss something, on her knees in the dirt, in her tattered uniform, trying to save the man she loved. They were waiting for her to face the futility of his recovery. Most of all, they were waiting for her to finish so they could cut off his right arm, which would end his career.

To his credit, Wilson did check John's breathing and his pulse. The other doctor simply stood, arms folded over his chest as Ruth pulled John's belly together and sewed him closed. She pulled the catgut tight and knotted it off. Only then did the tears come. She brushed them away with her bloody knuckles. She refused to cry in front of these men.

"If you would be so kind," she said to the nurse, who was now watching her in undisguised amazement, "find a stretcher. We need to take him back to what's left of the hospital."

"And tend to his arm," said Wilson.

"And tend to his arm," whispered Ruth.

CHAPTER THIRTY-SEVEN

Elise was third in line as the ambulances returned to the Hotel St. Jacques from the triage stations. As soon as they came through town, she could tell something was wrong. In the distance, a column of smoke rose into the cloudless evening sky.

A soldier was directing traffic, and he pointed Elise to the left to follow the other ambulances.

"I have to get to the St. Jacques," she shouted out her window. "My sister's there."

"Sorry," said the soldier. "Everyone's being rerouted to the hospital in Kortrijk."

Kortrijk was about twenty miles north. A train ran from there, taking the wounded straight to Calais, on the French coast. "But that's an hour away!"

"Sorry," repeated the soldier. He had very little air of authority about him, and Elise considered accelerating the ambulance past him, barreling down to the hotel anyway. But if there was smoke coming from the building, they weren't going to be interested in seeing her or her cargo.

"Just tell me what happened," she said.

"Move along," said the soldier.

"Oh, come on," said Elise. "You can at least do that."

The soldier waved his hands in resignation. "They were bombed, so I hear."

"How badly bombed? A lot of casualties, or just damage to the building?"

"They had to evacuate. That's all I know. Now will you please move along?"

Other ambulances were honking at her. Elise stomped the accelerator, and the ambulance coughed forward.

The drive to Kortrijk was achingly slow, and the road was full of potholes. One of the men in the back claimed to be a lieutenant, and every fifteen minutes, he would pound on the thin metal partition between him and the cab, and demand she go faster.

"I can only go as fast as the girl in front of me," Elise would shout back, which was true. From the lorry ahead of her, the wounded stared at her with dead eyes, crushed together, bathed in the lorry's exhaust as it crawled forward.

"Men are *dying* in here," shouted the lieutenant behind the partition.

"I know," said Elise, under her breath. There wasn't a thing she could do about it.

Eventually he was silent, and she wondered if he, too, had died.

It took all of an hour to get to the hospital at Kortrijk, and by the time Elise got there, she was truly rattled. Ruth had been bombed. John had been bombed. Here she was, with no way to find out what was going on.

She assumed her ambulance squad would be sent to the hotel to ferry the wounded to the hospital in Kortrijk. Without waiting for orders, and without waiting for Hera, she turned and drove along the bumpy road at full speed toward Lozer as night fell.

The wooded road was empty and dark, and except for one or two road signs, she might have lost her way. At last the road widened. She recognized a lorry on its side, off the road, and a broken stone wall, and knew she was no more than five minutes from the hotel. Elise slowed, afraid she would break an axle on the uneven dirt road, and finally came upon the moonlit ruins of the hotel.

She slowed even more, certain there would be wounded lying in the overflow areas in the circular drive in front of the hotel, and there were. What she wasn't prepared for was the shadowy crater in the center of the drive and the slow realization that the men sprawled on the ground weren't wounded at all, but dead.

Elise shut the ambulance off and got out. Beyond the dead men, the hotel was mostly dark. Candles lit the windows on the second floor, but that was all. Crickets chirped and night birds sang as she made her way to the hotel's front door, bombed to a heap of rubble. She smelled wet ash as she scrambled over the remains of the broken portico and strained to hear voices inside. She slid into the remains of the hotel's lobby, now a dusty crumble of plaster and stone, brushed herself off and stood.

"Hello?" she called out. "Hello! Anyone here?"

A nurse looked down at her from the second-floor balcony, just a shadow in the glow of candles.

"Oh, thank God," she said to someone behind her. "The ambulances."

Elise ran up the stairs.

The second floor was packed with men, in beds, lying on stretchers, taking up every square foot of space. Nurses picked their way around the ward. There were doctors, too. Two of them were stitching up a man right on the floor while one nurse stood by holding instruments on a white towel and another knelt with a candle so they could see what they were doing.

In the half light, Elise thought she recognized John, down on his knees.

"John?" she said. But it wasn't him.

"You're looking for Doweling?" said the doctor. "I have bad news for you."

"What do you mean?" said Elise.

"He was shot today," said the doctor. "Strafed by the bastard who bombed us."

"John's *dead*?"

"Not dead," said the doctor. "Not yet anyway."

One of the nurses looked her over. "You're Duncan's sister, aren't you?"

"Yes. Yes. Is she—is she all right?" Elise's heart throbbed in her throat.

"She's not hurt, but you should come and see her."

The nurse led Elise to another set of stairs—what would've been the servants' stairs—and took her up a flight to the third floor. Here it was darker. There were only a dozen or so men, bandaged and dozing. The walking wounded, Elise guessed, and then she saw Ruth.

Her sister sat in a chair beside a bed in the corner. John was in the bed, a drainage tube coming out from underneath the sheet, emptying into a flask on the floor. Elise could see his chest moving with each breath, but his eyes were shut.

Ruth's dress was torn, and her head was bare. Her short

hair stuck out in all directions. Tears had washed tracks in the dirt on her face.

"Oh my God," said Elise. "What happened?"

"Dr. Doweling went out during the attack," said the nurse who had brought her upstairs. "I guess he thought it was over. He was strafed right in the drive. Your sister went after him. I saw the whole thing. The aeroplane flew just over her. He could have mowed her down. She's lucky to be alive." The nurse sat on the closest bed as though the explanation had taken everything out of her.

Elise hurried over to Ruth and grabbed her cold hands. "Are you all right?"

"Yes," whispered Ruth. "I'm so glad you're here."

Elise turned to the nurse. "Can you get me a damp rag for her face—or something?"

"Yes," said the nurse, "of course."

She left, and Elise turned to see John's right arm, or what was left of it, lying on top of the sheet. They had cut it off, just below the elbow. She couldn't say anything. John's whole life had been in that arm.

Elise swallowed hard. "Is he going to be all right?"

"I don't know," said Ruth. "He's running a fever now. I'm trying to keep him cool." There was a basin of dark water beside her, and she squeezed out a cloth to lay over his forehead. "I think we'll know by morning—" she took a shaky breath "—if he'll make it."

CHAPTER THIRTY-EIGHT

To Ruth's dull surprise, people came to check on her and John all night long, even as the hospital was evacuated. Someone brought her a clean uniform dress and a veil for her head. Someone brought morphine for John. Ambulances came, but Elise didn't leave with them. The candles burned down to stubs, and someone brought more.

Nurses came up to retrieve the walking wounded, and gradually the floor cleared of everyone but Ruth and Elise and John. Outside, Ruth could hear the ambulances leaving, lorry by lorry, until the hotel seemed to be empty.

"We'll get him to the hospital in Kortrijk in the morning," Elise said at some dark point in the night. She was sitting on the edge of John's bed, wiping his forehead, his neck and his chest. Ruth checked the drainage flask again. So far, she thought, everything looked all right, but she wasn't optimistic.

"It's an hour to Kortrijk," Elise told her, "but I'll take it slow, so he doesn't get bumped around too much. So, maybe an hour and a half."

Ruth wasn't really listening. "They'll send him to recuperate in England." *If he survives.* She couldn't bear to say that out loud. Even under the dreamy influence of morphine, patients sometimes remembered what people around them said.

"You'll go with him," said Elise, as though it was already a fact.

Ruth nodded slowly. "You'll come, too," she said, in the same tone. To her surprise, Elise hesitated.

"I don't know."

Ruth frowned. "What's the matter with you? Don't you want to get out of this miserable hellhole?"

"I do," said Elise, and now she was looking at the floor. "But I have this pact. You know. With Hera. We watch out for each other. She saved my life when I got shot in the leg. She stood by me. We're friends." She leaned forward on the bed, gripping her hands together between her knees. "We're more than friends."

Did she want to know more, Ruth thought, or was it better for Elise to live with her secrets locked up inside her? Ruth shut her eyes, judging her own strength. She had just enough left to ask the simplest of questions. She opened her eyes. "Are you in love with her, Elise? The way I'm in love with John?"

Elise wound her hands together, tighter, and didn't say anything.

"Does she feel the same way about you?" Ruth asked.

"I don't know," said Elise, to the floor. "No. Yes. Maybe she does. I don't think I'll ever know."

"You won't unless you ask her."

"Oh," said Elise. "I can just imagine that. She'd never speak to me again."

"Well, then," said Ruth, "you'd better come with me to England."

Elise just shook her head. "I can't. I have to stay with her. Whether or not…you know." She didn't say anything for a long while. "How did you know?"

"I think," said Ruth slowly, "in a way, I've always known."

Elise wiped her eyes. She straightened and reached for the damp cloth on John's forehead. "He doesn't feel as warm to me."

Ruth touched his forehead, his throat. She ran her hand across his chest and finally pulled the sheet and blanket away to examine his belly. The incision was ugly and swollen around her stitches, but the fluid in the tube, which she had so carefully placed, was clear.

"This is going to be a miracle," said Ruth, "but if he's still stable by daylight, we can move him." She pulled up the covers and tucked them around his shoulders. John sighed in his sleep, his face slack with morphine.

"What'll you do in London?" said Elise.

"Take care of him," said Ruth.

"You'll go to his house and be his live-in nurse?" said Elise. "What'll his parents think about that?"

Ruth shrugged. "We'll get married. We've talked about it."

"What about medical school?" said Elise.

Ruth caressed his right shoulder as lightly as she could. "His arm. That changes everything."

"Everything?" said Elise. "Are you sure?"

"How can it not change everything?" said Ruth. "He'll never do surgery again."

"But he's still a doctor. They can't take that away from him."

"Surgery was what he loved," said Ruth.

"I had a doctor without a leg when I was in London," said

Elise. "He did just fine. You can't write him off, Ruth. If he was awake, he'd tell you the same thing."

Ruth let her eyes rest on John. Elise was right. She'd given up on his future without even consulting him. "But who'll take care of him if I'm in school? If I'm not his wife?"

"Another nurse," said Elise. "His mother."

Ruth bowed her head. "I can't marry him, can I?"

"Of course you can," said Elise. "You just have to wait. Do you think he'll wait?"

"Yes," said Ruth. "I do."

CHAPTER THIRTY-NINE

In Kortrijk, as Elise had expected, the hospital was jammed. Ambulances were parked three rows deep in front of what had been someone's pristine white mansion, with more coming in from all directions.

Elise drove down the gravel road that led to the hospital's entrance. The road had been widened by something with deep treads—possibly a tank—and her lorry bumped across the rough ground as she pulled up to the front of the building.

In the back with Ruth, John was awake. He claimed not to be in any pain, but he sounded woozy and disoriented to Elise. On the drive to Kortrijk, which had indeed taken an hour and a half, he had woken up three times. The first time, he'd discovered that half of his right arm was gone, and he'd fainted. The second time, Elise had heard him weeping. Now, struggling out from under the morphine, he seemed stoic and quiet, as Ruth spoke to him in soft tones about surgery, medicine and his future.

Elise stopped in front of the hospital, and two bearded old men came down the dirty marble stairs with stretchers. They hurried around the back of the lorry to find one patient and one nurse.

"Be careful with him," she heard Ruth say sternly. "He's a doctor."

As they carried him away, Ruth rushed over to the driver's side window, in tears.

"My God, don't cry," said Elise. "The worst is over, isn't it? He'll be all right."

"I just don't know." Ruth pressed her hands against her eyes, as though forcing the tears back in. She took a shaky breath. "What'll you do now?"

"I've got to find my squad," said Elise. "Take care of him. I'll look for you later."

"I love you," said Ruth, tearful again.

"I love you, too," said Elise.

Ruth turned and hurried up the stairs after John. Elise put the ambulance in gear and headed into the confusion of traffic, trying to find a place to park.

Elise found Tippy under the bonnet of her ambulance, tinkering with her fuel line. Tippy was oily up to her elbows, but threw her arms around Elise the minute she saw her.

"Oh, happy day," she cried. "When you weren't here for roll call, we thought you'd been killed. You should've seen us, crying like idiots. Especially poor Hera." She let go, leaving a smear of oil on Elise's neck. "Matron will be furious to see that you're alive. She smoked all her cigarettes when she thought you were dead."

Elise smiled. She was too tired to laugh. She wasn't sure when she'd last slept. "Where's Matron?"

"I'll take you to her," said Tippy. She pushed the bonnet

down. "We've been bivouacked in the stables. I say, the straw is nice and cozy at night. A decent change from those bloody old bunks in Ypres."

"I'll bet," said Elise, thinking how far her compatriots had come since their featherbeds at home. "Where's everybody else?"

"Running patients to the trains," said Tippy. "The Powers That Be are getting them out of here as fast as they can. They're sending them to Calais, and from Calais to England."

John, thought Elise, would be on a train today, if The Powers That Be could manage it. And Ruth, too.

When Tippy got her to the stables, Matron actually wiped her eyes, then gave Elise's hand a good hard shake. "Welcome back, Duncan," was all she said, and handed Elise an envelope with an official-looking stamp on it.

"What's this?" said Elise.

"Orders," said Matron in her cigarette voice. "They're breaking up the squad now that the Germans are on the run. We've all been reassigned."

Elise tore the envelope open. Inside was a folded piece of paper with Volunteer Aid Detachment written in fancy print across the top. Below was her name and squad number. Below that was the letter that read:

Dear Miss Duncan:
This is to inform you that you will be joining the 120th Ambulance Squad in Calais at once. You will report to Matron Bellingham and be bivouacked at the Hospital St. Martine.

Sincerely,

At the bottom was an illegible scribble, as though whoever had signed the letter had signed a hundred just like it.

"I'm going to Calais," said Elise wonderingly. Calais was across the Belgian border, in France, at the edge of the sea, far, far away from the front lines. She wouldn't have to worry about being bombed or shot at. "I have to be there the day after tomorrow."

"Half of us are going to Calais," said Tippy. "We've decided it's best to drive there in a group." She and Matron exchanged a glance, and Matron clapped a hand to Elise's shoulder.

"Including that idiot, Montraine," said Matron. "Just in case you were wondering."

Elise swallowed. Did *everyone* know? "Thank you, Matron," she managed to say. "Do…do you mind if I tell my sister about my orders? She'll be leaving on the train today."

"Go," said Matron. "And change into a clean uniform. You look like hell."

Between the men marching in formation and the lorries kicking up dust, Elise could see what a grand place the mansion at Kortrijk had been. Broken windows were framed by marble arches. Two grand staircases ran down from the front entrance to the gravel drive, now occupied by ambulances.

Elise felt raindrops and glanced up at dark clouds in the morning sky. Wonderful. In addition to everything else, this dust would soon turn to mud, and she would get soaked. Elise pulled up her collar and dodged between marching troops, hurrying to reach the hospital before the downpour. She got to the gravel drive and had to slow down. Ambulances were pulling in, pulling out, stopped in the middle of everything, blocking traffic. Horns were honking. Women shouted at each other to get out of the way. The rain started to come down harder, and Elise huddled into her inadequate collar, wishing she could remember where she'd left her hat.

An ambulance without doors drove past and splashed her bare shins with wet filth. In a tired fury, she yelled after it. "Watch where you're *going*! You stupid woman! Can't you see that *people* are trying to get *through*?" She turned her attention to the next obstacle—some other careless driver—but to her dismay, the stupid woman hit her squeaky brakes and slid to a stop. Elise saw her feet as she got out of the lorry and wished she hadn't said anything—were those fighting words? She hurried to get behind the next ambulance, and the next, as traffic slowed to a crawl and horns sounded at the stupid woman.

"Hey!" shouted someone. "Get a move on!"

Elise made her way across the crowded drive, taking advantage of the slow-moving chaos. The rain began falling in sheets. In moments she was soaked, through her uniform and into her shoes.

"Wait!" a voice shrieked from behind her. "Wait! *Elise!*"

Elise slowed and turned in the downpour. She stopped between the front end of one banged-up ambulance and the empty end of another. A cloud of choking exhaust rose up from around her ankles. Rain drummed at the gravel, and Hera burst into view, hatless, her hair plastered down around her head, rain—or tears—streaming down her face.

"Elise!" Hera stopped in her tracks, panting. "Oh my God, I thought you were dead."

Does she feel the same way about you? Ruth's question vibrated in Elise's head. The answer seemed plain, right in front of her. "I'm all right," she whispered. "I'm all right." She reached out, expecting Hera to take her hand, but Hera grabbed her and pulled her close. Her arms went around Elise's waist. Their wet faces were close. Then, just for a second, Hera's lips brushed hers.

Elise, shocked by the electricity of the kiss, pressed her face against Hera's neck, eyes squeezed shut, not moving. Hera's arms were tight around her. She sobbed into Elise's ear.

Elise opened her eyes to see the woman in the banged-up ambulance get out and pull the brim of her hat over her eyes. Separating herself from Hera was like pulling apart two magnets.

"Look," the woman said gruffly, "I hate to break up your little love scene, but some of us have work to do."

"Love scene?" Elise said as Hera wiped her eyes.

"It happens." The ambulance driver gave Elise a funny little smile. "It happens all the time. Now get her out of the road. Go on." She grinned and tipped her hat. "Good luck, girls!" she shouted as Elise and Hera stumbled back toward Hera's ambulance in the crowded, muddy drive.

CHAPTER FORTY

Outside John's hospital room, rain came down in a deluge. Inside, water dripped from the ornate ceiling into a rusty washbasin. Ruth, sitting in a gilded chair beside John's bed, eyed the basin and noted that she would have to empty it soon, probably out the broken window.

A dozen other men were in the room as well, some lucky enough to get a bed—officers, she guessed. Others were on stretchers on the floor. Everyone was waiting for the ambulance that would transport them to a train, which would take them to Calais, where they would wait for a ship to England. Every once in a while, a nurse would rush in with two orderlies and a list of names on a clipboard. She would read off a name and find the right man, and the orderlies would take him away. As time passed, Ruth began to wonder if there was any order to the names—they certainly weren't alphabetical. Nor were they taking officers first, or she and John would've been long gone. The list didn't seem to have anything to do with the severity of a wound either. As far as Ruth could tell, the list was completely random.

She pulled up a corner of the blanket covering John's wound. The tender skin was bruised around the stitches, but the doctor who'd examined him when they'd first come in had pronounced him stable and ready to travel. Ruth's impatience had started then. The rushing nurse couldn't hurry fast enough for her, even though she knew it was pointless to be impatient. The war, even with the Germans in retreat, moved at its own pace.

John opened his eyes. "Ruth?" he said thickly.

"I'm here." She leaned over and smoothed his hair away from his forehead. "I'll get you some morphine."

"No," he said. "Not yet. Where are we?"

"In Kortrijk," she said. "We got here this morning. They're getting ready to put you on a train to Calais. You're going home."

"What about you?"

She had told him all of this before, in Elise's ambulance. The morphine made him forgetful. She wondered if he remembered what had happened to his arm. "Of course, I'm coming with you."

He let out a long sigh, as though every word was a Herculean effort. "You'll need orders," he whispered. "You can't just leave."

Morphine dreams, Ruth told herself. "Don't worry. I'll get orders. Are you in any pain?"

He shook his head slowly, and his eyes closed as she stroked the stubble on his cheek. "Don't tell my mother," he murmured.

"About what?" said Ruth.

"About my arm," he whispered. His head rolled to one side, and he was asleep again.

A long time seemed to pass, with just the sound of the rain and the breathing of the men. Ruth emptied the basin out the window and set it back in its wet place on the parquet floor. She was just sitting back down on John's bed when there was a motion at the door. Ruth looked up, expecting to see the rushing nurse, but it was Elise, with Hera right behind her.

The two of them were soaked through. Despite the fact that they both looked like drenched cats, they were smiling. It'd been a long time since Ruth had seen Elise smile—*really* smile—and she wasn't sure she'd ever seen Hera crack a grin.

"Here you are, finally!" said Elise, and they came over to John's bed, avoiding the men on stretchers on the floor.

"We've been all over this wretched building, trying to find you." Hera pushed wet hair out of her eyes. "Is he all right?"

"He's stable," said Ruth. "Hopefully we'll be on a train for Calais soon. I think the hospital there is better equipped."

"Anything would be better than this," said Elise, eyeing the broken windows, the dripping ceiling.

"Aren't you two supposed to be driving patients to the train?" said Ruth. "Maybe you could take us."

"Actually," said Elise, "we just got new orders. That's what we came here to tell you. We've been reassigned. We're leaving for Calais." She smiled the shyest of smiles and reached over to brush Hera's hand. "It looks like we'll all end up in Calais, together."

Ruth blinked in amazement as Hera gave Elise the same smile, like a reflection in a mirror. Ruth didn't know what to say. *Does she feel the same way about you?* The conversation echoed vaguely in her head.

Ruth shook off the vertiginous feeling that her sister was in love. She'd *known*, but never imagined something would ever come of it. It was disorienting, and she looked down at John to steady herself. His eyes were half-open.

"Calais?" he asked.

"Not yet, but soon. Listen," she said as Hera and Elise hovered over him. "Can't you get us to the train before you leave?"

"Only if your name is on the evacuation list," said Hera. She knelt beside the bed. "We can't take anyone who hasn't been checked off."

"How do you get checked off?" Ruth asked.

"Well," said Hera, "first your name has to be on the list. Are you two on the list?"

"John must be," said Ruth. "They wrote down his name when we came in."

"What about you?" said Elise. "Did they take your name?"

"No," said Ruth. "But I'm going with him, list or not."

Elise and Hera exchanged a glance. Ruth could see the doubt in it.

"I hate to tell you this," said Hera, and for a change, she sounded like an adult. "But there are over a thousand men in this hospital, and there's only space for so many litters on the trains. It's standing room only, and they're making one-legged men stand. That's a six-hour trip. Do you think John could do it on his feet?"

Someone else came into the room, but it wasn't the nurse. It was a doctor. He was a slight man, with an oversized white coat, wild white hair and outsized ears. Ruth almost didn't recognize him, and then she did. She stood up in disbelief.

"Dr. Mouse?" she said. "I mean, Dr. Emmanuel!"

"Sister Duncan," said The Mouse. He came over and shook her hand. No embrace. He didn't even seem surprised to see her. "I heard you were at the St. Jacques when it was bombed."

"I was," said Ruth. "I was…lucky." She motioned at Elise and Hera. "This is my sister, Elise, and her…friend. They're ambulance drivers."

"True heroines," said The Mouse, and he shook their hands

gravely. His eyes traveled to John, half-asleep under the covers. "Who's this?"

"My fiancé," said Ruth. "John Doweling."

The Mouse nodded. "I remember. The sawbones up at Number Three who should've been doing abdominals with us." He drew the covers back and eyed John's belly, his arm. "I see," he said quietly.

"He was shot," said Ruth. "He's going home."

"And what about you?" said The Mouse.

"I'm going with him, of course."

The Mouse sat down on the corner of the bed. He was so light, the mattress barely moved. He reached into a pocket in his white coat and pulled out an envelope. "This is for you," he said, and handed the envelope to Ruth.

She opened it slowly, knowing what it was. Her orders.

The letter inside was short and to the point. Numbly, she read it aloud.

Duncan, R.: reassigned to the Mobile Unit of Hospital Number Four, following the infantry as it moves east toward the Hindenburg line. This assignment is effective immediately. Report to Matron Heflin at Medical Headquarters in Kortrijk.

"The Hindenburg line?" said Elise. "But that's miles from here."

Ruth sat heavily on the edge of the bed, ready to tear the orders to pieces. "I can't leave John."

"You can," said The Mouse, "and you will. I wanted to talk to you before you got underway."

"I'm not going anywhere but England," said Ruth breathlessly, and Elise put a hand on her shoulder. "I just need to go and talk to this—this Matron Heflin. I have to explain what's going on."

"I understand," said The Mouse, "but listen for a moment. The mobile unit you've been assigned to—Flying Squads, we're calling them—was supposed to be headed up by Dr. Doweling."

Ruth looked at John, eyes open, still hazy from the morphine, but following the conversation.

"Since he has been so grievously wounded," said The Mouse, "we've tried to find a physician to replace him. We did not succeed."

He was being so careful with his words, Ruth thought, and wondered why. Surely there was an adequate doctor somewhere. There was always Fellowes, the Drinker, for God's sake.

"I—" said The Mouse "—we, that is, are aware of your aspirations in the medical field. We know that you've worked on your own in the operating theater, against convention, and frankly, against orders."

John put his single good hand in Ruth's.

"Since we have no doctor to head up this Flying Squad," said The Mouse, "we've had to look to the next most qualified individual. And that happens to be you."

Ruth stared at him. Was this a joke? "You want me to take John's place?"

"More or less," said The Mouse. "Under Doweling, this particular squad would have specialized in abdominal wounds. With you in charge, it'll be strictly amputations."

Ruth swallowed hard. She couldn't bring herself to say anything.

"This is an honor," said The Mouse. "You could consider it a field promotion."

"It's not something they'd give out lightly," said John in a hoarse voice.

"Not at all," said The Mouse. "In fact, there are people at Medical Headquarters who've put up quite a fight for you to have this position."

"There are?" All Ruth could think of were the generals who'd thrown her out of the operating theater.

"Let's just say, there's at least one general on your side, plus several matrons of nurses. Dr. Doweling also advocated for you, of course, whenever he had the chance." The Mouse let his expression soften into a smile and nodded at John. "I know him well enough to be sure that his opinions about your skills were on the mark."

Ruth bit her lip hard. Tears rolled down her cheeks.

"Listen now," said The Mouse. "This is no time for despair. The Germans are on the run, and we must be out there, supporting the men. You've been here long enough to understand that."

"Yes, Doctor," whispered Ruth.

"Then I suggest that you pack your things and report to your matron right away. Honor your fiancé. Do what needs to be done when the war needs you more than ever."

He patted her hand, got up from the bed and walked out the door. As soon as he was gone, the rushing nurse with the clipboard and her orderlies were back. She came over to where Ruth, Elise and Hera were surrounding John.

"Captain John Doweling?" she said, and the orderlies moved forward. One of them held a stretcher, rolled up and balanced over his shoulder.

"Yes," said John huskily.

The nurse made a quick check on a piece of paper. "You're on your way to Calais, sir," she said. "Say your goodbyes, please. We have no time to waste."

John squeezed Ruth's hand with enough strength to make her bones ache, not just in her hand but through her entire body. She bent to kiss his lips, his cheeks, his forehead.

"You'll be all right," she said as the orderlies unfurled the stretcher.

"I know," he whispered. "I love you."

"I love you," she whispered back, and edged away as the orderlies pressed in.

CHAPTER FORTY-ONE

Ruth held Elise's hand as they followed the nurse and the orderlies down the mansion's sweeping staircase to the elegant front doors. Hera came behind, close on Elise's heels as though she was afraid to lose sight of her in the crowd of nurses, limping patients and officers in wet wool coats, all hurrying in different directions.

Outside, in the rain, John's ambulance waited for him, its sides streaming with water, up to its wheel rims in mud. The orderlies put him in carefully while the rushing nurse watched, still for a moment, shielding her eyes from the rain with one hand, hunched over her clipboard to keep it from getting wet.

"That's it, then," said the nurse.

The ambulance driver, a woman Ruth didn't recognize, shut the back gate of the lorry and got in the front seat. The engine started with a roar, and without any more ceremony than that, John was gone, off to Calais, and from there, home. The next ambulance pulled in, and Ruth, Elise and Hera stood aside as more men with stretchers came out the doors and into the rain.

Elise squeezed Ruth's hand as they watched John's ambulance disappear into the gray distance. "You can't worry about him," she said. "As soon as we get to Calais, I'll check on him. I'll make sure he's getting the best care."

"I know you will," said Ruth.

Hera came forward so she was standing next to Elise, half in the rain, half out. She was already so soaked, Ruth noted, rather remotely, that it almost didn't matter she was going to get drenched again.

"We should go," Hera said to Elise, with urgency in her voice. "We have to pack and get ready. The squad is supposed to leave by three, and it's already two."

Ruth wondered how it'd gotten so late. Hadn't she and John and Elise arrived just a few hours ago?

Ruth looked down at the crumple of paper, her orders, still in her hand. "I have to find my unit."

"The mobile units?" said Hera. "I can show you where they are. Follow me."

She led them along the side of the mansion, under the sliver of roof, to where the massive building gave way to a decimated formal garden. Hedges and rosebushes had been mowed down. Flower beds showed muddy tracks. In the middle of the garden were more than twenty ambulances, lined up in the mud, loaded down, not with patients, but with folded cots and crates of medical supplies. Canvas and tent poles hung out the backs, darkening in the rain. Orderlies were loading boxes, while a woman in a slicker seemed to be giving directions. A motorcycle with a red cross painted on its sidecar was parked at the head of the line of ambulances, as though ready to lead them all into the bedlam of the front. Ruth's heart pounded. She'd had medical guidance from The Mouse, or from John, from the beginning of her time in Belgium. Now she would be the one in charge, deciding whose arm or leg would come off, with no one to answer to but herself. She thought of Fellowes, sawing limbs with alcoholic abandon. She thought of all the men she'd worked on at Hospital Four, thought of John lying on the ground, bleeding, outside the St. Jacques.

She had been calm. She had been focused.

She made herself take a deep breath.

"That must be the matron," said Elise, pointing to the woman in the slicker. She gripped Ruth's hand. "Are you ready?"

Ruth nodded.

"Then this is where we have to say goodbye," said Elise. She wrapped her wet arms around Ruth's neck and kissed her hard on the cheek. Ruth held her tight for a long moment and then let go. "Take care of yourself," said Elise. "Write to me in Calais. Let me know where you are, and I'll tell you everything I can about John."

"I will," said Ruth. She was ready to step out of the shelter of the building and into the downpour, when Hera caught her hand and shook it with tremendous energy.

"Good luck, Dr. Duncan," she said. "Godspeed."

The two of them ran off into the rain. Ruth took a breath through her teeth, and walked toward the ambulances. As she got closer, she could see that, under her slicker, the matron, Heflin, was dressed entirely in a man's motorcycle leathers, from her jacket to her trousers. She was a tall woman with thick eyebrows, and when she saw Ruth sloshing through the garden mud, her eyebrows furrowed.

"You must be Sister Duncan," said Heflin.

"I am," said Ruth. "Do you need to see my orders?"

Heflin took the crumple of wet paper without even glancing at it. "Don't you have any luggage?" she said. "Where's your coat?"

"Everything I had was at the Hotel St. Jacques," said Ruth. "It was all burned in the fire."

"I see," said Heflin. "They say you were the one who stood in front of the aeroplane and frightened the pilot away."

"I don't know if that's how I'd put it." Ruth wiped water from her face. "But yes, that was me."

"Well," said Heflin, "I hope you saved some courage for this assignment. You'll need it. Come with me." She took Ruth's arm. "We'll find you a blanket and get you to your Flying Squad."

Heflin led her down the line of ambulances until they got to the last three vehicles. Two older men, two nurses and a bewildered-looking VAD girl got out and stood at attention in the rain. Ruth wanted to tell them to please get back inside, but Heflin snapped out orders before she could say anything.

"This is Sister Duncan, your lead medic," she said, and pointed at one of the men, burly, his red beard streaked with gray. "Get her a blanket."

"Yes, Matron," replied the man, and went to the back of an ambulance.

"There's no time for introductions," Heflin said to Ruth, "but you'll get to know each other soon enough."

"It's all right," said Ruth. "I know some of them." She recognized Greta Porter, who had been one of the night nurses in Ypres. Greta had a reputation for efficiency. One of the nurses was Davidson, who had been at the St. Jacques. The VAD girl was dressed in a brand-new ambulance driver's uniform and had a name tag—Witcover. The two men were too old to fight, and she guessed they would be the orderlies. The man with the red beard brought her a blanket and draped it over her shoulders.

"There you are, Sister."

"Thank you," said Ruth. "Mr....?"

"MacBride," said the man, smiling with missing teeth. "Hugh MacBride, at your service."

"Follow the rest of the ambulances," said Heflin. "Your squad will move to wherever the fighting is. Word is, the front is exceedingly mobile right now, and very volatile."

MacBride took Ruth's elbow. "Come, Sister," he said. "You'll ride with me."

CHAPTER FORTY-TWO

September 1918

Elise's orders took her to France, to the abbey of St. Martine, in a town of the same name, twenty miles northeast of the port of Calais.

The ambulance convoys were different so far from the front. For one thing, she wasn't picking up patients fresh from triage. Now the men had spent at least a week in the abbey's convalescent hospital. There was no more screaming—just quiet acceptance of circumstances. Men without a leg or an arm, or with even worse injuries, sat in the rear of the lorry, enduring miles of rutted roads on the way to Calais, talking quietly, smoking cigarettes, drinking liquor if they had it.

The routine was so safe, it soon became boring. There was no blast of the matron's whistle at midnight, no shells to dodge. They were all tucked into their sleeping bags by ten o'clock, and mealtimes were regular. Even the food improved. The only thing that didn't change was the quality of their quarters: the stables, where they ate and slept.

During tea one afternoon, Hera started complaining about the lice, and said she was thinking about cutting her hair short, like Ruth's.

"But your hair is so beautiful," said Elise. Not that they saw much of each other's hair. Mostly they kept it tightly braided and bound up so as not to get it tangled in the engines or grabbed by the wounded. A girl driver with long hair swinging around was just asking for trouble.

"It'll grow back," said Hera. "I'm just tired of trying to comb out the damned lice. It's impossible." She touched the bun of hair at the back of her head. It wasn't exactly tidy, and it was easy to see where its length was tangled into knots. "I'm filthy," said Hera. "Bathing with a rag and a pan of water just isn't enough."

The conversation around them turned to something else, and Elise sidled over to her.

"What if I told you I knew where you could get a bath in a tub?"

"I'd say you were a liar," said Hera unhappily. "Where would we possibly find one in this hole?"

"The abbey," said Elise. "There's a wing reserved for the nurses and doctors. I'll bet they have a full bath."

Hera looked at her with a doubtful sort of respect. "We'll have to sneak in and find out."

"Are you brave enough to do that?"

"I'm desperate," said Hera. "I'm brave enough to do anything."

"Get a towel," said Elise, "and some soap."

The two of them walked through the overgrown gardens behind the abbey and found the servants' entrance. Now it was the door for the surgery, where the wheelbarrows of arms and legs went, and where the bodies were stored for burial.

"I'll never feel clean after this," said Hera with a shudder. Dead men were stacked like cordwood, wrapped in sheets, ready for their coffins. Elise and Hera went in the door and then immediately to the right, where a narrow stairway led upward from floor to floor. They passed several doors before Hera made Elise stop.

"Do you know where we're going?" she asked, out of breath.

"No—I'm just guessing."

"Well," said Hera, "why don't we just find the servants' quarters? There's bound to be a bath up there."

"What about the servants?" said Elise. "Don't you think they'll mind?"

"Dear Elise," Hera said with a laugh. "Everyone's staff is off to war in one way or another. There isn't a servant for miles. My mother complains about it all the time in her letters."

"Okay," said Elise, "but where're the servants' quarters?"

"Upstairs," said Hera. "Follow me."

When they got to the top, they were both breathing hard, and to Elise's ears, loudly. But the door to the servants' quarters was wide-open. The floors were dusty and untracked.

"It's possible," whispered Hera, "that no one's been up here since 1914."

"Then why are you whispering?"

"I don't know." She tucked her towel under her arm. "Let's find the bath."

They found the butler's room with a closet full of fancy jackets, a maid's room with hardly anything at all, and finally the bathroom, small and neatly tiled, with, to their delight, a huge claw-foot tub.

"Lock the door," said Elise. "Let's see if we can get any hot water." She leaned over the tub and turned on the spigot. At first there were only hollow-sounding groans. Then the water came, cold and rusty.

Hera regarded the water. "This is how low I've sunk," she said. "I would wash with that."

Elise held her hand under the flow. "I think it's getting warmer."

"And clearer?" Hera knelt beside the tub and clasped her hands. "Oh, please, God, let us have some hot water. Please, God, let us wash this filth from our bodies."

"Keep praying," said Elise. "It's almost hot."

"Dear God," said Hera, "I swear I'll become a nun if You'll give me a tub of hot water."

"A nun?" said Elise. "Aren't you tired of bad food and a hard bed?"

"Even nuns get to wash," said Hera. "Besides, we're in an abbey. It's an appropriate promise to make."

The pipes moaned, and hot water came out in a rush. Elise pulled her hand back with a yelp. "Your prayers are answered!" She adjusted the cold water and turned to see Hera stripping off her ambulance uniform.

"Put in the plug!" said Hera, throwing her clothes on the floor. "We'll wash each other's hair! The lice will *die*!"

"Quiet down," said Elise, but she couldn't help but laugh. "You'll have every soldier boy in the place up here."

"Let them come," cried Hera, now completely naked. "I'm a nun!" She pulled the pins out of her hair, letting it uncoil into a tangled braid that reached her waist. She grinned, happier than Elise had ever seen her.

Hera put one foot into the quarter-filled tub and then the other. She settled her bottom into the hot water with a sigh of relief, unbraided her hair and leaned back. Her small breasts were already puckering from the heat. A peculiar thrill went through Elise's body. It seemed to start in her stomach, as if she'd just crested a steep hill and was speeding weightlessly down the other side. Hera ducked her head under the running water and sat up in the tub, her hair trailing around her face and body.

"Help me wash my hair, will you?" said Hera. "Where's the damned soap? I've been saving it for something like this."

Elise knelt by the tub, found the soap and, unable to say anything, put her hands in the water, rubbing the soap into a froth. Hera leaned over the edge of the tub and presented her head. Elise sank her fingers into wet hair, scrubbing, strong, but not too rough, while Hera picked up the bulk of her hair and pushed it to the top of her head. Together they spread the soap around, fingers dashing past each other, until her hair was one big frothy mass.

"When I was a civilian," said Hera from under the soap, "I had the best lady's maid. Her name was Charlotte, and she loved doing up my hair. Once I threatened to cut it, and I thought she was going to cry."

"I'd cry, too," said Elise, with feeling.

Hera laughed and put a hand over her mouth to shush herself. She spit out suds and scrubbed her face with both hands until her face was as soapy as her hair. "Hand me my washcloth—it's there with my towel. I want to get the grime off the rest of me."

Elise found the washcloth and gave it to her. Hera snatched it away with a soapy grin. She splashed water on her face and looked up again.

"You still have suds on your chin," Elise informed her. "Like a beard."

"Do I?" said Hera, and mischief sparkled in her eyes. "Why don't you get in here and wash it off for me? There's plenty of room." She slid down into the tub until she was entirely submerged, stretched out along the bottom, then sat up with an explosive breath, splashing water on the floor, on Elise. "Come on," she said, and reached for the top button on Elise's jacket with dripping hands. "I want to wash your hair for you. When was the last time you washed your hair?"

Elise looked down at her jacket, watching Hera's nimble fingers. "I don't know."

Her jacket was open now, showing her dirty blouse underneath. Hera's fingers traveled to Elise's blouse, to the buttons there. She started to open them. Elise steadied herself, holding on to the edge of the tub. Her stomach felt exactly like she was driving downhill too fast. She shut her eyes to see if there was a sensation of danger, but there was none. Only her heart pounding.

She opened her eyes to find Hera looking into her face. Her blouse was open now, narrowly, from her neck to her navel. Hera rested her hands on Elise's. Their warmth was overwhelming. All Elise could think about was that brush of a kiss in the rain. All she wanted was to do it once more. For a long moment, the only sound was water dripping onto the floor. Then Hera leaned over and touched Elise's lips with hers, ever so lightly, warmly. To Elise it was like kissing a flame.

Hera drew back slightly, like a mermaid in a pool. "Is this something you want to do, Elise?" she whispered.

"Yes," Elise whispered back.

Hera moved her wet hands up to Elise's shoulders and pushed away the jacket and blouse. Elise's bare breasts were cold and her nipples rigid. Hera leaned forward again and kissed Elise's throat. Elise kissed Hera's ear, her soapy hair, the side of her neck. Hera let out a breathy laugh, seized Elise's face in her hands and kissed her on the mouth, longer this time, her lips rich and tender.

"Get in here," she said.

Elise pulled off her muddy shoes and struggled out of her

skirt. She got to her feet at the edge of the tub, abruptly self-conscious. Skeins of filth covered her legs and arms. She was more embarrassed by how dirty she was than her nakedness.

"Get in here," Hera said again, softly, and moved to make room. "I'll wash you clean."

Elise put a foot in. The water was so hot. She sank like a lead weight into the heat of the bath, onto her knees, covered with goose bumps.

"Are you cold?" murmured Hera.

"No." Elise could hardly speak. "I mean, yes."

Hera got to her knees, too, waist deep. The water in the tub sloshed back and forth. She put her arms around Elise's shoulders, holding her tighter and tighter, until they were pressed skin to skin, breast to breast, belly to belly, breathing into each other's ears. Elise's hands moved hesitantly up Hera's spine to her shoulder blades. Everything was so familiar. In her stomach, the rushing down a hill feeling turned into the amazing impression that she'd done this before. She was trying to imagine where or when that could possibly have been, when Hera's fingers began traveling down Elise's spine.

"I want to touch every inch of you," Hera whispered in her ear.

"Me too," Elise whispered, wet palms still against Hera's shoulders. "But I don't know where to start."

"Then do what I do," Hera said, her voice husky. "Just follow me."

Her hands floated to Elise's hips, resting there, waiting for Elise to do the same. Hera's back was slick with soap, trailing with twists of hair. Elise followed the twists downward, past the intimate curve of Hera's waist, past the surface of the water, until her fingers touched the velvet stretch of skin over her hip bone. Elise swallowed hard and stopped, waiting for direction. The impression of familiarity had vanished, replaced by a certain heat. From her navel down, everything was heat, raising the temperature of the water in the tub, almost boiling where her belly pressed against Hera's.

"Can you feel that?" Elise whispered. "How hot the water is?"

Hera's teeth grazed Elise's ear. She nipped the lobe, and Elise, forgetting she was supposed to do the same thing, gasped. Her hands, all on their own, left Hera's hips and caught Hera's breasts, still pressing against her own.

Hera's hands came up to caress Elise's knuckles. Her fingertips moved with excruciating slowness to Elise's breasts, tracing invisible lines up, down and around. The tracery was like icy lace, or trails of fire, Elise couldn't decide which, but she had to watch what Hera's hands were doing so she could do it herself. There was space between them now, just a few inches of air, and Elise breathed into it, dizzy. She put her palms against the warm swell of Hera's chest, cupping, touching and finally letting her thumbs brush Hera's pink nipples. Hera let out a breath, arched her back and quivered in the hot water, and now Elise knew she could do no wrong thing. She leaned into Hera's neck, and kissed her, tasting skin, soap, strands of hair. She could taste Hera's desire, as well as the essence of every man who'd been in this spot before. She could taste how they'd been tested, evaluated, dismissed, because this spot, this skin, this body, this woman, had been waiting for Elise and only Elise.

Hera collapsed backward in the tub with a moan, pressing herself against the white enamel. Elise fell between her knees, her belly brushing the roughness between Hera's thighs. She braced herself against the bottom of the tub, and her own roughness touched Hera's. Elise's heart expanded to fill her entire chest. She could hardly hold herself up, but to let go would be to drown, too soon.

"My girl," breathed Hera, sounding amazed, "you've done this before?"

"Never," whispered Elise.

"Not even with yourself?"

"What?" said Elise.

"Never mind." Hera pulled her closer in the water until their bodies were pressed together again. "Do you trust me?" Hera whispered.

Elise nodded into her shoulder.

"Then close your eyes," Hera murmured in her ear.

Elise obeyed, and Hera's hand moved, slow and caressing, gentle but firm, past her breasts, her belly, until her fingers touched the curly edge of Elise's own roughness. Fingertips rested there a moment, and Elise felt Hera's heart pounding as hard as her own.

"Don't be afraid." Hera kissed Elise's ear. "Just let it happen. It's the most sensational thing."

"What is it?"

"It hasn't got a name," said Hera, and she moved her fingers into the soft, pliable part of Elise's body that Elise had never explored. All at once, something drove through her, a pure, fiery spike, igniting every nerve. The fingers, knowledgeable and strong, made their way through labyrinthine folds, pausing for a sensation here, pressing for an entirely different feeling there, but always moving. Elise clenched her thighs tight around Hera's hand, panting against Hera's neck. She felt like she would fly apart, like a shell in the night sky. Burning pulses matched her pounding heart, and she exploded, arching in the tub, and exploded again. Breathless and reeling in the water, she thought it was over, when, with a merciless pinch of her exquisite fingers, Hera had her squirming, surging, letting out terrible, helpless cries every time the fire shot through her.

Finally, Hera took her hand away, and Elise collapsed against her, amazed, bewildered.

"Oh," said Elise breathlessly. "Oh."

Hera stroked her back and spoke into her hair. "You're a wild little thing."

Elise swallowed. "What *is* that? Where did you find out about *that*?"

"Would you think I was sinful if I told you I discovered it for myself? In my bed, late at night?"

Elise pulled away, just a little, to see if she was joking, but her smile was a serious one.

"It helped me sleep," said Hera, almost apologetically.

Elise quivered in the bathwater, in the throes of aftershocks. "Do you—" she said hesitantly. "Do you want me to do *that* to you?"

"Oh, yes," whispered Hera, and she slid into Elise's arms. "I want you to do everything."

CHAPTER FORTY-THREE

The village of Mecklin was a ruin of small buildings. Hardly two stones sat on top of each other. They were two and a half miles from the front. There was a well in the square. There was no phone, no electricity, no X-ray, and they might have to operate by candlelight, but at least they had water.

To Ruth's relief, the wounded came to Mecklin in a trickle, not a flood. She had time to repair limbs instead of wholesale cutting them off. The pace of things might change, she warned herself as she mixed plaster for a cast, but between her, Porter and Davidson, the operating theater was efficient and smooth, as though they'd been working together for years. There was none of the jockeying for position as among the men, she noticed. For example, when Porter questioned something, there was no running off, tight-lipped, to follow orders. She simply asked, and listened to the answer.

Ruth missed John to the point of desolation, though, and

she wrote imaginary letters to him. In her mind, while she tended the wounded, she described the scenery, the surgery, her team, how making the decisions about whose leg would come off—or not—was an enormous burden. Often she wished he was there to tell her what to do, a feeling she did her best to shake off.

Early in the first week, she got a quick, scrawled note from Elise.

Dear Ruth,

Have seen John in Calais. He is recovering well, though I can tell he's very upset about the arm. They'll put him on a ship to England tomorrow, and he's been told he'll be in a convalescence hospital in London. I've written to his parents to let them know what happened, since he can only scribble with his left hand. He sends his love to you. I am well, stationed at an abbey in St. Martine, driving fifty miles a day to Calais and back. The food is much better here. Hope you are weathering the storm. We hear the Germans are retreating, but otherwise, awful things about the front.

Your loving sister

As soon as she could, Ruth sat down on her cot to write to John.

My Dearest John,

Elise says you've been evacuated to England by now, and I hope that you've seen your parents. I'm so sorry I haven't written to you sooner, and that this letter is so short, but we are up to our ears in wounded coming from the Hindenburg line. In a way, being here is a lot like being in Ypres. The guns are very close, and it is difficult to sleep at night.

Ruth stopped. She couldn't tell him about her experience sawing off arms and legs, or how Greta Porter had admired her speed one afternoon. She couldn't have him thinking that perhaps she had encouraged Wilson to take off his arm. There had been no choice about that, and she had stood by, tears running down her cheeks, while Wilson made his razor-quick cuts, and John's arm joined the others in the wheelbarrows. Ruth wiped her eyes at the memory and started writing again.

My dearest, I miss you so much. They say the war is nearly over, and if that's so, I'll be with you as soon as I possibly can. In the meantime, I'm covering this inadequate letter with kisses for you. I'll write again soon.

All my love,
Ruth

She kissed the paper, kissed the envelope and sealed it. She addressed it to Captain John Doweling, London. The letter would find him wherever he was. It would go out with the post when the ambulances came in from Kortrijk tonight to pick up the wounded, and be delivered in a timely fashion. Such were the ways of the British Postal System.

There was a motion at the entrance of the tent, and Greta Porter came in. "Oh, you're writing," she said. "I'm sorry to interrupt, but it's time for rounds."

MacBride proved himself invaluable, both in the ambulance and among the men. When he'd finished his runs, he would bluster into the tented ward and lighten the mood of the wounded soldiers with tales about the Bosch running away in the face of Allied forces.

"Laddies, you should'a seen 'em," he would say. "Like deer,

they were, leapin' and soarin' from one trench to the next. You couldn't see naught but their tails between their legs!"

Though Ruth doubted that MacBride had actually witnessed anything of the kind, it cheered the men, and he often had the entire ward laughing at his antics as he acted out the retreating Germans. He was a one-man show, and the troops, no matter what shape they were in, appreciated him.

Once, after a particularly quiet night, he went out scavenging in Mecklin with Witcover, and brought in a working gramophone with an armload of records. Most of the music was waltzes, but there were also two records of American jazz, and these were played ceaselessly. When one side was done, any man who could would get up and turn the record over. The music never got old for the patients because they were evacuated every afternoon when the ambulances came from Kortrijk with food and medicine. With the ward empty, Ruth, Davidson, Porter and the two orderlies would hastily clean and remake the beds while Witcover prepared dinner. Dinner was often rushed as well, but occasionally they all got to sit down together.

On one of those nights, Ruth said, "I think we're finally down to a routine here."

Witcover nodded, mouth full. She had become less shy in the past few days. Probably driving down to the front had scared the timidity out of her. Perhaps she had hardened, as Davidson thought she should.

"I'm not so afraid of getting lost in the dark anymore," said Witcover.

"She just follows me," said MacBride around a slice of mutton. His cigar was perched on the edge of the table, still smoking. "I always know where I'm going."

"I don't know how you do it," said Porter, who was always

kind and good-natured toward Witcover, as if trying to offset Davidson's impatience. "All those wounded men."

"They're so brave," said Witcover with obvious admiration, "they hardly make a sound."

"It's because you're a girl," said MacBride, "and a pretty one at that. They'd never show a shred of weakness in your lorry, no matter how they felt."

Witcover blushed at this and focused on her plate. Ruth looked at Porter, who grinned. Was it possible that MacBride was sweet on this little slip of a thing, less than half his age? Ruth had to push a forkful of mutton into her mouth to keep herself from smiling.

Porter, however, laughed. "How do they behave in your lorry, MacBride?"

"Now," said MacBride, "it's no joking matter. My men scream at me to hurry the 'ell up and get them to the bloody 'ospital, if you'll excuse my language, ladies. None of them are coy about it." He took a puff on his cigar to keep it from dying. "Sometimes I feel like a bloody taxi driver."

Everyone laughed, especially Witcover, who seemed relieved to talk about life in the cab of the ambulance. "I drove an ambulance for the convalescent soldiers in London," she said. "I definitely felt like a taxi driver there."

"What made you come out here?" Ruth asked.

"The adventure, I suppose." Witcover pushed her plate away. "I thought I could do more for the war effort. All I was doing was ferrying fellows from place to place. It was important enough, but there were plenty of others who could've done it. Not everyone can drive to the front and back. So I volunteered." She blushed again. "My mum's most proud of me."

Outside, under the constant, distant noise of artillery, came the unmistakable roar of a motorcycle. It pulled into the courtyard of their little collection of tents, and the engine stopped.

"Heflin," said MacBride abruptly, cocking his head.

"But she's not due for days," said Ruth.

"I'll bet good money we're about to pull up stakes," said MacBride. "Some of the boys in the ambulance were talking about the lines moving forward again." He slapped his fist into his palm. "We've got them on the run now."

Ruth stood up and pulled the tent flap aside. Sure enough, Heflin was there, stripping off her gloves and goggles.

"Duncan!" she said to Ruth. "Good. I'm here to tell you that you'll be moving forward tomorrow, about five miles." She gave Ruth a grin. "That means no sleep for you, my dear."

"None of us sleep anyhow," said Ruth. She would have gone into the tent and made the announcement, but Davidson, Porter, MacBride and Witcover were already outside, wiping their hands, ready to wade right in.

By midnight, every tent in their little Mecklin hospital had come down and was stowed in one of the ambulances. By the light of lanterns, Ruth, Porter and Davidson took apart the operating theater and packed all the surgical equipment in as sterile a condition as they could, into another lorry. Their personal effects went into the third—cots, blankets and pillows, extra clothing and suitcases—everything down to MacBride's galoshes. By five in the morning they were ready to move out, Ruth and MacBride in the lead ambulance, Porter and Stephano, the Italian orderly, following, and Witcover and Davidson bringing up the rear. Ruth felt sorry for Witcover, driving Davidson around the devastated countryside, no doubt having to listen to a never-ending critique of her driving, her character in general and the Germans in particular.

Before leaving the hospital site, Witcover had made a pot of strong tea and distributed it among six cups. Ruth sipped hers and held MacBride's for him as he steered around shell holes in the road. They were following the troops, just like the last time. There were columns of marching men and a scattering of lorries hauling artillery. Everything was moving at the pace of a quick-march, which wasn't very fast at all. Ruth thought it would take hours to make the five miles to the new front, hours more to set up, and then hours of surgeries on the wounded who were probably waiting for them even now.

MacBride seemed to be having the same thoughts. "You should sleep while you can," he said. "We'll be at work as soon as they put us down somewhere."

"Who'll hold your tea if I go to sleep?" said Ruth. "Who'll keep you awake with clever conversation?"

"Conversation about what?" said MacBride and he nodded at the bleak scenery. The pretty wooded hills had been stripped of their trees. Any surviving plants had been blackened and shriveled by gas. Villages had been bombed flat. Burnt-out lorries with cockeyed guns littered the landscape, most with the Bosch cross. There was even a burnt-out ambulance, lying on its side, the bodies of men spilling out as though they had tried to get away and then been shot. It made Ruth's ordinarily iron stomach turn to think of what had been done to those men, German or not.

MacBride followed her gaze as they crept past the tableau of havoc. "Ah," he said, when he saw the ambulance on its side. "It's a bloody barbaric war. Not like the old days when men on both sides had some honor in them."

Ruth let out her breath, queasy. "Where do you think the honor went? I mean, it couldn't have just disappeared."

"Oh," said MacBride, "I think it disappeared in the blink of an eye. Men are brutes when you get right down to it. Take that bloke who invented the machine gun. Was he thinking about honor?"

"Probably not," said Ruth.

"I don't even know if he was a good old Englishman or a bloody Bosch," said MacBride, "but I'm betting on the Bosch. They've made war into a machine that grinds up everything in the way." He nodded at the devastated land around them. "In the old days, there were at least civilians. You didn't go about killing off all the peasants just because they were in the way. Who would plant the crops for the victors? Now even the ground is ruined. It doesn't make any sense. Not to me anyway."

CHAPTER FORTY-FOUR

Having made love with Hera made Elise forget about practically everything else. It made her forget how scratchy the straw was in the stable where she slept. It made her forget to grumble about the food. But mostly having made love with Hera made her forget to be careful.

The new matron, Bellingham, was a doddering, old-fashioned creature, so unlike the matron in Ypres as to be a completely different breed of human being. She walked with a cane and slept in the abbey, with the doctors and nurses. There were days when she didn't show up in the mornings and the squad members had to roust themselves. This made them late for breakfast and the subsequent runs to Calais. When Tippy and Victoria complained about this, Bellingham wept profoundly about the war, the wounded and her late husband—who had died before the war even started—but didn't seem to register the resentment of her squad. Tippy and Victoria reported this back to the rest in disgust, and everyone was filled with righteous indignation, except for Hera and Elise, who could hardly keep from smiling. Sleeping late in straw, in a bed or on rocky ground—nothing mattered to them except being close to each other.

They kept the bathtub a secret for about two weeks, but couldn't hide how incandescently clean they were compared to everyone else.

Finally, just before dinner one night, Tippy said to Elise, "You've been scrubbing down somewhere." The two of them were under the bonnet of Tippy's habitually troublesome ambulance, Elise wiping down spark plugs, Tippy working on the fuel line, which she had finally learned to fix on her own. "Don't think we haven't noticed. Back in Ypres, you were the greasy one. Now even your fingernails are clean."

Elise didn't know what to say. "'The greasy one?' That's a nice way to talk about the girl who fixes your lorry."

"I meant it in the nicest possible way," said Tippy. "God knows, we couldn't have gotten to the front without you—and *thank* you very much for that—but now you have to confess. Where are you washing? Not in the horse trough out back of the stables."

"No," said Elise, slowly. "I have to tell you, though, I'm sworn to secrecy."

"Secrecy?" said Tippy. She picked up a wrench from the ambulance's toolbox and shook it threateningly. Her hands were so oily that the tool slipped in her hand. "Look at me, Elise. Do I look clean to you?"

Elise glanced up from the spark plug, wide-eyed at Tippy's tone. Tippy was streaked with oil, down her cheek and up to her elbows. She was actually angry.

"Do you know," said Tippy, "that I have engine grease on my body where no woman should *ever* have engine grease?" She took a breath, and Elise thought she might burst into tears. "This war is nearly over," said Tippy. "I want to go home to my husband as clean as I can be. I'm not a mechanic. I've never wanted to *be* a mechanic." She shook the wrench again. "Tell me where you're bathing, Elise, before I have to beat it out of you."

Elise blinked. A feeling of unfairness settled over her. Didn't she and Hera deserve some privacy now and then? But, on the other hand, Tippy had desperation in her eyes. And on the other hand—if there was another hand—wasn't it a luxury the two of them could share?

"All right," said Elise. "Let's finish the lorry, and then I'll show you."

Of course, Tippy told everyone else about the claw-foot tub, and it wasn't long before Matron Bellingham had the cleanest ambulance squad in the region. The bathtub boosted morale immeasurably, except for Hera and Elise, who no longer had any privacy—just a line of women waiting to submerge themselves in hot water.

"You had to tell her," said Hera grumpily one evening as they were cleaning the ambulances.

"She threatened me with a wrench," said Elise. "She was about to cry. What could I do?"

"Let her cry?" said Hera. She came over to Elise's ambulance and sat on the tailgate while Elise sponged off the sides. "Honestly. You're too softhearted. But that's probably why I like you so much."

Elise looked around in the early dark. The rest of the women were busy scrubbing their lorries. No one was watching. She leaned over and kissed Hera on the lips, briefly, and felt herself blush.

Hera giggled. "Why do you like me so much, Elise?"

"Well," said Elise. "You risked your life to save me."

"There were no bullets by the time I got to you," said Hera. "You were just lying on the ground. I couldn't very well leave you there."

"I distinctly remember bullets," said Elise.

"I distinctly don't," said Hera. "Perhaps you'll have to find another reason to like me." She slipped her hand into Elise's and lowered her voice. "Perhaps one day you'll say you love me."

"I'll say it today," whispered Elise. "I love you."

"Even if we never get a chance to bathe together again?"

"Even if," said Elise, and she kissed Hera, this time without looking around. It was even darker now. Who would see?

Hera pulled away with a sigh. "I got a letter from Mother today."

"Oh?" said Elise, warm from the inside out, and not really listening.

"She had some interesting things to say," said Hera. "None of which I really liked."

"What do you mean?"

"I mean, my dear, she's picked out a husband for me."

Elise stifled a laugh. "A husband? Do you mean you're— you're betrothed, or something?"

Hera shrugged. "He's a major. He's had his leg shot off in the war, but only below the knee." Her mouth tightened. "I'm sure Mother only told me that to let me know we could still have children together."

"Children?" echoed Elise.

"I want three or four," said Hera in a practical tone. "Two boys and two girls would be best."

"I can do a lot of things for you," said Elise slowly, "but you know I can't give you children."

"I know." Hera squeezed Elise's hand. "I don't know how I'm going to explain you to Mother."

"I can't imagine how I'll explain *you* to Father," said Elise, "much less Grandpa."

"What about your sister?"

"To tell you the truth," said Elise, "I think she already knows."

"How?" said Hera, and she slid even closer, thigh to thigh. "You told her?"

"No," said Elise. "She just sort of…guessed. She asked me if you felt the same way about me as I felt about you."

"And what did you tell her?" whispered Hera.

"At the time I didn't really know." She let her hand rest on Hera's knee. It was very dark now, but a romantically full moon was coming up over the eastern horizon. All she could hear was the distant chatter of women finishing up their lorries.

"Well," said Hera, "if she already knows, then you can tell her. I love you." She kissed Elise's lips, taking her time. Her touch made Elise so dizzy, she almost fell back onto the floor of the ambulance. Hera wrapped an arm around her and laughed into her mouth. "Steady, girl, steady."

"Steady indeed," said Tippy's voice, out of the half-lit moon shadows. "What in the world are you two doing?" She stepped into full view at the back of the ambulance. She sounded incredulous, like she couldn't believe her eyes.

Elise and Hera untangled themselves as fast as they could. In an instant, Hera was on her feet.

"We're not doing anything," Hera said, challenging. "What did you think we were doing?"

Elise, speechless with fear, couldn't bring herself to say a word.

"I'd say you were snogging," said Tippy. "My God, Elise, I knew you could fix cars like a man, but I didn't know… And you, *Hera*…" She took a step back. "My God," she said again,

and hurried off in the direction of the abbey, where the matron's quarters were.

"Where are you going?" Hera shouted after her. She glanced
back at Elise. "Come on, quick!" She ran into the dark after
Tippy, and Elise, clumsy and sweating, followed as fast as she
could.

They caught up with Tippy about halfway to the entrance
of the abbey. "Where are you going?" Hera demanded again.
"What're you going to do?"

"What do you think?" said Tippy, striding ahead.

"You're going to tell Matron," said Hera. "You'll get us
kicked off the squad."

"She won't kick Elise out," said Tippy scornfully. "Who
would fix the lorries? Although she probably should. Imagine! You two! Don't you know this sort of thing spreads? Like
a disease! What if *I* should catch it? What on earth would I
tell my husband?"

"You're too old and ugly to catch it," snapped Hera. They
were almost at the doors to the abbey, and Tippy stopped in
her tracks.

"Old and ugly?" she snapped back. "And what about you?
Young and pretty? I don't think so. Everyone knows you're
a loose woman. You should've been sent home a long time
ago. And *you*." She turned to Elise, who was trembling now.
"*You're* just a—a wolf in sheep's clothing!"

She turned on her heel and fled for the door of the abbey.
Elise took a step to follow her, but Hera caught her arm.
"Don't," she said.

"What do you mean?" said Elise. "We have to defend ourselves!"

"We can't," said Hera. "Maybe with our other matron, back
in Ypres. She would've laughed in Tippy's face. This one will
believe anything she's told."

"So, let's tell her Tippy's lying!"

Hera let out a laugh. "By the time we convince her of that—if we can—Tippy will've told everyone else in the squad about us. We can't win this, Elise. Believe me. I know."

Elise blinked in the moonlit dark. "What're you talking about?"

"I mean," said Hera heavily, "I *am* a loose woman. I've been kicked out before—finishing school, girls' clubs. All sorts of things. For chasing after boys. They all said I had bad morals." She touched Elise's shoulder. "The whole time I was just trying to find you."

Elise took her hand and squeezed hard. "But what're we going to do?"

"We'll wait and see what happens," said Hera. "What's the worst Matron can do? If she kicks me out, you can quit, too. We'll go to England on the next ship. Poof! No more war for us." She smiled in the moonlight, but she didn't look happy. "We'll go to my mother's house. I've written to her about you. She'll welcome you with open arms."

"Until she finds out about us."

"Elise," said Hera solemnly, "we will be *very* careful."

The abbey's front door opened, letting out a shaft of yellow light. Two figures stood there, casting long shadows. Tippy, standing up straight, and the matron, bent over her cane.

"There they are," said Tippy, pointing, and the matron beckoned.

"Come here, girls," she said, and turned, expecting the two of them to follow.

They did, passing Tippy. Tippy didn't bother to look at them, just headed straight for the stables, to spread the truth about her and Hera, Elise thought. Hera was right. It wouldn't take any time at all. All that fellowship, all those shared terrible meals, the blood and the gore, would mean nothing.

"In here," said the matron, and she pointed with her cane, directing them into a small, sparse office lit by a single kerosene lantern. There was a desk but only two chairs. Matron eased herself into the one behind the desk. Hera sat in the other. Elise stood, her knees shaking. The matron looked like she had been in the middle of dressing for bed—and her bed was in the small office, too—her uniform jacket off, a nightdress draped across the blankets. There was a glass of milk on her desk. Elise couldn't imagine where she had gotten it.

The matron leaned over her elbows on the desk. "Is this true, what I hear?" She eyed Hera.

"Tippy is lying," said Hera, but to Elise's ears, she sounded desperate.

"I've found her to be an honest woman," said the matron. "I don't know why she would lie about something so serious."

"She's mistaken," said Elise. "She saw us—we weren't doing anything."

"*Kissing* another woman?" said the matron, sounding shocked now. She leaned back in her chair. "She also says you bathe together."

"Lots of the women bathe together," said Hera. "It's impossible to wash your own back."

"But that's an innocent reason," said the matron. "What you two were doing was not innocent, but sinful. And I shall not have sin in my unit." She opened a drawer in the desk and took out two sheets of paper. "These are transfer orders. Tomorrow morning you will each report to a different squad. The numbers and locations are here." She pushed the orders toward them as though even the paper was too dirty and sinful to touch.

Elise took hers with numb fingers. Her new squad was the 415th, stationed in Liette, still in France, but about twenty miles east of the abbey. She glanced at Hera's orders. The 234th, in Thierry, miles and miles in the opposite direction.

Hera turned to the matron. "Why don't you just kick us out?" she demanded. "If you don't want sinners, why would anyone else?"

"In order to avoid embarrassment to my unit," said the matron, "this stain shall not be applied to your records. My hope is that you will forget about each other and remember that you have a duty to King and country. Besides, even if I wanted to kick you out, as you say, I cannot. You're committed to service through the end of the war. If you want to leave of your own accord, that is your business. But rest assured, this filthy indiscretion will follow you if you do. I shall personally see to it. Is that understood?"

"Yes, Matron," said Hera.

Elise could only nod, stunned to her core by the vindictiveness of this little old woman.

"You are both dismissed," said the matron. "Pack up your things tonight. You'll leave after roll call tomorrow morning."

Instead of going straight to the stables where there would be nothing but stares and scorn, they went back to Elise's ambulance and sat in the cab, holding hands, watching the moonrise.

"There's only one road to Calais," said Elise. "No matter how far apart she tries to put us, we'll probably pass each other every day."

"I don't want to be two ships passing in the night," said Hera.

"Neither do I," said Elise.

Hera turned in her seat. "When this is all over, we should go to Paris. I hear people are more tolerant there. We could learn to speak French. If we find the right set of sinners, we could fit right in."

Elise thought of the woman dressed as a man, back in Baltimore. She hadn't told Hera about her experience that night, not yet. "I know where to find them at home," she said. "Maybe we should go to America."

Hera kissed Elise's knuckles. She pushed up Elise's sleeve, leaned over and kissed the inside of her elbow. "Do you really think we're sinners, Elise?"

"No." Elise wrapped her arms around Hera's shoulders. "It doesn't feel evil to me. It feels right."

Hera breathed in her ear. "Let's stay in here. We'll collect our things in the morning and be on our way, but tonight I want to have you to myself."

CHAPTER FORTY-FIVE

October 1918

Ruth was having an afternoon cup of tea in the mess tent in Charleroi, taking a break from cleaning the operating theater. Charleroi, where Heflin had dropped her Flying Squad, was even more devastated than Mecklin had been, and was identifiable only by a bullet-riddled sign and the flattened remains of the town square.

There was a well in the square, but when Witcover looked down into it, she'd screamed. MacBride had pulled her back hastily, and peered down into the hole himself.

"Blimey," he'd said. "There's a German helmet floating around down there."

Ruth and the rest of the squad had gathered around the hole in the ground to see if there was a German, too, but the only visible thing was the helmet, upside down, half-filled with water.

The bucket for the well was a few feet away, and MacBride lowered it to bring up the helmet. It was in good shape, and the water in the bucket seemed clean, but Ruth insisted that they boil the water for fifteen minutes instead of the usual five. They added squirts of iodine, just in case. The iodine made the tea taste strange, but it was better than nothing.

Ruth sipped at the iodine-tasting tea, her aching feet up on a chair. Witcover was with her, peeling potatoes for supper. The ambulances from Kortrijk had already picked up their patients, and the wards were empty. MacBride and Stephano were out with two of the ambulances collecting wounded from the front. Davidson and Porter were in the ward, making it ready for the next wave. Things were calm for the moment, except for the hushed voices outside the tent.

At first she thought it was Davidson and Porter. Then she realized that these voices were speaking German.

Ruth shot out of her chair. Witcover stopped in mid-peel and dropped the potato into a pot of water. Her eyes went to Ruth, wide and unbelieving.

Ruth crept over and inched the tent flap open, just enough to see who was speaking. Two German soldiers were standing outside with backpacks and rifles. One had his arm in a bloody sling and was leaning on his companion. Neither of them could have been more than sixteen years old. They both looked scared to death.

Their fear gave Ruth the courage to step out of the tent. "Get away!" She shooed them with both hands. "Get out before someone shoots you!"

The one who wasn't wounded pointed at her and made a cross on his chest where the red cross was on her apron. Then he pointed to his friend's arm. *"Bitte, ihm zu helfen."*

Ruth didn't understand a word of German, but she knew what he was saying. "Go to your own hospital!" she said. "I can't help you." She wondered how on earth they'd gotten this far behind the Allied lines without getting their heads blown off. "Get *out!*"

Maybe they would have. They seemed to understand what she was saying. The wounded boy took a step away. His friend tried to hold him up, but he staggered and fell to the ground in a dead faint. His friend knelt beside him and looked at Ruth with beseeching eyes. He threw down his rifle.

"Bitte!" he said. *"Helfen!"*

By this time, Witcover was standing behind Ruth at the opening of the tent, and Davidson and Porter had come out of the ward to see what was going on.

"Good God," said Porter, taking in everything at a glance. "What're you going to do?"

"I guess I'm going to fix his arm," said Ruth. She turned to Porter. "You'll help. Davidson—"

"I'm not helping any damn German," Davidson snapped.

"I was going to suggest," said Ruth, "that you try to run this other one off. He doesn't have a gun anymore. It shouldn't be too difficult."

"That I'll gladly do," said Davidson, and she picked up the rifle that was lying on the ground and pointed it at the uninjured German. "Get out of here!" Davidson shouted at him. "Go on!"

Ruth and Porter dragged the wounded German into the tent that housed the operating theater. They could hear Davidson shouting as they got him onto an operating table. Her shouts turned uglier, but it didn't seem like the other German had any intention of leaving.

"Maybe they're brothers," said Ruth, unwrapping the ruin of the boy's arm. "They sort of look the same."

"Blond hair and blue eyes?" said Porter. "They all look the same if you ask me." She washed the wound with sterile water, then alcohol. "This isn't good."

"It'll have to come off," said Ruth. "I don't care where he comes from. This arm is a loss." She took a tissue knife from the surgeon's kit. "Put him under," she said to Porter. "Let's get started."

By the time they were done, Davidson's tirade outside had stopped, but when Ruth stepped into the mess tent, the other German was sitting there, having a cup of tea while Witcover nervously peeled potatoes, and Davidson sat in a chair nearby, pointing the rifle at him.

"He wouldn't leave," said Davidson tersely. "But I didn't think I could shoot him without permission."

The German eyed Ruth. He was so young and worn out. *"Ist er in Ordnung?"*

"Your friend, or your brother, or whoever he is, has lost an arm, but he's all right," said Ruth.

"Okay?" said the German.

"Yes," said Ruth. "He's okay."

"Ja? Gut." He put his hands up over his head, and Davidson took a quick little gasp and tightened her grip on the rifle.

"For God's sake, don't shoot him!" said Ruth. "He's surrendering!"

"Ich gebe auf," said the German.

"I give up?" said Witcover, who had a death grip on a potato. "Is that what he said?"

"I think so," said Ruth. "Davidson, put the rifle down. MacBride'll be here any minute. He'll know what to do."

Davidson reluctantly put the rifle on the table. The German carefully put his arms down and resumed drinking his tea.

When MacBride and Stephano got back with the ambulances, MacBride took one look at the German in the mess tent and shook his head.

"The wounded one can go to Kortrijk with the rest," he said, "but this one is a prisoner of war."

"Prizonner uf var?" said the German. *"Nein. Ich bleibe bei meinem Bruder."*

"Do you have any idea what he's saying?" Ruth asked.

"I think he wants to stay with his brother. Isn't that German for brother, *Bruder?*"

"Well, we can't do that," said Porter. "We can't just send him out in an ambulance if he isn't wounded."

"Vounded," said the German, and he suddenly turned pale. *"Ja. Ich vounded."*

"You're not wounded," said Ruth. "You're fine." She was about to go on when the German pulled a pistol from under his jacket. Everyone froze—even Davidson.

"Ich vounded," said the German, very loudly, and aimed the pistol downward. Before anyone could stop him, he pulled the trigger and shot himself in the foot. He let out a scream, and Davidson managed to shoot the rifle. She put a hole in the tent right next to Witcover's head. Witcover hit the ground. MacBride swooped down on Davidson and grabbed the rifle.

"Oh my God!" cried Davidson. "Did I hit her? Witcover!"

Ruth rushed over to where Witcover was just picking herself up.

"I'm all right," said Witcover. She brushed herself off as if to make sure.

"Everybody just calm down," said MacBride, and he grabbed the bleeding German by the collar. "This is the second one today."

"What're you talking about?" said Ruth.

"There's word of an armistice," said MacBride. "The Germans are coming over to our lines to give themselves up. I have another foot wound just like this one in the ambulance right now."

"You brought us another German?" Davidson exclaimed.

"Well, we couldn't very well tell him to walk home, now, could we?" said MacBride. "They're deserting, and they don't want to be shot for it."

"An armistice?" said Ruth. "But when?"

"No one knows," said MacBride, "but the rumors are thick at the front, let me tell you." He gave the German a shake. "You're last in line, you," he said. "Now if you'll excuse me, ladies, we have ambulances to unload."

An armistice! Ruth wrote in a letter to John in the wee hours of the morning. *So far, all we've heard are rumors. Perhaps you've heard something more? Please let me know.* Ruth put her pencil down and lit a new candle as the old one guttered. She'd spent most of an hour writing to him about the German brothers. She'd tried to make the whole experience seem as comical as possible, not wanting him to think they were suddenly being overrun by the enemy, but it was difficult not to be nervous about the whole thing. She kissed the letter and set it aside for when the ambulances arrived to ferry the wounded to Kortrijk.

To Ruth's surprise, Heflin came by the next day. She was red-cheeked when she got off the motorcycle. Ruth couldn't decide if she looked childlike with glee or just windblown and tired.

"What's going on?" demanded Ruth. "We've been hearing all kinds of rumors."

Heflin smoothed her leather riding gear. Her breath steamed in the late October chill, and her boots were spattered with mud from the road. "The good news," said Heflin, "is that the war is coming to an end. The bad news is that you have to wait until November 11 for it to be over."

"That's three weeks from now," said Ruth. "Why do they have to wait so long?"

Heflin shrugged. Ruth's second guess as to her state of mind was the right one, she decided. Heflin was worn out. Ruth could see it in her eyes.

"It gets better," said Heflin. "The fighting'll stop at precisely eleven o'clock on the morning of the eleventh. It's poetic, don't you see? The eleventh hour of the eleventh day of the eleventh month."

MacBride was standing beside Ruth now. "Lucky we don't have to wait for the eleventh year of the war."

"You're both so cynical," said Heflin. "Can't you see this is a good thing?" She didn't sound all that convinced, and Ruth wondered if she was going to cry.

"Do you have time for a cup of tea?" Ruth asked.

Heflin's shoulders sagged. "That would be lovely," she said. "I missed breakfast. I've been trying to get the word out as fast as possible."

"Welcome to our palace," said MacBride. He bowed and swept aside the dirty drape of the tent. "Come in and have a lovely cup of tea."

Yesterday's biscuits were stale, but not quite hard. Heflin took one, dipped it gently into her tea and took a bite. She swallowed, closed her eyes and let out a heavy sigh. "It's such good news," she said. "Why do I find it so exhausting?"

"Because it's endless," said Ruth. "What general came up with that?"

"To be honest," said Heflin, "I think they had to make a deal with the kaiser, and you know these old-world types."

"They can't just bring things to a stop," said MacBride, "like sane folk."

"They haven't been out here to see what it's really like,"

said Ruth. "How many more men have to get blown to bits before the eleventh?"

"And who gets the honor of being the last man killed?" said MacBride, grimly.

Heflin took a long sip of tea. "Try not to blame the messenger."

"We're not," said Ruth. "Sorry if it sounds that way. But who has the energy to fight for another three weeks?"

"Everyone," said Heflin. She finished her biscuit and drained her cup. "Wherever the fighting stops on the eleventh, it'll be Germany's new borders. It's important that we keep advancing until the very end. And even though they're retreating, the Germans know that, too. They'll fight as hard as they can for every inch."

"They're using boys and old men," said MacBride.

"And veterans from the Russian front," said Heflin. "It won't be an easy three weeks. In fact, one of the reasons I came by was to tell you to be ready to move in the next two or three days." She stood. "The front is surging forward, and so shall we. Shan't we?"

"Yes, Matron," said Ruth.

John's letter came in that day with the ambulances, supplies and post. Ruth was surprised to see it. Their letters rarely crossed in the mail. She waited for his and he waited for hers. She felt momentarily guilty for not sending her last one sooner—but it had only been a couple of days since she'd written. Hadn't it?

Her address, Miss Ruth Duncan, Hospital 4, Mobile Unit, c/o Kortrijk, Belgium, was typed this time instead of written in someone else's hand, and she was seized with happiness that finally he had found a typewriter and could put together a letter himself, without an intermediary.

When her work in the operating theater was done for the day and she had cleaned herself up as best she could, Ruth hurried to her cot, sat down alone and opened the letter. The whole thing was typed, with X's and strike-throughs where he had hit the wrong key, left-handed.

My dearest Ruth,

I want you to know that my health is good and so are my spirits. I am in the company of a number of other wounded doctors—they have given us a special ward. We talk and play cards and entertain each other. We have been promised prosthetic limbs by the Royal Army Medical Corps, but having seen how useless and ugly they are, we will donate ours to soldiers who need them more than we do. Overall, we have decided, we would prefer to present ourselves in public the way that we are. If we are to be pitied, let us be pitied for what we are—cripples.

I do not seek pity, and the rest of this letter is not to make you feel sorry for me, but to enable you to move on with your life. As I have said, I am healthy and in good spirits, so none of what follows is a result of depression or nerves.

I have known for a long time that without my right arm, I am incapable of continuing my work as a doctor. Obviously, I am incapable of performing surgeries, but the day-to-day activities that make a good physician are also beyond me. This understanding will enable me to devote time to my parents, as they age, and are in need of more assistance. That being said—and this is the most difficult part of this letter—I also feel that I am incapable of fulfilling my promises to you. I said that I would never hurt you, but I'm afraid that this news will be more than hurtful. If I am not a doctor, I cannot support a wife. I know that we discussed alternatives to marriage while you went to school, but circumstances—and I know you will try to argue against this—have changed. I will not marry as long as I live.

My heart will always belong to you, but you must continue to move forward without me. I urge you to write your next letter, not to me, but to the Women's Medical College, and apply for acceptance for the spring term. Even in our little out-of-the-way ward, we hear rumors of an armistice. Now is the time for you to pursue your dream. You are eminently qualified. They would be lucky to have you as a student. As one who loves you, I insist that you seize this moment.

As one who loves you, I must also say that I freely give up any hold I may have had on you, romantically, or physically. I will treasure the time we had together forever; and will never forget you. I will always remain your friend, but you must open your eyes and your heart to whatever and whoever comes after me. Please know that I look forward to meeting the man who will be able to give you happiness with all his body and soul.

Your friend forever,
John

He had signed it with his left hand, a barely legible scrawl. Ruth let the letter rest in her lap, absolutely sick to her stomach. She wanted to scream. She reread the last line... *I look forward to meeting the man who will be able to give you happiness with all his body and soul.*

"Oh my God," said Ruth, too loudly. "Oh my *God.*"

She put the letter to one side and got down on her knees in the small tent. Greta Porter always kept writing paper under her cot, along with all her correspondence. Porter wrote endless letters to her mother and husband and got almost daily messages in reply. Ruth scrabbled around in the tied-together stacks of envelopes until she found a piece of writing paper. She pulled out Porter's lapboard and a pencil, and started to write.

Dear John,
I don't care about your arm, your plans to give up on medicine or anything else, and you should know that about me by now. All I care about is you,

not some unknown man in the future. For me, nothing has changed. I will
be your wife and you will be my husband. My time in medical school will
give us a chance to work out any problems you have with this. Tell THAT
to your doctor friends in their little ward of self-pity. Tell them you will
be away from their awful opinions as soon as possible, and back to your
parents' house, where they will hopefully talk some sense into you.

Your fiancée,

And, on impulse, she scrawled her name with her left hand, too.

She sent the letter the next afternoon when the ambulances came from Kortrijk. As evening came on, MacBride, Stephano and Witcover went out as usual for the wounded at the front, which left Ruth with Davidson and Porter to clean things up for the next wave.

"Well," said Ruth to Davidson, "now that we know the war's going to be over, what'll you do on November 12?"

"I'll be on the first boat to England," said Davidson over the boiling trays of instruments. "And when I get to Dover, I'll be kissing the ground."

"What about you?" Ruth asked Porter.

"I don't think we'll be going anywhere. There'll still be wounded coming in. We'll have to tend to them. I'd say we won't be out of this hospital for another month after the eleventh. I say none of us sees England until December."

"Another winter in a tent?" said Davidson. "I don't think so. I have chilblains as it is."

Ruth had never considered Davidson as the optimist in this tiny group, but when she thought about it, she realized that it wasn't optimism at all. On the morning of the twelfth— or maybe at 11:01 on the eleventh of November—Davidson would simply pack her things and leave. If the war was over, why would she stay? Why would any of them? Ruth had a sudden, awful vision of herself and MacBride as the last two standing in this tented hospital, MacBride assisting while Ruth sawed off the last limb of the war.

As soon as her duties were done, she went back to her cot, found a blank piece of paper and wrote a letter to Elise.

I hope by now that you've heard the good news about the war coming to an end on November 11. I am at a loss as to what to think. The war seems like such a normal state of affairs at this point, I can hardly believe this will all be over. On the other hand, I thought we would be closer together at the end, not so many miles apart. If you are still ferrying soldiers to Calais, we should meet there and try to get on the same ship to London. I hope to hear from you soonest.

Your loving sister

The letter couldn't go anywhere until the ambulances came down from Kortrijk the next day with supplies, so she folded it up and put it under her pillow.

She took out another piece of paper and addressed it to the Women's Medical College in London. Ruth sat on her cot with the paper, trying to conjure the letter she needed to write, the one she had hoped John would help her with. She wondered whether to start it *Dear Sir* or *Dear Madam*.

Slowly she wrote,

Dear Madam:

I am a nurse in a Casualty Clearing Station (CCS) who has been doing a surgeon's work. Because of my skill level and a lack of doctors to fill the position, I have become the head of a unit on the Hindenburg line. I am writing to apply to your medical program. I have written before, but only the nursing program was available then. With the end of the war in sight, I hope your course of study has changed, and you are once again training women as doctors.

Yours most sincerely,
Ruth Duncan

She found an envelope under Porter's cot, and after a moment of consideration, wrote the Dowelings' return address on it.

Two days later, she had a reply from Elise. Heflin had been right. The fighting was becoming more fierce as the two sides battled over inches of ground, and she didn't have a chance to open the letter until a full day after it came. Ruth read it by candlelight at approximately midnight when all the surgical cases were taken care of.

Dear Ruth,
Writing this in haste, as we are overwhelmed with rush cases. Yes, I have heard about the end of the war. I've just been transferred to a hospital in Liette, but I drive to Calais every day. Let's be optimistic and plan to meet there on the twelfth if we can. If we can't, we will write to each other and make alternate plans. I have a lot to tell you. Hope to see you soon.

CHAPTER FORTY-SIX

November 4, 1918

With only a week until the armistice, Elise tried her best to stay busy and not think. Liette was a small town in France, at the foot of a forested hill. Its streets were lined with old sycamores. The buildings were intact, and for the first time, Elise had a sense of how the countryside used to be.

The hospital was a converted spa, which had previously been used for tuberculosis patients. There were a thousand wounded men here, Elise had been told by her new matron, a thin woman with a high-society accent. Still, there was room for the ambulance drivers to sleep in beds, not on straw or in wooden bunks. The beds were in a garage, which wasn't heated, and the beds were so close together that the twenty or so drivers could hardly walk between them. Still, Elise had no complaints, except, of course, that Hera was miles away.

To Elise's relief, Matron Bellingham had kept her word, and talk of "snogging," whatever that was, had not preceded Elise's arrival. The other drivers were welcoming enough, but with only a week to go, Elise didn't feel compelled to make friends. Her focus was on two things: writing to Hera, and finding her in Calais.

My dearest,

I miss you so much, I can't even describe it. I was in Calais yesterday afternoon looking for landmarks where we could meet. As you probably know by now, the ambulances line up at the docks, where everything is such a mess, we will never be able to find each other. There is, however, an old lighthouse about a mile south of the docks, where the Red Cross is giving out sandwiches and tea. If we could decide on a time—say, noon—we could meet there, stay awhile and then drive back.

I hope you're not sleeping on some cold floor. I think of you all the time.

She mailed the letter after supper that night, at a picture-perfect little post office that had been part of the spa since the last century. Like everything else at the hospital, the post office was busy. She waited in line behind a nurse in a bloody smock until she got to the clerk, a harried little man with a fringe of white hair. He took her letter, glanced at it and tossed it into a sack marked Thierry.

"Hey," said Elise, before she could be pushed aside by the soldier behind her. "Do you have anything for Duncan?"

The clerk turned to a wall of alphabetical boxes. He went to the *D* box and pulled out a handful of envelopes, shuffled through them and took out two. Elise's heart jumped. One was probably from Ruth, but the other had to be from Hera.

Near the post office, Elise found a decorative little bench with a streetlight beside it. She sat down and tore open Hera's letter first.

My dearest love,
Oh, how I miss you! I'm enraged at Matron Bellingham
still, the same level of rage as when we were transferred.
*   Calais is a nightmare, and I don't know how we'll*
ever find each other there. We must make a plan to meet
each other there or in London. I have written my mother's
address below. Keep this letter (next to your heart) and
if we can't meet before the twelfth, we will meet on the
thirteenth at her house. Even if you get there first, she'll
be delighted to see you.

I send you all my love—
Hera

Elise tried to picture herself arriving first and introducing
herself to Hera's mother. The whole scene, as she saw it in her
mind, was…awkward. *Yes, your daughter and I were bosom bud-*
dies in the war. Elise opened the letter from Ruth.

My dear sister,
We are in a complete rush here. I may not have time to write to you
between now and the armistice. Yes, let's be optimistic about the twelfth, and
do our best to meet in Calais. If we don't see each other there, I'll be at the
Dowelings' soon after.

That answered one question, at least. Ruth wasn't planning to stay in her hospital after the war was over. Orders or
not, she was planning to walk off the field of battle and go
straight to London, which made Elise wonder, uneasily, how
John was dealing with the loss of his arm.

Elise slid both letters back into their envelopes and put

them in her breast pocket. She got up and made her way to the chilly garage to get some sleep before daylight and the four-hour drive to Calais.

CHAPTER FORTY-SEVEN

November 10, 1918

In the cab of Elise's ambulance, on the way to Calais, was a young American soldier by the name of Arnold Jones.

"Shot through the lung," Arnold told her, for the fourth time. "Only been here for three months. Got shot through the arm once, twice through the leg." Here, he showed her the wound stripes on the sleeve of his uniform, again. "Always went back to the line. But this lung. I guess I won't be playing baseball anymore once I get home. Used to like playing baseball with the fellas. Do you like baseball, baby?"

"My name is Miss Duncan," said Elise, also for the fourth time. "And no, I don't really care for baseball."

"Well, baby," said Arnold, "what *do* you care for?"

She wondered what he would say if she told him what she really cared for was a little blonde ambulance driver from London. It wouldn't shut him up, she was sure of that. She thought again about stopping, making him sit in the back of her crowded ambulance, and picking out one of the more proper, English patients who wouldn't call her *baby*. They always seemed more polite than the Americans. She'd had one elderly officer who'd told her all about grouse hunting, one Tommy engineer who'd survived the Somme only to have his leg shot off at the end of the war, a number of morphine sleepers who were no company at all, and now this. For three more hours. Elise revved the ambulance's engine, but there was no way to go faster than the lorry ahead of her. She was in a long line of ambulances, and the road was narrow, curvy and unpaved. Everyone was being careful, slow, even though every single driver and every single patient could hardly wait for *tomorrow*, the end of the war.

"Well?" said Arnold, again.

"I like fixing cars, if you really want to know," said Elise. "I was the lead mechanic in my last outfit."

Arnold gave a one-lunged snort. "That doesn't sound very ladylike to me."

Elise thought of some choice swear words she had learned from the Tommies, but didn't say anything.

"What did you do before the war?" he asked. "Did you sew and cook?"

"No," Elise said flatly. "I don't know how to do that kind of stuff. I fixed my father's car."

He didn't seem to be listening. "Now, me," said Arnold, "I was a salesman. Sold brushes door-to-door. Made good money, too. My customers *loved* me because—" and here he leaned closer "—I'm such a charming guy."

"Really," said Elise. She wished she could hit a big rut in the road, jog him over to his side of the bench seat, but there were the men in the rear to think of.

"Really," said Arnold. "And good-looking, too, or hadn't you noticed?" He took off his uniform cap and smoothed his hair, which was an almost blue-black. He had a thin little mustache, too, which she decided she hated.

"You must have a lot of girlfriends," she said.

"No, no girlfriend," said Arnold. He leaned back in his seat with his arms behind his head. "I could have had affairs with a whole lot of housewives, but I never did."

She wondered if this was anywhere near the truth. After all, his customers loved him.

He let one arm fall onto the seat back behind her. "What about you, baby? Boyfriend waiting at home?"

"No," said Elise, which was at least honest, but she had a lie for him, one that she had formed at the beginning of this endless ride. "He's waiting for me in Calais." She nodded. "He's a big, strong British soldier. He's killed a hundred Germans. Some with his bare hands."

Arnold hesitated, then moved his arm. He put his palms on his knees. "Oh," he said. "What's his name?"

"Montraine," said Elise. "And besides that? His father is a lord."

"Oh," said Arnold. "You going to marry him?"

"Yep," said Elise, "and if you put your hands over here one more time, I'm going to tell him all about you." She tried to imagine Hera beating the snot out of Arnold and had to smile.

"What's so funny?" said Arnold in a sulky tone.

"Not a thing," said Elise.

He shut up for the rest of the ride.

Finally she crested a hill, and the docks of Calais came into view. Freighters and warships lined the wharves under a wintry sky. Ambulances were parked in rows a dozen deep. Between the ambulances and the ships, doctors, nurses and orderlies were getting the wounded on the ships as fast as they could.

Beside her, Arnold let out his breath between his teeth. It came out as steam. "Finally," he said. "I'm getting out of this damn country."

At last, thought Elise, *you're getting out of my damn ambulance.*

When her ambulance had been unloaded, Elise drove to the spot she had written to Hera about. The lighthouse, about a mile south of the docks, was a ruin, like practically everything else. Its top had been knocked off, and there were shards of glass all through the sandy grounds. The sea stretched out behind it, cold, gray and choppy. In the distance were warships, moving toward a stormy horizon. By this time, Elise knew that bad weather blew in from the west, and now she expected snow on the drive back to Liette.

The wind tugged at her hat and scarf. One thing she'd gladly received from the ambulance crew in Liette was a warm woolen coat. Her bare shins and ankles were still cold, but the rest of her was warm enough to stand in the wind with her back to the ocean. Elise hugged herself, and stood where she could see every driver as they got out of their lorry. The weather started to turn from wind, to wind and flurries, and from flurries to actual snow. Still, there was no sign of Hera. Elise glanced at her watch. She'd been here for almost an hour, well past noon, when they were supposed to meet. Maybe Hera was still on the road, stuck in traffic from Thierry to Calais. Maybe she was held up at the docks—the lines had been long.

Elise brushed the snow from the shoulders of her coat and walked slowly up to the crowd around the lighthouse, searching every face in the long queue of people waiting for a sandwich and a mug of tea. She made her way to the parked ambulances and peered into every cab. She found two women in VAD uniforms sleeping against each other, covered in a blanket, breathing out steam, but no sign of Hera.

Finally, at almost two o'clock, when Elise knew that her squad would leave without her, she went back to her own ambulance, started the engine and, through the whipping snow, drove back to the docks.

At the assembly point, Elise was the last one in line. The matron, an impatient woman who was no older than Elise herself, leaned into Elise's window and checked her off on a clipboard.

"Cutting it close, Duncan," she said.

"I was just down at the lighthouse," said Elise. "The queue was long today."

"We were ready to leave without you," said the matron.

Elise wished they had.

"A sandwich isn't worth a demerit." The matron made a little circle on the clipboard.

"A demerit?" Elise couldn't help herself. "The war's over tomorrow. What kind of demerit can you give me?"

The matron just pursed her lips. She took a whistle out of her coat pocket and blew it piercingly. "Move out!" she shouted, and the line of ambulances surged forward.

On the way back to Liette, Elise shifted gears, trying not to worry about Hera and not to tailgate as the convoy began climbing the first substantial hill. Now that the end was so close, she found herself having dreams about Paris. She had never been, but in these dreams, there was a country house with a dozen children underfoot, all of them, oddly, the same age. Elise saw herself on a porch swing, like the one Father had put up on the front porch in Baltimore. And it was a good dream until Elise looked over at the other presence on the swing and saw, not Hera, but Father. "Fix the car!" he'd snap, and she'd wake up in a sweat.

Elise spun the steering wheel, avoiding slicks of ice on the road. Moving to Paris would mean never going back to America. Wouldn't it? Moving in with Hera and somehow producing a dozen urchins would mean never seeing either of their families again. She desperately wanted to talk to Ruth about all of this. Ruth would at least make an effort to understand. She always did. But Ruth had her own problems right now. Like a boyfriend without an arm, and the promise of medical school. If she got in, and Elise had no doubt that she would, it would mean years of study in London, and then marrying John. At any rate, it would mean not going back to America anytime soon. That would mean Father and Grandpa on their own for another however many years, with Grandpa getting older and Father more bitter. Elise tried to picture the two of them on a steamer, coming to Ruth's wedding, or her graduation in London, and couldn't do it. She tried to imagine Father coming to see his grandchildren in Paris, and had to wipe away tears when she couldn't do that either. If it hadn't been for the woman dressed as a man, so long ago in Baltimore, she would have thought of herself and Hera as completely alone in this dilemma, but there were others.

She knew it.

As the ambulances crawled along, the weather grew even worse. Snow fell in clumps, covering the road, the lorries, the burnt-out buildings. Elise tried to think about cheerful things, like a nice fire blazing in the hearth at the Dowelings'. She shivered in her seat as the wind blew through chinks in the old lorry. Her wipers didn't work, and she had to reach out her open window to clear the windshield with her bare hand. Any heat that had accumulated inside her cab went out the window. Elise cursed the weather, and wondered if she would catch pneumonia and die, a final slap in the face from the war.

The snow was so thick, she could barely see the back end of the ambulance in front of her. When it came to a stop at the crest of the hill, she nearly ran right into it.

Stopping at the top of a hill wasn't uncommon, especially when the down side was so dangerous. Each ambulance driver gave the one in front a chance to get down safely, but this wait stretched on and on.

She stared at the ambulance ahead of her and counted to a thousand. Still no motion. In fact, she now noticed, there was no smoke coming from the tailpipe. The driver had turned off her engine and was just sitting there. The whole column was at a dead stop.

Elise turned off her engine and set the brake. She got out into the ankle-deep snow and slogged up to the driver in front of her.

"Hey," she said, rapping on the door. "What's going on?"

The driver, a woman from her squad whose name she didn't know, just shrugged, bundled up in a coat and scarf. "An accident, I think," she shouted through the window, not opening it. "Matron told me to stay where I was."

Elise looked down the hill. This was a place where accidents had happened before.

"Who was in front of you?" she shouted at the driver.

"Just Matron," said the driver. "She said it wasn't anyone from our squad."

"Which squad was it?" said Elise.

"How in the hell should I know?" said the driver. "Nobody tells me a bloody thing."

Elise straightened and looked down the hill into the swirls of snow. Where was Hera? For all she knew, Hera was stuck, just like she was, in a line of ambulance traffic that stretched halfway to Calais. On the other hand, it would be just like Hera to have a crash at the very end of things, because she was thinking about a house full of children instead of the road in front of her. Elise pulled her coat tighter and started down the hill, a feeling of dread in the pit of her stomach. Even if it wasn't Hera, there would be something she could do to help—she hoped—and if it was Hera... Elise slid down the hill, hurrying, stepping in between the tire tracks until she was at the bottom.

She met the matron, who was coming out of the thickly falling snow, on foot.

"Duncan," snapped the matron. "What're you doing out of your vehicle?"

"I heard there was an accident," Elise stammered in the freezing cold. "I wanted to see if I could help."

"You can help by getting back into your ambulance," said the matron. "She's pinned. We've been trying to get her out."

"Who is it?" said Elise, teeth chattering.

"Some idiot from the 234th," said the matron. "Probably never driven in snow before."

Elise pushed past the matron and started to run in the steadily deepening snow.

"Duncan!" shouted the matron, *"Duncan!"*

Elise ignored her and ran on, snow in her shoes, following the matron's tracks until she smelled smoke and engine oil. Ahead, finally, was the ambulance, rolled onto its side, its frame bent against a burnt tree, its red cross flapping in the chill wind like a flag of surrender.

Two other women were there, kneeling in the snow on either side of a third, who was lying on the ground. Elise recognized her blond head immediately.

"Hera!" She slid to the snowy ground on her knees. Hera's left arm was pinned beneath the edge of the cab. There was no blood that Elise could see, but the arm was clearly broken, and Hera, pale as a ghost, was already in shock.

"You know her?" said one of the women.

"I do," said Elise, shaking now. "She's my friend."

"Oh, Elise," whispered Hera, tears leaking down the side of her face. "I'm so sorry."

"Don't be sorry," said Elise. "We're going to get you out."

"We've been trying," said the woman, "but the lorry's too heavy. Your matron went to see if she could find some men to help us."

"There aren't any men for miles," said Elise. "Let's try again."

The two women stood, and the three of them dug their hands under the edge of the cab where Hera's arm was pinned.

"Get ready to slide out," Elise said to Hera. "One, two, three, *lift!*"

The three of them strained to raise the cab, but it didn't budge.

Elise positioned herself for a better grip and maybe more leverage. Her feet were deep in the snow, right next to Hera's head. "Let's try it again. Ready? One, two, three—"

Again, the lorry stayed right where it was. Hera was sobbing now, her free hand over her face.

"Maybe if there were four of us," said one of the women uncertainly. "Or five."

"Go," said Elise, and it was abruptly clear in her mind what had to be done. "Find some other drivers and bring them here. But the engine's weighing this thing down. It has to come out."

"Then we definitely need a man," said the other woman. "I don't know how to do that—do you?"

"I haven't done it before," said Elise, "but I know where the bolts are. Now run! Get help!"

The two women hurried off, and Elise went to the back of the overturned lorry to find the toolbox. The metal box had fallen from its rack and sprung open, tools scattered everywhere. Elise crawled inside the torn canvas canopy, looking for the wrench she would've used to change a tire, and finally found it. She grabbed a blanket, too, and crawled back out to kneel next to Hera.

"You're going to be all right," she said, covering her with the blanket, tucking it around her shoulders and legs. "This could be much worse."

"I know," said Hera, trying not to cry. "Please hurry. I'm so cold. I can't feel my arm at all."

Elise went around to the underside of the lorry's bonnet, easy to get to now that the ambulance was on its side. She'd seen mechanics remove engines from cars in Baltimore and she knew there were only four bolts she needed to find to release the crankcase from the frame.

The undercarriage of the lorry was covered with oil and dirt and dirty snow from its slide down the hill. Elise brushed filth away from the engine with freezing hands and felt around for the bolts that held the crankcase in place. She found two right away, adjusted the wrench and pulled with all her strength to get the first one to move. It wasn't easy. The bolt had been there since before the war, back when the ambulance had first been put together, but she managed to get it to turn and turn and turn until the bolt dropped, an oily weight, into her hands.

"I've got one," she called to Hera, out of sight on the other side of the lorry. "Three to go."

"Oh, Elise," said Hera, her teeth chattering. "I'm so sorry I wasn't at the lighthouse."

"It's all right," said Elise.

"I was held up at the d-d-docks. Then we had to turn

around right away." She gasped for breath. "Oh, Elise. I'm so afraid I'm going to faint."

Elise seized the second bolt in the wrench's jaw and hauled on it. It didn't budge. "You can't faint," she grunted. "You'll freeze to death or—or something. Besides, it would be cowardly."

"C-c-cowardly?" echoed Hera. "Is that what I said to you when you got sh-sh-shot?"

"No," said Elise. She wiped her greasy hands and tried again, hanging on to the wrench with all her weight. This time it moved. She pulled harder and harder until the bolt began to loosen. She unscrewed it as fast as she could with fingers she could barely feel. "I don't really remember what you said to me when I got shot," she said, to keep Hera talking. "Do you?"

"Of c-c-course," whispered Hera. "I called you my truest love and told you that if you d-d-died, it would kill me."

Elise found the next bolt. It loosened far more easily. "You never said anything like that to me," she said. "I would've remembered *that*."

"Well, I th-th-thought it."

"Even back then?" said Elise. She threw the third bolt on the ground and started on the last one. "We hardly knew each other."

"You s-s-see," said Hera weakly, "you were nice to me. N-n-n-nobody else was. Wh-wh-when I saw you in the road, bleeding to death, I j-j-just knew."

She was quiet for a while. Elise leaned into the fourth bolt, frozen hands slipping on the cold metal of the wrench. She had to stop and catch her breath. She tried to warm her hands in the folds of the woolen coat, but her hands were so cold, it didn't do any good. Elise looked around the snowy patch of burned woods and wondered where everyone else was.

Surely the women she'd sent away could've been back with reinforcements by now.

Elise set her weight against the wrench and tried again. "Hera?" she grunted, "are you still there?"

"Yes," whispered Hera, barely audible.

"Do you know when I knew?" The bolt wasn't budging. Elise yanked on it as hard as she could.

"When?" said Hera faintly.

"The first time you washed my back," said Elise, panting now. "In the bunkroom, with those awful tubs. Do you remember that?"

"I remember."

"There were so many naked women," said Elise, and she let out a breathless laugh. "I was so scared." She hauled on the bolt again, listening, but Hera was quiet. Elise started to panic. She tried to control her racing heart, to really examine the engine, to see if she had missed something. What she saw was that the weight of the crankcase was hanging on this one final bolt, and that it would take a muscular man or a torque-wrench to free it. She had neither.

"Hera?" she said. "Are you still there?"

Hera didn't respond.

Elise swallowed hard. She kicked around in the snow until she found a good-sized rock, and pried it up from the ground. She locked the wrench into place around the bolt and held it with one hand. With the other, she hit the end of the wrench with the rock, harder and harder, until the rock fell apart. But the bolt had moved. She found another rock and banged away at the end of the wrench, the thudding ring of rock against metal echoing through the snowy patch of burnt woods. The bolt moved, and moved again with each successive blow. She could see the crankcase starting to sag against the frame. She pounded again and again until she was sweating in the cold.

She shook off her coat and began hitting the wrench with all her strength, all her rage against the war, the stupidity of it, which had left her in this place, at this time, with Hera freezing in the snow. She hit the wrench so hard that it actually bent, but it swung as it bent and the bolt came free. Elise twisted the damn thing off and gave the crankcase a good hard push. It fell heavily into the snow, and broke open, spewing oil like blood.

Elise rushed around to the other side of the overturned ambulance. Hera was blanketed with snow. Big flakes had mixed with her hair and were melting on her face. From up the hill, Elise heard women's voices, coming closer.

"Hurry!" she shouted.

This time there were five of them, including two of the biggest women Elise had ever seen in the corps—not fat, but muscular. They all ran over and grabbed the snowy, grounded edge of the ambulance with gloved hands and heaved. The chassis groaned, and the cab door flapped on its hinges, but in a minute, they had raised it off Hera's arm. Elise ran to pull her free, but the two women kept pushing until the ambulance fell back onto its wheels again, crooked, broken, but upright.

One of the big women dusted off her hands. "That wasn't so hard," she said in an American accent. "You girls could've done it yourselves." Then she saw the crankcase on the ground, leaking black oil into the snow. "Ah. No wonder it was so light. Who the hell did that?"

"I did," said Elise, kneeling beside Hera, still without a coat. "Now help me get her to an ambulance. She's got to go to the nearest hospital."

Two of the women ran to get a stretcher. Elise could see their ambulance, parked at an angle, and the rest of the column, passing by. She wondered where her own ambulance was, or if the lorry behind her had simply pushed hers off the

road. She wondered how many demerits she would get for
saving Hera's life, and knew, deep down, that she would never
see her matron again. She held Hera's cold hand, blue at the
fingertips, as the women gently loaded her onto the stretcher,
and hurried along behind as they took her to the ambulance.

One of the heavy women seemed to be the driver. "You
coming along?" she said, and patted the passenger seat. She
smiled an easy smile, and Elise flushed. Here was a woman
just like her. She hardly knew what to say.

"I'll ride in back," she said.

"Good idea," said the woman, and she smiled again, knowingly. "Get yourself a blanket, dear. You're half-frozen."

The hospital was no more than a ten-minute drive from
where Hera had wrecked. The building was someone's ram-
bling old country house, where soldiers were being evacuated
to Calais, just like at Liette. The doctors looked at Hera's arm
right away, forced some whiskey down her throat and then
wrapped her up in a cast. Elise sat in a chair, watching it all,
so deeply grateful that the arm didn't have to come off. She
had to wipe the tears out of her eyes again and again.

Later, Hera was given dry clothes and put in a hospital
bed. Elise found a wooden chair and pulled it up next to her.
The ward was warm and full of activity, and they watched
together as nurses bundled up soldiers for transport. By now
it was dark outside.

The big woman who had driven them to the hospital came
over to Hera's bed and nodded to Elise. "How's the patient?"

"She's going to be fine," said Elise. "Thank you so much
for your help."

"Thank you," said Hera. "Where are you from?"

"Boston, Massachusetts," said the woman, and she took off
her cap to reveal hair as short as a man's. She smoothed it back

and replaced her hat, grinning. "I'm catching a ship home in the morning, thank God. What about you two?"

"We're going to London first," said Hera. "Then Paris."

The woman smiled. "If you're ever in Boston, look me up at a bar called the Marble Fawn. That's where I work, and I have a lot of friends there." She winked. "Good luck, girls," she said, and walked away, heading for the front doors of the hospital.

Hera turned to Elise as soon as she was gone. "She *winked* at you," she whispered.

"She winked at *us*," Elise whispered back. "She's one of *us*."

Hera stared after the woman for a long moment. "Oh," she said, finally. "I see."

CHAPTER FORTY-EIGHT

On November 11, Ruth was just washing up in the operating theater when she heard engines approaching. A lot of engines.

She checked her watch. It was two in the morning. The ambulances from Kortrijk weren't due for hours. She turned her whole body toward the sound. Could it be the Germans? A last-minute assault?

"MacBride?" she said.

He answered through the canvas, from outside, "Yes, Sister?"

"Who is it?" she said.

"I don't know," he said. "I can only see headlights."

She heard a *click* and she realized that he had a gun. A gun he'd never shown her or let on that he had. For a moment she was grateful, and then she was afraid. Without even tying her apron, she ran out of the tent and found him in the dark. In the near distance, headlights came around a curve in the road.

"Is it the Germans?" she asked, her voice shaking. "How could they get behind our lines?"

"Whoever it is," said MacBride, "they'll have to deal with me."

Suddenly there was honking. Someone was shouting over the noise of the lorries, *"Victory! Victory!"*

"Oh, God," said Ruth. "It's the ambulances from Kortrijk. But they're so early!"

MacBride waited until the first of the ambulances pulled up in front of the tent and then pushed the gun into the waistband of his trousers.

"What's going on?" said Ruth to the nearest driver, an old man with stick-figure limbs and muttonchop sideburns. He grabbed her hands and danced a little jig of joy.

"We've won!" he cried. "Haven't you heard? The whole bloody war is over."

"Not until eleven o'clock," said Ruth. "Why're you here at this hour?"

"To pick up your wounded," said the old man. "To empty your hospital. Your ambulances will have to be down at the front by eleven, and that'll be the end. Here," he said, and handed her an envelope. "Your orders."

Ruth tore it open. Inside was a piece of paper with Heflin's neat handwriting. She turned so she could read it by the headlights.

1) Prepare wounded for evacuation.
2) Pack up all equipment and return to Kortrijk as soon as possible.
3) Report to hospital at Kortrijk for further orders.
Many thanks, Sister Duncan, for your service.

The drivers were already inside the tents. Lantern light cast a mass of shadows rushing back and forth as orderlies lifted

groaning men from their beds and moved them outside. The
ambulances creaked as they were loaded, and in the dimness,
one of the wounded men gave Ruth a weary wave.

"Thank you, Sister," he called as he was carried away.
"Thanks for everything."

Ruth waved, and stood, doing nothing in the bustle all
around her. She felt like those German gunners she had seen
in the trenches, chained to their posts, glued to the spot where
she was standing.

Victory! she thought to herself and tried to smile. Out of the
predawn darkness, MacBride and Witcover came over to stand
next to her. MacBride put his arms around their shoulders.
The ambulances departed, honking their horns and flashing
their lights. The shouts of the men diminished in the distance.

"Victory," said MacBride, and he took a deep breath of the
early morning air. The sun was just coming up, flat and gold
against the eastern horizon.

"We'll celebrate when we get to Kortrijk," said MacBride
later, in the mess tent. "But I want to be at the front lines when
the last shot is fired. That'll be something I tell my grandchildren about." There was no clock in the mess tent, but all of
them had watches. It was ten fifteen now. It would take half
an hour for the ambulances to get to the front, and the drivers were impatient.

"You should come," Witcover said to Ruth. "It'll be his-
toric. You could ride with me."

"I'd just take up room you'd need for a patient," said Ruth.

"No, you won't," said Witcover. "I don't think it'll be bad.
Yesterday it wasn't bad. Everyone knows the war's about to
be over, and no one wants to get shot."

Contrary to Witcover's opinion, the big guns had been

going all night. Ruth was sure the ambulances would have their fill.

"I think it'll be worse than ever," said Ruth, "but all right. I'll go with you."

MacBride, in the first ambulance, led them at full speed over the rocks and bumps in the narrow country lane that led to the front. Oddly, they met no soldiers, either coming or going. Ruth guessed that everyone had been told to hold their positions until the very last minute. MacBride made a sudden right, up a hill on an even smaller, muddier track. Ruth realized, as she held on to her seat with both hands, that they were going up to where the big guns had been placed to get the best possible view of the end of things. Witcover downshifted, spun the steering wheel and followed him upward with the skill of a race car driver. Behind them, Stephano veered off and headed directly for the front lines, either disinterested in the final shot, or angling for a closer view.

"Shouldn't we stay together?" Ruth asked, watching Stephano disappear into the distance.

"Any other day, Sister, I would have said yes."

Ruth looked at her watch. It was 10:39.

MacBride pulled over to park on the trampled grass beside a half-dozen lorries. Witcover pulled in beside him. Already on the hill were a pair of colonels, a cluster of troops and the immense, gray, almost abstract shapes of the big guns. The sound of the shelling was so loud, it was hard to make out what anyone was saying. The colonels, in their freshly polished boots and battle ribbons, were speaking into each other's ears.

Ruth, MacBride and Witcover made their way to the edge of the hill, close to where the colonels were, and looked down.

Below them, the trenches were shallow, not like the built-up encampments in Ypres. There were hundreds of men, stretched thin here, bunched up there. Rifles and bayonets bristled like a porcupine. The smell of smoke and gunpowder wafted over everything. No man's land was barely a quarter mile between the two sides and scattered with bodies in uniforms from both sides. Barbed wire coiled in front of the trench lines, and reached as far as the eye could see. From above, on the hill, the big guns fired as fast as the gunners could load them, but the shells were falling far away from the German lines, somewhere off in the eastern distance. From below, a lone German gunner was firing his machine gun into the British lines, not hitting anyone as long as they kept their heads down. No one was firing back.

"Why aren't they shelling the Germans?" Witcover yelled to MacBride.

"They're just blowing off ammunition before the end of things," MacBride shouted back. "But that fellow down there—" he indicated the machine gunner "—he means business."

Witcover checked her watch. The colonels, MacBride and Ruth, checked theirs. It was 10:48. Ruth hoped everyone was synchronized, especially the German machine gunner.

Ruth peered down the hill for wounded men, but there were no stretcher-bearers or white bandages to be seen. She couldn't even see Stephano's ambulance. She dared to think that Witcover might be right and that all anyone was concerned with today was not getting hit by a bullet. She watched in horrified fascination as the German machine gunner swept the lines of huddled British soldiers, bullets flying harmlessly over them. She checked her watch again. Another eight minutes of this. The colonels were watching the gunner with binoculars now. One had pulled a man forward from the group of Tommies standing with them. The man had a long rifle, and Ruth guessed he was a sharpshooter. She looked down the hill again and wondered if this German would be the last to die. No one said anything for a long while. Ruth's watch crept minute by minute up to 10:58.

One of the colonels went up to the artillerymen who were still loading shells and told them to stop.

The big guns went quiet. The only sound in Ruth's ringing ears was the chatter of machine gun fire in the valley below.

The other colonel looked impatiently at his watch, down at the troops, over at the sharpshooter and back at his watch again.

Ruth's watch said 11:00.

The sharpshooter took aim. The German gunner appeared to glance at his watch. He stopped firing, unfolded himself from behind his machine gun and stood up straight. He was in the line of fire from every Tommy, but no one fired.

"No," said the colonel to the sharpshooter, who lowered his rifle.

The German machine gunner brushed off his uniform, then took off his helmet, and with great grace and ceremony, he bowed to the line of British troops. He turned and sauntered away from his machine gun nest as though it had been part of a stage and now his scene was over.

The Germans began to stand up. The Tommies, too. No one fired. No one said anything. Below, the soldiers began to crawl out of their trenches, each in their own direction. Ruth heard them start to cheer. MacBride joined in. The colonels looked stoic, but shook each other's hands. Witcover began to jump up and down. The artillery crews cheered as loudly as they could, just to hear themselves, Ruth thought, poor half-deaf things.

MacBride grabbed her arms. His beard met her face, and he kissed her hard on the cheek. "It's over!" he shouted. "It's over!" And he grabbed Witcover and kissed her, too.

★ ★ ★

It was hard for Ruth to believe there weren't any wounded. The three ambulances returned empty to the tent hospital at Charleroi, and Ruth searched the camp for Davidson, fully expecting her to be gone. Ruth found her in the nurses' tent, packing a very small bag.

"If you help take down the hospital," Ruth said to Davidson's back, "you'll get a ride to Kortrijk. Otherwise I'm afraid you'll have to get there on your own. It's a long way to walk," she added when Davidson didn't answer.

Davidson turned, red in the face. "The walk'll do me good," she snapped. "I should be able to remember every inch of ground we had to fight this useless war over. I should be able to remember every man whose blood I mopped up off the floor, but I can't. Do you know that? There were too many of them. Just too many. Did you know I lost my husband at the Somme? He was shot for cowardice when he didn't go over the top with everyone else. The poor man only wanted to go home. He never wanted to kill anyone and he'd gone over the top plenty of times before. *Cowardice?*"

Ruth, taken aback by this explosion of feeling from a woman who had been so bottled up until now, wasn't sure what to say.

"What a useless waste of time we've all had," said Davidson, furious. "What a useless waste of lives. And this—" She waved her hands at the hospital tent. "I say leave it to fall in on itself. Leave it here as a monument to the futility of it all. Mending men just so they could fight again. Shameful! And you—" She stabbed a finger in Ruth's direction. "You never questioned any of it. You were saving lives, and I'll give you credit for that, but you never questioned for an instant what you were doing. All you ever think about is becoming a doctor. Well, I for one would never come to you. You haven't the ethics to be a doctor of any kind." Tears began to stream down her red face. "All those young men. All of them, dead now. People say it's an entire generation."

Ruth took a step toward her, to put a hand on her shoulder, but Davidson jerked away.

"I don't want your sympathy," she said. "I don't want anything to do with the tidying up. I can't even say it's been a pleasure working with you because it *hasn't*. It's been anything but." She snatched up her little suitcase. "Goodbye," she said. "I hope I never see you or any of these other people again."

She ducked under the drape of the tent and stalked off across the barren landscape, heading for Kortrijk, a good twenty-five miles away.

Ruth went outside to watch her go, dumbfounded at the amount of venom the woman had hidden all this time. Part of her was deeply wounded by the things Davidson had said. Patching up soldiers just so they could go to the front lines again. Wasn't that the agreement of war? Soldiers fought, doctors cured and nurses held up the middle between them. She was guilty of some of the things Davidson had said, but she tried to shake it off. The war was over, for God's sake. Of course there were still dead men to be buried, still wounded men to hover over in the convalescent hospitals, but it was over. The last bullet had been fired. Wasn't that some cause for celebration? She was suddenly sorry for Davidson and wondered how the woman would live the rest of her life with such a profound bitterness.

Ruth turned to find Porter standing beside her, shading her eyes at the distance and Davidson disappearing into it.

"Did you hear any of that?" Ruth asked.

"All of it," said Porter. "The walls are thin. I think everyone heard it."

"Do you want to walk back to Kortrijk, too?" Ruth asked uncertainly.

"Not me," said Porter. "I say we break this place down as fast as we can, pack it up and go someplace where they're serving champagne."

CHAPTER FORTY-NINE

November 12, 1918

By Ruth's watch, it was midnight when they got to Kortrijk, and it had started to snow. What should have been a three-hour trip stretched on and on as she and MacBride got caught up in column after column of marching men, lorries, horse-drawn carts, even tanks. Until sunset, she had been able to keep track of Witcover's and Stephano's ambulances, but as it got darker and snowier, she lost them in the endless traffic and glare of headlights.

"I hope they're still behind us," she said to MacBride in the cold cab. Her breath came out as steam. "We're all supposed to arrive in Kortrijk together."

"They'll get there," said MacBride. His beard had ice in it. "They know the way."

"But we're all supposed to meet Heflin at the hospital," said Ruth. Her cloth coat was too thin for this weather. She'd taken a blanket from the back of the ambulance and wrapped it around herself for the ride. Her bare hands, tucked into the edge of the blanket, were freezing. "She'll give us our orders, and we'll be able to get on the train to Calais."

"If Heflin thinks we'll find her in this mess, she'll have to think again," said MacBride. He gestured at the pelting snow and the jam of cars, men and machinery. "She may be stuck out here as well. Not too comfortable on that motorcycle, I'll bet."

By the time they got to the outskirts of Kortrijk, the snow was churned to a cold, icy muck, and the ambulance spun its wheels, barely able to get traction enough to move. More and more vehicles seemed to be deserted, and more and more men passed them on foot, shouting and laughing as they marched through the slop. Then traffic came to a standstill. Ruth checked the time: twelve thirty, twelve forty-five, then one in the morning. MacBride had long since turned off the engine to save gas.

"I'm going to see about Witcover and Stephano," said Ruth.

"You'll do no such thing." MacBride caught her arm as she opened the passenger side door. "You'll get lost. This ambulance looks like all the others. You'll get lost out there and never find your way back. You'll end up walking into Kortrijk alone. Listen to them," he said and nodded at the crowds of men winding their way through the lorries toward town. "Half of them are drunk. It isn't safe."

"I'm a nurse," said Ruth in surprise. "They won't do anything to me."

"Things are different now," said MacBride. "Yesterday they were soldiers. Now they're just men with guns."

Ruth looked at him curiously in the faint light. This hardly sounded like MacBride. But then she thought back on their conversation about honor, and how it had evaporated. "Well, what would you suggest?" said Ruth. "Should we sit here until sunrise?"

"No," said MacBride. "I'll go with you."

The two of them got out of the ambulance and waded through the slush. They headed against the advancing flow of men, past abandoned lorries, a chuffing tank, even loose horses. There were more ambulances in the mix. Two were empty, tilted sideways, trapped in the snowy mud. The other three still had drivers, but none of them were Witcover or Stephano.

Ruth leaned into the driver's side of one. "Which hospital are you from?"

The driver responded in French.

"Were you under Matron Heflin?" Ruth asked hopelessly.

The driver just shook his head, smiled and offered her a bottle of something boozy. He was obviously going to stay put, soaked with alcohol, until morning.

Ruth wiped snow from her face and turned to MacBride. He'd been right about finding her own ambulance again. She had no idea where it was.

"Sister," said MacBride, "we might as well just walk into town with everyone else. You could look for hours and still not find them. If they're smart, they'll leave their lorries and get to the hospital. At least it'll be warm there."

"You're right," said Ruth, discouraged, cold and very tired. She hooked her arm into MacBride's. He clamped her cold hand to his side. She huddled into her blanket, and they started the walk into Kortrijk.

When they arrived, it was close to two thirty, and the town was caught up in a huge celebration in the middle of a freezing night. Cafés had opened their doors to all, officers and men, and were pouring drinks freely. Mobs of singing, shouting, drunken soldiers, half of them wrapped in blankets, like Ruth, blocked the narrow streets. Some were already over-come and lying on their faces in the snow.

"They'll freeze to death," said Ruth, her teeth chattering.

"That may be," said MacBride, holding on to her as they pushed through the tight jostle of the crowd, "but at least they survived the war."

At last, they found the mansion-turned-hospital, candles lit in only a few of the first-floor windows. Ruth had expected a driveway full of ambulances, rousting out the last patients for the train, but there were only a few lorries parked in the main courtyard, and the party in the main part of Kortrijk was nowhere to be seen near the mansion.

The two of them went in through the ornate front door to find the hospital almost entirely deserted. Here and there, soldiers were sleeping in beds—dressed in their uniforms and muddy boots—some snoring, some quietly unconscious from drink.

"Where's everyone else?" Ruth asked as they stood in the main hallway at the foot of the dark stairs. Her voice echoed off the ceiling. "Where're the doctors and nurses?"

"And Heflin," said MacBride accusingly. "Where's she?"

Behind them, Ruth heard the door open, and she turned to see three soldiers, practically in rags. One had an arm in a sling. One had a dirty white bandage over one eye. One was muddy but seemed unscathed. All three of them were hold-ing bottles of beer, which they hoisted in Ruth's direction.

"Victory!" cried the one with his arm in a sling.

"Victory!" echoed the other two, and all three of them took a swig.

"We're very happy about that," said Ruth. She spread her arms at the empty wards. "But where is everybody?"

"They shipped th' wounded out this mornin'," said the

uninjured soldier in a thick Cockney accent. "All th' doctors and nurses, too. Wozn't even a place on th' train. Ridin' on th' roof, it woz so packed."

"When's the next train?" MacBride asked.

The men started to laugh. "Whenever it gets here," said the one with the eyepatch.

"But I have to be in Calais today," said Ruth. "I have to get to London."

The men laughed again. "Good luck, Sister," said the man with the eye patch. He came over and tried to hand her his bottle. "Forget about that, Sister! Drink with us! Celebrate!"

MacBride gave him a push that sent him to the floor and knocked the beer out of his hand. The soldier staggered to his feet and drunkenly put up his fists, but MacBride placed his bulk between him and Ruth.

"Get out," he said, deep and commanding. "Go back to your bar. *Now!*"

The other two soldiers grabbed their companion. They dragged him out of the mansion without a backward glance, but Ruth could hear them laughing as the big door shut behind them. The candles set in the arched windows flickered in the draft.

She and MacBride stood in silence for a long time.

"Heflin's never going to get here," said Ruth.

"No," said MacBride. "I don't think so."

"No one has any orders," said Ruth, suddenly dizzy with the realization. "We can get on the train without them. We'll just wait at the station until it comes."

"We'll go together," said MacBride. "It's a madhouse out there."

It was another mile to the train station, and the weather was getting worse. The snow, where it hadn't been ground into frozen mud, crept into Ruth's soaked shoes. Snow fell into the narrow space between the collar of her inadequate coat and her neck, and chilled her to the bone. The blanket, still draped around her shoulders, was damp and frozen. MacBride's arm was the only warm thing. She clung to him as he plunged ahead, pushing aside soldiers and officers, all slogging toward the train station. She kept her eyes open for nurses or VAD personnel, or drivers, but all she could see in the snow were soldiers, dragging their feet, dragging their rifles in the dark hours of the morning, heading for the bright lights of the station.

"Look there," said MacBride as they got closer. "Ambulances."

Sure enough, ambulances were parked in a neat row along the road to the station. There were dozens and dozens of them, as though they had lined up, disgorged their cargos and been abandoned. They weren't quite abandoned, though. Solders had taken shelter in the backs and here and there. Lanterns lit the insides, showing men in tattered uniforms sleeping on the racks of cots, or drinking, just out of the snowfall.

"This way," said MacBride, and he angled her toward the bright lights of the station. Ruth could feel him shivering, but his voice was steady. "Let's see if we can get inside."

They made their way along the snow-covered train tracks until Ruth could see the platform, where there was a roof. The roofed area was packed, barely sheltered, and the men were huddled together. Snow covered their shoulders and hats, as though they had been standing there for hours. The revelry in the main streets of Kortrijk was missing here. If there was drinking, it was quiet.

MacBride managed to get the two of them up onto the concrete platform, lifting Ruth by her waist. He climbed up beside her, panting, his beard dripping with icy water, his eyebrows crusted in white.

He took a breath and looked around at the soldiers crushed up against them. For Ruth, it was warmer here, in the press of bodies, and no one seemed to be grabbing at her or pushing a bottle of beer in her face.

"Sister Duncan," said MacBride, "this is where you and I part ways."

"What?" said Ruth. "No! I mean, aren't you coming to Calais?"

MacBride shook his head. "Not tonight. I'll wait for another train tomorrow, or the next day. I don't have appointments in London. There's no need for me to rush." He gave her an awkward bow. "It's been my esteemed pleasure to have worked with you all these weeks. I think you're the best nurse I've ever known. You'll make a fine doctor one day, and if Davidson can't see that, it's her loss entirely. I hope you'll excuse me now, as I intend to get roaring drunk with my compatriots."

"Yes," stammered Ruth. "Yes, of course. Thank you so much for your help. I could never have done half of it without you."

MacBride tipped a nonexistent hat at her and eased himself down off the platform. Officers in their greatcoats made way for him, and soon MacBride was disappearing, against the flow of the crowd, into the driving snow.

One of the soldiers standing near her was watching him, too, a stained bandage around his head. "Excuse me, Sister," he said in an American accent. "Do you know the time?"

Ruth looked at her watch. "It's almost four. Do you know when the next train comes?"

"They said they would send one every six hours," said the soldier. "I've been waiting here since yesterday afternoon. But the station master got a phone call a while back. They say the train's coming anytime now."

Ruth wondered how often that rumor had circulated since

the last train left. She wondered if there was anywhere to sit down and rest. And when the train did come, how long would it take to get to Calais? She was so cold and tired. She couldn't remember the last time she'd had more than four hours of sleep, and being warm seemed like a dream from long ago.

"You're an American," said the soldier. "So am I. Where are you from?"

"Maryland," said Ruth. "What about you?"

"Mississippi," said the soldier. "I've never seen snow before."

From farther up the platform, someone gave a shout. In the distance, Ruth heard the chug of a train, and a cry went up all around her. Dampened spirits evaporated into shoving and shouting. Ruth was caught in the surge of the crowd and felt her feet lift up from the ground in the press of shoulders and chests. The soldier from Mississippi vanished behind her, and she let herself be carried along by the rush of men toward the train. Before she knew it, she was reaching for the handles of the doorway of one of the cars. One soldier spread his arms against the tide of his fellows so she could navigate the steps in her long, dirty skirt, but only for a moment, and then the rush was on again, pushing her up the steps, inside and into the passageway between the seats. An officer, already sitting by the window, both his hands bandaged, stood up for her and wordlessly offered his seat. In the din and the crush, she fell into it and sat, breathing hard, looking out the window at the men still trying to get on. She saw no one she recognized, not a doctor, a driver or even a patient. It occurred to her that she didn't actually know where the train was headed. She turned to the officer who had given her his seat.

"Excuse me," she shouted over the ruckus. "Where does this train go?"

"Where all the trains are going now." He, for one, seemed perfectly calm. "Calais."

CHAPTER FIFTY

It was just dawn on the first day after the end of the war, and Calais, from Ruth's point of view, was a tightly controlled riot. At the train terminal, military police were everywhere. Handfuls of able-bodied soldiers were sitting, smoking and drinking as they waited to board the only ship Ruth could see, the *Mary Beth*. Farther away, the wounded were lined up in rows, on stretchers on the ground, feet and hands wrapped in rags against the cold. Ruth could see her breath as she hugged the blanket around herself and hurried over to the ranks of the wounded. Surely she would find Elise somewhere over there, or someone who knew Elise, or where she was.

Ruth made her way over to the stretchers and soldiers who could still sit upright. Every wound imaginable was there for her to see and Davidson's words came back to her—the waste of an entire generation. There were hundreds here and more coming in every minute. It shouldn't have surprised her—it wasn't as if she hadn't seen all this before—but somehow this was different, more awful. Part of it was that she didn't know what to do for these men. They had already been bandaged and made ready for transport.

She stopped, breathing hard, and realized that what made this whole scene so unnerving was that she could no longer hear the big guns.

A VAD girl with a muffler wrapped around her throat came rushing by with a mug of hot tea in each hand. Her breath steamed out over the muffler. The tea steamed in her bare, red hands.

"Wait a minute," said Ruth, and the VAD girl stopped in her tracks.

"Yes, Sister?"

"Who's in charge here?"

"See that tent?" The girl, who could not have been more than eighteen, indicated a dirty white tent about a quarter mile away. White smoke rose from a pipe in the side. "That's where the matrons and the doctors are."

"Thank you," said Ruth, and the VAD girl hurried off.

Ruth picked her way toward the tent. To her right, the ambulances dropped off ever-growing numbers of men. To her left, the sea of wounded stretched almost to the docks. The tent seemed very far away, and she had to step between stretchers to get to it. Men begged her for water, for a blanket, which she gave away immediately. Cold wind picked up her nurse's veil and crept down her neck. It blew under her skirt and made her legs feel pinched. The sky was leaden, and it looked like snow might start at any minute.

The closer Ruth got to the tent, the more activity there was. Orderlies picked up stretchers and carried them in the direction of the ship. Nurses fluttered around the wounded, distributing blankets. Doctors were there, too, wrapped in greatcoats, kneeling by their patients. There were priests as well, their cassocks blowing in the cold wind, delivering last rites out in the open, scattered like black birds, crouched over those who had made it this far but were going no farther.

Ruth entered the tent and was both surprised and unsurprised to see Matron Heflin there in all her bustle and glory.

"Duncan!" she said. "You made it! Congratulations! Where's the rest of your unit?"

"As far as I know, they're all still in Kortrijk trying to catch a train," said Ruth. She didn't want to say *we were in Kortrijk—where were you?* Trying to hold MacBride back from his celebrations would have been impossible. She didn't want to talk about Davidson. She had no idea where Witcover, Porter and Stephano were.

"Never mind, then," said Heflin. "You look done in. Sit down and have a cup of tea." She had a cup of her own, and she poured Ruth one from a kettle on a woodstove, the source of the smoke. Ruth sat heavily on a nearby chair.

"Matron," said Ruth. "I have to find my sister. She was driving the wounded here from a hospital in Liette."

"Hmm," said Heflin. "I'll see what I can find out. It may take a while. In the meantime, you can see if you recognize any of the drivers. I'll put you on duty with the incoming wounded. You'll be giving out blankets." She gestured at a pile in the corner of the tent.

"Yes, Matron." Ruth started to get up.

"But not right now," said Heflin. "Drink your tea. Have a biscuit." She pointed to a stacked plate. "Rest a bit and then we'll get you started."

Heflin ducked out of the tent, and Ruth sipped the tea, which was bitingly hot. The biscuits were stale, but she didn't care. She ate three, not remembering her last meal or having any idea where her next one was coming from.

As the heat of the tea crept through her, she felt a little more enthusiasm for what was going on around her. People were gathering here. People were going home. The war was over. Sometime soon she would sleep in a proper bed, not on a cot. She would be eating food off a table instead of a plate in her lap. There was civilization on the other side of the water. She would see John. For the first time in a long time, they would have a chance to talk.

Ruth finished the tea, took blankets from the corner of the tent and went back out into the cold.

There were so many ambulances coming in, unloading and leaving again, Ruth hardly knew where to start. She dispensed her blankets to shivering men, the unconscious, the ones still waiting from the night before and covered with a light dusting of snow. It was endless, Ruth thought, as she headed back to the tent for more blankets. This stream of the wounded. What would it be like in England when they all got home? Who would take care of them then? How would their families cope? How was John's family coping? She couldn't imagine.

Ruth worked her way farther and farther from the tent, until she was close to where the ambulances were discharging their loads. She was surprised to see soldiers driving some of the ambulances, not the usual women. One lorry pulled up right next to her, and a British soldier leaned out, grizzled with days of stubble, dark circles under his eyes. He had an unlit cigarette in his mouth.

"'Ello, Sister," he said to her. "'Ave you got a light?"

"Sorry," she said. "I wish I did."

He looked disappointed and gestured vaguely to the wounded men, lying on the ground or on stretchers, lined up in neat rows on the snowy grass. "Where do you want 'em?"

She pointed to the end of the closest row. "I'll help you."

"No need," said the Tommy. "Mine are all walkers. Aren't you, boys?" He slapped the side of the ambulance, and affirmative voices mumbled in the back. The tailgate banged open, and the men started to get out. Most of them were arm amputees, though a couple were bandaged for head wounds. Ruth tried not to think of John. She made sure they all had a blanket and showed them where to sit. One by one they thanked her.

"'Ow long before they can get on a ship?" asked the Tommy.

"It could be hours," said Ruth. "I've seen men who've been here all night."

"Well, it's bloody better'n being in a trench," the Tommy said, mostly for the benefit of the men. "Pardon my language, Sister."

"It's all right," said Ruth. "Where were you driving from?"

"St. Martine," said the Tommy.

She'd hoped he would say Liette. "My sister's driving an ambulance. She's stationed in Liette."

"At the spa?" said the Tommy, and he let out a whistle. "Lucky girl."

Had Elise ever mentioned that she was running the wounded from a spa? Ruth really couldn't remember. Maybe she had the name wrong. "I'm seeing more and more men driving," said Ruth. "Where are the women?"

The Tommy gestured at the ship in the harbor. "They're goin' home, Sister. Now that there's no more war, they're puttin' soldiers in the ambulances, and the girls are leavin'. I'll tell you wot." He eyed her. "Maybe you should, too. You don't sound like you're from around 'ere."

"I have to find my sister first," said Ruth.

"And I have to find a light," said the Tommy. He gave her a sloppy salute. "Thanks for your service, Sister."

She watched him drive off, and hurried to meet the next ambulance as it came jouncing over the field. There were at least ten more behind it, and Ruth began to wonder how she would ever find Elise. To plan to meet at Calais was one thing—to actually find each other was another. It began to dawn on her that the only sure place to find Elise was at the Dowelings'. Maybe Elise was already there. Maybe the Tommy was right. She should get on a ship and go.

Ruth stopped in the snowy field as the ambulances approached, and turned to look behind her at the wounded men, packed together, past the tent where Heflin was, all the way to the docks. There was nothing she could do for these men but give them a smile and a blanket. She was out of blankets, and she didn't feel like smiling. She could get on a ship, and no one would care.

Ruth shut her eyes and stood where she was for a moment, the wind blowing down her neck. She was freezing, and she wanted to see John so badly. Wanted to know at least what he would say to her now that he'd had time to think. She opened her eyes, ready to walk away from the incoming ambulances, when she saw four nurses running toward her, each with an armful of blankets. One stopped and breathlessly handed Ruth half of her stack.

"Come on," said the nurse, "no time to waste." She started running again, expecting Ruth to follow. Ruth turned reluctantly and hurried along behind. She was committed to this day, at least.

If there was one thing she'd learned from the British, it was that duty was duty, after all.

Ruth spent the morning wrapping men in blankets, smiling as best she could and going back to the tent for hot tea when possible. At noon, one of the VAD girls brought around dishes of stew, which, though cold and meatless, gave Ruth the energy she needed for the afternoon. She had asked every ambulance driver she saw if they were from Liette, and if they knew Elise. Many of the drivers were French orderlies who had taken the place of the women, and just shrugged at her English. Finally one of the women drivers told her that the ambulances from Liette were late because of the snow, and would probably be in closer to two. Eagerly Ruth asked her about Elise.

"The one who crashed yesterday?" said the driver.

"What?" said Ruth.

"Slid down a hill," said the driver, a woman with round glasses, swaddled in a gray scarf. "Pinned under her lorry. Had to remove the engine to get her out from under it. Quite a fantastic feat."

"Did she survive?" said Ruth. It was the hardest question she had ever asked.

The woman squinted behind her glasses. "Dearie, I just don't know. I assume she did. I know they took her to hospital."

"Which one?" demanded Ruth.

"Not sure, dearie, not sure. Be a love and find me an orderly or two. Got sitters in the back, don't you know."

Ruth swallowed hard and went to find a couple of orderlies. It was one o'clock now. If Elise wasn't here by two thirty, with the other drivers from Liette, surely they would know what hospital she was in. Instead of getting on a ship, that's where she would go next. The dreadful picture in her mind of Elise pinned under an ambulance kept her sweating for the next hour, when a long line of ambulances, nineteen in all, came into the field to unload.

Ruth ran up to the first one. "You're from Liette?" she said to the driver, a woman dressed in a matron's uniform.

"We are," she said. "We've been on the road for five hours. The men are freezing. Have you any tea?"

"I'll make sure they get some," said Ruth, "but first tell me about Elise Duncan. Is she all right?"

"Duncan?" said the matron. "I have no idea, and furthermore, I don't care. She deserted her ambulance and her squad yesterday. She can go to hell."

"But she crashed her ambulance," said Ruth, hardly believing her ears.

The matron looked at Ruth like she was out of her mind. "That was someone else, Sister. Do you have any tea, or don't you?"

"We do. Of course we do." Ruth should've run to find a VAD girl, but instead, she ran to the next ambulance. The driver had parked and was just getting out, beating her arms against her body with the cold.

"Do you know anything about Elise Duncan?" demanded Ruth.

"Of course," said the driver, shivering. "She saved a girl's life yesterday. Bad crash and all."

"But she wasn't hurt," said Ruth.

"*She* wasn't," said the driver, "but I heard they had to take off the girl's arm. Real shame, here at the end of the war and all."

"Do you have any idea where Elise is?" Ruth asked.

"No idea," said the driver, "but I know she was ahead of us. She should've been here hours ago."

Hours ago? Ruth turned and looked at the ships again. Was Elise on board already?

"Say," said the driver. "Any chance of hot tea and blankets?"

"Unload your men," said Ruth. "I'll make sure you get some."

She headed down to the tent. Had she been looking for Elise in the wrong places? Was it possible that Elise was wandering around in the rows of wounded looking for her? A cloud of nurses surrounded the tent, running in and out with blankets. Ruth elbowed through them, found two VAD girls inside and instructed them to take tea up to the newly arrived ambulances. The girls were hurrying to obey, when Ruth heard someone call her name.

"Ruth!" shouted a woman's voice from just outside the tent. "Duncan!"

Ruth turned to see a bundled-up woman with her arm in a cast. She was holding a cup of steaming tea in her good hand. A knit cap was pulled down over her head, almost covering her eyes. She was dressed in an oversized officer's coat. Ruth tried hard to recognize her. A nurse she'd worked with in Belgium? No—that wasn't right.

The woman shouldered her way into the tent. "It's me, Ruth," she said impatiently. She put down the tea and pulled off her hat. Yellow hair spilled out.

"Hera! Where's Elise?"

"Just outside—come on!"

Ruth followed on her heels, past men in bandages, past women in uniform, past Heflin still perched by the stove. Outside, amid the sitters, was Elise, wrapped in a scarf and a tattered woolen coat, scratching her head and looking around. Her cheeks were pink, and her body was whole. Ruth felt relief rush over her. She pushed past Hera and caught her sister's cold, bare hand. "Elise!" She fairly screamed it.

Elise swung around, and the two of them grabbed each other. Tears ran down Ruth's face. "Elise!" she said in her sister's ear. "I thought you'd wrecked your ambulance!"

"Not me." Elise pulled away to wipe her eyes. "Not me—it was Hera. My God, Ruth, you look like hell. What happened to you?"

Ruth glanced down at herself, her skirt, dirty to the knees, torn in places, bloody in places. She reached up to adjust her nurse's veil, and discovered she'd lost it. Her hair seemed to be sticking out at all angles, like a madwoman's. She tried to smooth it down. Why hadn't anyone told her she looked like hell? Ruth glanced around at the other nurses and realized that they *all* looked like hell. No one looked rested or fed or clean—except for Elise and Hera, who were positively glowing.

Something in the way they were looking at her—with sympathy—pity—and pride, made Ruth's knees weak. Even though it was freezing cold, her whole body began to sweat, from behind her ears to the soles of her cold feet. She leaned against Elise, dizzy, trying not to fall into the trampled grass and frozen mud.

"Are you all right?" Elise murmured in her ear.

"I'm just so glad to see you," Ruth whispered. "I was afraid for you so many times."

Elise hugged her tightly. "When was the last time you slept?"

"I don't know," said Ruth. "Before the end of the war? What about you?"

"Well," said Elise, "last night I slept in a chair, but Hera got a nice clean bed in the hospital."

"I would've been glad to sleep with the other drivers," said Hera, "but they insisted." She tapped her cast, which reached from her shoulder to her wrist. "Doctors, you know."

"Right," said Ruth. She pulled away from her sister, steadier now, and tried to smooth her hair again.

Elise eyed her. "What're your orders? Are you supposed to stay here?"

"I don't have any orders," said Ruth. "I have no idea what I'm supposed to do. I was handing out blankets, waiting to find you."

"And then?" Elise prompted.

"And then I was going to get on the ship." Ruth gestured weakly at the harbor. "What about you?"

"We've been replaced by soldiers," said Elise. She touched Hera's good arm. "We're leaving." She hooked her other arm into Ruth's. "Are you ready to go?"

"But what about all of these men?" said Ruth. "They're freezing. Who'll give them a blanket?"

Elise cocked her head at the tent, the flurry of nurses, orderlies and VAD girls, in and out, all carrying blankets. "Maybe you've been replaced, too. Maybe you've done your time. You've cut off their arms and legs. You've taken bullets out of them. You've sewn them up. The war is over, Ruth. It's time to go."

"But what about duty?" whispered Ruth.

"What about Dr. Doweling?" said Hera. "Isn't he waiting for you?"

"Yes," said Ruth. "Yes." One way or the other.

"Then let's go," said Elise. She pulled Ruth away from the tent and toward the ship, and Ruth went willingly.

CHAPTER FIFTY-ONE

With Ruth's arm locked in one hand, and Hera's hand in the other, Elise marched them toward the ship. As they approached the *Mary Beth*, Elise could see that the biggest problem they were going to have was finding a place to stand for the three-hour voyage to Dover. High above them, leaning over the ship's railing, were soldiers, sailors, even pilots, by the looks of their jackets, crowded together, not so much for warmth as by necessity. Elise had seen what a thousand wounded men looked like in the wards of Liette. This ship had that many, and more getting on every minute. It was just a question of time, she thought, until the ship was declared full, the gang-plank was raised and the *Mary Beth* sailed away.

"Come on," she said to Ruth, who was lagging. "Hurry up."

"I'm hurrying," said Ruth.

"Hurry faster," said Elise, and pulled the two of them along, down the shallow hill to the harbor.

They wound their way between stretchers and wheelchairs where legless men sat and smoked cigars. Orderlies and soldiers were everywhere, carrying stretchers up the wide gangplank, pushing wheelchairs. Nurses at the top of the gangplank waited for the next patients. There was no crowd of pushing men, as Elise had expected, just a line of orderlies and their charges, waiting for their turn to board.

"Look up there." Hera freed her good arm to point. "It's so full, they're standing on the lifeboats."

The ship's horn sounded, deep and low. It vibrated through Elise's body, and she pulled Ruth even closer. "They're getting ready to leave. Let's go."

Together they trudged up the creaking gangplank. No one gave them a second glance until they got up to the top, and the nurses saw Ruth.

"You're a sight," said one of the women, eyeing Ruth's dirty, torn uniform dress, her bare head and her hair. "Find yourself a place to sit, Sister. I wish we could offer you a chair, but…" She spread her arms at the number of men.

"It's fine," said Ruth. "Thank you."

"There might be places by the rail on the far side of the ship," said the nurse. "Maybe some gentleman will give you his seat."

"Thanks," said Elise, and the two of them followed Hera, holding hands, filing through the press of wounded men. Elise wished she could find a place for Ruth to lie down. Her sister seemed almost ill with exhaustion. Hours on this ship in the cold and hours more on a troop bus to London would put them in the city by nightfall. By then, Ruth might actually be sick.

From wherever the troop bus let them off in London, they would have to get to the Dowelings' home. Elise wondered if they could do something as ordinary as take a cab, and realized that she had no money to pay for a cab. In fact, none of them did. It occurred to her that she'd had no money since the beginning of the war. Everything—food, clothing, shelter, an ambulance—had been provided for her, no matter how poor it was. She looked down at her tattered coat, her snow-soaked shoes. This was all the war had left her. Wasn't it? She looked up at Hera's blond head as she led the way to the far side of the ship. Maybe she had more than just a few articles of clothing and a head full of awful memories. Maybe the war had left her with a future.

The far side of the ship was just as crowded. Men stood together in large groups, huddled against the wind, talking and smoking. Some, Elise noticed, had hip flasks they were passing around. The deck was wide, perfect for huge groups of people, but open to the weather. Elise, searching for a sheltered spot, saw none.

"I say," Hera said to Elise. "I do believe I see a lifeboat."

"We don't need a lifeboat," said Elise. "We need a place to sit."

"We'll sit underneath the lifeboat," said Hera. "It'll be less windy." She pushed through the crowd, her hand still wrapped tight around Elise's, Elise's hand still locked on to Ruth's, until they managed to get to the first of five or six lifeboats. There were ropes coiled underneath, and there wasn't much room, but no one was sitting there, and Hera was right—it seemed more sheltered than the rest of the deck.

The three of them sat on the cold, hard ropes, their heads now at hip height to the men who surrounded them. Ruth slumped, shivering against Elise, and Hera cradled her broken arm protectively. One of the men standing right in front of them turned and bent down. He had a broken arm, too.

"Sisters," he said, perhaps mistaking them all for nurses. "Would you care for a blanket?" He had one draped around his shoulders, and he took it off, offering it to Elise.

"Don't you need it?" Elise asked. "It's just going to get colder."

"I'll manage," said the soldier. "But the three of you look like you're freezing."

Elise took the blanket and draped it over Ruth, tucking it in at the edges. It was scratchy and thin, but Ruth huddled into it and stopped shaking quite so much. "Thank you," said Elise to the soldier.

"No trouble at all," said the soldier, and he disappeared into the churning mass of men.

The ship's horn sounded again. A billow of smoke rose from its smokestack, and a cheer went up across the deck.

"We must be casting off," said Hera. "We're on our way home!"

"Thank God," said Elise. "Ruth? Did you hear that?"

"Thank God," Ruth croaked. She moved just enough to put her feverish head in Elise's lap, and fell asleep.

The short passage seemed endless to Elise. Snow clouds obscured the sun, making it a cold, hard disk that never seemed to budge, no matter how many hours went by.

"Do you know," said Hera, who was trying hard to keep up a constant chatter, "Father's yacht does this trip in two and a half hours? It's quite exciting, with the sails out and the sea foaming around the bow. Naturally, we don't do it in the dead of winter, like this."

"When do you do it?" Elise asked absently, stroking Ruth's hair. She liked hearing Hera talk. She just wasn't paying attention.

"In the summer, obviously," said Hera. "You'll be coming with us, of course, when we sail to the south of France." She sighed. "If there's a south of France left anymore."

Elise didn't want to say anything, but she was fairly sure

Hera's parents would disown her as soon as they figured out what was going on between the two of them. The thought made her depressed on this, what should have been the least depressing day in the history of her life.

"Hera," she said, and prepared to ask the question that had been nagging at her. "I know you want to have a hundred children and live in Paris, but have you thought about how we're going to pay for that? I mean, I suppose I can fix cars, but that'll never be enough to support us."

Hera just blinked at her out from under the knit cap. "Darling," she said. "Haven't I ever told you? I have an allowance from my grandmama. It's ten thousand a year. We can afford whatever we like."

"But what about your parents?" said Elise, and she lowered her voice. "When they figure out what's going on…"

"Pooh," said Hera. "Let them. They can't take that away from me. It's my inheritance."

"So," said Elise slowly, still not sure what ten thousand a year would buy, "what you're saying is that you can do whatever you want with this money."

"I'm not rich," said Hera modestly, "but we can be well-off."

"Well-off," echoed Elise.

"I have a plan," said Hera. "We'll go to Paris as soon as my arm is healed. We'll find a perfectly wonderful house in the First Arrondissement, big enough for a dozen war orphans. We'll be close to the museums and galleries so the children will be exposed to all the best art. And the best food, naturally. We'll hire a maid and a cook—they'll have to be sympathetic to our cause, of course—because we may even take in a German orphan or two. My goodness, there must be thousands, but we must all do our part to make sure this sort of war never happens again. We'll start with the very youngest," she went on, barely taking a breath. "And then take in a few older ones, especially the girls, around fourteen and fifteen. They're so vulnerable at that age. I know *I* was, and I imagine you were, too. And who knows what awful things have happened to them."

"You've given this a lot of thought," said Elise, taken aback.

"Someone had to," said Hera quietly, and she leaned closer. "I knew you were only thinking about me."

CHAPTER FIFTY-TWO

Ruth woke abruptly, curled up on a mattress of ropes, stiff from the cold. Elise was shaking her.

"Wake up! Wake up! We're here!"

She pushed herself to her knees, ears ringing, throat raw, nose dripping. She felt terrible. Elise grabbed her arm and pulled her to her feet. Ruth dropped her blanket and tried to steady herself on the rolling deck. Everyone, all the wounded, were cheering their lungs out. "Where are we?" she said thickly.

"Dover!" shouted Elise. "You can see the cliffs!"

It was sunset, a dark, brackish sunset. It was impossible to see anything except the backs of the men in front of her as they pressed for the railing.

"Get up on the lifeboat." Elise grabbed Ruth by the waist and lifted her. From above, a man's hands caught hers and pulled her upward. The ship rolled. The lifeboat swayed, but

Ruth ended up on her feet, standing on the heavy canvas life-boat cover, steadied by a soldier with a patch over one eye.

"Over there, Sister." He pointed to the right, and she could see them, distant white cliffs darkening as the sun went down, stretching for miles along the coast.

Elise and Hera clambered up, stood and held on to each other for balance.

"There's the harbor," shouted Hera. "Look at the lights! It's like Christmas!"

Ruth, Elise and Hera sat squeezed together on a bench seat meant for two as the bus pulled out, stinking of diesel. The only reason they had gotten a seat was that they were women, Ruth thought, although her hacking and sneezing might have been part of the motivation behind the two soldiers with their arms in splints getting up and making room for the three of them. She leaned her head against her sister's shoulder, pledging not to sleep as she listened to Elise and Hera whispering something about the children they would have. It seemed like a dream, and it probably was. The two of them seemed so happy together. Elise's secret life was not so secret anymore. Elise's love life, looking up when her own seemed so bleak in comparison.

The bus jerked to a halt at one in the morning in front of Victoria Station. Ruth opened her eyes and looked out the window, frosted with her own breath. The station was garishly lit, nothing like the blackout darkness of Belgium, but it was what was on the street that caught her sleepy attention. There were dozens of people out, all dressed in coats and hats, all waving little British flags, and she could hear them singing "Rule, Britannia!" The street seemed heaped with snow, but people were throwing handfuls of confetti, and slowly Ruth

realized there was confetti on the street, left there from previous crowds. Crowds that must have numbered in the hundreds. Possibly more.

"Elise?" she mumbled, and elbowed her sister. "Do you
see that?"

"They're welcoming us," said Elise. "They've been lining
the streets since we got into London. There're thousands of
people out there." She peered at Ruth. "How're you feeling?"

Ruth coughed into her hands. "Better." In fact, all she
wanted was hot tea and a place to lie down.

The bus's doors creaked open, and the singing got louder.
People outside were cheering, throwing their hats into the air.
The wounded started to get up, crutches, casts, bandages and
all. Hera was already on her feet, grinning from ear to ear.

"We're home!" she crowed. "We're home!" She planted a
big kiss on Elise's cheek.

Elise got up awkwardly and pulled Ruth to her feet. Ruth's
head spun, from fever, from waking up too quickly, from
standing too fast. She leaned on the seat in front of her as the
soldiers filed off the bus, singing and shouting into the night
air. She wanted to wait until everyone else was gone and not
get caught in the shove of the crowd, but there was no chance
of that. With Hera in the lead, the three of them waded into
the press of eager soldiers and were swept down the narrow
aisle, up to the front of the bus and out into the damp night.

Outside, people were calling out the names of their sons,
brothers or fathers, running back and forth along a line of
perhaps thirty buses. Confetti drifted into Ruth's hair. Hera
started laughing—a sound Ruth couldn't remember hearing
before—and kicked at the confetti as though it really were
snow. An old man in a peacoat leaped from the crowd and
caught Hera around the waist, leading her through a few
waltzing steps. He left her spinning and danced over to Ruth.

"Welcome home, Sister!" He grabbed her hands and spun her around. He waltzed over to Elise and spun her, too. He let go and started dancing with a soldier who danced back with a huge grin on his face, letting the man in the peacoat lead, and everyone laughed.

Hera took Ruth's elbow as she wobbled in the street. "Do you want to stay for the party?" she said over the celebratory noise. "Or go to John's house?"

"I want to stay," said Ruth, "but I want to go."

"You're awfully sick," said Elise. "We should go."

"The party'll be on for days." Hera pointed away from the station. "Can you walk for a while? We're not far."

"I can do it," said Ruth, and she took Elise's arm.

The next thing Ruth was aware of was the sun. She was lying in a bed with the covers pulled up to her chin, and she was warm. The sun was shining weakly through a window to her left. On the wall beside the window was a painting of a sailboat leaning over in a deep blue sea. It was the room she and Elise had stayed in the last time they were here. She was aware of someone at her side, and for a moment she thought it was John. When she managed to turn her head, she saw Elise, covers thrown back, dressed in a flannel nightgown, softly snoring, with her long brown hair everywhere.

Something moved to her right. She shifted and saw John and his mother in the doorway. John was holding a basin with a cloth draped over the side. His mother had a breakfast tray that smelled of bacon.

"Good afternoon," said John. "You're awake."

Ruth swallowed, her throat sore. Her stomach growled loudly enough that John and his mother both smiled. The sound must've woken Elise. She rolled over and sat up, rubbing her eyes.

"I was dreaming about artillery," she muttered. "Is that breakfast?"

"Call it breakfast and lunch," said Mrs. Doweling. She came in and placed the tray on the edge of the bed. The plate on the tray was heaped with eggs, toast and bacon, and a cup of steaming tea.

Ruth struggled to sit up and found that she, too, was wearing a nightgown. Her nurse's uniform was on a chair in the corner of the room. Who had undressed her? Hera and Elise? Probably. Elise looked like she'd washed. Ruth realized she had been bathed.

"Elise," said Mrs. Doweling. "There's more food downstairs. Come put on a robe and slippers. Your friend is already up. Let the doctor tend to his patient."

Elise smiled sleepily. "You survived the night," she said to Ruth. "Good for you."

Ruth tried to say, *I'm not that sick*, but it came out as a phlegmy whisper.

There was a chair beside the bed. John put the basin on the bedside table and sat down. He was wearing a white Oxford shirt and trousers. He touched her forehead as Elise and his mother left, closing the door behind them.

"Your fever's broken," he said. "Eat something and drink some tea."

"Do I have pneumonia?" she whispered.

"No," he said. "Just a bad cold. Don't try to talk." He dipped the cloth in the basin and squeezed it out, left-handed. He wiped her brow, her neck, cool and calming. She had a vague memory of him doing this all night long.

"Have you slept?" she whispered.

"No," he said, and smiled. "Now don't talk. Eat." He angled his head at the tray heaped with food at the foot of the bed. "Can you pick it up? It's so awkward with one hand…"

"Of course." Ruth reached for the tray and pulled it onto her lap. She went for the tea first. It was hot and soothing. After a couple of sips, she thought she might get her voice back. After a few mouthfuls of eggs and toast, her stomach stopped rumbling. As she took another forkful of eggs she noticed there was something else on the tray—an envelope addressed to her in care of the Dowelings. The return address was the Women's Medical College. Her hand froze midway between the eggs and her mouth.

"That came for you a few days ago," said John in a soft voice.

"Can I open it now?" Ruth asked hoarsely.

"You can open it whenever you're ready."

Ruth put the fork down and tore the thin paper of the envelope, trying not to rip the equally thin paper inside. She unfolded the letter and skimmed it. The letter was brief—something about the formality of an application. At the end was a handwritten note.

We very much look forward to having someone of your experience in our program.

"Oh my God," whispered Ruth. "They want me."

"I'm not surprised," John said steadily. "How could they say no?"

She put the letter down. John was sitting up straight in his chair, like a man at his own execution. She could imagine what was going through his mind. What woman would want a man with only one arm? Why would she want a man who had been a doctor, but now couldn't even lift a breakfast tray by himself? What did he even have to offer anymore?

"Do you know what my question is?" she said hoarsely.

He swallowed and shook his head.

"Do you want me?" she whispered. "I mean, do you really want me? Body and soul?"

"Of course I do," he whispered back. "But I know what I can't have. I know you'll go to school. I understand how important it is for you."

"Did you get my last letter?"

"The one where you chastised me?" He gave her an unhappy smile.

"I apologize for that," she said, "but you can't feel sorry for yourself. And you can't give up on me."

"I don't feel sorry for myself," he said, but his voice broke. "And...I haven't given up." There were tears in his eyes.

Ruth put the breakfast tray to one side. She patted the bed beside her, and he came over and sat so that his hip was pressed against hers. He smelled of aftershave, and she wanted, badly, to bury her face in his chest and weep. There would be time for that, she knew, but that time wasn't now.

"The war is over," she whispered. "You showed me so much. You taught me. Now I need you to show me one more thing."

He looked at his feet and blinked, and tears ran down his face. Without a word, he unpinned his right sleeve with his left hand. The empty fabric fell.

John wiped his face with the back of his hand. "It's ugly."

She shook her head. "That doesn't matter."

"I can't," he said. "You would be utterly repelled."

"Would I?" She touched the front of his shirt with her fingers and began on his buttons. She could see him swallow hard. By the time she had unbuttoned down to his belt buckle, he was trembling. She pushed the shirt off his shoulders and to his elbows. On the right side, the shirt fell to the bed of its own accord, revealing the scars, the harsh marks left by the cauterizing iron. She had cut off so many arms, just like this, that she thought she could look at it analytically. Wilson had done a good job. The amputation was clean, ready for a prosthetic. But it was heartbreakingly ugly, and all she could think of was the men she had sent home with ugly scars for their wives and lovers to see. What were they doing right now, at the first sight of it? Ruth took John's arm in both hands and raised the wounded end to her lips. His skin was rough and chapped. The scars from the cauterization had healed as hard blisters. She kissed him there until he started to cry, like a child, in great sobbing gasps. He wrapped his good arm around her back and held her so tightly, she could hardly breathe.

"I missed you so much," he wept. "I was so afraid you would leave me."

"I'm never going to leave you," she said in his ear. "And you're never going to leave me." She put her hands against his hot chest and pushed away just enough to see his face, raw and red and streaked with tears. She kissed him until he stopped crying so hard.

"Will you have me," she whispered gravely, "and not worry about medical school?"

"Ruth," he said, "I'll do whatever you want."

"I love you," she whispered.

She got up and stood in front of him. The nightgown had three buttons at the throat. She undid them one by one until she could push the nightgown off one shoulder so that the top of one breast showed. She waited for the hot flush of embarrassment. She had never stood naked in front of any man. Instead of embarrassment, though, she felt a whole different kind of flush, one that started in her belly and spread downward.

John got to his feet and kissed her, on the lips first, then down her neck, then to her bare shoulder. He pushed the nightgown away, and the soft flannel fell to her hips, leaving her upper body, and his, bare. She pressed against him, finally skin to skin. He held her tight, and they stood like that for a long time, breathing against each other. At last, he ran his hand down her back and pushed the nightgown away from her hips so that it fell to the floor around her feet. She wasn't wearing anything but the pearl at her throat, and she leaned into him, trusting, waiting for him to do the next thing. He fumbled with his belt buckle, and she let him fumble. To help would not be useful. In a moment, his trousers slid to the floor along with her nightgown, and she could feel him, hard and warm against her.

"I don't want to rush you," he whispered.

"Let's lie down then," she whispered back. "I want to get to know you again."

She let go long enough to move the breakfast tray to the floor. He locked the bedroom door and took off his shoes and socks. They lay on the rumpled bed, naked together for the first time. With the tips of her fingers, Ruth touched the fine curls of dark hair on his chest, the flatness of his belly. His hand traveled down her neck, to her shoulder, to the edge of her breast. The presence—and now for the first time she could see it—lay against her thigh. Unwillingly, Ruth thought of the men she had stripped bare in the operating theater. She had seen everything, but never touched so intimately, so gently. The heat in her body expanded, up into her chest, down through her thighs. She touched him, and he grew harder. He moved his hips, ever so slightly, like an impatient animal, at her touch.

He watched what she was doing, hand on her waist, and looked up into her eyes.

"May I?" he said quietly. All his tears had dried.

The silent language from their time in the woods caught in her throat, and all she could do was nod. He watched her face as he moved his hand, warm, along her body, from waist to hip, to the small of her back. Her hesitated there, at the base of her spine.

"Go on." She shut her eyes and leaned against him. "Please go on."

He grazed her rear with his fingertips. The sensation made her tremblingly aware of the dense heat at the crux of herself. What had been dry and consuming in the woods was now molten against her thighs. His fingers trailed across the horizon of her hip. He moved closer, and she opened her thighs for him. Without clothing between them, everything was different, pure, rich. Ruth pressed her teeth against his bare shoulder to keep from making those sounds that no one could hear in the woods. His fingers explored her, leaving behind whorls of sensation. Behind her eyelids came silent explosions. He found the deepest opening of her body and circled it gently, round and round, first with fingertips. Then he was there, full of heat, and strength, and primal knowledge. He pressed against her, burning through a door she'd never even imagined.

Ruth wrapped her arms around John's shoulders.

He was over her. He was in her.

There was a quick, piercing pain, and then there was sweetness, only incredible sweetness.

EPILOGUE

Ruth adjusted her shapeless robe again, and her cap, the square black pasteboard cap with the tassel.

"You can try," said the woman next to her, also dressed for graduation, also an American, "but you'll never be able to make this getup look glamorous."

Ruth pushed her hair behind her ears. After two years, it was long again, not the spiky brush she'd kept short because of the lice. There were no lice in the Women's Medical College, but she still had terrible dreams about vermin in her hair. Glamour, she reflected, smoothing the long black robe again, was really not what she was after.

A smiling, elderly woman in an equally black dress, clapped her hands for everyone's attention. "Ladies!" she shouted. "We must move to the stage! Quickly now!" She opened the door of the lecture hall. Outside, the English spring had turned sunny, with a few perfect white clouds. A far cry from last week, when Elise and Hera had arrived from Paris with two of their orphans, trotting down the gangplank in the pouring rain. This morning Elise had driven to Southampton to pick up Father and Grandpa, who had spent almost a month on a ship from Baltimore to arrive for her graduation.

Ruth followed the rest of her classmates into the large, bright garden where guests were gathered and the stage had been built. She hesitated by the door, looking for Father in the crowd. Letters over the last two years had been sparse, tense. She still wasn't sure if Grandpa had forced him to come along, or if he had finally accepted that his daughter, the nurse, was about to become his daughter, the doctor. She didn't know if she would be getting that familiar stern glare when she saw him, or if—and here her imagination failed—he would congratulate her.

Ruth made her way down the marble stairs into the garden, into the cheerful press of other peoples' families, and almost instantly bumped into Elise.

"There you are," said Elise. She was dressed in a sprightly pastel Parisian outfit, the most feminine clothing Ruth had ever seen her in. "Hurry up. Grandpa wants to talk to you." She caught Ruth's elbow and pulled her into the thick of black jackets and frilly frocks.

Ruth grabbed her pasteboard cap to keep it from falling off. "The stage is *that* way. Doesn't he know I'm about to graduate?"

"It's all he could talk about," Elise said over her shoulder.

"What about Father?" said Ruth.

"What about Father?" said Elise, in a way that made Ruth's heart sink.

She spotted John's parents first, beaming and waving as Elise pulled her toward the chairs set in rows at the edge of the stage. John's mother threw her arms around Ruth's neck.

"We're so proud of you!" she whispered in Ruth's ear. "We *just* could not be any prouder."

She let go long enough for Mr. Dowling—Ruth could never make herself call this terribly proper man by his first name—to pump her hand. "Very proud," he puffed.

"Thank you so much," said Ruth, "for everything," because she and John, secretly married for the last two years, had been living under their roof while she went to school. She was about to say more, when she saw Father and Grandpa, standing with John and Hera, and two of the girls Elise and Hera had taken into their household. Ruth took a deep breath as Mr. Dowling released her hand.

"Hello, Father," she said. "Hello, Grandpa."

Father was just standing there, hands clasped behind his back. Grandpa came over and embraced her without a word. She could feel that his face was wet as he pressed against her cheek.

"Don't cry," she said, about to burst into tears herself. "Not yet."

"Congratulations," he said in a choked voice. "I always had faith in you." He pulled away, wiping his eyes. "Come see your father." He took her sweaty hand and led her over.

"Now, son," he said.

Father surveyed her. He looked so sad, Ruth thought. "Father?" she said.

He swallowed. "Daughter," he said, "you've changed."

Three years of war, she thought. Two years of school. Five years since they'd seen each other. "I don't think you have," she said. From his black coat to his short beard to his stern eyes, nothing that she could see was different.

He took a step toward her. "I would like to congratulate you," he said stiffly.

"Thank you," she said, tears hot in her eyes.

He took another step and held out his hand. His eyes seemed to be glistening with tears, but she couldn't be sure. He reached out and took her hand. She thought he was going to give it a good hard shake, but he didn't. He pulled her close instead.

"My God," he said, squeezing her hand hard. "Are you pregnant?"

She nodded, unable to speak. Of course he could tell. She'd only told John this morning, and he'd wept over her belly, great heaving sobs. In another month she would be showing. Another graduation secret.

When he let go, it seemed to be the signal everyone was waiting for. Hera and Elise and the two girls raced over, enveloping Ruth in their arms and covering her with kisses. Only John stayed back, his uniform jacket pinned up at the sleeve, looking on with what Ruth knew was nervous relief. All these years, waiting for this moment. All those nights, poring over her books. He had done everything for her, and still she had felt, not once but many times, that he never wanted anything to do with medicine again. She looked at him and smiled. He seemed so tired, but he smiled back. Was there a new and hopeful light in his eyes? She couldn't tell.

"You remember Amelie?" said Hera, who was wearing an even fancier dress than Elise. She held the girl's shoulders while Amelie curtsied prettily.

"I remember you perfectly," said Ruth. "Are you still thinking about becoming a doctor?"

"Yes, madam," said Amelie. She smiled with her plain face. She was about sixteen now. She had spent her time during the war tending to wounded French soldiers, from the time she had lost her family to the Germans when she was twelve. In her eyes, Ruth could tell how much she had seen in her short life.

"I think you'll do very well," said Ruth gently. "I have no doubt."

"Merci, madam," said Amelie. "I will try."

"And Greta," said Hera, guiding the second girl forward. Greta was blonde and astonishingly pretty, about fourteen or so. In her letters, Elise had told Ruth that Greta and Amelie had been practically joined at the hip since they'd met.

"So good to see you again, Mademoiselle Greta," said Ruth.

Greta curtsied. "Congratulations, Madam Doctor." Her accent, Ruth noted, no longer sounded so German. She had been found, alone and filthy, in the ruins of some bombed-out village as the German troops retreated. She was one of the dozen orphans now living in Hera's dream house located in the heart of Paris.

Ruth smiled at her. "Have you decided what you want to be when you grow up?"

"Yes, madam," said Greta brightly. "I will be Amelie's head nurse!"

Everyone laughed. Even John smiled.

"Graduates!" cried the elderly woman in the black dress, now standing on the stage. "Graduates, to the stage immediately!" She clapped expectantly. "Right away, please!"

"I have to go," said Ruth. She squeezed past Hera and Elise and held a hand toward John. "Will you walk me to the stage?"

"With pleasure." John took her hand and pressed it against his heart. Ruth couldn't help but notice, again, how his nails were bitten to the quick. She leaned over and kissed him soundly on the lips. She was so worried about him. These days, now that her studies were complete, he had very little to keep him occupied. He'd said he wanted to write a book about the war, but all she'd seen him do was stare out the window with a pencil in his hand.

John offered his arm, and together they made their way

to the stage. Ruth's classmates were already there, waving to their families and blowing kisses. Familiar faces, after two long years, filled with joy.

Ruth stopped at the stairs and turned to John. "Are you all right?"

"I'm perfectly fine," he said. "I'm more than fine."

She leaned closer. "You're going to have a son," she whispered. "I can feel it."

"I can, too," he whispered back.

She pulled away a little. "I'll be right back."

He nodded and let her go.

On the stage, Ruth found her seat between Jane, who was going to be a pediatrician, and Hannah, who was going into obstetrics. Ruth had joked with them about Hannah delivering Jane's future patients, and they had laughed, but then told her, with obvious admiration, how impressed they were by her intention to be a surgeon. Ruth reached out and took their hands, and the two young women smiled at her. They were not the only battlefield nurses here. Everyone on this stage had been touched by the war, but they had survived, mentally, physically, and come out stronger. Ruth felt a solidarity with them that she wished John could feel. She released Jane's hand and let her fingers brush her own belly. So much hope inside her body.

A new beginning might heal everything.

★ ★ ★ ★ ★

ACKNOWLEDGMENTS

So many thanks to everyone who had a hand in this novel, from my beloved writing group (Ellen, Rachel and Stephanie), to my extraordinary agent, Richard Curtis, and my marvelous editor, Nicole Brebner.

This novel got its start at The Sewanee Writers Conference, where the first chapters were critiqued, and where I made a number of lifelong friends, but this acknowledgment would be incomplete without including Virginia Hartman's class at The Writer's Center in Bethesda, MD.

Thanks so much to Kathleen Oudit and Elita Sidiropoulou for the cover, and to my publicist, Lia Ferrone.

No acknowledgment is complete without thanking my wife, Vicki Sipe, my first editor, whose skill as a librarian has saved me innumerable times from just making things up. That being said, I have tried to respect history and geography when they served my purposes as a novelist, but wherever they did not, I have cheerfully, or with regret, ignored them.

SOURCES:

For an excellent read about the lives of women ambulance drivers during WWI, have a look at Helen Zenna Smith's *Not So Quiet: Stepdaughters of War* published by The Feminist Press, 1989.

For an amazing look at the Great War and its artifacts, visit the Imperial War Museum in London. Thanks to my friend Katie who suggested that we see the Trench Exhibit there.

Many thanks to the following authors:

Vera Brittain—*Testament of Youth*

Dr. Sean Lang for his books about the First World War

Dorothy and Thomas Hoobler—*The Trenches*

Mary Borden—*The Forbidden Zone*

Dorothea Crewdson—*Dorothea's War*

Anne Powell—*Women in the War Zone*

Sebastian Faulks—*Birdsong*

Arch Whitehouse—*Heroes and Legends of World War I*

For me, a picture really is worth a thousand words. Thanks to Time-Life and American Heritage for their collections of photographs.